THE STILL POINT OF THE TURNING WORLD

THE STILL POINT OF THE TURNING WORLD

A Novel

SHEHERYAR B. SHEIKH

4th

First published in India in 2017 by Fourth Estate An imprint of
HarperCollins *Publishers*
Building No 10, Tower A, 4th Floor, DLF Cyber City, Phase II,
Gurugram Haryana – 122002
www.harpercollins.co.in

1 2 3 4 5 6 7 8 9 10

P-ISBN: 978-93-5264-381-3
E-ISBN: 978-93-5264-382-0

Typeset in 11/14 Adobe Devanagari
by Jojy Philip, New Delhi

Printed and bound at
MicroPrints India, New Delhi

For Jani Chacha, collector of stories

For mom and dad, and for their kids,
but more so for their grandkids

For Sheema, with love

At the still point of the turning world. Neither flesh nor fleshless;
Neither from nor towards; at the still point, there the dance is,
But neither arrest nor movement.
And do not call it fixity,
Where past and future are gathered. Neither movement from nor towards,
Neither ascent nor decline. Except for the point, the still point,
There would be no dance, and there is only the dance.

—T.S. Eliot, 'Four Quartets'

The Vice Chancellor's Opening Remarks

Students. Parents. Faculty. Staff. Friends.

As vice chancellor, I welcome you all to the Lahore University of Social Sciences on this rainy, and not altogether happy, occasion the night before this year's graduation ceremony.

As you well know, this kind of gathering has never been observed on our beautiful campus before. However, it is also true that never, in the forty-two-year history of this institution, has an event of this nature and magnitude come to pass, either here or at any school or university in the entire country.

Given these circumstances, I feel it is appropriate for our academic community to collect here tonight. For each other, and with each other. Tonight, I am glad we are all here.

But we have not gathered here to talk about bombs and explosions. We have discussed tragedies all our lives in Pakistan, it seems, though I have vague memories of prolonged periods of peace and prosperity. The reality is that we live in harsh times, and we may be talking about guns, violence and extremism for a long time to come.

But, tonight, let's just talk about the two people we have lost. What they meant to each of us and what they represented for each of us. For, I am sure, seeing all of you here and having talked to many students, their parents and families, Sara Shahjehan and Omar Kayani are in all our hearts tonight.

Before we proceed, I would like to thank the staff who worked tirelessly all of yesterday, through much of last night and all day today to make this gathering possible. In order to accommodate the entire student population, rather than just the graduating class, we have had to arrange for extra budgeting through the finance office, for which I would like to thank Mubbashir Naqvi, our interim CFO.

This space had already been earmarked for the annual graduation concert, but I am glad that the music society and the theatrical society have decided with good taste to forego the tradition this year. I would like to thank the band Passion's Creed for accepting our last-minute cancellation with fortitude. And even though legally they did not have to return the funds that were collected for the concert, they have graciously donated them so that tonight's gathering could be made possible.

I should also mention our pro-chancellor, Mr Anjum Ali Khurrana, for all his support to our students and their parents during this difficult and trying time. Mr Khurrana is here with us tonight, and we are glad you could come, sir.

Last, but not the least, I would like to especially thank our current graduating class for their effort in helping the rest of the community understand what happened here this week. The outgoing seniors of our illustrious institute have brought all of us together tonight by insisting that we not forget two of their best. I am grateful for the support they have shown to each other and to the families that have been affected by the tragedy.

But tonight is not about the tragedy of what happened. It is about remembering and celebrating the two people we knew.

Sara and Omar were precious members of our little community, and they will be sorely missed by all of us. We knew them as students, as friends and as teaching assistants. We knew them as active members of the community, as teammates in sports and as joyful individuals who had beautiful futures laid out for them in the stars.

Personally, I remember Omar as an early morning shadow on the running track. And Sara, I remember, as a girl who impressed us all with her courage and grace in the face of adversity. People full of life; lives that could have been. That's what I remember.

Before we go further, let us please observe a moment of silence and pray for both of them…

And now, without hogging the podium any longer, I would like to invite some of Sara and Omar's friends to speak about them, and share with the rest of us the stories of their lives in and outside the Lahore University of Social Sciences.

Before you ask them or me—and I'm sure you have many questions—I will confirm that an official investigation into this week's events is under way. And it will go on for some time, I am told. We are cooperating with all the authorities involved. The results of the investigation, should they not be considered a matter of national security, or otherwise liable to confidentiality, will be shared with our community at an appropriate time.

So, please, while keeping your speeches as long as they need to be, do let them focus on the lives of your friends. That is my only request for tonight.

There will be three main speeches, and then members of the audience may briefly share their stories of Sara and Omar. Dinner will be served in the Khurrana Gymnasium right after. I urge you all to attend, and make the untiring efforts of the staff worth your time.

Once again, before handing the podium over to the close friends of Sara and Omar, I want to say a few words about the people who have been directly responsible for making this gathering possible. I know you probably don't want to hear things like sponsorship messages at a time like this, but it is our responsibility to appreciate our corporate helpers. There is no way that we could have come together under this tent without the efforts of Daud Ashraf at Pepsi, Najamul Haq at Ping Telecom and Sultan Dar at the *Daily Times*.

When Sultan heard of the incident, he insisted on being involved every step of the way. He has known Sara's family personally, and she even interned with him at *Daily Times* during the summer before she started college. Sultan would have liked to be here and talk about the potential that Sara had as a journalist, and how Pakistan has now lost a bright, young star. But Sultan is at a conference in the United States where he is chairing an international panel supporting democracy in Pakistan. He was torn between coming here to be with us and leaving for Boston and chairing the panel. I was able to convince him that Sara would have wanted him to go and be the voice of reason representing Pakistan at the conference.

Similarly, Daud Ashraf, vice chairman of Pepsi's publicity in Asia, who has been involved with our university for over two decades, and is himself a graduate of our illustrious institution, was told of Sara and Omar's story by a friend of the university. Daud called me up, crying. He said, 'Najam, we must do something for the two kids. We must do something for their friends. We must do something for our university.' We have Daud Ashraf among us today. What has he not done for the university, I ask you. How much more can one person give? And yet he keeps on giving more and more. I only pray that he is showered with a million times more of what he already has as he shows us the immense depth and capacity of his love and generosity.

Now, I think it's time to give the podium up to people who know exactly why we are here, and for whom we are here. But before I leave the stage and become part of the audience, I want to take one long look at all of you, and thank each one of you.

Your being here would have meant the world to Sara and Omar. I don't think there is a soul in Lahore among the people from our community who is not here today. If anybody isn't here, it's because they had to attend to urgent matters in their own lives, and we wish them well.

It has taken the lives of two of our best to bring us together like this. Sitting together with our heads bowed, praying, crying softly, wondering why this had to happen. I know what you are all thinking. 'What is the wisdom behind this?' I am thinking that too.

I do not claim to know much about theology. It is not my forte. I am a professor of physics. Atoms and quantum particles are my comfort zone. They give me the meaning that I seek in life.

But I never discount the wisdom that God Himself has provided us with in His holy books. No matter what belief you have, even if you lie on the agnostic and questioning side of the spectrum of belief, it is hard to deny that the Almighty—or call it the Universe—works in mysterious ways.

Thank you for being here tonight.

Here to share some of her thoughts, I would like to welcome Nadia Shirazi. She has been a close friend of Sara's since early childhood and will be among the seniors who graduate tomorrow.

Nadia, please come and say a few words.

Thank you.

Freshmen

Boom

Sara's hair was in a bun on top of her head, tight and cocked, and she felt the numb heat of it piled up like that. She listened intently to the sound of shuffling feet around her, with students climbing the steps, and she shifted her attention away from the boys smoking and staring at her and her two friends. She knew they were watching Nadia's ankles, the s-curve of her feet in platform shoes, and her pigeon-red painted toenails. Nadia liked to put her feet on display, and some of the students walking up the steps had to work their way around her outstretched legs.

Sara wasn't paying attention to Mehreen, who was telling Nadia and Sara about her mother's latest idea: to start a restaurant and catering service on the LUSS campus.

She also wasn't paying attention to Nadia not paying attention to Mehreen. Nadia's smile seemed forced even as she said, 'Mmhmm', for the fourth time. The smile was directed at the least attractive of the smokers: a tall, muscular but geeky-looking bespectacled kid—stylish, rectangular spectacles, metal braces on his teeth, lots of hair on his arms, and a moustache and some hair on his chin—who leaned against a pillar, wearing dirty flip-flops. Flip-flops in the morning, before a ten o'clock class.

Sara sat and continued to listen to the sound of shuffling feet, and looked directly in front of herself, at the four boys who had now come to stand in the middle of the steps leading to the entrance. Why couldn't they stand on one side? Why did they have to display their bonding rituals for everyone to see? They would slap each other's backs and hiss muted curses as though they were the kind of cool kids who almost didn't care if any girls were around them. Almost.

'Eff, man, I can't think of going to class,' one of them said, stretching his arms as he yawned. His T-shirt rose, and Sara saw a flat belly with some black, frizzy hair. She looked away, then back at it again, and then the T-shirt came down as the boy stopped yawning, and that view was gone.

'So don't go, motherf—,' the short one with a massive pimple over his left eyebrow said. He had a beard, but it wasn't one of the religious types of beards. Just an elongated scruff.

'Your sis—, what if there's a quiz?' asked the first one again.

A quiz on the first day of class? Sara wanted to ask, but she didn't. None of the other boys did either. They must be thick. Or maybe their teacher was a hard ass.

Sara, pretending to look elsewhere, focused on them through all the peripheral vision she could muster. But a lime green polo shirt caught her eye. It wasn't the colour she noticed, but the jutting out chest of the girl wearing the lime green polo shirt. It was someone she had shared a bench with at the dining hall during orientation week. They hadn't exchanged names even though they were both freshmen. Sara didn't want to make new friends outside of her group just yet. There were politics to consider. She'd made mistakes before.

Sara's friend Mehreen said something about 'design', then something about a 'logo', and then she said 'corner spaces'.

The stiff and curved chest moved past where Sara sat.

'Effin hell,' a third boy on the steps said. The girl with the big chest and negligible waist had to bend around the boys on the stairway. They deliberately swayed in her direction, leading with the pimple, but without surrendering their spot.

They'll never leave, Sara thought, they'll remain here all morning, stuck to the stairs, bothering everybody. There should be a rule against these kind of people.

'Sixteen tables,' Mehreen said. Sixteen tables? Right, the restaurant Mehreen's mother was opening at LUSS. Feed the kids junk, and grab their cash.

The wind picked up, and Sara's hair in its bun swayed reluctantly. She loved this moment. The drama and nonsense of high school was finally over. This was the first academic day of college. She was not invested in the mundane play of reality being acted out by the people around her. Things were happening around her that she had no control over, and that was perfectly okay. She was prettier than many of the other girls in the LUSS freshman batch, though not prettier than Nadia. There was hardly anybody prettier than Nadia on campus though, and she was Sara's friend. So that said something about her. Plus, Sara had a good sense of style. Plus, looks were just the base. Sara knew she had far more to offer.

But offer to whom? Why even think this way? For reassurance, for a backup plan of hooking a boy in these four years in college in case academic pursuits didn't quite pan out, of course. Right, right. The cynic in Sara's head was having a laugh.

'Yeah,' Nadia said to Mehreen. She said it in a drawn-out way, which indicated she might say something more. But now she was looking deliberately away from the smoking boy who was no longer leaning on the pillar and was stubbing out his cigarette. He gave the back of Nadia's head a meaningful smirk that Sara saw.

'Is he looking?' Nadia asked Sara. Was that a hint of desperation in her voice? Did she like this kid? She *liked* him, didn't she?

Sara could play with Nadia now; she could say *yes* or *no*, and she wanted to lie because she thought that would make the game more fun. But she said the truth through pursed lips so the boy couldn't figure out what she said.

'Yes,' Sara said, and something in her ached to say 'at me'. But she didn't, even though she smiled at the torture and ambiguity she could inflict. 'Who is he?' she asked instead.

The boys on the stairs slapped each other's hands and backs. Presumably at the sight of that big-chested girl who had just walked by the pimple-host.

'So, that's the initial concept,' Mehreen continued. Her curls did a celebratory dance as she finished narrating her mother's idea, and Sara's tied-up hair felt tight looking at those free curls. She squeezed the muscles in her head together and relaxed them deliberately, to contain the playful vibe of not wanting anything at the moment. She wanted to continue being wantless. But she did want to let her hair down.

This was the first true day of college after four days of ridiculous icebreaker games during orientation the previous week. She had no class today, nor did Nadia or Mehreen. But they'd wanted to come and be here, check out the campus, the boys, the library, the food, the atmosphere, and just be away from their homes. To feel like college students.

'Is he really looking? Tell me!' Nadia demanded. She *was* desperate. Definitely desperate. My God, Sara thought. Is *this* what happens? Is *this* what college is about? Will there be four years of *this* between the students?

The boy was no longer looking, and he had gone from smoking to stubbing out his cigarette on the brick wall to staring at Nadia's head to giving her a once-over to turning around and heading into the college building with his smokers' entourage; two of the five boys who followed him were much better looking than him. There, Sara thought, there I go judging people based on their looks again.

'Who?' Mehreen asked. Sara wanted Nadia to answer Mehreen first, so she would know who the boy was too. She didn't remember seeing him on any of the orientation days. He might not be a freshman.

Nadia raised her eyebrows, bristling with her own question: is he *really* looking? Sara looked at her friend and concealed her pity for Nadia behind the layer of indifference that had now come over her. Why was Sara feeling so out of it? Was she dehydrated? The sun was beating down quite heavily. Was she having a heatstroke? No, Sara thought. It's just all so absurd. We're playing at being college kids. We don't really know what it means. It's our first day here and we don't know how to act. We could just be rehearsing a scene from a sitcom that hasn't been made yet. Nadia is acting out something she believes she *should* be feeling. There is no *actual* feeling. This desperation is fake.

But Sara couldn't express this lucid and utterly logical thought to Nadia without appearing ridiculous to someone living within the play acting. It would come across as either bizarre or unfriendly. Perhaps even both. You can't break the fourth wall from outside.

'He's gone,' Sara said.

'Gone where?' Nadia asked. 'Is he walking here?' Her eyes widened, her pupils contracted and the dots in the middle stared through Sara with panic.

'Who, dammit?' Mehreen asked, leaning towards Nadia.

Sara looked at both her friends. She wanted to get up and walk away very calmly, to leave Nadia and Mehreen to play the hottie-and-sidekick roles. They were suited for it. Mehreen could be such a tube light sometimes.

'Mother-eff, check that piece out!' one of the boys on the stairs said.

Three girls in hot pants came up the steps: purple with a white button-down shirt, navy-blue with a sea-green kurta, and white with a grey t-shirt. Nadia was prettier than all of them put together, and Sara felt she was better looking than at least the two walking closer to her. The third one was very fair, though. But none of them was the 'piece' the boys were checking out.

All four of the boys were facing, like a prayer group, the one girl further along who was sashaying up the path slowly. She was showing the most skin Sara had ever seen in real life other than at sleepovers at Nadia's house.

'Zafar,' Nadia said.

'Zafar who?' Sara asked without thinking. She knew Nadia would want her to be interested. So she feigned it by forcing a grin with arched, questioning eyebrows.

The girl coming up the path had a deep and blossomed cleavage, and Sara felt the inadequacy of the bumps on her own chest as visceral insults. Nadia's bust wasn't up for debate, though. She was a hottie. She could be a model. She *should* be a model.

But the carriage of this girl, with the catwalk-pendulous sway of her hips in sync with the pulse of hormones streaming through the boys' veins, and the nakedness of her barely sandalled feet, juicy calves, and through the patched and torn designer jeans, glimpses of her creaseless knees and thighs, and the raised shirt revealing the hint of a bellybutton, one shoulder in the sun with the black strap of her bra exposed, and the other shoulder barely covered by the white cut-off t-shirt that said 'Cornell University', and the sunglasses with silver-blue lenses as big as tennis balls—

What kind of parents did this girl have? Rich, for sure, Sara thought. Parents that don't care, parents without values.

She wished she could switch parents with this girl. Not to take advantage as this girl was obviously taking of the freedom given to her, but just to feel this liberated, for once.

But did it matter? In the end, there wasn't much dissonance between Sara's own life and her parents' rules. So no, she did not need this girl's parents; she could keep them. Who was she anyway?

As much as she was revolted by the obvious—freaking obvious—scream for attention that this girl's get-up was letting out, Sara herself wanted to have this swagger in her arsenal of moves, to get the boys to swoon.

The bun on her head seemed an antique from the sixties, something she wanted to release right now, to feel relaxed again. But there were just so many pins.

'Zafar,' Nadia repeated. 'He's a sophomore.'

On the steps, the darkest boy looked down. He was slowly turning a deep crimson-black, the colour of crusted blood. The rest of the boys stared at the girl, and kept quiet until she walked past Sara. Nadia further extended her left foot but the girl stepped right over it and did not look back. Her hips swayed this way and that without missing a beat. She disappeared into the Social Sciences building. The perfume she left behind was intoxicating.

'What about him?' Mehreen asked.

The boys had become quiet and they weren't looking at each other. Each of them felt separately lost, Sara thought, and none of them knew how to share it with the others. It was written on their faces.

Watching people who were watching other people was much more satisfying than just watching people. This added layer of observation was the one that allowed judgement to be less flawed. At this thought, Sara wondered if there were other layers behind her, of watchers watching the watchers, who in turn watched the people who watched her watching the boys watching the girl. Was everyone at some point or the other watching someone and did it so happen that the entire LUSS campus was at one point under observation by itself, in an intricate web of voyeurs and victims? But it didn't have to be simultaneous, did it? No, that was too neat an equation and life was a far more sophisticated puzzle. There she went, catching herself in another conundrum she had created to assure herself that she could think on the meta level, to convince herself that while she was not *above* it all, she was possibly *beyond* it all.

The pimpled boy on the stairs was biting his lower lip and looking up at either the sky or the roof of the building. The darkest one couldn't take his eyes off the building's entrance, the one into which the girl had disappeared. They had seen something they could never possess. Never. And they didn't know how to deal with it.

'Nothing,' Nadia said meaningfully.

'Yeah, right,' Mehreen said, poking Nadia's shoulder and then her rib. 'Tell me.'

How could Nadia and Mehreen not see that there was more going on than just themselves, I mean, look around, Sara thought. That girl just glided over Nadia's foot and walked away without getting harmed, and she destroyed the lives of four boys.

Speaking of which, two more boys came out of the dining hall from breakfast, and approached the once-loud group on the stairs. They hugged, slapped backs and shook hands. The necessary ritual; like dogs sniffing each other's backsides. Something not forego-able. Girls don't need that. They don't need to do so much touching to exhibit their friendship.

Sara wanted to stay within the moment as an observer, but she felt Nadia smiling forcefully at her, as if prodding Sara to tease her more about this 'Zafar'. The pimpled boy stood around, not hugging anybody. Maybe the rest were afraid of bursting his pimple, that's why they didn't hug him. How much blood was in that pimple? Sara smiled from the queasiness of that thought. Pus too. She squirmed.

The pimpled boy moved to the side a little, and Sara saw two girls sitting on a bench behind him. She had not noticed these girls before. Her view had been blocked. But there was nothing special about them. They were clearly the super-conservative types. She could see one's face through a scarf and, through a slit in a black burka, the other's eyes only. *Ninja*, Sara thought by reflex.

'I'm going to class,' said the very boy who didn't want to go to class. He just rendered the time with his friends meaningless, didn't he, Sara thought. She wasn't judging, not at all. Simply making an observation.

'Eff, man,' said the darkest one, and they both made their way towards the dark entrance to the building, and Sara could now see the space behind the spot where they had stood.

'Come on,' Sara said to Nadia. 'Tell us about Zafar. How do you know he's a sophomore?' She tried to keep her tone playful and teasing. Instead it felt like it came from a newscaster announcing his seventy-first thousandth break for commercials.

The two boys who had just vacated the stairs unblocked Sara's view of someone else. It was a boy sitting on the pavement with a cigarette in his hand. The cigarette wasn't lit. The boy wasn't that great looking. There was a bench in front of him, but he wasn't sitting on it. Was the bench wet? But it hadn't rained recently. Maybe it had fresh paint or some dirt on it. He was alone. Maybe because he wasn't that good looking. Sara felt ashamed for thinking that; something so obviously bigoted about the concept of looks being important to ensure company. But she didn't flush for long. That wasn't it, not in this boy's case. He was alone by choice. His posture said it all: slumping forward into a curl and leaning an elbow on one of his stretched-out legs. He wasn't faking this posture.

'Zafar who? Is he cute?' Mehreen asked. She was always preventing other people's questions from being answered by asking her own stupid questions right after a more decent one had been asked. She had to chime in. Sara forgave her this time. But one day, she promised herself, before it *truly* got on her nerves, she would warn Mehreen about this annoying habit.

But for now, this lonesome boy and his unlit cigarette seemed to distract her.

'Hmmm?' Sara smiled, showing that she was playing her part in needling Nadia.

The boy's cigarette had an orange filter and white paper. He was looking at it like it was the only piece of a missing puzzle and he was trying to figure out what to do with it. He would roll it between his thumb and two fingers, and then turn it around to look at it from the tobacco end. He put it on his lap and let it roll a few inches. He would grab it again and turn it around, and then put it between his lips only to take it out again. He did everything with it but light it.

His black t-shirt and regular dark-blue jeans were a very dull, if reliable, combination, and he was wearing blue-grey canvas shoes that looked like a favourite pair considering how frayed they were.

'Let's talk about this later,' Nadia said to Mehreen and Sara, but Sara didn't acknowledge this. The boys on the stairs were also no longer points of interest. Except that pimple, which was hideous and ripe, and could not be ignored.

The pimple itself had a white top that was round and seemed to be—though it wasn't—oozing pus from the body of the boy standing on the steps. It was like a discoloured nipple. Or the stump of a miniature tree with white sap congealed at the top. Sara did not know which one was the distraction: the boy and his virgin cigarette, or the pimple on the other boy. Her focus was uneven, maybe indirectly proportional to her level of disgust. She drew a mathematical equation of her interest in the vagueness of the moment, and it came to nothing.

Also, would the boy sitting on the pavement light up his cigarette? It seemed as if he was deliberating, but what if he didn't have a lighter? He did have a lighter. It was sitting on the boy's lap, and he knew it was there. He tapped his fingernails on it.

Sara wanted to ask Nadia if she knew the boy with the cigarette, but she was sure Nadia wouldn't tell her or would make too much of it. Anything to tease Sara. She decided she would ask Mehreen later, so she would know what name to call him. She couldn't just call him 'the boy with the cigarette'. It felt right and important that she should find out his name. But Sara was not ready to bring so much attention to herself. Not on the first day of college.

'No,' Mehreen said, 'tell me now.'

The ground shook. Right in front of her. The stairs seemed to sway one way, and then the other. An earthquake?

Two seconds later, a loud thud followed and it was more physical than sound.

Flecks of dust flew up from the grassless patch of ground near the stairs.

The smell of wet sewage laced with gunpowder and dust sprang into the air. The sun stayed high and bright, and there was no cloud cover.

The boys on the stairs looked in the direction of the university grounds.

Sara's eyes didn't leave the boy with the unlit cigarette. She thought the pimple had burst. All things being equal, it must have burst.

⚜

Omar was not playing with the cigarette. He was playing with Sara. The finger acrobatics with the cigarette were his means of piquing her interest. How contrived the pose and his deliberation on the cigarette was.

At first, it was a performance meant for an audience, any audience really. Spying on all the students from the corner of his eye, hoping to hook a viewer, secretly wanting the performance to at least *appear* natural, even though it wasn't. He didn't want to announce his intention. He just wanted to play his part.

He was lonely as fuck. All his friends had left for the US, the UK, Canada or Singapore. All gone for college, starting new lives in new cities, while he was stuck in the same old Lahore, waiting until they came back and told him about life in the outside world.

He was an Aitchison boy at LUSS, tagged with the elite high school's legacy of snobbishness just by having attended it, universally hated by the non-Aitchison crowd for having that exclusive scar on his transcript. The LUSS crowd forgave much, but one of the things it didn't forgive was schooling at Aitchison, where the boys were trained to believe they were the best and deserved the best, whatever that may have meant. This meant bullshit to Omar. But he didn't know how *not* to be from Aitchison. He didn't want to be at LUSS any more than he was wanted there and planned to transfer out within the first year, or maybe after three semesters. This time he wouldn't let the application deadlines whiz by.

Orientation was over and now it was all about putting his head down, and achieving the grades that would get him out of LUSS, out of Lahore, out of Pakistan. To the West, to the open societies, which promised legal bars and genuine American accents.

Hitting the books was the first step. His grades would follow from that. He knew the drill. He had five A's in his A Level high-school exams. Several Aitchison kids had that, but nobody had more. He'd been a top dog back at Aitchison—prefect of his house, editor of the school magazine, second lead role in the annual play. It was no wonder he had run out of time to fill out his applications.

But LUSS was an alien place, disconnected from both the surrounding city of Lahore and from any kind of reality. And here, Omar was a nobody.

His head was down, but his eyes refused to focus on the cigarette. He had already snatched glimpses of Sara from between the boys on the stairs. He did not know her name, but the out-of-time-and-place hair bun on her head already held his attention and became a point of curiosity for a few seconds. That is all it took to keep him there while he pretended to play with the cigarette in his hand.

Omar heard the boys on the stairs cussing and whining through the muddle in his own head. He was thinking about the Aitchison boys, his core group of eight friends, who were all in real colleges like Yale and Amherst. Not this imitation institute.

He was trying to attract Sara's full attention, to seem interesting to her because she appeared interesting to him. He twisted his knee at an awkward angle that he thought made him seem more flexible and athletic. I'll tell the boys later on about this girl, he thought. That she had her hair up in a bun, and she was friends with the hottest girl on campus. Maybe, he thought, taking a picture could be possible with his phone held between his legs. He could get a candid shot of Nadia and send that to the boys. One of his Aitchison friends knew Nadia through family connections. Omar could make him jealous.

The dry tobacco rustled on the inside of his cigarette. Omar had rolled the thing around enough to form creases on it and soften the paper.

Nadia's beauty struck him as bland, there was too much of it. It was an unquestionable thing. But the girl with the bun, she was the question mark. Was she really, really pretty and didn't know how to show it well? Or was it that she couldn't care less? A bun, in this day and age, Omar thought. Either of those things—whether she didn't care, or whether she didn't know how—struck him as crush-worthy, in different ways. It was as if she had something beyond her looks to vouch for her. Maybe she was as alone as he was. Maybe they were alone in the same way and could spend the rest of their lives filling each other's silences with meaningful things to say. Maybe they could just be alone and quiet together.

I should put it in my mouth, light it up, then look up at her and breathe in the smoke deeply, hold her in a stare and not breathe out for three seconds, and then puff out a cloud, thought Omar.

But he didn't want to smoke. He wanted to share a joint with his Aitchison buddies in a basement with Xbox 360 rounds of Halo 3 Deathmatches all night long. Or, he wished, if not for that basement scene, that he could be in his buddy Aneeq's room, lying on his massive bed, reading a good Hemingway or Nabokov novel.

Omar wasn't ready for the real life that college was supposed to prepare him for.

He was worried in the way that being abandoned in a forest would make a six-year-old. He was thrilled and petrified at the same time. He saw colours more vividly than any of the twelve times he had smoked up with the Aitchison boys over the summer that had gone by.

The grass was divided into distinct blades that had separate existences. Thin single leaves and knotted stems, hidden clovers lay flat against the dark mud, under the blades of grass. Everything had an individual ethos, a trampled sense of self that could never be understood until examined up close like this.

Omar's disposition oscillated, in that cigarette shuffling moment, between the tolerance of his situation and the rejection of it, without settling. He would forget to exhale, and then he would let the air out all at once. The same with his inhales. Smoking without smoking, holding his unlit cigarette.

The girl's cheeks were less round than the curve of her hair bun. Her cheekbones were hidden partially under a layer of baby fat. He guessed her hair was long enough to reach her shoulders if let down, and that her waist under that white shirt was thin enough for him to wrap one arm around her and crush her to him. He wanted to pursue that thought.

But the grass shook like a carpet, with the army of blades moving one way, then another.

Strands of tobacco fell out the cigarette's open end into the grass.

A loud *boooooof* of air and sound hit Omar. He thought someone had played a sharp note on a hideously out-of-tune trumpet.

⚜

Omar watched the grass.

Sara watched his hand dropping the cigarette.

He looked up from the grass to see the other students looking in the same direction the sound had come from—the back of the campus.

She looked at him and kept sitting where she was and didn't blink.

He wanted to get up but, once he saw that she was looking directly at him, he couldn't move.

Her mouth was open and she was looking at his mouth and his eyes watching her, as if *he* had made the sound. The terror in her eyes was compounded by his having discovered her among this mass of people at the entrance to the college.

With some effort, his eyes stayed on hers as he stood up and stayed standing by the bench.

The boys on the stairs hesitated, said a few mother-sister cusses, and went in the direction of the sound, running but then shuffling quickly along. It was too hot to run. Someone older, with shit-brown-coloured trousers, came out of the college entrance and was followed by boys and girls with backpacks full of course books. Some of them rushed for the college gates.

Omar lost Sara in the crowd. He got up on his toes to see if he could find her again, or if not, then to see the boys who had gone to the back of the college. He put one foot on the bench to climb it, but then decided not to. He could see her get up and come down the stairs. He shook himself internally to regain some composure and tried to act casual, just casual enough to also seem alert about the big noise. With his shoulders raised, breathing with his mouth open, he looked with concentration in the general direction of the commotion.

'Fucking hurry,' Nadia said, grabbing at Mehreen's purse. Mehreen ran faster than Nadia, and ran into her, pushing her along.

Sara knew she would have to pass him on her way out. Nadia's car was parked outside. Sara didn't want to leave the campus, though she didn't want to explore the source of the sound and the earthquake either. It was probably some electricity pole that had got its wires crossed or fallen into a pool of water. It was surely nothing. But she was still unsure of what she wanted. A few minutes ago, she would have liked to know the name of the boy with the cigarette, and before that she had wanted nothing. But she didn't remember wanting nothing anymore. She wanted to stay in the college even though she knew she couldn't. What if it was a bomb? Her parents would kill her if she decided to stay. Follow-up explosions might kill her if she stayed. Maybe even a mob, and there were chances of rape wherever there was a mob. That, above all, scared the shit out of her.

Omar held his breath as she came up the pavement near him. He wanted to say something. He had to. He asked, 'Are you okay?' but the shouts in the distance drowned him out. So he said, louder this time, 'Are you okay!' like a command, and immediately regretted it. He wished his Aitchison boys were around, or he was standing in a crowd rather than alone with these girls walking past him. His position struck him as supremely awkward.

She stopped near him and answered, 'Yeah, did you hear it?' and immediately felt abjectly stupid and she didn't want to seem so stupid to him, of all people, because he had held her interest, even her divided interest, however briefly.

Nadia looked back from the gate and saw Omar and Sara in a world separate from the world at large; she was the first to see them as they really were. But Nadia completely lost it. 'Fucking, what are you doing? Sara!' Nadia screeched.

Sara looked at her as though from within an aquarium.

Sara, so that's her name. Omar smiled at the solution appearing before the problem could manifest itself. 'Yeah, I heard it. What was it?' he asked her.

But Sara wasn't looking at him. She knew she had done it now. Nadia would think there was something special going on between her and this boy. Sara didn't want Nadia to be part of anything important, and this was definitely not important. So she decided to ignore Omar's question, and Omar too.

Some of the boys had reached the back of the college, near the hockey and cricket grounds, and they were shouting loudly. It was muffled in the distance.

'Sara!' Nadia shouted. 'For God's sake!' Sara started to move away from Omar.

He almost followed her.

She looked at him, shook her head and said, 'Good luck,' and smiled. She was uncomfortable at leaving so impolitely. Why did I wish him luck? She stayed on that thought and pushed Nadia and Mehreen along out of the gate.

Omar nodded and acted rigidly cool, as if just brushing off an encounter with someone he knew well. He pretended as though Sara and her friends were his friends from before LUSS, and that he had just escorted them safely out of the gate and could now relax, now that he had done his duty towards his female friends. He had rescued the damsels; now he would see what all the fuss was about. He had this entire narrative ready, should someone ask. He would have said, 'I heard something and these girls were coming down the track. I had seen two of them look like they were in shock. I asked them to tell me if they were okay and they wouldn't reply, so I was getting ready to slap them, in case they were in shock, but just to check if they hadn't heard me because of all the noise, I loudly asked the one with her hair in a bun if she was okay, and she nodded. So I nodded and let them all know that they should not let curiosity get the better of them and that they should get back to their homes. Preferably just one of their homes, and call their parents and let them know that they are okay.'

Lucky for him, nobody was looking at him. Had anybody asked him at that point exactly what he was thinking, he would have collapsed from the exhaustion of keeping up the appearance of not being lonely as fuck.

The bun on Sara's head brushed against the ceiling of the car when she got in. She wanted to, but didn't reach up to adjust it. She let the itch remain unscratched and sat behind the driver. Mehreen came and sat in the middle from the other side, and grabbed Sara's hand without saying anything. Sara gave a squeeze back, but let Mehreen's tight grip keep their hands together.

They were in Nadia's Civic. The driver started the car. She got in, and Mehreen's other hand grabbed Nadia's thigh.

Sara's eyes were wide with horror. She couldn't believe she was leaving college on the first day of classes, fearing a terrorist attack. Is *this* what it was going to be like? Or was anything ever going to be bigger than this? In the rear-view mirror, she caught a glimpse of her lopsided bun. Oh, God.

'Do you know the EMS number?' a tall boy with a long beard asked Omar.

'EMS?' Omar asked. He was still reliving the brief exchange with Sara in his head. He didn't know which way around the Khurrana Sports Complex he had come. He didn't know why he had come or how long it had taken him. He only understood the present moment; it was here, in the cricket ground, with a crowd of students and janitors converging on a single spot.

'Emergency Medical Services,' the boy answered patiently.

'Is someone hurt?' Omar asked.

'Dude, do you *know* the number?' the boy said, losing his patience. He did not wait for Omar to answer and moved away. Omar bristled with anger and guilt for being put on the spot and then dismissed. He wanted to say he was a freshman, but didn't know if it was a valid excuse for not knowing about the EMS. There was a session on emergencies during orientation that he had skipped. Maybe he should have gone to attend it.

The crowd was spread out and when Omar reached the edge of it, he elbowed past the first few people and saw, over the shoulders of a boy with a blue bandanna, the hole in the ground. It was a large hole. The earth seemed to have been sucked into the ground, and not uniformly. But there was a kind of pattern. The boundary of the hole was circular and the end closer to the school buildings was deeper. A boy was sitting on the edge of it, dangling his legs in the hole. Some of the other students were taking pictures with their cell phones. Despite the cussing in Urdu and English, it seemed rather quiet when there was such a large crater in the ground. Around thirty people stood around it, just staring.

'EMS?' someone standing at Omar's left asked. 'What's that?'

'Emergency Medical Services,' came a reply.

'Motherf—, that's huge!' someone shouted. Two professors of anthropology and one of economics stood in the crowd of boys and staff, and gaped like the students. The freshmen would look at them and then at the other students for guidance on how to act. Omar was observing the freshmen, judging their confusion and his own to see if they matched. Curse words flowed and were even endorsed.

There were seven girls in the crowd and two of them had nerdy engineering boys rubbing up against them when the pretext of leaning closer to the hole.

Omar pushed further up and saw that the bottom of the pit was not smooth like he had imagined. It was also not very deep. Maybe five feet at the deepest points. And it was just dirt and roots of grass with no blood. The hole was on the inside of the running track that surrounded the cricket field. But the pitch and boundary lines had not been redone since the monsoons, and the hole seemed like the only marker all around.

'Who is hurt?' someone in a lab coat asked. Nobody replied. 'Anybody hurt?' the young man in the lab coat repeated, his voice cracking. In his hand he held a dark leather valize, which looked like it could contain a first-aid kit. But he did not look confident enough to handle emergencies. With his nervous fidgeting, he wasn't giving anybody any assurance.

A girl in navy blue hot pants standing next to the man in the lab coat asked him, 'Are you from the EMS?'

'No,' the young man in the lab coat answered. 'My friend is. He's on his way.'

'Okay, then don't act like you're from the EMS,' the girl said. Omar stared at the two having this exchange, and though it struck him that this girl in blue was pretty and had character, perhaps even a strongly defined personality, it was not enough to dislodge the still vivid memory of Sara from his head.

'I'm only trying to help,' the young man said. He was sweating from his forehead now, and his handbag no longer seemed like a first-aid kit. More like a briefcase full of useless papers.

'I know,' the girl said.

'What happened?' A tall boy, the tallest Omar had seen on campus so far, asked as he came to the edge of the hole. He was three feet from Omar and must have been at least 6'5". A giant.

'Hey,' Omar said, 'I think there was a bomb.' He didn't know what made him say it. But it just seemed appropriate to say something that nobody had yet said.

'I'm just saying,' the girl with the blue hot pants said, 'don't act like an EMS representative unless you are one.' The pitch of her voice had climbed a notch.

Two security guards had arrived and they were working their way from the opposite end, pushing the students back, away from the hole in the ground. The student dangling his legs didn't get up immediately.

'A bomb?' the giant asked.

'I wasn't impersonating anyone,' the lab-coated young man said defensively.

'It's okay,' the girl said.

The guards shoved a boy back and there was a scuffle, but only for a second. One of the guards was way too big to take on.

'Get back please!' said the guard. 'Get back!'

Omar stayed quiet. He didn't want to give too much credence to his own theory of the bomb. But there was nothing else around that could have caused the loud noise, the tremor, and this cavity in the ground.

He was busy looking at the girl with the blue hot pants. She was trembling and clutching at her throat, taking deep breaths.

Her mouth was twisted in a snarl. Some of the other boys were also looking at her.

'Motherf—,' the tall boy said.

'It's okay,' the girl said to the lab-coated young man. 'I'm sorry.' She seemed to be calming down. She breathed with less effort. But she still had a grimace stuck on her face.

'It's probably a suicide bomb,' another student whispered on Omar's right.

But why would a student take their own life with a bomb in the middle of a field? Did the student—or was it a faculty or staff member, or even an outsider—decide not to blow up the bomb near other students at the last minute? Plots of recent terrorist films raced through Omar's head. None of them conformed to the current situation. It just didn't make sense.

The short boy the guard had roughly brushed aside was mouthing off the big man from behind and stepping back up to the crater. The guard looked around at him but decided to ignore him.

'I'm sorry,' the girl in the blue hot pants repeated and Omar looked back at her.

'It's okay,' said the young man in the lab coat, though he was clearly not showing that it was okay. Omar could sense the young man's embarrassment creeping into his own body. But Omar wasn't worried about him. He was more concerned about the girl. Someone needed to look at her, someone with medical and psychological expertise. Her eyes were red and dripping with tears.

'I'm sorry,' the girl shouted this time. It was quite loud, and the students were all looking at her. She was in shock. So this is what shock looks like. Omar, had he been closer to her, would have deliberated between shaking her by her shoulders or giving her a tight and quick slap across the face. A few seconds of debating would have made him choose a good thwack. But he was too far away. The lab-coated young man did nothing. Instead, he folded his arms around his bag and pretended he did not hear the girl.

The guard was only ten feet away from her. She began to curl up and shouted again, 'I'm sorry.' Nobody got it.

A plump professor of economics moved closer to her, but he didn't want to be inappropriate and touch a girl student, so he just spoke softly to her. Omar didn't hear him say, 'It's okay, please calm down, it's okay,' but that's what Omar imagined he was saying.

The hole in the ground did not seem significant to Omar. It didn't look like the site of an explosion, and it didn't appear to be the scene of any crime. It was important for other reasons. For collecting people and bringing people to it. For drawing wide varieties of attention. But that was all in the back of his head, waiting to be accessed.

For now, in the moment, he watched the girl gather her breath and shout again, 'I'm sorry.' It was even louder this time and she bent further forward than before. Her knees were buckling. The economics professor had his hand out in front to catch her if she fell forward, but she stayed arched and suspended. The lab-coated young man on her other side had unfolded his hands and stood staring at her with mad eyes of his own, looking worried that he might be partly to blame for her losing grip on sanity.

Omar knew she needed a slap. Or a hug. And nobody was giving her either.

In the centre of the circle formed by human bodies was the crater. The hole seemed to gape back at everyone staring at it. Some dirt crumbled off the edges, the people around it nudging and toeing the precipice of solid earth. At any moment, the gap could widen and swallow more level ground.

The giant student had shoved forward, stood next to Omar, and then kneeled down next to the hole. Omar watched him reach inside and touch the mud.

The girl in the blue hot pants, when Omar looked back at her, was still in the process of falling.

'The soil is cool to touch,' said the giant student, his long arm and extended fingers reaching low into the hole. Given the cool soil, did that mean it wasn't a bomb? Did the earth just cave in? Some other students grabbed handfuls of dirt while others brushed the grass roots that showed.

Minutes passed. Omar stayed near the hole, as did many others. The tall boy and Omar got talking, but they mostly sat there like two loners thrown together by circumstance. The tall boy said Omar could call him Qasim or QT.

The crowd swelled. A few clouds passed and covered the sun. People came and went. An hour went by. Then more time. At some point, the girl in the blue hot pants had disappeared. She wasn't missed.

Someone brought a handful of sandwiches and passed them among friends. More people were now sitting around the hole than standing around looking into it. Food was distributed even among those who were not friends with the person who had brought it. Some crows gathered to get at the crumbs too. They snatched at the paper and plastic wrappings, and came back for more.

QT and Omar listened to the conversations that ranged from the World Trade Center attack in New York to the Taliban and Al Qaeda, on the pitiful hole in the cricket ground, and the incredible threat it posed to everyone's safety. 'Imagine if one of us had been walking here…' someone said, and trailed off.

When the police and ambulance sirens could be heard in the distance, it was already well past noon.

LUSS
The Campus

It is unfortunate to be named so: the Lahore University of Social Sciences—LUSS—in a country not known for letting such nearly vulgar titles go unscathed. An absent 'T' at the acronym's end is often vocalized by the students, staff and faculty within their own coteries, and more often by outsiders, jealous of the premier university's symbolic status. There are also issues with the double 'S' at the end. 'Seduction Sciences' and 'Sex Sciences' are the cruder pokes. 'Lahore University of Sell-out Slaves' is yet another track of derogation.

But there is nothing unfortunate about the campus, which sprawls across a hundred acres of prime land in Lahore, forty miles from the Pakistan–India border. It is a hundred acres of former wasted overgrowth, which begins as a series of office buildings before being converted into a college campus.

The trees have grown rich canopies. In the fall semester, LUSS is the most beautiful place in Lahore. In the brief spring, with its manicured and blossoming flower gardens and lanes of yellow-and-purple-flowered trees shedding just the right amount of petals on the gray tarmac, it is the amongst the most picturesque places in Pakistan, even counting the virgin mountains and valleys in the north.

The phenomenal success of its initial Social Sciences and Humanities School enables unprecedented expansion. From its twenty-fifth to its fortieth year, a School of Engineering takes root, a Business School sprouts forth, a School of Education branches out, and a Law and Public Policy School blooms.

Given the exponential increase in the areas of the university's academic research and inquiry, the vice chancellor has taken up as his main mission to get the name of the university changed. He wants to have it officially renamed Lahore University or LU. If not that, at the most, TLU: The Lahore University. He refuses to call the place by its current acronym for fear of making it sound like Lust. The institution deserves better.

Sara and Omar see each other for the first time at the entrance to the college, and this is the same place where, in the right corner of the base of the stairs, the foundation stone with its handprint of a German education ministry official is preserved in unpainted concrete.

Male students from the supposedly secret society (LUSS Secret Society or LSS) have, as part of their rite-of-passage, urinated on this preserved handprint before graduating for over thirty years. This desecrating act is usually completed in the junior or senior year.

LSS members meet twice daily by the carpentry and mechanical repair sheds located behind the engineering building to smoke fresh hash from Peshawar, and to devise new ways of creating trouble. They rarely rant about 'the system' or Marxism after sophomore year.

Severe lack of space for girls and boys at the university to freely make out keeps hormones on the campus at an elevated level. Dark corners and dark times at night do exist. Power blackouts are frequent and the generators take time to start up. But the cricket and hockey grounds don't have canopied trees around them to allow any secret rendezvous. The buildings are all locked up at night too.

⚜

When the vice chancellor hears about the peeing tradition, he wants to disband the not-so-secret LSS. He does not know how many people are part of the society and nor does he want to know. He guesses fifty, and that guess seems to him an educated one because he thinks he can spot the society's members on sight. The kind of boys the LSS attracts are potheads. Though all potheads are not LSS members, all LSS members are potheads.

⚜

Two of the LSS boys once dress up as girls, with make up and wigs, and make it past the guards at the gate leading to the female hostel. They lose their nerve once they are let in past the front door and decide to turn back. The lack of a game plan after initial success keeps them from going further after crossing the threshold.

⚜

Sara once makes it all the way past the security in one of the boys' hostel, asks the way to Omar's room and finds his door open. She knocks on it, twists the knob, enters, and locks the door from the inside.

⚜

The large hole that appears after the explosion in the cricket ground is cordoned off first by tape, then quickly by screens, and eventually by a large wedding hall tent. Teams of police and army investigators arrive on the scene later that day. Some of them are equipped with gas masks, radiation suits, even Geiger counters, but others among them seem not too fussed with those things. Nothing is disclosed to the media by the administration or the authorities, but a brief ticker at the bottom of the GEO News channel shows 'Grenade attack on college campus', for an hour in the evening.

The tent disappears on the Monday of the second week of classes, though the yellow tape remains. Guards are posted there through day and night, in rotating shifts, for four weeks.

But the hole is visible again, and some students stroll up to it between classes and in the twilight hours. They will look in and see grass and dirt, and they will share stories of the noise, and recall the feeling of the tremor from their various vantage points on the day of the explosion. They will rehash their old conspiracy theories.

Time passes, and once dinner is served in the cafeteria, there are quizzes and assignments that press down hard on everyone, along with memos and presentations, deadlines to work out. There is already so much to do this early in the semester.

The hole is filled with mud on the third weekend after the semester starts. Grass seeds sprout fresh blades, and within a few months there remains little but the trace of a story about the hole.

For four years, no student attempts suicide on the LUSS campus. But then a sophomore is emotionally compromised; his journal is read out by his roommate to the entire student body of the men's Hostel 2.

It is 2 a.m., close to the average hostel bedtime. But friends are roused from floor to floor, building to building. Calls are made across campus to the girls' hostels. This is good, they promise, the journal is worth it.

The guards at the various gates see over a hundred pyjama-clad and hooded people march in ragged formation over to Hostel 2. Curious, they send one of the junior guards over to investigate. He does not yet have a paunch like most of the veterans and his blue uniform fits him well, though his belt hangs low. A walkie-talkie, the knobs of which he keeps fiddling with, makes scratching sounds as he stands with the students looking up.

'What's happening?' someone asks.

Omar and Sara, still freshmen but closer now, stand next to each other, she in her pink and baby-blue-striped pyjama bottoms and the gray hem of a long t-shirt peeking out from under her black shawl. She is staying overnight with a friend at the hostel to study for a midterm.

It is the first time Omar sees her dishevelled. He then looks up at the second-floor window with four people framed in it.

'He's going to fucking jump,' someone says. Curses fly. 'Mother' this and 'sister' that! A girl screams genuinely and a boy in the crowd shrieks.

'Hey everybody,' one of the boys, a senior, shouts down from the open window. 'Hayyan doesn't want to jump anymore. Thank you for coming. Good night.' The window then slams shut. A curtain is drawn, but the lights stay on, and the crowd refuses to disperse.

What is this farce? What is this place? What kind of a university allows something like this? Questions and answers and more questions go on for a while, but hushed ones, out of respect for a near miss.

Sara and Omar walk away eventually after getting tired of craning their necks to look up. They stroll over to a bench near the hockey grounds and sit there, not wanting to go back to sleep, not wanting to study. What if something happens once they leave?

She pulls up her feet and sits contemplating the bloody as well as bloodless ways to commit suicide, and the possible personal and public reasons to do so; whether it is an act of ultimate bravery or ultimately an act of cowardice. She thinks all this is either too morbid or too irrelevant, and for both those reasons shares none of her thoughts with Omar. Instead, she keeps injecting trite spirals of 'I hope he's okay' and 'He needs professional help' and 'I hope none of us end up like that' into the silence.

Omar, meanwhile, does his best to appear caring and sensitive with considered responses, mostly drawn out ones like 'hmmm' and 'yeah'. But he feels awkward to be so alone with her in the dead of night, and feels responsible for her in a way he does not want to be. He will begin to get up, but then won't, and the hours until sunrise are long and tedious, weighing down on him like boulders. To conceive of staying awake all night on that uncomfortable bench rubbing into his thighs is difficult, but he keeps up his end of the vigil. She is his only real friend on campus.

A year later, they will look back on this as the beginning of something. Another year will pass before they will have built so much fog around this night that it won't matter who was supposed to have jumped off the building, or why he didn't.

Interest in the hole wanes. But metaphysical interest is not so easy to remove. LUSS is tainted with the act and imprint of violence. No longer can it claim to be safe from the rest of Pakistan's social upheaval and political muck. Somehow, some day, another act of violence will occur here, and make a pattern of the isolated incident.

Sixteen guards work on rotating shifts throughout the campus. They are paid the minimum wage, and worked until even their sweat runs dry and becomes embossed in their skins.

One of the guards works for eighteen years at the gates and in the halls. He is saluted and greeted by many students, and he lovingly cleans and irons his uniform every night before going to sleep, while recalling for his childless wife the events of the day. One month before his retirement, he is fired for a minor lapse in vigilance: thinking this must be a student, he lets in a sharp-looking cigarette salesman through the gate. That lapse is the excuse the administration uses to save a little over Rs 700,000 in pension.

Over the course of forty years, four students succeed in killing themselves on campus. Three, in the early years, hang themselves from the rafters in the male hostels. Those deaths are attributed to inordinate academic stress—LUSS in its early days calls itself the 'MIT and Harvard, combined, of Pakistan'.

A fourth student slits her wrist on a long weekend in one of the female hostels. It is most likely a plea for attention, which doesn't arrive in time because of the long weekend's two extra holidays.

Students swear to have witnessed strange things on campus. A dark corner along the back wall is rumoured to be haunted, as dark corners are apt to be. Legends say a faculty member's wife was killed by her husband and buried there. Legend splits the cause of the haunting into two versions, to encompass an amorous rival as well as lands and properties as the focus of the dispute.

On moonless nights, a haze of a woman in a green sari with red flowers can be seen walking amidst the broken flowerpots and the dense, unkempt bush.

Snakes frequent this nook in the middle of summer, and they are an empirical threat that keeps the verifiers of the legend at a safe distance.

Two assistant professors of economics, both buddies on the surface, become rivals at everything. They go to the gym together and squabble over who can stay longer on the treadmill, at a higher incline and faster pace. They invite each other with their wives and kids to their campus apartments on alternate weekends. Their wives will have to try and elicit unguarded praise for the food, changes in the apartment's decor, as well as their children's special gifts of eloquence or athleticism.

At work, the two professors vie for things such as better student evaluations, and downplay each other's chances with quasi-hostile banter while they try to convince their department head to give them goodies like sabbaticals, research projects and pay raises.

One's hair is receding, so he is needled by the other into getting a hair transplant. The other's gut begins to show after a week off from exercise, and his friend nags him into going to the gym twice a day for a month.

One of them leaves for a conference on oil economy in Dubai for a week. In that week, the one who stays on campus unwittingly spreads rumours of his buddy perhaps having a girlfriend in Dubai. The rumour escalates in status to news, and keeps circulating for a week, especially since the conference ends within the first two days. What could be keeping him there? There's nothing to really see in Dubai. The department head takes notice of the matter, and once the assistant professor returns from Dubai, he is confronted by his wife as well.

A weekend goes by without any invitations from either side. Then two such weekends. The Dubai-returned, maligned assistant professor recedes into his own world, goes to the gym at odd hours in the middle of the night, and refuses to talk to his once best mate.

Eventually, the gossip even reaches the students. Female students seem to avoid the assistant professor's company and boys sneer at him at the gym, calling him 'sir' with apparent sarcasm. His friend tries to make amends without, and then with, an apology but it is too late. The wheels have fallen off the cart of this rising star of the academy. More than pushed, he is *willed* out of the university by the collective that moralizes against him. Weeks pass, then months and even years. The news of him dwindles into rumours of divorce and ruin. He is remembered as a budding genius cut down in his prime, all of it precipitated by a supposed affair during a foreign conference.

Meanwhile, on campus, life continues. The remaining professor befriends other members of the department. The side-by-side competitive spins on the gym's stationary bikes begin once again, as do the squash matches, dinner invitations at the best restaurants, and car-buying one-upmanship.

Onward slicks the campus groove.

❦

For Omar and Sara, the open fields are part of the campus as much as the buildings, the pavements and the parking lots. It takes them only a few weeks of walking around the campus with each other to have the map of it in their heads. And from then on, like satellites honing in on their signals and targets, they remain in orbit around each other as much as they can.

Omar can sense when she is on the premises. He can gauge her whereabouts and know at any point—just know—if he will run into her within the next two minutes. It is as if he feels possessed by a different set of atmospheric conditions when she is nearby.

Sometimes, he will be off-kilter with this additional radar because he mistakes his infrequent bouts of anxiety as an indication of the proximity of Sara as well.

Sara's sense of Omar is a lot less traumatic. She finds it easy to read him and his moods. She finds it easy not to mistake his intentions. With all his pretences and shields, he is like a solved puzzle for her. She can look at him and see the core of what he wants. It is easy to see herself at that core. She can't sense his presence or absence on the campus. She doesn't need to. It is a small enough place anyway.

Probability and his searching gaze make sure they keep meeting. Enough meetings and run-ins by chance and circumstance take place, and they know they can be friends despite what keeps them tethered and apart for reasons of magnetic push and pull.

❦

There is a dark green patch of grass and pavement outside the men's Hostel 4 where Omar, once, walking back from class, stands reading a seemingly dense passage in Milan Kundera's *The Unbearable Lightness of Being*. These are the words he reads: 'Anyone whose goal is "something higher" must expect someday to suffer vertigo. What is vertigo? Fear of falling? No, vertigo is something other than fear of falling. It is the voice of the emptiness below us which tempts and lures us, it is the desire to fall, against which, terrified, we defend ourselves.'

Omar knows he is missing something. He reads through it four times without understanding it, and is ready to give up and turn right, in the direction of the dining hall.

He is first showered with water from a bucket, then a bag of granulated sugar is thrown at him, and it doesn't miss him enough. Then comes a pail of green paint. All three by different hands from adjacent windows, so the succession of substances is instantaneous, leaving him with little time to react.

He stands there groaning, for the book in his hand is now ruined, wondering where to turn to try and save it. He doesn't think to look up and identify the boys who have done this. He doesn't want to know *who*. He wants to know *why*. The answer to that can't be an easy one. Boys will always be boys.

But the answer *is* easy. The purpose is simply laced with malice. The mastermind is a freshman who hates boys from Aitchison because an Aitchison boy once stole his girl in high school. The boy sates himself against the girl's betrayal with the splatter of things on this Aitchison boy, Omar, who is an easy target because he is always alone.

The paint does not completely come off Omar's hair and skin for three days.

The book's most obscure pages are ruined, but otherwise it dries out in the trashcan outside the hostel, eventually becoming part of the LUSS weekly haulage down to the city dump closer to the Indian border. It will take four years to decompose and be obliterated in that muck, making sweet compost for the ferns that take root on the canal's bank.

❦

The 'sex spot' is a bench enveloped by two wings of the social sciences building, and has never seen any carnal action. Neither boy-girl, nor boy-boy.

Girl-girl carnality is confined to hostel sleepovers.

Boys with homosexual tendencies prefer not to disclose them out loud. They fear danger from the overtly Islamic students and professors on the campus. Brutal cases of assault against suspected homosexuals are still rampant in the country.

There have never been any transsexual or 'other'-gendered

students at LUSS. The cordoning-off from society is thorough. But sins don't need permission. They thrive on not being permitted.

In one group of friends, the leader shows his approval by slapping across the face of whomever among his minions pleases him through action or comment. By extension, they take it upon themselves to slap each other and laugh about it. That is the closest LUSS comes to having a goth or sadomasochistic club.

There is a faculty apartment up for hourly rent to students from all departments. Only the seniors know about it, and they find out about it as a gift from the graduating class. This den of debauchery has all the ingredients that the bulk of people at LUSS consider the lowest depth of depravity: bottles of homemade wine, locally cultivated Peshawari marijuana, a fresh supply of Murree Brewery beer cans, and a corner room with a mattress on the floor, dim lamplights, a scent close to lavender incense, and, in a large black handbag, a variety of imported condoms.

The faculty member who rents out this apartment teaches Persian, commutes fifty minutes each way to LUSS from the Mall Road, and his wife of thirteen years doesn't know he spends a fifth of his paycheck to rent and maintain an on-campus apartment.

Omar goes with a group of QT's friends to this apartment twice in his sophomore year—the only sophomore to ever visit the place.

Sara, Mehreen and Nadia try half-heartedly in their senior year, for curiosity's sake, but never make it to the room in the back with the mattress on the floor.

The campus mosque has been mirred in controversy for forty years. For fifteen years there is no mosque on campus, and that is a point of contention. After it is created, the next twenty-five years' debate revolves around what kind of Islam should be preached in the Friday sermons.

The fundamentalist professors and staff on campus refuse to be in camouflage. They sport beards and hike up their salwars. Many students become fundamentalists by 'getting brainwashed', or 'getting convinced of the true nature of this world of illusions', depending on who is asked.

You can't pray without the lefties questioning the soundness of your mind, and you can't *not* pray and still be considered a good Muslim by the fundamentalists.

A high-school Islamic studies teacher makes it past the HR filters to get hired temporarily at LUSS. Not being versed with the intellectual rigour required to debate with people questioning their own faith in times of doubt, the teacher physically attacks a girl in class.

She asks, 'Who is Mohammad compared to God? He is nothing. So why should we follow the hadith if, and when, they contradict the Quran?'

Not realizing that such questions are allowed, expected, and even encouraged in any class on Islam among students just beginning to think for themselves after years of memorizing without understanding, the instructor, flummoxed, climbs the three stairs between him and the girl in the aisle seat of the fourth row, and lets her have a forehand strike across her face. The slap is muffled and unsatisfactory for the temporary fix of the teacher, and he goes on a tirade about the blasphemy law, and how it should be invoked on LUSS students who think about the Holy Prophet with such disdain.

Some professors and students think along those lines. A few even have the national blasphemy hotline number saved on their phones.

❦

The city's grid does not generate enough power to keep the supply constant. The founder of LUSS, Mr Khurrana, has the vision years ahead of the countrywide electricity shortages to install a power generation unit on campus. One acre of the hundred on campus is taken up by the fuel-and-sun-charged energy plant near the male hostels.

The space between the turbines, though fenced off, provides the most easily accessible but dangerous make-out spot in the middle of the night. This is also a convenient doping area during the day. And during exams it is the favourite place to study for a notorious nerd who refuses to share his notes. The electric hum of the idling generators provides the ideal pitch of static noise by which to memorize equations of physics and facts of history.

❦

A business professor will go around campus after dinner with a torch, hoping to find students in compromising positions. He feels blessed and graced with this divine duty, which he carries out only because he is the most pious man on campus.

❦

In that faculty apartment, with the mattress in the back room and frequent student visits, some faculty members take their relationship with students further than the classroom allows. Discretion is implicit.

The whole campus knows such faculty members by name and

face. But they live in auras that the administration cannot touch. There are no official complaints.

One of these faculty members is a woman. She undresses many boys and men on campus with her searing gaze, but falls in love with none of her conquests.

A young, unmarried assistant professor of chemistry falls head over heels for his gorgeous teaching assistant. Gossip spirals out of control after they are once seen together in the parking lot in the dark. They end up marrying though. It is a good match. Their marriage results in the gossip fizzling out and then dying.

Woken up just before dawn by an ache in his chest and throat, fearing heartburn or a panic attack, Omar jumps out of his bed in the hostel and rushes for the hockey grounds, which have the most open space on campus. He hurries along, and remains out of breath.

There is nobody around at 4 a.m. It is hot and muggy outside. The running track around the cricket field is on the way to the hockey ground, and Omar stops at its edge and forces himself to cough. The pain, increasing with every intake of air, feels like a mesh of fine barbed wires hooked on every cell in his heart and lungs.

It hurts to breathe. It hurts to have a beating heart.

Please, God, he thinks to himself as he doubles over, looking wildly around with tears in his eyes. What the hell did he do last night? Was it the food? Not a single breath comes easily. He has to fight and suffer. At least the exhales are better.

He thinks about calling the Emergency Medical Services, but he still doesn't know their number and has left his phone upstairs on the windowsill by his bed. He can't think of climbing the stairs now. He wants Sara to be there with him.

No, in fact he definitely doesn't want her to be here. He wants her to see him being brave, not squealing.

He squats. It is getting worse. *Please. Please, God.* The barbs are sprouting veins and arteries of pain, and they are radiating to his arms and down into his stomach.

It isn't yet first light, but it is close. He stays squatting there, but manages to raise his head. *Please, God, please. Just please.* He can't remember focusing on anything this intently in his life.

Every bloody inhale is a fight. He wants to amputate his heart.

Birds begins to chirp around him. Fucking birds. It is so beautiful here. So beautiful that, maybe, death is on its way.

'Please, God,' he finally says out loud because maybe thinking it just isn't enough to make it a prayer. He is praying. He hasn't for a while. Can that be the reason for this pain? Did God want him to come out grovelling from his hostel before anyone else is awake, to kneel and scratch his knees on the clay and gravel of the running track?

He decides to take the next breath without squeezing any of his muscles. He is ready. He slowly exhales and spits out a gob of saliva that has collected in his mouth, releases his t-shirt where he has clutched it, and lightly taps his chest where the pain is. Ready, inhale.

It doesn't work. The needles dig deeper than before.

'Please, please,' he says, and spits again, his sight blurred with tears now. 'God, God, God.'

The birds have not stopped chirping. More than a thousand people are asleep on campus and a few hundred are just waking up for their morning prayers. Some runners and walkers will soon arrive at the track and notice him. He imagines them seeing his sprawled-out, lifeless body. In the span of half a second he envisions the boring process and ritual of his own funeral attended by the whole student body at LUSS, and the speeches they will give before putting him to rest. He will be the first student at LUSS to die of a heart attack. Or food poisoning. Whatever this is, this awful affliction.

Or, what if he survives? What if this only paralyses him? It could be a stroke too, Omar thinks. A stroke at eighteen, then seventy years of being able to move just his eyes. Maybe his neck. Maybe half his face, while the other half drools away. 'Please, God, please.'

Someone passes by within hearing range of the track at that point. It's a security guard cycling the 50 metres between the business school building and the social sciences building. It is time for the change in guard duties. The cycling guard doesn't look in Omar's direction. The night lamps are still on, and their series of spotlights is the glow within which he sees the guard wheel away.

Omar thinks he could shout and get the guard to come back. But does he dare?

He gauges his pain. No, he doesn't want to risk shouting. That might cause something inside of him to burst.

The sky has begun to grow lighter. The burn in his breath and his blood vessels is still there.

He says, 'Okay,' and decides to stand back up on the next exhale. Inhaling slowly and deeply, holding the air in, he flattens both feet on the ground and begins to get up, exhaling as he straightens himself. Inside, he has not stopped saying *Please* and *God*, and sometimes, *let me live*, and once he is nearly upright, he wonders why God is punishing him at all. What has he done to deserve this?

Omar is covered in sweat. He can see the flitting birds that are making the racket of chirps. His exhale is almost over and he is standing tall again.

There is someone behind him on the track, heading his way, 30 metres away.

He feels the slap of shame at once, for being scared of pain, something so invisible. He begins to move his arms over his head to stretch and carefully avoids looking directly at whoever it is on the track coming up behind him.

The early morning walker is wearing jeans and has white earbuds on. It is a bald, middle-aged and unfit man with spectacles. He doesn't look at Omar. Omar inhales. The pain is still there; but it begins to feel better. He exhales, this time with his arms reaching for the skies. He inhales again.

Yes, the pain has decreased. The attack of something has passed.

Omar feels dizzy, fatigued.

Maybe the stretching helped? *Thank you, thank you.* Was it just a minor thing then? Could have been just a scare. Maybe heartburn. Yes, that's what it must have been.

The bald man walks past the point where Omar stands. Scratches of music escape his plugged-in ears. They are orchestral sounds. He ignores Omar who ignores him right back, but five seconds after he passes Omar starts walking tentatively behind him. Slow, very slow, like each step means a new kind of movement, a new kind of living.

But: is he going to die before his first year of college is even over? He doesn't tell anybody about the pain. For many weeks, he feels conscious and troubled about keeping it from Sara. But it is a weakness he doesn't want to expose.

Days pass and the pain doesn't return. Omar is scared of looking it up online. For a month, he wakes up at sunrise or stays up all night, and walks around the track. Even if it means missing the morning class because he has to come back and catch up on his sleep.

This is the beginning of his drawn-out laps around that 400 metres of gravel, grass and dirt; round and round the field and the filled-up hole in the ground.

One day, frustrated by the amount of time it takes to walk the distance he feels is the minimum he needs to cover, he jogs a quarter of the way, and saves four minutes from the ritual. The next day, he shaves off another ninety seconds.

Some serotonin release mechanism kicks in. The fatigue wears off, and euphoria drops into a slot in his life that has always felt its absence.

This is how Omar begins to run.

Walking between classes, eating food with his roommate, discussing life with QT, seeing Sara from far off, Omar wishes to remember how alive he felt with the pain, how vital and focused it made his thoughts feel. He wants to keep that as a readily accessible memory.

Time will win, and it will pass. Sharp edges of the pain in his memory are rounded off. Like a once-favourite song overplayed beyond its capacity to be played and remain a favourite, the event dulls out, not meriting recollection. The pain, which in its moment of occurrence was like a thousand shards of glass in his throat and chest, does not remain a part of his memories, the ones he imagines make up his real history.

For QT, his first year of college is his loneliest. In his second year he grows used to the feeling, even embraces it. He takes it as a given condition as he studies, sleeps, eats quietly at the corner table at the cafeteria and keeps to his side of the hot hostel room.

QT is the tallest boy to ever attend LUSS. Thin, with a hiker's body, he doesn't smoke, smoke up or drink alcohol. An ex-girlfriend, still in high school and studying in London, keeps peppering his inbox with emails, and the LUSS hostel's uncensored Internet ensures he isn't frustrated. But his romantic, charged-up heart lies boxed up.

The reason he sleeps early every night for the first two years at LUSS is because he can't bear the thought of being alone when it is dark. So he attempts to shut the night out.

In his junior year, on the first day of classes, the first explosion shakes the LUSS campus, and tears open a hole in the fields at the back. Because of that hole, he meets Omar, and they become friends.

Things change after that. His loneliness is still a constant, but it is separated from being alone.

Every year after classes end at the close of spring, a contingent of the more well-off students sign up for a trip in May to the leading edge of the Himalayan mountains in the north of the country. Queues to sign up start seventy-two hours before the ticket counter even opens. They need to, though. Only 250 seats are up for grabs for a student population of 3,000.

Omar manages to get tickets during all four years at LUSS, but he only goes twice.

Sara never stands in line for tickets, but is offered them during all four years. Boys will offer or Nadia will, and at the end of her junior year, Omar stands in line to buy tickets for himself, for Sara, and for her friends too.

Sara finally decides to go that one year.

On the bus, Omar sits just behind the driver, with a young business school professor, who has unfortunately forgotten to put on any deodorant that day.

In the back, Sara sits on a single seat across the aisle from Mehreen and Nadia.

As they are in Pakistan and this is such a massive trip with them travelling 1,500 km each way, the organizers are thorough with their checks and double-checks. The eleven buses linger inside the campus for five hours during the checks, and then the snake they form takes twenty minutes to uncoil its way out of the gates. Most passengers are already asleep by then.

Omar is awake because of the irrepressible pungency of his seatmate.

Sara sits watching the back of Omar's head, and waits for Nadia and Mehreen to fall asleep before making her move.

Freshmen
Floating, Rising

A large number of cats were taking over the LUSS campus. Four of them lay sprawled out in the central courtyard in the glare of the mid-morning sun. An orange one with long whiskers chewed at a piece of chicken breast wrapped in a piece of thick and sticky paper, trying to separate the meat.

The pavement, grass, air and corridors felt as if they would never see humans, never be squelched under shoes, never suffer the exhaled smoke of cigarettes or tobacco. Little did they know, though. A gush of noise and traffic was brimming over in the classrooms. The students were about to leave their 10 a.m. classes.

Sara came out of the library and squinted in the bright sunlight. With one hand covering her eyes and a patronizing smile at Nadia's text to call back urgently, Sara walked down the steps and looked around. Four students stood smoking around a fifth passive smoker, and one by one they scanned Sara up and down. One of them was in her intro to econ class. Two of them she knew by face, even through the scruff that hid their jaws, clearly showing they hadn't shaved in weeks.

Her smile disappeared so they wouldn't fathom her smiling at them, for them, with them or near them. She couldn't allow this unwashed bunch the comfort of thinking they could approach her with ease.

Omar sat at a table at the other end of the cafeteria after finishing his omelette. He had been speaking to his roommate for the past fifteen minutes and the boy seemed, on the surface, unaffected by Omar's monologue criticizing the campus, its food, students, teachers, girls, grass, and all the other things which made him uneasy. 'It's so absurd that they call this place a university,' Omar said.

Omar's roommate, Basit, nodded and looked out of the window, then back at him and smiled and looked down at the textbook in his lap again. His eyes rolled, but Omar didn't catch that.

Omar said, 'No way am I going to stay here. How can anyone stay here?'

Basit's family was from the southern Punjabi town, Multan. Admission to this university had been his life's goal for the past five years, and to him Omar's words against LUSS were like insults. He would brace himself for each sentence pouring out of the spoilt brat sitting across him, but his stare was feeble and he would keep having to fight back tears of rage when he looked up, away, and back down at his textbook on the introduction to financial accounting.

Omar did not take the hint. He raised his eyebrows at the other students in the cafeteria who were involved in gulping down the chickpeas on their plates. 'God,' he said, again testing his roommate's resolve, 'what kind of people can study in this mess?'

Basit looked secretly at his watch and promised himself that if Omar didn't shut the hell up in five minutes, he would get up and leave. That was it. Five minutes.

Omar stayed seated, took a toothpick out of its paper wrapper, and put it in his mouth to feel the thin piece of wood against his teeth and tongue. It helped mask the smell of stale grease that he could almost taste. He then looked at Basit staring down at his textbook through his thick glasses—hair full of dandruff and grease, no concept of cologne or deodorant—and Omar cringed. 'Dear God,' he said softly, with pity.

Sara stood on the veranda of the social sciences building. She dialled Nadia's number and kept a lookout for the boy with the unlit cigarette from Bomb Day. She had seen him twice since then.

Once, she saw him from far away, heading for the male hostels.

But the next time, he had passed by her in the hall, looking so straight ahead, without returning her nod and smile, that she knew he was deliberately avoiding her. When he walked past, she turned around to look at him going plumb for a pillar; she saw his shoulders visibly slump, and he walked around the pillar with the hem of his dark blue jeans brushing the base of it. All she wanted was to have her nod and smile returned. But she got something more interesting instead. He was now swimming in her thoughts, this awkward boy whose name she still didn't know.

Nadia finally answered Sara's call. It wasn't serious, though. Nadia wanted to talk 'Zafar this, Zafar that'. Regular Nadia stuff. So Sara performed her duty.

She listened with half her head occupied with the explosion and hole in the cricket ground that everyone was building and sharing theories about, while the other half was occupied with the absence of cigarette-boy from the hallways for the past two days.

Muffled voices turned louder, classroom doors opened into the hallways, streams of students came pouring out with their mobile phones beeping through the corridors. Most students scraped their shoes, sandals, clogs or heels without lifting their feet.

Corners were turned without looking. Students, tech staff and teaching assistants bumped and weaved; middle-aged paunchy as well as gangly professors looked down at their feet, or lifted their noses in the air as they made their way back to their offices.

Two janitors, finished with their morning duties, sat smoking on the roof of the engineering building six floors above the ground. They looked down and passed comments on the rat race all these elite, bastard students, teachers and staff of the university were stuck in, blessing their own luck for having such cushy jobs and such easy lives, before they cracked up with the sarcasm and jealousy that brought them close to tears even through their empty chuckles. They eased away from the edge of the roof, and of their despair, by palming a soft high-five.

Taking two more paper-wrapped toothpicks from the holder, Omar got up from the table. 'Sorry, man,' he said to his roommate. 'Time for class.'

Basit nodded and gave a thumbs up, looking up at Omar's black button-down shirt but not his face; he didn't trust himself to say anything to Omar that wouldn't be a scream, his head boiled so hot and hard.

Omar shifted the toothpick from the left corner of his mouth to the right, conscious he was losing some of his disgust with every step he took away from the table. He felt partially weakened in his resolve to hate LUSS without Basit's ready ear, and partially less sure of himself as time drew closer to having to enter his history of war class.

He did not want to engage the professor, though he knew there might not be a choice. He might get called on this time.

In the previous session, considering himself more knowledgeable than any LUSS history professor, Omar had answered a few questions incorrectly. He didn't realize that answers in college weren't as simple as the memorized ones from high school. Instead of 'World War II ended in 1945,' the answer the professor had been looking for was, 'World War II is not the universally recognized name for the conflict; many nations did not participate in the so-called World Wars—in fact, the wars were known by other names and other dates in accounts from non-Western sources.'

The other students in the class listened to the professor grind Omar like an elephant would a gnat.

Most of all, it was the professor's disdain that stung him.

Omar wanted not to care. He would be transferring out within a year, he reminded himself. He had kept reminding himself of this over the next two days because what the professor had said still bothered him. It pricked him enough to make him consider dropping the course in the 'add/drop' fortnight. But it also stung because what the professor had said made so much sense. This conflicted with something Omar had memorized in high school, taking for granted that the information was correct.

He wanted time to stretch out so the noon class wouldn't begin until he had readied himself. He also wished his roommate Basit had echoed Omar's own anger at LUSS and the system of things in general.

He was further, probably most, troubled because he had even deliberately avoided Sara, and walked right past her after the previous history of war class, too ashamed to face her. He felt almost as if she had seen him crumble in class, even though she obviously had not.

Paper so wet and stuck this close to the bone and flesh was a fresh experience for this orange cat. The other cats had abandoned the piece of chicken breast and bone after minimal effort. But this one stuck to the job; she clawed and gnawed at it, fibre by fibre, freeing the piece of meat from the paper.

Very few students who passed by the cat paid she any attention. It was just another orange-and-white-striped one working its way through the scraps some students threw away.

No one noticed this one cat struggling for fifteen minutes, nor could they feel the throb and ache in its lower jaw from all the effort it was putting in. The students walking past would look at her, register a feeble movement, look away, and instantly filter the cat from their conscious thoughts.

There were classes to attend, text messages to send, idling and gazing and rehashing the explosion and its meaning to be done outside the tuck shop, or on the university's front steps.

Sara saw Omar walk past the orange cat while she was still on the phone with Nadia. It seemed to her that she had been anticipating this fortunate encounter; the image in front of her nearly matched the one in her head.

The toothpick sticking out of his mouth was something new, though the clothes checked out. He looked good in his black button-down shirt loosely hanging outside of his jeans. He had a spiral-bound course pack, a paperback novel, and a notebook in his hand. He flicked the toothpick from one side of his mouth to the other. That didn't suit him, the movement. He was nervous. He looked twice at his black-strapped watch too. Yes, nervous.

Meanwhile, she walked back and forth between the shade of a pillar and the clean sunlight, and 'hmmm'-ed at the appropriate moments when Nadia's voice inflected upwards and there was a pause. She was still going on about Zafar.

Nadia was crushing on Zafar like she had on George Clooney after watching the *Ocean's* series during a Saturday binge last year.

After that, Nadia had collected Clooney quotes, posters, postcards, interviews, magazine articles, fan site bookmarks, t-shirts he had worn, the works.

Now, given her new focus, she was collecting the intangibles associated with Zafar: moments when he looked at her during their intro to political science class, sightings of Zafar anywhere on or off campus, his various colognes ('he always smells different; sometimes like citrus, sometimes like aged mahogany, but always warm and amazing'), the fit of Zafar's clothes over his 'gorgeous muscles'. Nadia was still such a high-school girl.

Sara mumbled, 'Yeah', and stepped out into the sun, knowing exactly where Omar stood inside the hall, keeping him in her line of sight, but not looking directly at him.

If—when—he looked at her, he would see Sara on the phone with the sunlight forming a faint halo around her head. He would look at her any second. It just hadn't happened yet, but she knew it would. She felt the force of serendipity coursing through her, and it brought her closer to the verge of hanging up on Nadia.

Omar stopped outside the classroom and flipped open the paperback in his hand. He sensed the girl next to the pillar, the one in red and white, looking at him while talking on the phone.

He pretended his Marquez novel was a textbook that he needed to consult before class, just in case there was a quiz. He had this story ready but nobody asked.

A crowd of students swam around him while the cat continued to lick through a tear in the paper wrapping that old piece of chicken.

He stole a glance at her, and knew the girl didn't catch it. Was it Sara? It looked like her, but he hadn't seen her so up close before in a salwar kameez, with her hair hanging loosely. She even had bright red lipstick on. Could a face change this much from a swipe of lipstick alone? It could, couldn't it? Yes, it was most definitely her.

She turned around so he could see the back of her head. There were no ribbons or curls in her hair. It was just straight. He looked back at his novel, swivelled, and faced her. He could go late to the class, if needed.

She stepped into the shade and looked directly at him.

He saw her come out of the light like an angel coming to him from a realm of infinite grace. She was beautiful. It startled him, thinking that. He didn't know how to undo this thought. Somehow something clicked inside him that couldn't be unclicked. Beautiful. Simply beautiful. That word beat through his thoughts like panic, with a rhythm of its own.

'Okay, I'll call if I see him,' Sara promised Nadia over the phone. 'Bye, babe.' She hung up and looked at Omar with the hint of a smile. There he was.

He smiled uneasily at the word 'babe'. He had not expected to hear that word from Sara. It came out of nowhere. It just didn't fit. He was looking directly at her, and then quickly tried to pretend he was looking through her. But that didn't work. He was beginning to smile with guilt.

She waved and felt comfortable enough to walk up to him. She chose an introduction in her head, but immediately rejected it. 'Hi, I'm Sara,' had no charm.

Omar did not wave back. He nodded at Sara and widened his smile to rid himself of some of the nervousness. He tried not to blush. She had waved, and so initiated contact. It was on her now, whatever was to follow. But he had to take the lead and do something. He decided to walk over to meet her halfway, as casually as he could.

There was a boy in shorts and slippers leaning against a wall nearby, talking on his phone and checking Sara out. Omar stepped between the boy and Sara. The gentleman at his core was ready to rescue at a moment's notice. A regular Don Quixote, needing to play the hero where it was not even called for. He scolded himself and said, 'Hi.' He felt smart for stopping right there and not saying anything else. It was just right.

'Hi,' Sara said, grateful that she didn't have to start the conversation; but she was a bit irritated as well. He hadn't said his name. She didn't know his name. At some point, she would have to say 'I'm Sara, and…' just to know who he was.

'You heard it was a bomb, right?' Omar asked instead. He felt like following that with a 'duh', because the entire campus was talking about nothing else of value.

'I thought it was a drone strike,' Sara said on reflex. She didn't want to think it could be a bomb. She preferred to believe it was an accidental drone strike, far away from the terrorist hideouts in the northwest of the country. It seemed like a more welcome, a more one-time explosion. She clung to that end of the speculation.

In the absence of an official confirmation or denial, everyone had an opinion, or a conspiracy theory. People either had no clue, no interest, or had a short memories and lots of reading to get through before the next quiz, and had no time for theorizing explosions at the back of campus.

'Yes, that's also possible,' Omar said, 'but it doesn't make sense.' He closed his book and gave her his best sympathetic look, his forehead pinched and lips puckered. 'I'm just glad nobody was hurt,' he said. A sliver of fear ran down his spine. Had he just closed the conversation? This was his one chance to develop a friend from scratch; no formal introductions, just a natural friend—and he had wasted the chance. After this they would pass by each other on the campus with little acknowledgment and successively dissipating awkwardness, until they wouldn't know each other at all, not even in a long forgotten memory.

But she didn't seem to react, didn't say anything; she just stood there, looking at him, at his book, at his hand and his arm around the book, at his bedhead hair, his pretentiously creased forehead, his eyes. He felt like opening his eyes wider just so she could look further in.

Sara took a chance. 'What do I call you?' she asked. She liked saying that. She felt secure with something vague like that, without the word 'name' in her question. She was asking not for his name, but his essence, distilled in a word.

The orange cat had managed to remove the paper from one corner, and she was able to lick away a tear. She gnawed at the tear, widened it, and began to feast on the chicken tikka masala.

Someone wearing heavy black boots nearly stepped on her tail. But she was exhausted, hungry and oblivious.

'Call me Omar,' Omar said. *Call me Omar*, he said in his head again as if he had come up with something entirely original, entirely unprompted. This was something he would use again, if asked what his name was. Though in his head he gave some credit to Sara. He would remember her whenever he said it. 'And you're Sara, right?' he asked.

She stared at him like he knew everything there was to know just because he knew her name.

He looked at her like he had deduced, without any clue, her name. That he had plucked it out of thin air. That he had, in guessing her name, named her all over again.

'Yes,' she said. Good, we're past the introductions, Sara thought. I know his name now. How did he spell it? He said it like it started with an 'o'. Now she knew him, and she was catching up, since he already knew her name from the bomb day.

Or drone day. Or gas pipe explosion day. Or leftover landmine day. In the absence of an official confirmation, some people had even started calling it the land fart day. Nobody had a clue.

Sara had also heard a fringe theory that someone had lobbed a grenade from outside the campus. But who could throw that far? In every direction, the campus stretched at least 100 metres from the crater. So that meant it was probably someone from the inside. A student, faculty or staff bomber. Could it be? The jumble stayed indecipherable. Sara couldn't unravel it.

'Do you have class right now?' she asked Omar.

He had to say yes. It was time.

The shuffle of the crowd behind him had thinned out, the sun had arced westward a notch, throwing more shadow over the two of them from the pillar. The yawn of time in which they stood was coming to a close.

'Yeah,' he said, 'history of war.' He felt he said the word 'war' like it was a robust and attractive thing, something macho men went for, people with too much brawn. So he modified it by saying, 'It's about tactics and the evolution of strategies.' He waved the books in his hand casually as he said that, and felt silly for trying to prove that he read books.

She nodded. 'I don't have class until four,' she said and paused, thinking. Mehreen was going to leave campus at three, and Nadia wouldn't come today because she didn't have class on Tuesdays and Thursdays. That meant nobody would find out what Sara was going to do today.

The pause niggled Omar. He had classes until four. He almost said a desperate, 'Do you want to hang out at six, after your class?'

But she said something first. 'There's the drones talk at six. Are you going for it?' she asked. She had opened another equation, and she didn't know the other side yet. He was going to have to do a calculation, come up with the right words, in the right order, with a suitable tone so she didn't feel he was being too clingy or too aloof. He had to strike a balance. She was testing him, giving him a little bit of rope.

He felt the passage of time expand as they stood there. Sara was inviting him, opening a door. But maybe she was opening a door she wasn't going to walk through herself. She had said *going*, not *coming*. *Are you going?* she had asked. This could mean she was finishing the conversation right now and giving him a chance to speak to her later, with an update on what the talk on drones was about. He could take that, and wait for the next time they ran into each other randomly. But no. He couldn't just rely on chance again.

'Are you?' he asked her instead. This was like a game of tennis. He had returned the serve in an area she could easily reach.

'Yeah,' Sara said. She would have to call her mom and say she was staying on campus until eight, but she wouldn't tell her about the drones talk, or about Omar. Sara's mother was unwell, and had been undergoing a lot of tests, so there was that set of logistics to consider. She would have to burden her conscience with the guilt of lying to her sick mother, and not being there for her. But it was okay; of course her mom would be fine. 'See you there?' she said, but regretted the question she had made of it, as if she was eager.

But wasn't she? Not desperate of course, but eager for sure. She even wanted to tell him it was in Auditorium 9, the biggest one, but she held back. She didn't want to invest more than she already had. He would have to find the information and show up on his own.

'Cool. I'll be there,' Omar said. Without thinking about it, or even pausing to consider the options with which he could have assented. She was *going* as well. She had asked an inclusive question, not an off-putting one. But he had to make sure it was inclusive. 'I'll save you a seat,' he said. Thereby saying *I want you to sit next to me*, as if they were both toddlers.

He pictured that: her as a two-year-old, coming into a daycare, with him already seated there in a corner, the only one with the empty seat next to him. He pictured her looking around with her little eyes, seeing the empty seat, and him putting his hand on it saying, 'This one's for you,' in a baby voice. The scene passed in an instant though. He smiled inside, but on the outside he waited for her to say something so he could go to class and think about her.

'Yeah, save me a seat,' she said, giving him some marks for that.

He half-turned, and waved his books a little to indicate a goodbye. 'See you then,' he said.

'See you, Omar,' she said, taking hold of his name and saying it for the first time. She had named him back. He fit the name now that she had called him that.

The two hours of the history of war whizzed by. He could only absorb one thing, one strategy. Between thinking about the distance from the tips of her long, straight hair and the floor—two-and-a-half feet—the old-school Nokia phone without a touchscreen she held in her hand as she talked to him while otherwise just standing there, and the way she had said his name, like it was spelt with a 'u' and not an 'o', he also absorbed and assimilated into his thoughts a singular concept passed on by the professor of history of war, without raising his hand or offering even an internal challenge to the strategy, and he applied it to something happening vividly in his present: the Encirclement. From its first known recorded use in the battle of Thermopylae in the fifth century BC, through occasional use in medieval and contemporary wars, it was used in the two 'world wars', and more recently in the Arab Spring as well, in Syria and Libya. The click in Omar's mind hardly took any time.

Infantry approached the opponent in a wide-open line, and enveloped the enemy from all sides. What ensued was a 360-degree fight against a force that had prepared to fight only on one front. Variations included the box formation, in which the curves were replaced with straight lines.

The Encirclement was obviously a tactic used outside of war and, by direct analogy, without recalling any specifics, Omar's mind centred on romantic comedies: the woman encircles the man, cutting him off from his friends, and from his access to freedom as a single man.

She moves in with him. She sees the clothes flopped on chairs, toilet seats raised, day-old plates stacked in the kitchen sink. She panics at this, a laugh track in the background.

A montage follows: the woman cleaning, sorting and organizing in fast-forward and in skip-reel.

Comedy is how they get you, Omar thought, his heart-rate picking up to match the pace of the laughter and the woman's panic in his imagined montage. Everything is cleared, organized and new.

The man arrives home and shades his eyes from the sparkle of things. He goes out again and checks the number on the door to see if it is his own house. He goes inside and takes a tour of his home, afraid to sully anything by touching it. He gingerly opens a drawer where he used to dump all his clean spoons and now there's not a spoon in sight among the washed and folded dishtowels there. He opens another drawer, the one where he kept cereal bowls. There, he finds toothpicks and chopsticks—items he would never, ever, put together. The woman has cleaned the kitchen of his presence. Without going to the bedroom, he knows his favourite pair of faded blue jeans is no longer draped over the desk chair in the corner. It will either be folded, without its character-lending creases, on a shelf in the cupboard, or else tumbling sacrilegiously in the washing machine.

Comedy and romance both disarm the male, thought Omar, and before he knows it, the woman has taken over all his time and space. He knows nothing other than what she lets him know. Like Encirclement in a battle, the only resources allowed in to the defeated army—the subdued man—is what the suppressor allows.

The man, once enfeebled, turns helpless. Because he thinks that while he is being surrounded he is battling hard in pursuit of glory and fulfillment. Little does he know about the war beside and behind him, a war that is being won by the woman.

Omar's nostrils flared. He felt sweat inside his shirt collar and under his armpits. The starch of the shirt stuck to him along his torso. His back felt creased and weak. He sank low into his chair with the weight of the conceptual disaster playing out on the screen inside his head.

What he wanted most was to recall seeing Sara, as she had stepped out from under the shadow and into light, haloed in the autumn sun. What he was able to access through memory was her standing in the shadow but as soon as he would make her move into the light, her face would distort.

He noticed he was clicking and unclicking his pen. The soft noise masked the air conditioner's metallic drone, the history professor's baritone lecture, the squeaks and scratches of chalk on the blackboard, and the *click-clack, click-clack* of another person in the middle of the room doing the same thing as Omar, with a louder pen.

The other students seemed transfixed by the professor, his measured gait and cadence, his ability to disentangle truth from fiction about the World Wars and the US–Korea war and thus render everything they considered fact back into the realm of conjecture.

Hot and cold dwelled Omar's mind on thoughts of Sara. Maybe she was going to take over everything. Maybe she was going to open him up and make him into something he otherwise would not, or could not, become. Maybe she was a passing figure, like a hobby he wouldn't ever take to.

Or she might not be at ease with him, ever, just as he was always uneasy with himself.

The only time he was able to relax and forget about being conscious of his awkwardness was with his Aitchison boys, now flung far across the wide, open world.

How would she ever fit into his life? He now wished he did not have to meet her in a few hours.

Time, inevitably, passed. Class ended and the professor left, taking with him a knot of students asking questions about the mid-term exam and the final essay.

The room became nearly empty. A girl in the back row opened a box of Tupperware on her desk and shared half her sandwich with another girl. They talked about the explosion in monotones between bites, then picked up their things and left. He was now alone.

Omar did not step outside the classroom for another ten minutes and reached his next class just before the TA closed the door and locked it. He went and sat at the back, and even raised his hand once or twice to show his participation.

There were three hours to go until 6 p.m., and he was already numb with the range of possibilities Sara meant and offered. In his head he was already on the long route to a marriage in which bitter fights and solace both figured in equal measure. And he even fleshed out versions of the other route, where they became more distant and awkward with each passing day, and dreaded seeing each other on campus until years later they happened to meet in a crowded market, followed by introductions to spouses and kids. Or the still more variant version, when years later one of them kept waiting to run into the other but it didn't happen. Or maybe even an alternative future possibility in which somehow they both reached the vantage point of not remembering the other.

The sliding door which would open to the true future was at least three hours away. Or it had already slid one way, and the rest was a formality, waiting to happen in due course as had been planned by fate.

Omar exhausted himself by fleshing out all the different possibilities.

He refused to cut up past and future anymore. What would be, would be. Even this freshmen rhetoric class he was sitting in—how could it possibly be duller or more exciting than it already was?

Two hours and forty-five minutes to go. Then Sara. Then life. Que Sera Sera. Que Sara Sara.

⚜

She was positive that he would show up at Auditorium 9, and she was certain that he would show up late. Given the amount of talk the panel on drone strikes had generated since the posters went up two days ago, Omar/Umar would not find seats for them.

She anticipated that the two of them would have to stand at the back of the large hall, squeezing themselves between thirty or forty eager listeners. She imagined he would grow more insecure by her side, that he would begin to fidget while she kept absolutely still, and there would be supreme awkwardness between them while they stood at the back of the large hall, listening to a lecture neither of them really cared much about.

To avoid pitying him, she would have to leave early, excusing herself, and at night while eating dinner it would occur to her that without letting Nadia and Mehreen know about Omar/Umar, she would not be able to socialize with him at LUSS. But by then it would be too late because he would have failed both of them by not having saved a seat for her like he had promised.

She had gone back to the library after Nadia's call, and after speaking to him. In front of her, on the table, lay her book, *Introduction to Macro and Micro Economics* on which she could not concentrate. The supply-demand curve did not make sense to her. Why would it shift up or shift down once it was where it was? The overly simplistic explanations in class didn't help either because she never learnt well when she was being spoken down to.

Sara had heard that the concepts and the teaching would get more intricate and harder to understand with time. All the patience would be used up here, in the beginning of the term, and then the professors would disinvest themselves—they had kids at home and issues other than teaching to worry about.

She kept thinking she probably shouldn't have come to LUSS, that she would have been better off as a tried and failed artist at the National College of Arts than the bored and numbers-oriented economics or computer sciences graduate she was going to become.

The detachment that took over her stemmed from not being invested at LUSS. It came like a wave of energy and stayed like a force field which protected her and gave her strength and immunity. Being at LUSS, she felt she was on a road she was never meant to travel. Somehow she had stepped into an alternative universe, an experimental one, and the real one was continuing along the correct, the official, trajectory. The weight of things, the weight of being, was more tangible in that real reality.

Here, in the version of reality that she found herself waiting for, and dreading her intro to econ class, she would feel the pain and effect if someone pinched her, but it seemed not to matter for now.

It would matter soon though, she knew. She would have to embrace the role of this Sara, the one who had chosen to go to LUSS with Mehreen and Nadia rather than start over, with zero friendships, at the arts college. She would have to accept this Sara, who sketched and painted only late into the night, with no guidance except her own instinct and whatever rudimentary tricks she had learnt at school.

The textbook lay open in front of her. All around her, in the library, the stacks and stacks of books stayed shelved and charged with knowledge. Some of the students were gathered around the sofas at the front, reading newspapers and magazines.

The supply-demand curve shifted down somehow.

The stacks and stacks of books remained unmoved. One of the students put down a magazine and went to the shelves to pick another one. Another made a show of turning his newspaper's page.

Somehow, the supply-demand curve shifted.

Pretending that it was only a doodle, over the next hour Sara sketched, in the margins of her textbook, the shift of the supply-demand curve, as witnessed by a bewildered young girl.

Omar entered Auditorium 9 while it was being set up for the panel discussion. There was still an hour to go until the talk. He had his copy of *Love in the Time of Cholera* with him. Time would pass with reading. He would get past the tenth page, the one he had been stuck at the last time he had picked up the book.

The auditorium was V-shaped, and the stage was its focus. Two aisles separated 500 seats into three allotments. He chose the middle set, crossed over and sat in what would be two rows behind the centre. He set the textbook and his notebook on the seat to his right, and picked up the Marquez novel. He opened it to page 10 and read this sentence:

'He would spend an hour in his study preparing for the class on general clinical medicine that he taught at the Medical School every morning.'

Reading the sentence made him think of his own schedule at LUSS, and he paused to wonder what schedule a Pakistani medical school would follow. That took him out of the book.

He looked up at the stage where they were setting the microphones in place. There were three microphones for three speakers at the table but no chairs yet. Another microphone was already set up at the podium. The attendants ignored him.

The stage seemed to loom directly in front of him—it suffocated him. There was nowhere to look but at the stage. Omar didn't like this. He didn't want to sit with Sara here. He gathered his things and stood up.

He climbed the steps to the back of the centre aisle and looked towards the stage. This was too far away and he didn't want to hide in the back with her either.

He stepped over to the right, moved down a few steps from the back, sat on an aisle seat and put his things down on the adjacent seat. Before picking up the novel again, he leaned over to check whether the seat he would offer Sara was not broken.

A pendulum inside him oscillated between panic and calm, and the full spectrum in between. She might not come, even though she had said she would. She could decide to enter from the other side, and if there was too large a crowd by then, she would not be able to see him and would quickly have to find a seat away from him.

If that happened, if she sat on some other seat, he would have to give up the idea of talking to her today because he did not want to come across as desperate for her attention and friendship. He would have to bump into her some other day and casually mention how he had enjoyed the lecture, or not enjoyed it, and found it full of insights or not driven by insightful thinking.

On the flip side, however, was the calm that overtook him. So he would not get to sit next to her today during this lecture and he would not make her a friend or ally at LUSS. So what? No matter. He was going to transfer out of LUSS anyway. What difference would it make if both of them did not have a future in which they spent any time together? Life would go on. It was sure to.

Oscillating between the panic of Zen and the calm of surrender, he never got past the same sentence on page 10 which he read four times while sitting in the auditorium, waiting.

The hour passed.

In that hour, students walked in and took up seats in the middle and the two side pockets. They came in groups of at least three, and they looked him over and wondered why he had come alone.

The centre seats, where Omar had first thought to sit, were taken up by five boys who unrolled a large parchment in their laps and passed whispers from one end to the other and back.

Other students arrived and chose seats according to algorithms of preferences that took into account distance between others already in seats, distance from and angle to the stage, access to an exit, just in case, and the ability to be seen or not seen.

Unseen technicians tweaked the lighting to find the correct shade between theatre candlelight and classroom phosphorescence. On-stage staff tapped microphones in turn and said, 'Hello, check, check, check, one-two-three, check,' into each of them, and another unseen technician adjusted dials to equalize the volume. At the podium was a laptop computer with which a technician fiddled until the screen behind him filled up with a Panasonic logo, and then faded to show a Windows PC desktop, with the bland default wallpaper. Then he shut off the projector with a remote and the screen went white again.

A buzz began to build up in the auditorium; students piled in and seats became scarce. Soon the few seats that remained were those reserved for the panelists, the guests and a handful that some students had saved for their friends.

Omar's things lay prominently on the seat he was saving and only once did someone come up and ask if he was saving it for someone. That did not go well because he almost lifted his things, for at that moment he was as certain—as he was of the incessant passing of time and the unquestionable movement of spheres against the blackness of the galaxies—that Sara would not come sit next to him.

That crest of doubt was the only time in the whole hour that he sat waiting for her when he did not have a story ready for why he was there by himself; whether he was saving a seat, or hoping against the march of fate to be rescued from becoming a lost cause in the swelling and buzzing crowd.

⚜

It was 5.55 p.m. Sara left the washroom after fixing her hair and taking a good look at herself. She had no books or bags with her, having left all her things in her locker at the library. She walked in through the open door to Auditorium 9 and excused herself past the two boys blocking the entrance. They let her pass but she now had to walk through the students kneeling and squatting on the floor.

At the back of room stood another fifty or sixty students. The air was thick with a dissonant mix of sweat and perfume.

The panelists were at their assigned seats on stage, getting microphones fixed to their lapels. A bald, bearded and chubby professor stood at the podium. The session hadn't started yet, but the room was silent. A titter here, a whisper and a cough in the middle somewhere. Close to a thousand people in the room, and those were the only sounds she heard in the first few seconds it took to adjust her eyes.

Omar was not standing in a row at the back.

She scanned it twice to make sure and kept running her eyes against the students leaning against the back wall even as she searched the room. She looked farthest from herself, not believing he could have found a seat close to where she had entered.

The crowd swelled as one as she took a breath in. But there was still no sign of him.

Would she have turned around and left had she not found him?

But just then, closer to her than she expected, was his hand raised with a closed fist, except with one finger pointing to the ceiling. His eyes were locked on her. She had to negotiate past a few students seated on the steps, and into the aisle full of boys. There was a loud cough from the podium that was echoed by the speakers. She glanced up at the stage, and kept walking. Then she was there, standing next to him, and he had his things on his lap and the seat next to him was empty.

As soon as she was within reach, he held a hand out and she understood he was reaching out for her phone, and she gave it to him. It felt natural and uncomplicated, this flow of the phone from her to him. She saw where, on the back of his head, his skin showed through the black tangle of his hair. He punched a few keys, and handed her phone back to her. The screen showed 'Omar Kayani' and his number starting with 0305 and ending with 89. She had his number now, and Sara slowly sat down next to Omar.

The boy on her other side took his elbow off the armrest between them. She had a choice to lean either way now.

'Welcome, ladies and gentlemen,' boomed the speakers all around the auditorium.

Sara chose to not rest her elbows on either side and pressed a button on her phone.

The speaker continued, 'I am Professor Rasheed—' and he garbled his last name with a cough.

The silence thickened and pulsed.

Sara leaned left and whispered, 'I'm calling you,' to Omar. She felt as though the whole student body in the auditorium could hear her say that and she blushed.

Omar nodded, and with his left hand touched the pocket of his jeans as he waited for his phone to vibrate.

Professor Rasheed enjoyed his baritone filling the auditorium and he stretched out the vowels of every word, and trilled the r's, as he said: 'I am professor of law in the School of Law and Public Policy at the Lahore University of Social Sciences, and I have the great honour of hosting today's panel discussion. Our topic for the evening is the legality of drones, as they are used, in all their capacities all across the world. Since this topic is one close to home for all of us, I am glad to see how much interest it has generated. I have never seen this large auditorium filled to the brim, but it is fuller than capacity today. I thank you all for being here this evening.'

Omar's pocket vibrated and he took out his touchscreen Windows phone and noted the time. 6.01 p.m. Sara had called him at 6.01. It was significant, even if he did not know how or why.

She hung up and rested her hands in her lap.

On Omar's phone, the number started with a 0300 and ended with an 811. He saved it as Sara, the only Sara on his phone.

'Joining us today as panelists are three remarkable people,' continued Professor Rasheed. The loudspeakers bellowed. Otherwise not a stir, a cough or sneeze sounded. One thousand silences. 'Their record as advocates and champions of the truth is long and lustrous. Their service to the community is redoubtable. And the grace they lend our stage here at LUSS is immense.' Professor Rasheed then paused, as if for applause, but none was generated. The audience was not there to listen to his bombast.

Omar leaned his body left, but his head right. The imperceptible and equal angles of twist made him feel as though he was sitting straight up, and he thought it was best to stay like this, within reach of her whisper but not too close to scare her away.

An hour ago he could not have imagined himself without panic at the thought of sitting next to her. But sitting required no energy; what needed energy was the effort not to fidget. He didn't shake his legs or fiddle with a pen. The pangs of his worry, which had peaked minutes before her arrival, had dissipated like a myth and in their stead was the assurance of Sara herself sitting next to him. As if the panic were part of a process to bring her here and, having served its purpose, had bowed out. Exeunt, stage right.

On stage, at the podium, the professor waved at the three panelists and introduced them as 'journalist, Ghaazi Sikander, former Member of Parliament, Gulminay Dost, and educationist, Jehangir Saulat, all very dear and close friends of mine,' without allocating to them individual paragraphs of praise, qualifying their championship of the truth or delineating their services to the community. He then went on, 'Our format for the evening is as follows: Ghaazi Sikander will speak about his book-in-progress on drone policies and usage, and the legal implications of drone activities throughout the world. Then we will open the discussion to our panelists. Since Gulminay Dost has plenty of experience working on legislation against drone usage in

Pakistan, I am sure she will contribute to our understanding. As will Jehangir Saulat, who is addressing terrorism at the grassroots level by introducing a curriculum reform and the formation of new schooling systems in the areas being targeted by the US-led drone strikes in Pakistan.'

Sara recognized two of the three panelists. Ghaazi Sikander came on television every night at nine. Her dad thought that Ghaazi was an army stooge masquerading as a voice of reason. Gulminay Dost, an alumnus of LUSS, was supposedly a 'clean' politician, but that only meant her party did not have any power. Sara did not know Jehangir Saulat and she rested a fragment of idealistic hope on his contribution to the panel.

She was not thinking about the explosion at LUSS anymore or about sitting next to Omar, which now felt like something that was always meant to be. What concerned her instead was peace in Pakistan. There was a larger picture, of which she felt a part, even if as a pixel on the colossal canvas of it all. She leaned over an inch and said, 'Good seats,' to Omar.

He nodded and waited for things to progress.

A scatter of claps started and fizzled out as Ghaazi Sikander rasped a breath into the microphone on the table that he brought closer to himself. Meanwhile, Professor Rasheed stepped off the stage and sat down on an empty chair in the front row.

'Before we begin,' said Ghaazi Sikander, his voice gravelly and deep, his words coming out in a put-on American accent, 'I would like the following fact to be understood: I am not here to talk about drone attacks in Pakistan. They are of no interest to me as a journalist and researcher.' He took a long pause and scanned the room to wait while his words sank in.

Some in the audience looked at their phones to recheck the topic of discussion, some checked for emails and texts, others shifted but most didn't do anything at all.

'Good,' said Ghaazi Sikander. 'Once we have moved past that point, I want to tell you what I am actually going to speak about: the legality of drones. The subtitle of my talk is: "Can we ban the tin cans?" I am sure you understand that the tin can refers to the drones and also to the aphorism that empty cans make the loudest noise. It's a simple play on words.' If he was waiting for laughter or a note of appreciation, Ghaazi was at the wrong place at the wrong time. He received nervous and uncertain stares from the audience. It was the best he was going to get.

Omar felt his feet uncross and then cross again. Why was he here? Would he have come on his own? Most likely not. Definitely not, in fact. He had no interest in the legality of drone attacks. They were illegal, so what was there to discuss? He took a chance and looked over at Sara, who didn't look back at him but raised an eyebrow. Omar took it as a positive sign, as her way of saying she was also wondering the same thing.

But he was quite sure, instantly, only for an instant, that they were not on the same wavelength, and he wondered if he should let that bother him.

But why let his insecurity ruin everything from the start? He decided to wait until after the panel discussion, when he would walk with her outside the auditorium. He could already see himself walking her to her car, or at least the gate, saying, 'See you later.' He would then turn around to walk to his dorm with a glow and a smile. It felt like a certain thing, this one-two walk-smile act, as if it was already in play and all he had to do was follow the rails laid out for him.

'Drones,' continued Ghaazi on stage, 'come in all sizes and shapes. They have proliferated among us to the extent that in five to ten years they are going to become ubiquitous. Every household will have three or four. One for the kids to play with, one for the surveillance of the house from an aerial vantage point and one to fetch your dad's paper from the front lawn.' He pressed a button on a remote. The projector turned on with a beep and the screen behind him switched to black, and an unseen technician turned the hall's lights down so the presentation became more visible. 'But before we get into all that, let's start at the beginning. What is a drone?' The black screen brightened slowly and a picture appeared out of darkness. It looked like a missile with wings and a tail. Ghaazi Sikander kept sitting and looked alternately at the audience and his laptop screen. 'Here's a typical one. This is the MQ-9 Reaper. It is used for hunting and killing specific targets.' He clicked a button and said of the next one, 'This is a similar one. The Predator, which can launch missiles.'

Someone in the audience whispered 'Damn'. Sara turned to look in the direction from which the voice had come.

Omar turned to look at Sara. Her eyes were wide open and her face was blank. It was as if she didn't even know he was there.

She turned her eyes back to the stage.

He looked at her hands resting in her lap. Omar felt a subtle force tethering him to Sara, coercing him to conform and become what she thought he was and it did not feel entirely good. He became absolutely still and watched the screen.

'Here,' Ghaazi Sikander said, clicking the remote's button, 'is another one.' This time a white spider-shaped hub with legs came up on the screen. 'This one is used for surveillance. It has two main cameras on its belly and four others under each fan.' Then a red and white helicopter showed up on the screen, hovering over fields. The picture transitioned into a video and the field was then shown from the perspective of the drone in flight above it. There was no sound from the speaker until Ghaazi Sikander said, 'And this one is used for information-gathering and pattern analysis of crops and water distribution in Massachusetts, USA.'

Sara coughed to clear her throat.

Omar wanted to turn but decided not to.

'Could we have the lights turned up again, please?' Ghaazi Sikander asked, and waited. After five seconds of silence and darkness, the overhead lights lit up. With another click a black slide appeared and on the top it said: Common Usages of Drones. 'Here are some of the common uses of drones in today's world. We will start here. Look at the past patterns of military and industrial development of similar technologies, and then examine what the future holds.' Bullet points faded in, one by one, and he read them out loud: 'Reconnaissance. Surveillance for activity. Surveillance for terrain examination. Delivery and pickup. Extraction. Surgical strikes—'

'Shut up!' someone in the hall suddenly shouted.

Sara turned her head.

Omar's hands gripped his own thighs. He also turned.

'You don't know anything!' shouted the voice once again.

It came from the centre of the audience where Omar had first sat down. It was one of those five people with the large roll of parchment.

'Excuse me?' Ghaazi Sikander said in a thinner voice than his presentation one.

The group of five who had come together were holding up a large banner.

The speaker was the middle one. He had, of all things, a red balloon in his hand. 'We will show you what drones really are,' he said with a snarl. He was thin and average in height, as young as a student, and he looked ordinary. He didn't have a beard or a turban. He was dressed in jeans and a polo shirt. So were his companions, who stood as they unrolled the banner.

'What is the meaning of—?' Professor Rasheed said from his seat in the front row, his torso twisted around.

'We will show you,' the boy cut in. He held the red balloon and released some of its string so it floated up, unspooling from his hand. Nobody else moved and the balloon floated up higher.

It was as if all movement were in fast forward and slow motion simultaneously. Time was out of sync with reality.

'Here, this is what drones do,' said the boy, releasing some more string from his hand. Behind him, the banner was unfurled and on it were pictures of faces with eyes closed, skins torn and bloodied. There were five faces with the sixth one lost in the folded portion on one end. One of them looked like the face of a little girl. The others were men or boys. The faces were separated in the middle by the words: THANK YOU, DRONES!

'Stop this!' Professor Rasheed shouted.

There was a stir at the back of the room. Some of the students there had ducked.

Sara's instincts told her that escape was impossible. She did not need to look around to know that there were at least forty people sitting between her and the door closest to her. She watched the balloon soar higher. It was four times the size of a regular balloon.

Twenty-five feet above the floor, it hovered.

'Watch this drone!' said the boy who held the string to the balloon. His companions held the banner high and stretched it wide. The people sitting around them tried to get up, tried to back away. No one wanted to be a hero; not yet.

The speaker among them, the one who held the balloon by its string, showed his other hand. He flicked something in it and a fire was created. It was a lighter. 'You want to know about drones?' he bellowed. 'This is what drones do. This is the bastard thing they do.' He brought the flame close to the string and touched it, released the string from his hand, and put the lighter out.

The fire on the string began to work its way up to the balloon, and the released balloon began to rise towards the ceiling.

Omar lost all thought of action. He was so mesmerized by the fire.

It grew bigger on the string and longer as it climbed up. The lower part of it unextinguished even as it engulfed more string.

Omar was expecting a bomb to go off when the balloon would burst. This was the end of it all. He thought the sound alone would be enough, even if there was no material explosion.

Sara took hold of Omar's arm.

The air conditioning worked the smell of fire around the room. The shouting started. Still no heroes. Not yet.

Professor Rasheed rushed onto the stage and grabbed a microphone. But he didn't say anything once he had it. Nobody was looking at him. The fire and the balloon were a few feet apart, and the balloon only a few feet from the ceiling.

Sara's clutch on Omar's bicep was like a bear's grip. He heard screams and believed for a second that he was also screaming. But he was only panting hard.

Sara waited for the loud noise that would shake her up and show her how real everything was. If it took an explosion to do that, so be it. She only hoped nobody was harmed.

The flame ran out of string. Above the string, there was rubber and helium.

The thousand people in the auditorium waited, some attempting to run through the thick mass of people. Others waited while standing their ground, blocking those who were trying to run.

One tried to be a hero, to take down the boy who had lit the string leading to the balloon. But he was not hero material, and two of the four who held the banner kicked and punched him away.

Omar put his free hand on top of Sara's, the one she had on his arm.

Reassured but alarmed at the same time by his hand on hers, Sara tightened her grip.

There was a gap in the screams, like an awkward pause in the conversation of fear. It felt like a moment of real time suspended outside of the jumbling chronology of events in play.

But that passed and everything was slow-motion-fast-forward again. Someone tripped and got his elbow stepped on and broken. There was a loud and hoarse scream. The doors at the back were forced apart.

The red balloon did not burst. The flame had run its course and died. The ceiling air conditioning vents contributed to that, as did air resistance on the balloon's upward climb.

Sara and Omar were among the many who stayed in their seats. He stayed because he was petrified and she because she wanted to be there, to hear the loud noise that was about to come.

Time kept ticking but the explosion never came. It was a dud.

And then, suddenly—inevitably—there were heroes everywhere. Two of them picked up the boy with the crushed elbow. Five others went from one side of the aisle in which those with the banner stood, and ten others came from the other side. The perpetrators were still looking up, baffled.

Without the long string, the balloon was less rooted. It lolled back and forth, and bounced up and down between two air vents on the ceiling.

Sara and Omar let go of each other's hands and kept looking at the mayhem.

He was utterly ashamed that he had not done anything.

She was still looking up at the balloon, waiting for the noise that would not come at all now.

'Please,' Professor Rasheed said on stage. 'Stop panicking.'

It looked like a scuffle was about to break out in the row from which the balloon had ascended. One of the boys, a senior at the university, had a knife on him. He held the four-inch blade with the confidence that it was enough to save him in any scrap.

Half the banner with the faces of the dead and bloodied drone victims lay draped over the seats while the other half lay on the floor. The five boys who had brought it with them stepped on it while trying to escape by climbing over the backs of their own seats to the row behind. But that row was still half full, and the clamber was interrupted by kicks, punches and slaps to their legs.

Two security guards appeared at the doors, followed by five who blocked the closest entrance and refused to let anyone leave. Students tried to shove past them, but were held back with thick staffs.

'Sit down, please, everyone. Listen, everyone, please sit down,' Professor Rasheed said. Some students sat down, while others kept standing near the entrance. The professor pointed at the five disrupting banner-folk and said, 'Grab them, guards. Grab them now. Do it now.'

Sara put her hand on Omar's shoulder and pressed down on it to keep him sitting.

She did not need to, for he had no intention of getting up to join the ruckus. That moment he had thought of bolting from the room after grabbing her hand had long since passed.

But she didn't know that.

There was a loud crack. The audience looked up at the ceiling again, but the fire under the balloon had not come back to life. It was not the sound of an explosion but the sound of wood snapping. It had come from the centre of the room, where one of the five boys with the banner had pried off the wooden armrest from a chair. He brandished the shard of wood like a weapon.

That did it. Now everybody decided to become a hero. Not because the threat of a weapon had woken up their heroic natures; but because of the 50,000-rupee fine that accompanied any damage to LUSS property, which the students were eager to impose on the outsider who had dared to show such violence to the furniture.

Someone dived into the aisle and brought down two of the perpetrators, along with three students. The other three did not stand a chance against the garrison of guards and students. One of them squealed, 'Drones are terrorism!'

'Who are these kids?' Professor Rasheed asked from the stage, into the microphone. 'Find out who they are. Bring them to security.' En masse, the righteous crowd dragged the five dissidents to the far exit. They were kicked and punched on the way, and held fast in the guards' iron grips.

Sara let go of Omar's shoulder and got up.

He stood up too and lined up behind her and the crowd that funneled out into the corridor.

The panel conferred on stage what to do. A handful of students stayed back to see if the talk would continue. But in the large auditorium their numbers looked bleak. After five minutes, the panelists were escorted out by three guards and they soon left the campus.

Since her car hadn't arrived yet, Omar did not walk Sara to the gate. Instead, she walked beside him as he headed in the general direction of his hostel. He only shuffled along. It seemed okay to just shuffle. A conflict between the desire to be encased and the fear of being trapped had taken hold of his insides, and the web grew thicker with each moment he lingered beside her.

'Were you scared?' he asked.

'No,' she replied, without thinking whether she really had been. 'It was only a balloon.'

'Yeah,' he said, 'that's true.' And he wondered now why he had been so afraid. Was it because of the blast last week? He felt a sense of danger in the night around them, in the students who walked past them in the darkness. In the distant sound of sirens of ambulances. He wondered if he was safer with or without Sara.

He did not question whether she was safer with him. But he wanted clarity on what he would have to do if they were both under threat because danger seemed to follow him everywhere.

'Whenever we meet, some terrorist comes along and makes it fun,' Sara suddenly said. She did not know why she said it, but she saw this as a cosmic joke, and looked up and wondered who was telling it.

He looked at her. She had read his thoughts. She was looking up at the darkening sky and shaking her head. She was smiling. How could she smile at a time like this? Didn't she know what she said was true? That the danger was real? Omar wanted to shake her until the smile fell off her face and she saw the reality of what she spoke, and had to choose, after knowing how dangerous it was, whether to keep walking with him or to turn around right now.

Because he knew. And he had made his choice. He was going to keep walking very slowly, maybe even take detours and U-turns just so he could spend time with her. It made him feel weightless.

And though he could not suspend time completely, the few hundred metres to his hostel could be covered at a slower pace. The distance could be divided into longer chunks of space and time.

And while saying the banal things he said, and choosing to hear what she said as multilayered and at least on some level profound, he wondered what it all meant. The balloon, the boys, their act of setting fire to the string, their desire to have everyone hear the ball of helium bursting into flames. Why do this?

And he wondered what his own reaction meant. Instead of jumping up to protect her by forcing his way, with her, out of the hall, he had sagged and turned to unmoving stone. Eventually, after all the action that had taken place in the room ended, Omar excused himself for not having moved from his seat. It had been, in retrospect, an act of bravery not to join the screamers or those who had done or said anything at all.

There was a buzz all across campus. Students were sharing the story and adding or removing details, already making it something it was not. Some dorm rooms' distant but loud Beyonce, Zeb and Haniya, and Arcade Fire tracks overlapped and provided a surreal soundtrack.

Sara matched steps with him, wondering out loud how many people had wanted to see the balloon burst. She did not lower her head while walking when she remembered she had wanted it to explode. But she did not share this with him. Instead, she punched his shoulder and half-joked about their run-ins with trouble.

'Don't worry, Omar,' she said. 'I'll protect you next time there's a terrorist on campus.' And she watched his frown pivot around and become a smile.

He laughed, picturing her holding a machine gun and dressed in camouflage with black face-paint.

She stopped walking.

'Sorry, sorry,' he said, and kept soundlessly laughing. 'I am imagining you as Rambo.'

She decided not to take offence, and not to pretend to take it either.

He put one hand up and another on his belly and kept heaving with dry chuckles, mouthing 'Sorry', and losing some of his fear and the gravity that wound him up so much.

She stood there wanting to hear him laugh louder. She also remembered wanting to hear the balloon burst loudly, like a wakeup call. What would it have felt like? Would it be like the moment after a loud clap of thunder?

There, waiting for him to overcome his spasms of amusement,

one of the plans for life she made, which she knew she would forget in the coming days, was to one day buy a big bundle of helium balloons, tie them overhead with a long tangle of strings dipped in kerosene oil, and then watch and listen as the knot of strings burnt away and the balloons tried to escape into the darkness of the night sky. It would lead to a sound she knew she would regret not having heard in the perfect acoustics of Auditorium 9 at LUSS.

Nadia called Sara within the hour and told her about the incident at the university, and Sara told her that she knew. Without going into too many details, Sara told her that she had been there, with Omar, when it had happened. When Nadia asked who Omar was, Sara said, with new boldness, 'I'll introduce you to him next time.'

That night, Sara had a deep and restful sleep in her own bed, miles away from campus. She had reconciled to the fact that no noise would equal the one she needed to hear.

Omar and QT had decided to meet up for dinner. QT's take was that the whole incident was a prank, a call for attention, and that there would be more of those.

'It could have caused a stampede,' Omar said.

'No,' QT said, chewing on his food and looking into the distance over Omar's head, 'we're too lazy to run.' He looked at Omar again and said, 'Plus, it's fun to stick around and see what happens after shit happens.'

Omar wondered if he had done exactly this—whether being too scared to move was just an excuse to stick around and watch the drama, no matter what the risk. He felt much less of a hero or a scared idiot. Now he felt almost evil because that meant he wasn't looking out for Sara at all.

The following week, Omar woke up with his chest hurting, and he remembered, at the instant of waking, the fire that had somehow seemed to vanish from the string. It felt like a magic transposition but he forgot the auditorium fire instantly.

The hot lava of pain in his throat and chest did not allow conscious thought. He ran down the steps out of the hostel and to the back of the campus. He was heading for the hockey fields, and he made it only as far as the running track around the cricket ground. It was the night his chest burnt up, the night he took his first long walk around the track, the one that started all the running in circles that he would become accustomed to later.

For the students, the administration's prolonged silence on issues of security was the worst thing about being at LUSS in those days. It confirmed that the threat to their lives was real; also real was the fact that there was no plan to deal with the threat. It was as though the administration had admitted defeat in facing the odds and had decided that the students were not worth the increase in security measures required to keep them safe.

As expected and as feared, in the days and weeks that followed that night, nothing official was said about the five perpetrators at all. Their names, their institutional link to LUSS and their agenda, whether they had any, were all swept away under some inter-departmental bureaucratic rug.

What remained for a brief moment in time was the red balloon. It stayed up there in Auditorium 9 that night, jostling back and forth with shifts in air pressure from the vents. In the morning, the janitors made numerous attempts to bring it down using the two inches of string still tied to its rubber knot. But the auditorium's ceiling was too high and they did not have a ladder long enough.

In the end, they decided to shoot it down. But using a guard's pistol or shotgun would have been overkill, not to mention alarming for all who would have heard it. They finally had to burst it with an air gun the following night. It took them three attempts to shoot the balloon down.

Until then, the balloon stayed up there, lolling back and forth while the 150-person introduction to financial accounting and the 220-person introduction to business studies classes went on underneath it.

Omar's roommate, Basit, didn't once look up to see the balloon. He knew it was red and he knew why it was there. But his textbook was down here, in front of him, and that mattered so much more.

Nadia Shirazi's Speech

Hi everyone.

Most of you know me. For those who don't, I'm Nadia Shirazi, Sara's best friend. Well, sort of. I'm her best friend in many ways. Her best friend on and off. Maybe that's the best way to describe our friendship, Sara's and mine.

All of us knew Sara, I'm sure. There's no way you could miss her. She was one of the smartest and most beautiful girls on campus. And she didn't even have to try. She was so naturally full of grace and charm.

She had it all. She really did.

I used to feel really jealous of the attention she used to get. Walking with her across campus was a really hard thing to do. All those stares, all the attention from the boys and the envy from the girls.

But that's the one thing I miss most. I wish I could walk across the campus with her now, just like I used to.

I miss Sara.

Well, what else can I say about my best friend? I don't know if it will make sense to any of you, or if you even believe in having best friends anymore since we're no longer in high school. But I'll tell you that having a best friend in college was the biggest blessing I ever received.

Sara used to listen to me. I could say anything in the world to her, anything at all. She would always be there, on the other end of the phone or the other end of the table or the other side of the car. Listening and offering advice. I'm not proud of telling you that she listened more than I did. She started listening to others in kindergarten, and never stopped listening. She was always ready with fantastic advice, some of which I took and some of which I didn't.

And I mostly regretted it when I didn't.

But I don't think she was perfect. No. Sara also had flaws. For instance, she didn't like to be held up against any external standards. She was always internally motivated. This made her seem aloof to most people, sometimes even to us, her friends. It's hard to describe what we felt, but it often looked as though she believed she was better than us.

Mehreen would agree with me on this. She and I talked about this many times.

But I want to say this: Sara *was* better than me. She cared about me and was honest with me like nobody else ever was or ever can be. I remember her now as the supporter I needed every time my heart was broken. Whether it was my mother who wasn't being reasonable or the massive load of assignments I couldn't handle, or my terrible grades or crushes that were killing my soul, Sara was always there to let me cry on her shoulder.

But while she gave me all this, she never gave me the chance to be the support that *she* needed. I don't know anyone she trusted enough to show her true self to. Maybe she trusted Omar that much. But I don't know.

I never got to know Omar well, even though I was so close to Sara. Perhaps I was closer to her than anybody, even closer than Omar. She never said though.

That's another complaint I have against Sara: she would never share things that made her vulnerable. She wasn't secretive, but I felt she never really showed us who she was. I still don't know her, even though she knew me as much as one human being can know another.

But then, maybe that is a good thing. Isn't friendship like falling in love too? You just can't choose who you're friends with, can you? I couldn't.

Sara and I first met when we were three years old and joined school together. I remember her clearly. I can picture her even now, in her blue frock, white socks and black shoes, coming in through the gate holding her mother's hand. Her mom stayed for five or maybe ten minutes, talking to our teacher, Miss Gul, and then she left leaving Sara there.

Sara didn't cry, but I could tell she was being left alone like that for the first time.

I was already best friends with someone else at the time and didn't need to make friends with Sara. But I went over to her anyway and I asked her if she wanted to play with us. She nodded very seriously, I remember. I led her to my friends. We spent the day playing some silly games and I told her all about myself: what my favourite colour was, what my mom cooked, the foods that I didn't like, how I hated my brother for having bigger toys even though he was younger. I told her I already had a best friend and I recommended someone she could be best friends with.

For the past seventeen years, I have been repeating that first meeting with Sara. I have been telling her who I am, what my problems are, what my favourite colour is. That I hate my brother because he gets to do all the things as a boy that I never get to do as a girl.

Sara would listen, and she kept telling me to be patient, to count my blessings and carry on. Sometimes she said it in an ironic way, as if telling me to rebel.

I never rebelled, of course. I'm more of a complainer. If I have the right person listening to me, I don't need to do anything about what's bothering me. All I need is the perfect person to listen to me. And Sara was my perfect person.

I know I've spoken mostly about what Sara has given to me rather than who she was. But I can't possibly describe who she was. She was gone before I could ask her. I wish I had. I wish so many things for her. So many things.

I can't even express what she means to me. I can't tell you how it feels to wake up and know she is gone. I know that if I ever have a daughter, I will name her Sara.

And I don't think I can stop talking to her. She's somewhere out there, listening, I know it. I can feel it. I can tell her anything and she won't judge me; she never did.

Sara, you will always be my best friend. I miss you.

Thank you.

Sophomores
Rage in Their Streams

The year passed. Even summer came and went. The year's August sun shone overhead. It was the third day of classes in their second year at LUSS.

Omar sat cross-legged on the outer edge of the rough circle their bodies made on the grass. Nadia, Mehreen, Sara and their friends Hayyan and Ali sat listening to Sara, and passing her phone back and forth while Zainab lay flat on her back, her eyes covered with her forearm, sleeping or maybe pretending to sleep.

During the summer after their freshman year, while Omar had gone back home across the city, Sara had left for New York and San Francisco with her parents.

Sara's mom had needed treatment and medical care, but that was something Sara didn't mention. Nadia knew, but nobody else did.

'It was so good,' Sara said about a roller-coaster ride, of which she was showing the group pictures on her phone. She had not yet had a chance to upload them on Facebook. 'So, so good,' she repeated.

Omar didn't take the phone when it came around to him. He only leaned in to look closely at Sara's face stuck mid-scare, smiled and leaned back again.

'Nice,' he said,

'Omar, it was just so good,' Sara repeated.

Each time she said the word 'so', she stretched it to two syllables. It irked Omar enough to want to hear it again the first time she said it, but the repetition of it itched under every exposed surface of his skin. His forearms, palms, face, eyes and even inside his nostrils. Everything cringed as he tried to smile wider for her sake.

'Show me,' said Nadia, and Ali passed her the phone. Nadia looked at the picture quickly and then passed the phone back to Sara.

In her bag, Nadia had a scarf and a pair of Simply Vera heels Sara had brought back for her. Sara could tell that Nadia didn't like that they were beige instead of black. But all the black ones had been more expensive and way above Sara's budget for gifts.

'What else did you do?' Mehreen asked. 'Did you eat pizza in New York?'

'All the time,' Sara said. 'It was ridiculous.' She could hear herself falling back into the patterns of her New York speech. Everything good was 'ridiculous' and everything bad was 'totally disgusting'. The same words over and over again. She had described Pakistan in those words to people she had met in Manhattan, people who had wanted to chat about how different she was. Doormen, waiters, passers-by, dog-walkers, doctors and nurses, even acquaintances of her parents who had left Pakistan a long time ago but kept looking back for one reason or another. The word 'like' had crept into every possible part of sentences, especially during conversations with boys and girls her age.

'Did you eat at Grimaldi's?' Hayyan asked.

'Yeah,' Sara said, 'I tried the Manhattan one, not the Brooklyn one.' She smiled at him for knowing what she knew.

'The Brooklyn Grimaldi's is the best pizza in New York,' Hayyan said. 'You should have gone there.'

Sara nodded and looked down. She knew that but he didn't have to rub it in.

All of them rot, Omar said bitterly inside his head, while his hands tore apart a blade of grass in long, thin vertical strips. They come back from a visit outside Pakistan and think they are somehow gifted with an insight on how the world works. This wasn't his judgement on Sara. He was thinking more of his friends from Aitchison. They had all come back after their first years at various US, Canadian and UK colleges, for the summer break. Omar had waited all year, making elaborate plans for it. The all-night gaming parties with endless munchies, some booze and some weed, catching up on each other's stories, playing cricket and tennis and going swimming, eating out and going to parties with the LUSS girls. The ideal summer had spread out before him three months ago. At the end of it all, eight of them would have bundled up in a couple of cars and gone up north to the hills for two weeks of blissfully cool weather and good times in the pure mountain air far away from Lahore. But that hadn't worked out.

'What about pizza in California?' Mehreen asked. Her mother's snacks and catering business had been up and running inside LUSS since early summer and she always had free treats for her friends since business was doing very well.

'Californian pizza doesn't compare,' Hayyan said before Sara got a chance.

'I don't know,' Sara jumped in, squinting, 'I kind of liked it.' Her thoughts stumbled over the stupidity of the argument. What pizza were they comparing? California was a state bigger than all of Pakistan. Without specifics, how could they argue about something on that scale? Though their visits to the US gave her and Hayyan authority over describing it to people who had never been there, she wanted to be more authentic in her description—but not too authentic.

For instance, she did not want to mention how many hours she had spent depressed and bored out of her mind in hospital waiting rooms; she didn't want to describe the awful spring mattress in the motel where she had stayed with her dad; while he had slept from exhaustion after getting her mother admitted to the hospital, the room next door had erupted with regular squeaking sounds, likely from an amorous couple's shenanigans. Sharing all this would have provided a modicum of authenticity but she didn't think she could share these with anyone.

'Oh man, I wish I could go to California,' Ali said, lying down on the grass and looking up at the white and grey clouds.

Sara felt like she had deceived Ali about her summer experience and given him false hope for a better place than where she had really been. She felt she had painted a false picture, and Ali was already dreaming about the wrong things. But she also knew that her summer in the US had been at least mixed with both good and bad experiences. She had pictures to prove it had been fun. She would have traded the staged, fake-smiling photographs for better memories though.

And everything with her mom was still up in the air. The doctors had said they wouldn't know anything for at least another three months. Would they have to make another trip in the winter? Sara hoped not. She hoped there would be an answer. But it felt wrong hoping for that. Would she rather her mom die quickly rather than linger over years of sickness, just to make the equations of life quick, closed and neat? It baffled Sara how cruel her mind was when left to its own devices. So utterly disgusting.

Her mood fell. California, New York, it all seemed so distant and so full of misery. But she kept the hint of a forced smile on her face. Appearances did not have to be honest.

'The San Francisco Bay Area is the most beautiful place I've been to,' Sara said. She meant that at least. She sensed how wistfully she said it, as if its beauty were something she had meant to experience but hadn't been able to.

Not everyone knew what the Bay Area meant. Omar nodded because he didn't want to ask and appear foolish. He also didn't want to ask, thereby showing he was engaging with *this* Sara, the one who had come to campus on the third day of classes because she had been jetlagged for the first two even though she had been back in Lahore for a week.

Nobody else asked what it was either and they all let the Bay Area comment hang for a few seconds.

'Okay,' Omar suddenly said, 'I have to get going. It's time for class.' He was lying. 'I'll see you guys later.' Then he looked at Sara in a neutral way before turning around.

Sara looked at the screen of her new iPhone. There were still fifteen minutes until the next set of classes. Why was he running away? He didn't notice that she needed him precisely now, did he? She thought about getting up and going with him, to take up those fifteen minutes before his class. But the moment passed and she stayed sitting without making that choice. So she stretched her legs out, leaned back on her elbows and her arm touched Nadia's shin.

'See ya,' Mehreen said to Omar.

Omar half turned and raised his arm, showing the back of his hand to acknowledge Sara's friend. Mehreen had thrown him a rope. Without that, he would have felt like an intruder again, like he had before the summer.

He didn't walk to class. He entered the social sciences building, walked past the room where his class would start in a few minutes, and found a spot of open courtyard where he knew none of the kids. Some freshmen lurked around but he was okay with that. They didn't concern him.

He sat on a raised ledge and took out his phone. He wrote Sara a text: 'Catch up later? Stick around if you can. I'll be done by 3.50.' Then he deleted the '3.50' and wrote '4' instead. Why be precise? It wasn't as if he wanted an appointment with her. She was his friend and he wanted to hang out, get some quality one-on-one time.

Maybe even tell her how annoying she was being. Or maybe—hopefully—not have to tell her that at all. Through some form of conversation and a walk around campus, he would coax the right Sara, the old Sara, the non-American-influenced-and-accented Sara out of her. He waited for her reply and stretched out his legs so that they were in the sun while the rest of him stayed under the building's shade.

Sara's phone buzzed and beeped. She looked down and read Omar's text.

'Is that Omar?' Hayyan asked with a smirk, teasing her. Maybe he was even a bit jealous.

'No,' Sara lied. 'It's my mom.' Why did she lie? And why did she have to bring her mom into it? Her poor, sick, mom who was maybe, God willing, going to get better. She should have ignored the tease. She didn't have to say anything and owed no explanation to Hayyan, who was after all Nadia's friend and who, it seemed, was trying very hard to be Sara's friend as well.

She felt the six feet of grass between her and Hayyan were not enough. And she didn't know what to write back to Omar. Of course she would stay. She typed 'Sure thing' and then deleted 'thing', eventually just sending, 'Sure'. She sent it without making it a thing she would overthink. To make sure she wouldn't have to lie again, she set her phone on vibrate.

'Anyone hungry?' Ali asked. 'My stomach is growling thinking about pizzas.'

'I'm always hungry,' Mehreen said.

'Stop trying to sell us your mom's sandwiches,' Hayyan said. No one was certain if he meant it as a joke.

'She isn't,' Sara said, coming to Mehreen's rescue. Something inside her was brewing up against Hayyan and she glared at him.

'I know, I know,' Hayyan said, and raised both hands briefly off the ground, in mock surrender. But he didn't say it in a way that came across as funny.

It looked as though Sara had killed his good humour. She felt sorry she had done that. But she didn't apologize.

'Well, we can always go out,' Mehreen suggested.

'I have class,' Nadia said. 'You guys go ahead.'

'So do I,' said Mehreen. 'We can go after class. Or skip.'

'Does your mom do pizza?' Ali asked.

'Dude,' Hayyan said, 'that sounds so wrong.'

'What?' Ali asked. 'Her mom doing pizza?' he asked, and cracked up. He kept looking at the sky and heaving with laughter. Hayyan shrugged, shook his head, chuckled, and looked at Sara.

She refused to meet his eyes or say anything to him. Let him look, she thought.

Omar saw the text from Sara on his phone. 'Sure.' He liked it because he wanted to like it. He could build up an elaborate narrative around it. There were so many meanings hidden in a word like that which a 'Cool, yeah', would have killed. There was an openness to this, a magnificent openness.

Soft whistles of the wind played around his collar while the leaves danced and rustled in the taller trees.

He let the threads of incipient narratives fall. It didn't mean eventual marriage or dissolution of friendship. The *Sure* was the only thing that was sure.

The knot in his stomach, however, wouldn't loosen, even the rest of him felt limpid and light. Maybe she was just saying 'Sure', and maybe she was feeling the same way about him as he was about her. Maybe he was too backward and too Pakistani for her now. The knot stayed. Wasn't that where the truth lay—in the gut?

He looked at the grey cat sleeping four feet away from him with its belly up to the sun. He looked at the cat's closed eyes and spaced out, thinking of the summer gone by and what about it he would tell Sara and what he would keep to himself. It all depended on how they would talk in real life after talking on Facebook or Google Chat whenever they had been able to. It was going to be different now. That was definite.

Hayyan, Ali and Mehreen went to get something to eat. Zainab looked fast asleep with her head on her bag, her forearm still across her eyes.

Zainab was Hayyan's friend, so Nadia and Sara didn't wake her up after the others left.

Nadia suddenly said, 'Zafar and I are sort of going out,'

'Oh?' Sara said, widening her eyes, pretending to be interested. She had wanted to talk about her mom since Nadia was the only person at LUSS who knew why Sara had gone to the US in the first place. But those conversations, Sara guessed, would have to remain on text messages and online chats.

'Yeah,' Nadia said. 'I didn't tell you the story?'

'Tell me now,' Sara said. Her mind drifted and she felt like yawning, but she knew an old trick: lick your lips to stifle an unwanted yawn. The trick worked, or at least it didn't look like a yawn.

'He's so cool,' Nadia gushed. She turned as red as her shirt and then back to her pale self. It was like seeing a sunrise in a time lapse. 'He asked me to come over to his place and we just sat in his room talking for hours.'

'You went to his house?' Sara asked. This wasn't just a harmless crush anymore. She felt the adult inside her take over and she knew she was going to interrogate Nadia now. For God's sake, what was Nadia thinking, going to a boy's house alone. And Zafar's on top of it. If Zafar asked Nadia to jump off a cliff…

'I did,' Nadia said. 'I wasn't alone, though. He had a few cousins. Some of them were girls.'

'Okay,' Sara prodded. 'And then?'

'Then nothing,' Nadia said. She pulled her legs close to her chest and wrapped her arms around them. 'We just sat together at dinner and talked about things.'

'When was this?' Sara asked. 'How do you know for sure that the girls were his cousins?' She was attacking Nadia with questions. She had a bad feeling about Zafar. Nadia was an idiot and Sara wished she could tell her friend what an imbecile she was for liking Zafar in the first place. The vibes. Didn't Nadia sense his slimy vibes?

She felt like pulling herself out of this friendship just because of how dumb Nadia was being. It felt like an insult that she could have such airheads as friends. Mehreen was a given; did Nadia have to follow suit just because of a stupid crush?

'Sara,' Nadia fought back with a sharp look, 'nothing happened. Okay? Nothing happened. We just held hands.'

'Okay,' Sara said. Holding hands was more than nothing, she wanted to say. But she became conscious at once that the sourness in her mood had appeared the moment Omar got up and left. Maybe it was her—Sara. Maybe she was flaring up because of her own issues.

'I do like him, Sara,' Nadia said. 'And I think he likes me too.'

'Okay, okay,' Sara gave in. 'But you know that you shouldn't go to anybody's house by yourself. Especially someone like Zafar's.'

Nadia didn't say anything but looked away into the distance. Sara had touched a nerve. She had let her judgement about Nadia's taste in boys show. She wanted to say something to take back the 'Especially Zafar's' but there was no way to.

She picked up a twig and twirled it between her thumb and index finger, and then let it drop. It lay on top of the grass. She tried to push it down, but the spring of the grass brought it back up. She picked it up again and looked at Nadia who was still looking away. A minute passed. Sara broke the twig into pieces and those pieces into smaller pieces. Yet another minute passed.

'You know,' Nadia finally said, 'you've changed.' She was still looking into the distance.

Sara could have nodded; she could have shaken her head. She could have brought up her mom's complicated treatments and possible imminent death, how that had made her reconsider who she was and how she acted around people, why and how she should change that and become more direct and assertive, and less of a coward in expressing her thoughts.

Or she could have said she had always been this way and Nadia had never known because Sara never let her, because Nadia wasn't worth it, because Nadia wasted her time on stupid bloody things like boys who were a dime a dozen, because Nadia would never see the bigger picture, because she wasn't meant to be one of the elect who could look beyond problems their own hormones created for them to the vast universe of possibilities contained in metaphysical laws that caused and effected both time and space and created multiple universes and infinite realities. That Nadia was a fucking bimbo.

But Sara didn't say any of those things in response. Instead she said, 'Everybody changes.'

Nadia looked at Sara. They stared at the glint in each other's eyes. Call it hatred, intensity; a moment of transference. Each knew the depth of the other, became the other's abyss. *How dare you trivialize my life?* Sara felt both sets of eyes asked that. Nadia tore away her gaze and looked at her watch. It was two minutes to 2 p.m.

Nadia got up, picked up her bag and notebooks while Sara kept sitting. Nadia turned to go and said, 'You know, I don't know how you can act like this when your mom is so unwell.'

With a flash of heat in her head, Sara remembered how she had been expecting to bring up the subject of her mom herself.

Nadia's words made her livid on the inside, but on the surface of everything that she called herself, she was nonplussed; caught off guard.

A voice within her sprang up saying, *How dare she talk about?* But Nadia had left by the time Sara recovered.

Nadia's words were meant to be bitter. She knew how to mess with Sara's head. She had known it since Sara had told Nadia her first secret back in kindergarten—that she had peed during recess in the boys' toilet. Something so innocuous now, which back then was the difference between good and evil. Nadia had told her mother within the week and Sara had been scolded into oceans of tears by her own parents for her transgression.

Later that week she had become friends with Nadia again.

But that first betrayal had festered for years like a recurrent sore between them. Through the years, at low points in their friendship, they had invoked memories of that original betrayal in contradictory ways. Sometimes to laugh at the memory and at other times to fuel a bit of hatred.

Nadia knew how to twist the blame around to hurt the victim. That's what she had just done. Sara, as usual, had been unprepared. Nadia always had the final word, the upper hand. Sara with her seething head, with no recourse.

She looked at Zainab who was still sleeping, breathing through her open mouth. Sara felt rage at being left alone with this log of a sleeping form. She searched for words but nothing came to her.

Her hands were cold and her shoulders ached from the pressure she was using to contain herself.

She got to her feet, picked up her things and walked away.

Alone, dreaming perhaps, and also perhaps having absorbed what went on around her on some mystical plane of transference of energy, the un-storied Zainab lay there a while, dressed in forest green, seeming to belong there, lying on the grass.

Over the next two hours, grey clouds invaded the skies. They spat at intervals on the ground, but the torrents of rain they threatened weren't yet let loose. Far away, even darker clouds loomed and in the shifty, uncertain flow of the wind, it was a guessing game whether the storm would reach LUSS or get redirected.

Omar walked up behind Sara on the track of which she had already taken nearly six rounds. She had texted him to meet here on the track because the weather was great and she wanted to walk while she waited for him. She was pensive, he could tell. Something was disturbing her.

'Hey,' he said, slowing down to her pace as he caught up.

'Omar, I have to say something,' Sara said.

'Sure, go ahead,' he responded.

'I don't want you to think I'm being mean or anything,' she said. She had her arms wrapped around herself as if she were feeling cold.

'Okay,' he said. This was it. She was going to 'break up' with him without them having ever being 'together'. This was 'the talk' where she would tell him she had moved on while she was eating Californian pizza and riding roller coasters and shopping and living the high life. She was going to say, 'Look, you've been a good friend...' That's how she would start. He braced himself and wondered how low and dirty he would get in his response. If it came to a head-on collision, he knew he had more material. He wasn't the one who had changed. That was a virtue.

'I think Nadia and Zafar are going to have sex soon,' Sara said, and she looked down and away from him to hide the glow on her face as she released the venom that had been burning inside her. Saying what she had been mulling over didn't feel like conjecture. It didn't feel wrong. It was very likely that Nadia and Zafar would go all the way soon. But it was still something Sara knew she shouldn't have said.

'Okay,' Omar said. He was taken aback, out of his self-centred thinking and realized there were more people in Sara's life than just him. She cared about Nadia, she really did.

'Yeah,' Sara said. 'I don't know what to do.' She fixed her face and channelled her anger at Nadia into concern for her. It was easy. So what if Nadia wasn't around to witness this catharsis? She looked at Omar.

They kept walking.

'Okay,' Omar said, and he wondered what else he could say. Should he offer advice? Is that what Sara was looking for? 'I understand,' he added, just to say something other than that one word.

'What should I do?' Sara asked. The crunch of gravel under their feet was the only answer for a few seconds. He didn't say 'Okay' again, so she ventured further. 'Should I do anything at all?'

'Hmm,' he said, not knowing what Sara wanted to hear. Not knowing to what extent this reached and how implicated he would be if he said what he wanted, which was: let it go, let her do what she wants, Nadia is a grown-up, it's her life.

'I don't know,' he said, 'I have never advised a female friend on whether or not she should have sex.' He could imagine Sara asking him next: what if I want to have sex, what would you say to me? He could imagine himself squirming with equivocation. *Have mercy.*

He would have to be strong, get his arms untwisted and say, 'It's up to you.' He was ready to say this.

The gravel was in some parts wetter and more silent as well. The crunch underfoot played its own rhythm with their walk, even as they kept a regular pace.

'Have you ever advised a male friend on sex?' she asked. She wanted to ask him if he had actually had sex, to put him on the back foot and see him squirm. But it was too blunt a question, even for how bold she was being by planning her intervention for Nadia.

'Have I advised a guy friend on having sex?' Omar asked, laughing. 'What kind of question is that?' He wanted her to laugh with him, to see that this could be a light moment between them. But Sara didn't crack a smile.

'It's a simple question,' she said. 'Has someone ever asked you for your opinion on sex?'

'Well,' Omar started to say, but then stopped. The shuffle and crunch of clay and gravel continued. He thought about it. He looked up at the dark grey clouds. They were heading this way and sooner or later it would rain. The wind was picking up and it was growing cooler. 'Hmm,' he started again, and couldn't come up with anything else. He shrugged.

'Never mind,' Sara said, and smiled at him, 'I don't want to know you and your boys' club fantasies that you fuel with pornos.'

He smiled back, not knowing why he was smiling at her insinuation that he had some crazy fantasies, which he didn't. Well, maybe one or two. But those weren't active fantasies, not even the one with … he shook them out of his head. 'Well,' he said again, pretending to play along.

She shook her head, smiled and said, 'I don't want to hear about it.' It had gone on long enough. She needed no further vengeance or catharsis. It was good to be back at LUSS, in Lahore, in Pakistan. The world made more sense here, with Omar by her side. He had been a constant thought through the summer, even though she had seldom reached out to him. Here he was now, though. Next to her. She only wished it weren't so cold. What strange weather for late August.

The late monsoon storm was going to hit LUSS that night. Omar would be a witness to this strange weather change. The gusts of wind coursed through the pores of his t-shirt and bathed him in fresh air. He felt cleansed of sweat, scentless. In the back of his head, he admitted to himself, he was thinking about the wind doing the same thing to her body. The platonic walk in circles around the age-old story—boy meets girl, boy falls and tries to make her fall, trip-tripping away—was layered over by the rhythmically complex crunch underfoot, years and years of boys talking about girls without knowing girls, and back-dropped by the face of the sun dying in whorls of rolling black clouds.

Leaves and polythene bags took to the air, swirls of dust rose and blasts of wind whipped her hair all about. She looked at him with what seemed to be a smile.

There was no other place or time he would rather be.

He decided to share something with her because he had already imagined several times over how he would tell her. There was supposed to be no wind like this, but this was somehow better. He pointed at a patch of brown grass coming up next to the track. 'Remember that spot?' he asked her.

She looked at the spot which he was pointing to. 'Is that where the bomb hit?' she asked.

'Bomb or something else,' he replied. 'The grass doesn't grow green over there anymore.' He said it like it meant something secretive that only he knew about.

'I don't want to talk about it,' Sara said. 'No bomb talk now. It's getting cold.' They kept going and walked past the site of the explosion.

Omar glanced back at the patch of brown grass, thinking he was the only one who spent so much time thinking about it. A significant portion of his life at LUSS so far seemed to revolve around it.

'Okay,' he said. 'What do you want to talk about?' He was amiable. She could talk about anything she wanted, as long as he felt this much at peace.

'I want to know about your summer,' she said. 'Did you have fun with your friends?'

'Yeah, yeah, it was fun,' he said because in retrospect it didn't seem so bad now that it was over, and the good feeling of telling Sara about it overrode the awful mess that he had survived. 'They all came back from their universities and we hung out a few times.'

'Yeah, that's what you said,' she said. 'But what did you guys do during these hangouts?'

'Well, you know,' he said, 'the usual. They mostly wanted to chill out.'

'Ah,' she said, and shook off a polythene bag that had wrapped itself around her leg, pressed to her by the wind. Her long shirt fluttered and her hair was a mess. 'And chill out means?'

He couldn't hold all of it back anymore. Something had to give. He tried to keep it all in, one last-ditch effort. But here it came, 'Boozing, doping, shit like that.' He remembered sitting in Aneeq's room in early May. Aneeq had just got back from the University of Toronto. After a couple of rounds of playing the new Halo, Aneeq had got up, bored and not trying too hard to hide it from Omar; the conversation, having grown stilted, sputtered and eventually stopped. Omar had left. Later that week he found out why this had happened when they all gathered for lunch at Zakir's. The boys, his Aitchison boys, had not changed. But they had definitely lost interest in hanging out with him. He tried several times to spend the night out with them or have them come over to his place. They had always turned him down. Then one of them told him the reason. It was something he could never tell Sara.

'And you did all that too? Drinking and doping?' Sara asked.

'Yeah, I did some,' he said, conscious not to come across as either an excessive user or a prude. The balance had to be just right. Her approval mattered very much. He had not touched alcohol over the summer but somehow he didn't think that was the right answer. 'But I stopped once it got too much,' he said, trying to enter the territory of truth again.

Aneeq had told him that some of them went to Las Vegas over the winter and one thing had led to another. Aneeq trailed off, but Omar had insisted. He had to know.

He didn't dare pique Sara's interest. He had to make it sound boring. 'You know how it is,' he said. 'It gets dull after a while.'

'Yeah, I guess,' she said. She was feeling much colder than she was letting on. Part of her loved this kind of monsoon wind, but she would have loved to be wrapped in a shawl. That would be perfect. 'So what did you do?' she asked. She wanted to know if he held her as a better friend than he did his Aitchison boys. But how could she ask him such a question that put loyalty on the line? 'With all the time, I mean. Three months is a lot.'

'I went running a lot,' he said, his voice barely louder than the wind. The track they were walking on was mapped out in his head. He knew the patches where it didn't drain well after the rains, so he had to either skirt inside or outside the track, on the grass. And he knew the wear of his running shoes was faster on this track than on tarmac, but there were no tarmac circles available.

'What else?' she asked.

He did not answer. He mused how easy it was to dismiss his running as just running. But how could he explain that to her—wasn't it completely experiential? If she never ran, especially here, while thinking of someone far away and about the whole of her life, trying to distill it into processes that mirrored the cadence of running, she would never know.

Going around this track again and again had been a source of finding himself. He had no words as yet to describe that.

'Well,' he said, 'I had a lot of time, so I read a few books and thought about a lot of things.'

She had hoped for more from him, and all at once. But this was like prying open a can with bare hands. He seemed locked up about the summer and she was impatient because she was growing colder. He had only a t-shirt on, so he couldn't be the hero to offer her a jacket either. And yet, with him on this track, going slowly around the grass field, she suddenly felt all right about nearly everything—her mom was ill, yes, but she might get better; Nadia was an idiot and a bitch, but that came and went; Omar was still here with her.

Sara had almost called him to the airport to pick her up, and then almost came to college earlier. But the flight back from San Francisco had weakened her mom and Sara had been needed at home. Just to stay around. In moments of weakness, as she sat by her wheezing and sleeping mother, Sara had almost called him over to her place. She had wanted Omar, not Nadia. But Nadia had rushed over the one time she had called her.

'How are your parents?' she asked Omar then.

They both saw at the same time a guard get up from a bench at the edge of the track and leave. He had been there all along, while they had assumed they were alone on this side of the campus.

'My parents are fine,' Omar said. 'They still want me to apply for a transfer.' That's all he had to say about his parents. It hurt him that this was everything it boiled down to these days: 'Omar, you need to transfer out of LUSS', 'Omar, you need to get into a good American university', 'Son, you need to think about your future'.

'I don't know what their problem is,' he said. 'It's not like I'm living with them and it's not like I won't be able to go to a great graduate school after LUSS. Anyway, I want to stay here now. I'm not going to apply for a transfer. I'll major in history and minor in business administration. That'll cover me for grad school applications in humanities and for MBA. My parents will understand eventually that living in Pakistan is fantastic for me because Pakistan is in the eye of history's storm right now.'

She noticed that he didn't have an answer for how his parents were doing either. The questions he had just answered were, 'How are you feeling about your parents?' and 'What part are your parents playing in your life right now?'

For a moment, using his words to hold a mirror to herself, she was out of excuses about why she was so cruel about her own mother. As soon as Sara had found out that her mother might die, she had withdrawn some of her love. A defence mechanism, clearly. Or so she thought. Maybe she was just selfish, greedy, without empathy. She wanted to tell Omar all this, but where should she start? Should she start with, 'My mom's been dying for over a year now'? What a sad conversation that would turn into.

'It's so cold,' she said. 'I wish I was still in California.'

She said it like a fact.

The cold sieved through his t-shirt, but her words went deeper and cut at him inside his blood vessels and nerves. All the magic that the late monsoon winds and rain had gathered for her arrival, all the joy that had been coursing through his body and his lifted spirit floating in the wind were popped by her words and it all began to collapse. He took a step forward and then refused to take another one. It was a perfect day. Right here, in Pakistan, it was a perfect day. What the fuck did she mean she wished she were still in California?

He could not understand what she had said from her point of view, that she had spent a month in 90-degree weather, become acclimatized to that, and she was now unused to this cold, and it was too sudden a shift. And he did not understand that, without knowing how she should have articulated it, she had also implicitly meant that she wished this walk, with Omar, had been on a warm day. Not to mention that it was just a wish, just something to say, to conceive, while feeling cold. He had no clue. Being stuck in his body and in his self-centred universe, having orbited this running track endlessly while thinking about her and processing what she meant to him, still not coming to conclusions—just delicious questions and alternatives—and, being who he was, he misunderstood her expressed desire to be somewhere else.

He stopped and stared at the back of her head, his lips parted, his eyes burning.

She walked another three steps, turned halfway around on the fourth and saw the look he was giving her. She stopped completely and turned around to face him. The wind slapped her hair against her face, forcing her to squint; her shirt clung tight against her and she had goosebumps all over. 'What?' she asked, with one eye open.

'You've changed,' he said. He almost growled it.

'No, I haven't,' she said.

'Yes,' he said. 'You have, Sara.' He then said, 'I love this wind,' and without knowing he would do it, he walked past her and started to run. Really run. If she wanted to be back in California, let her walk away from the track, leave campus, go home and buy a ticket and go back to bloody California. He felt animal blood in his head and the rest of his body went cold. That didn't matter. He just kept running. He felt the gravel push him forward as his shoes skidded. They had no tread. It was like trying to walk on water. He managed it like he knew he would, with effort and a lighter gait. He went halfway around and then slowed down. He didn't look back. It didn't matter where she was. She didn't want to be here anyway. He caught his breath and began to enjoy the different rhythm with his grip-less shoes and his jeans. It was more difficult, and very different. There was another beat to the whole thing. He panted, his mouth was open. The wind felt good, felt divine. His short hair felt caressed and his arms and legs were kneaded by the force of the gusts. He was more than three quarters of the way around. He slowed down to a jog, and caught his breath and he could see her still standing there on the track. She was waiting for him. Let her wait, he thought. He slowed down further and curved against the wind, enjoying the resistance. He looked straight at her as he ran the last of the distance to her, and saw one of her eyebrows was raised. Maybe the eyebrow had been raised the entire time he had been running. He slowed down to walking pace, but still kicking up his heels as he came up to her.

'Are you done?' Sara asked.

He came and stood next to her for a second. 'No,' he said, smiling, and turned from her to the track ahead of them once again. He bent low, grunted and dashed off again.

She felt the anger take shape inside her as a solid thing; it gathered in her stomach and from there it furred out in veins across the insides of her body. But in spite of herself, she laughed. He was being so ridiculous. Why was he doing this? Why was she letting him? Why was she waiting for him? It was freezing cold now. This was so ridiculous. She let herself frown. There he goes, loping and prancing rather than running. He was performing for her. He had thinned down over the summer in the effort of running, the way his body and the wind worked together, his leanness showed. She wished she could run too because it looked like it could help her have fun. Maybe it could help her lose weight, both literal and figurative. She waited. Any ill-feeling she had nurtured was beginning to dissipate; her muscles had woken up, shivering, to make her immune to how cold she felt. It was bearable. If she were to admit it, watching him run also had a warming effect. She watched him slow down when he got within range of her voice. She didn't say anything, but waited.

She hadn't told him about her mom. She was going to fix that though. Her head lowered, she looked at the ground, shook her head, sighed and decided she was going to be honest. She was going to give him everything. Omar walked over the last few yards. He stood next to her and she felt his gaze on her head. Let him look.

'Are you okay?' Omar asked.

'No,' Sara said. 'I'm cold and I've changed.' She didn't mean for it to come out so sharp and blunt. She had tried to make it softer, sadder. But she was scared to be sad with him.

'I'm sorry,' Omar said, and stood there like he wanted a cookie for his apology. He lowered his head, as if that made up for something wrong he had done.

'Don't apologize to me,' Sara said. She looked up to see him looking down at his feet and smiling. She felt a swell of fury take hold of her. He was so pathetic, so spineless. 'What do you think I'm saying when I say I've changed? Everybody changes, Omar.' Her voice was growing louder, shriller, matching the wind's howl.

'I know that,' Omar said as he looked up, furrowed his forehead and leaned back as if to dodge something.

'You don't know shit,' Sara said.

'What are you talking about?' he asked.

'You think this is jet lag, Omar?' Sara asked. 'You think I'm tired and cold and that's why I'm not being myself?'

'I—' He wanted to ask her why she was angry with him. But there couldn't be more than one person asking rhetorical questions here. The universe would flounder, split apart.

'This is not jet lag,' she interrupted. She shook a whip of her hair that had come across her face and it went flying to flail behind her in the wind. 'This is not me being tired or me changing.

Everything changes, Omar. And if you don't know that, you will one day.'

'What—?' He never got to complete his question.

'My mom is dying, asshole,' she said. 'This trip to New York and California wasn't a fucking vacation. It was an attempt to save her life.' Why was this anger directed at him? She could already tell it was misdirected. Even Nadia didn't deserve it. Did her mom? Maybe. Maybe part of it.

But there. She'd said it. She had come out with the truth. 'I didn't have a single day of fun. That is all fake in the pictures. Do you understand?' She stared at him, goosebumps erupting all over her skin because she was bristling with rage.

'Why?' Omar asked. 'I mean, how is she dying?'

She didn't answer him. She took a deep breath, released it and took another one, slowly letting it out.

'Next time,' Sara said, 'if you want to talk to me, be honest. Say what you mean. Don't, like, stand there pretending I'm this idiot who will get over what she feels and then you will be able to talk to who I really am.'

'Sara,' he said and shook his head. How would he make her see he was not the enemy? That he was as lost as she. That he could not have guessed about her mom. He didn't know what to say. Only a few hundred metres ago, this had been the best day of his life.

They stood there, Sara looking off to the side, her hands folded.

Omar felt drained. She was being unreasonable. He didn't know what to say or what to ask. His legs, his very foundation, were buzzing.

'I have to go,' she said.

Omar nodded. He decided to let her go.

She walked off the track and headed for the buildings.

He stood there, not looking at her, not wanting to. He could feel her absence growing because she had hooked him with it since the first day. His hands were warm from the jog. He waited, closed his eyes and turned to the wind. It attacked his short hair, blew dust and leaves at him. He tried to smile, tried to enjoy this last great blast of the monsoon for the year.

A minute passed. He slowly opened his eyes and looked at the space between the trees and the sports building.

Sara was gone. He could sense her on the campus, but she was leaving, going home.

Should he stop her? Say something? What was it that made her so angry all of a sudden? Was her mom really dying?

She had never told him about her mother being so ill. Why?

Let it go. Let it go.

But he couldn't. He had to use this.

All summer, running had been an escape from thinking, but not from feeling. Now he had to use what he was feeling. Or he had to run *off* the feeling. It was riding him. He needed to get on top. He headed fast to the hostel and was up the stairs and changing his clothes in his room without thinking. The motions were automatic.

The running shorts, the loose black t-shirt, his running shoes and a bottle of water. He gobbled up a banana before leaving. QT wasn't around, so he couldn't ask to borrow his iPod. But he looked in QT's desk drawer. There it was. Hopefully it was charged. Omar plugged in his earphones and put it on.

Awolnation's pulse-driven song '*Sail*' came on. It was just the fucking beat he needed. He would drown out the lyrics and focus only on the beat. He went downstairs again, loped to the track, stretched, put the water bottle on a bench next to the track and started running.

She had never told him her mother was dying. She could go to hell. She didn't know how good a friend Omar had been to her. She could go hang out with her 'Nadias' and 'Mehreens' and leave him the fuck alone. She never listened. All she did was impose herself on him. All she did was ask him to be here, be there, do this, do that, listen to this song, check out that video. Never talked about her mother. How could she be this shallow? There was nothing great about her anyway.

She was pretty. So what? Every girl could look pretty or even hot with makeup.

Fuck that. It's all a lie.

Breathe. Breathe.

He couldn't get his mind off the anger enough. His breathing didn't regularize even after his first three rounds of the track.

The wind splattered a few drops of rain. Then thunder sparked overhead. The first thick drops of water rushed to slap the ground all around him. Finally.

Here comes the storm.

Instead of slowing down to catch his breath, he bent low and doubled his pace.

'Fuck this!' he screamed.

Her dad pulled up at the curb outside campus. Sara sat in the car.

She asked, 'How's mom doing?' She didn't want an answer; she was just deflecting questions he may or may not have. She didn't hear what her dad said to her. It would have been something trite anyway.

It wasn't rage she felt now but indignation.

This was her share of things in life. A walk through *this* universe. Where the epic storm outside was nothing compared to the colossal one inside.

Sad music played softly on the radio and the wipers squeakily swiped across the windscreen. The road glowed yellow under the streetlights and thunder flashed in the distance.

Sara took out her phone and played around with her texts so her dad would not break the awkward silence with awkward conversation. She could tell he was doing his best. She didn't blame him. Not much, anyway. She let him have the silence. More than anything, her dad needed rest.

Why Omar then? Why did he have to bear the brunt of it?

The wind hurled everything it could at him. It broke the rain up into sheets, which splattered across his face and body. Omar wiped his eyes and kept running. Parts of the ground were beginning to get sludgy. Running on wet clay and gravel was going to be hard. His shoes were soggy from the outside and getting heavier. And his socks and feet were already moist.

He kept thinking to himself over and over again that he should have made her stay, should have talked to her, should have worried less about how the day had turned from great to horrible for him, and been more concerned about how she was feeling.

No. No. He should have told her to eff off and to stop treating him like a doormat.

He should have told her that all his Aitchison boys had cut him out of the group—and for what? For hookers. They had paid, through the entire summer, some poor and needy high-school girls to come to Aneeq's place at night, where they did whatever they had learnt to do in Las Vegas.

He should have told Sara that. He should have told her she wasn't the only one feeling fucked up. He was up to his elbows in shit.

The knot in his stomach had dissolved. But there were more knots in other places. Everywhere the water touched now, it pinged and stung him.

His friends had made the choice for him by not telling him.

Would he have chosen differently from them? Would he have been a prude if he had done that? He didn't know because he wasn't given the choice to know. So many things were not given to him.

While off the track, nothing was in his power. Nothing seemed like his own decision.

He had no ability to help anyone else since he couldn't even help himself.

He couldn't save Sara's mom from dying.

On the track he could choose the direction to go around the circle, and for how long and at what speed. Even then, he would tire out. Even this would fade out into nothingness eventually. Sound and fury, and then nothing.

But that's not how he ran. He ran like the run would never end.

❦

When she got home, her mom was asleep. So Sara went up to her room and sat at her desk to check her email and Facebook. There was nothing new worth looking at. Still, she clicked through things and watched portions of some videos linked by her friends.

Nothing held her interest. And she was too exhausted to lie down and sleep. It felt like sleep would never come.

She shut her laptop and took down an old sketchbook from her shelf. The one with eyes sketched on every page. Some straight on, some from angles. Eyes and lashes and brows. The effort she had put into each was apparent to her. The mistakes were more obvious than any semblance of skill. But even these mistakes were somehow someone else's fault, weren't they?

Sara began to think her mom was dying just to spite her. And Omar was going to suffer it all, wasn't he? She was going to channel it all in wrathful and vindictive bursts at him, wasn't she?

She took a dark pencil out of a set in her drawer and near the bottom of a full page, across one of her worst sketches of an eye in profile, she drew parallel, short, thick, straight lines. She drew ten and kept going. Darker and darker. She felt the effort in her shoulder and her spine. The eye disappeared under parallel dark-black lines.

It was too bad she couldn't leave this universe now. This Sara was meant to be here for as long as she would last. She had sprung out from the prototype of the original Sara, the one with all the potential of being an artist, a dancer, an actor, a woman of substance and skill. And since being sprung here, day by day, that connection to the original had severed just a bit more.

As within any single one of them, the collective alternate universes also expanded outwards, away from each other.

And Sara's mom was dying in every one of them.

She turned the page and drew fat lines across another badly drawn eye. Then another page. And so on.

❦

All factors considered, he should have felt miserable. He was thirsty, but that was the easiest thing to disregard. His socks were logged with water, but his feet were not in pain and any blisters wouldn't appear until after he stopped running. The back of his right shoulder was beginning to cramp, but he had run through cramps before. He could no longer hear the music; the storm also drowned out the sound of his heavy breathing and sloshing through the puddles. None of that was the bottom line.

He could not stop thinking that he had been wronged. This was why he couldn't stop running. The more he ran, the more redeemed his anger felt. If he stopped, wouldn't the anger stop as well? He didn't want to know yet. Of course, there was nobody near the track in the gale-strength winds and thunderstorm. So he couldn't even think in terms of playing out a story for an audience. His head kept pumping him with, 'What. The fuck. Have I. Done wrong?'

Being the rational idiot that he was, he did not know the significance of what Sara had done for both of them. While he might not reach out and play with her emotions too often, she could crack his defences whenever she wanted. This wasn't about who was to blame. It was about closeness. He didn't realize that she had done him a favour by using her fury on him. That this was a plus point for him. She was at home feeling utterly vulnerable and even though he could not access that part of her by volition, it was a gift she gave him: the ability to sometimes reach her core by fluke, and sometimes she just might let him in.

At some point while running that night, with music plugged into his ears, even though he couldn't hear it over the sounds of the thunder and the torrential rain, the track under his feet disappeared. He could no longer feel it. There was only the storm and him after that. And that is how he kept running.

Sara had crossed out half the eyes in her sketchbook. The rest she spared, even though she was proud of only one and it didn't look like something she could repeat.

She knew her talent had gone the way of the dodo. A shame, really, if she could have at one point drawn something like this eye. It looked off to the spine of her sketchbook, never at her, but she could see inside of that eye her own parallel universes.

All the other realities were different enough to not matter anymore. Only in this one would she have met Omar the way she had. Only in this one would she know that he had not decided to stay back just for the history major at LUSS, or for what he called living the historically significant moment within which Pakistan was centred. She knew a part of him had stayed back for her and it did not matter what percentage she had played in his decision. It was everything.

When she lay down in her bed and turned off the light, her anger simmered just under the surface. It was directed at herself just as much as at him, clearly misdirected.

Could she be angry at the real thing that she didn't understand?

Before she had known of the illness, Sara would plan the digressions in conversations with her mom and map out the network of relational material she had to share. Since the onset of her mom's disease, Sara had not been able, except in unguarded bursts of spontaneity, to talk to her.

Now the silence had grown as if she was wishing her mom … wishing something dire or grand, the miracle of suddenness rather than a slow, inexorable, gravitational pull to either side of life or death.

That last conscious moment before Sara fell asleep, there was no darkness and there was no rage. There was only the feeling that she was losing a war she did not want to fight.

Lahore
The City

In Italo Calvino's short book of conceptual fiction, *Invisible Cities*, Marco Polo entertains Kublai Khan with accounts of the cities he has visited on his journeys. All the descriptions turn out to be, in some way, that of the traveller's home town, Venice.

Calvino's Marco Polo measures a city by the number of ways it can be approached and still seem fresh. He gives fifty-five different ways to describe Venice and also calls it by fifty-five different names.

To reduce Calvino's book to the few sentences above is to reduce Lahore to as few as fifty-five cities.

Each city opens up as a different harem of ideas and artifacts, depending on the approach, the time of day and the mood of the traveller. Within any person's reason to journey is found the hook that colours and reveals the destination.

With a romantic's eye, coming in or leaving from the Old City, Lahore is a million different Lahores.

Omar and Sara inhabit different worlds in the same city.

Omar is from Lahore and chooses to live in the dorms so he can study without domestic interferences, and also feel like he is in college.

Sara knows the city better because her dad is an architect. She is tempted to become one herself, but sees how her dad stops enjoying his job dealing with the contractors who are always looking to undercut the budget and skim off the top. She thinks of architecture as a niche profession; it will always be so in Lahore, where it is the contractors who are the real moneymakers. Not many clients want to spare the expense of hiring an architect. Everybody makes engineering graduates do the load-bearing calculations for them, and then apply their own gaudy designs, or replicate easily duplicable layouts.

Omar's father knows nothing about city planning. He is a lawyer and he is moderately wealthy. There is always a deathly quiet as well as a sense of urgency in Omar's house. It is as if someone has just died or is about to fall off from somewhere. Omar can never figure out what it is. His father's breathlessness from asthma is either the cause or effect of it all.

⚜

At the end of the sixteenth century, Mughal Emperor Akbar builds the Lahore Fort. But does he really build it if he lays only the foundation stone? The rest is completed by the anonymous workers left to the decay of history's pages. They are made more anonymous by the twist in language that attributes the building to the ruler of the time.

Someone has gates and walls erected to protect the city. Their names are local and not kingly: Bhatti Gate, Mochi Gate, Lahori Gate and so on.

Many hands contribute to the construction of the Badshahi Mosque, which lies adjacent to the fort and may or may not stand on top of secret tunnels leading out of the city.

Mughal kings fight with their fathers and sons. Just like their European monarchical cousins, they build elaborate webs of deceit. They invent religions, but unlike the pharaohs they stop short of calling themselves gods.

Lahore is one of their capitals. A glint in the jewel, a spark in the abyss.

The Mughals die, and the fort is taken over by new rulers with a foreign language and foreign ways.

In British hands, the mosque becomes a relic. Lahore's notorious and culturally rich red-light district, Heera Mandi, blossoms under the shade of the Badshahi Mosque's tallest minar.

Population explodes; the gates, deemed too narrow, are widened. Some are even left permanently open. The Old City's wall is taken down and the city expands and blooms and decays and festers and flowers and creeps out of the past into the future.

The chaos of Partition comes calling. Neighbourhoods divide along the lines of those who are running off to India and those who will take over the property of the runaways. Religion is simply the excuse. Blame is laid onto ideologies, even though it's men who put the ideologies to shame. Many die in the chaos. Many are raped, while scores are abducted. Lahore becomes a blister at the border between the new countries.

Political chaos and the self-aggrandizement of the armed forces on either side of the border leads to three wars. Two of them roughen up the edges of the city. Each time, through post-war negotiations, Lahore is further shamed by jingoists and their braggart ways, all used to good effect by parasitic politicians.

Meanwhile, cinema houses, stadiums and commercial centres take root. Universities and hospitals are planned and then somehow executed worse than they can possibly be, given the ample budgets.

Food streets are built and then taken down. Cab schemes, underpasses and overpasses. Short-term fixes for a city spiralling above growth predictions.

A new airport is built every twenty years. The old ones lie fallow. More land is devoured and highways are carved out through the city and around it. It is finally dressed up and ready to meet the world.

Map this out: on a minute dot of a circle in a corner of Lahore, close to the Indian border, a boy goes round and round the track on a college campus. Round and round the track he runs like a trick on a spindle.

The city sprawls outward from this axis, flowing with streams of light and dust, with ant-like scurries of activity.

As if to prove every other part of the city inferior, the Mall Road's trees thrive on pollution. Tall oaks and sycamores, trees greener than those in a forest.

To go from one end of the Mall Road to the other is to travel through a time machine from the beginning of Lahore to a minute before just now. Other roads also stretch from the Old City to the newer areas, but they all have to wind and wend and twist underground or loop overhead. Only the Mall Road leads out straight and thick as an artery out of the city's aged heart.

Like most ancient cities, Lahore is built next to a source of clean water. The Ravi flows for centuries on its way to the Indus at one edge of Lahore, providing the city and its outskirts with drinking and irrigation water, natural sewage disposal and a shore lined with trees promising cool shade in the hot summers.

The banks of the river are grounds for epic love poetry. Naturally, some of the women in the poetry end up drowning along with their sorrows.

The twentieth century arrives, especially its later half, and the Indus Water Treaty allows Pakistan and India to negotiate how rivers and waters flow between their lands. Lahore suffers months of drought every year, followed by annual floods, because the Indian government chooses to use the Ravi in that way.

Not all of the new issues with the river are the neighbouring country's fault; its banks are garbage dumps, there is no sewage treatment, no mass-scale recycling facilities exist in all of Lahore, there is unchecked growth of industries along the river, and the majority of inhabitants on both banks are stateless squatters.

Whenever the government changes, the squatters are removed. They bide their time and begin moving up the river's edges by the second month.

A third-year LUSS student is assaulted off-campus in a fight outside a restaurant on M.M. Alam Road. He is defending his sister's honour against a group of high-school students from Aitchison who are out for a laugh.

The fight grows bigger, longer, nastier than any of the sides intends. Cars with headlights on full beam are flagged down while others stop because the road fills up with people. The restaurant's two guards try to break up the fight.

A gun is fired into the air.

Bats and hockey sticks are pulled out of the trunks of the cars and windshields are smashed.

Sirens wail in either direction and the mass of cars and people grows thick around the eye of the fight. Other scuffles break out in its periphery.

Without room to swing hockey sticks at the centre, someone hurls an empty 7Up bottle and the LUSS student's head is smashed. Blood spurts on a car's hood and his body falls to the floor.

The fight keeps on going and many others are injured, but none so critically as the third-year LUSS student. Once a stalemate is reached, he is eventually taken to the hospital by students from both sides in the fight.

The boy is in a coma for two weeks. His parents are filthy rich with suspect money. The boy doesn't require funds from LUSS students. No fundraiser is started after the obligatory vigil. There are even rumours that it was he who had initiated the fight by picking on someone's sister. His father's shady wealth prevents the campus from rallying forcefully behind his recovery. He is taken overseas for observation and treatment, and eventually the story of what happens to him is lost in a trail of rumours.

Lahore should be on the bucket list of every foodie in the world. An actual bucket might come in handy. Lahore is the city of dangerous and delectable street food. The worst that can happen is an exponential increase in the number of visits to the washroom and a bit of food poisoning. But on the bright side it means instant weight loss!

The taste far outweighs the risk. And food poisoning can happen from the grub in the posh restaurants on M.M. Alam Road as well. Worry makes the taste buds less effective.

This is on offer: nihari—beef cooked overnight in thick gravy and dollops of ghee; paye—trotters and tendons cooked until they melt in the mouth; kuttakut—you don't want to know what that is; tikkay and machli. For dessert there is kulfi, jalebi, gulab jamun and other diabetic delicacies.

And all of this is just the top shelf of items in a pyramid that is more richly layered than the one Maslow created of human needs.

The need for food is as deeply embedded in Lahore's consciousness as that of Punjabi poetry in any lover's soul in

Lahore. Food is what nourishes. Food teaches one how to show feelings.

No longer is the Old City the only place for the trade of the two oldest professions: food and flesh. There are options for all kinds of tastes in every part of the city.

From the air, Lahore at night looks well put-together despite its clover-like, amoeboid shape. Its sprawl is uneven, but bright lights against the black terrain can make any city a welcome set of flickers after hours and hours of flying in the dark.

Headlights swim through rivers of highways. Even at 1 a.m., with half the city fast asleep, the Old City is always clogged with traffic.

Pakistan's Army fights a war to save this one city. They are overwhelmed, and the Indian forces, many times the size of the Pakistani defensive, are said to be repelled from attacking by the power vested in the shrine of Sufi saint Ali Hajweri (also known as Data Gunj Bakhsh) in the heart of Old Lahore.

To the Indian side is attributed the quote, 'Muahahahaha. We will dine in Lahore tonight.' And to the saint, a silent and invisible shield that the enemy dares not cross. This is the city of the saint of averting bombs and ending wars.

The city shuts down late, and opens up bright and early. It breeds insomnia, nostalgia and myopia.

Its gates remain open to pedestrian and automobile traffic; but the Army has barricades crisscrossed and zigzagged throughout its sprawl. There is a price to pay if you are a main player in the war on terror: the perfunctory checks, the daily toll of some distant fight within the country.

Often, parts of the city, especially the airport, are shut down for security reasons. Cellular services are often disrupted on religious holidays for the same purpose.

All these security issues and impediments to daily life do not exist when Sara and Omar are growing up in Lahore.

Sara's house has always been in Model Town. From when she is eight years old until she turns fourteen, she wakes at dawn and rides her horse around a huge park near her house; often, she goes out alone, without her dad. Model Town is that safe during her childhood.

Then years go by without Sara riding a horse. The roads stop being benign. The parks are dangerous too. Being out there, seeing the city as her own playground, is something she misses dearly and diverts her own attention from. But sometimes Sara will linger on a piece of fruit and remember her horse Gallop's wet and rough tongue on her hand as, in her daydream of her memory, she offers him red and yellow apples—a quarter of an apple at a time to savour the moment.

When Omar is a child, his grandfather lives on Sarwar Road. Turning six, surrounded by grandparents who spoil him and cousins he cannot imagine living without, blowing out the candles on his Knight Rider-shaped cake, Omar believes the house has always existed, and he makes the folly of thinking that it is where he will one day grow up and live.

The white house with all his childhood's most precious memories is sold when he is nine so that his grandparents' bills and loans can be paid off and a new, smaller house can be built on less expensive land, at the leading edge of Lahore's Defence Housing Authority.

Later in his life, Omar runs by that old Sarwar Road house twice, but drives past it more often, always slowing down, driving close to the kerb, to take a look past the gate. He imagines some large family living there, creating cherishable moments. His wishes and nostalgia smother each other, and he drives on.

Sara secretly promises herself something: one day she will own a horse and teach her daughter to ride on it. She even knows what she will name it: Daisy.

She also knows, in a moment of clarity during a nightlong power outage in Lahore, that things will never work out between Omar and her, and that they never should.

So tightly packed are the buildings in the Old City that a person can walk from one end to the other by jumping across rooftops. It is like any overpopulated favela. Favela-havelis. Even the sound of the words is not that far apart.

But unlike the Brazilian favelas, the richest people in Lahore own most of the buildings in the Old City. Some of them continue to live there and look down their noses on the relatives and acquaintances who relocate to Model Town, Garden Town, or Defence.

In the early days of telephones, when only every tenth household can afford one, conversations are relayed via one person standing on the roof, shouting across the city's skyline, and through the relay of information back and forth, making of conversations a story that can be shared by the whole neighbourhood.

On hot summer nights, the residents sprawl out on their rooftops to sleep. They will continue to sleep in this way for as long as the Old City lasts.

Lahore's traditions include Basant, the festival of kites. Larger kites are flown with stronger string. Degrees of string strength emerge. Multiple shapes, colours and sizes begin to create a rainbow in the sky. Common varieties include the square-shaped Gudda, the daddy-sized Dhai Tawa, the effeminately tailed Pari, the androgynous Machchar, the curvaceous Patang and the Lucknow Cut.

As they are bound to, eventually, airborne strings tangle up; one is worn down by the friction and gets cut. The owner of the kite that still flies starts shouting to celebrate his victory. A kite-battle, a *paincha,* is born.

Strings are coated with glue and glass to give them more bite. The painchas get more serious and Basant morphs from a colourful festival celebrating the arrival of spring into one more kind of war for catharsis-hungry masses.

On the black market is available a string strong enough to cut through bone. It does cut through bone in fact. Loose strands of it trailing after defeated kites behead several motorcyclists as they ride without their helmets in the kite-battle zones.

A string even sharper than that one appears, for which the user has to wear chain-metal gloves while flying an invincible kite. The string is nicknamed the Atom Bomb. Basant death tolls escalate.

Add to that the deaths from stray bullets fired into the clouds to celebrate a victory, and kite-runners falling off rooftops, engrossed in air-fights and while chasing the kites whose strings have been cut.

The tradition of Basant gets laced more and more with death. A chief minister's inebriated son loses an arm after falling off his roof while flying a kite. Of course, the booze is overlooked and the kite flying is blamed.

Lahore's Basant is banned. The festival of spring, an occasion to fall in love as a kid, is taken away at the drop of a minister's son.

Omar has a vague childhood memory of crushing on a girl he once saw several rooftops away from the one he was standing on in the Old City. But who doesn't have such memories.

A young boy or a young girl, without a heart filled with the infinite weight of a first crush, has yet to live.

The quality of life improves steadily in Lahore from the 1940s through the '60s. Ava Gardener visits in the '70s, among other celebrities from Hollywood and the British royalty, and the decade is a cultural high point for the city and the country. The future seems bright.

Then Zia ul Haq takes over the country in a decade-long military dictatorship, and after him the louts Nawaz Sharif and B.B. and her husband play tug-of-country, followed by a military takeover by another army chief and his cronies. Then, rinse and repeat. It is the same old song and dance.

Also follow the apocalypse of 9/11, the war in Afghanistan, the import of danger into the country and the city, and up go all the blockades and security checks. Hope for positive change ethers away even as the city gets paved and spruced up like a whore.

What else dies? Lollywood, the Pakistani equivalent of Hollywood and Bollywood. It operates for some time out of the red-light district, eventually petering out.

Everything holy except the saint's shrine is exposed to decay and death.

What Omar sees on his late-night running circuits around the Defence Housing Authority close to LUSS: sprawls of green and thickets of dust; proud, displaced Arab palms, shrubs that bear brown leaves.

With their thin beds and blankets scattered under the open sky, corpse-like, tired poor people lie about, sleeping on the fringes of the sector divisions and the commercial areas' backplots.

Even here, the affluent live with slums pockmarking the spaces between their posh housing societies, and cracks and crevices show between all that glitters.

What Sara muses about while driving around the city is how ugly modern buildings are compared to the old Mughal monuments; the combinations in which life can exist in ways other than her own life's permutations stretched nearly to infinity; the fact that she will never know where the rickshaw drivers on the roads or the security guards of the Empire Center live, though she tries to picture and confine them in her mind in small hovels with three-pan kitchens; the kids on the street begging—are they genuine or faking their broken arms or paralysed legs, and should it concern her either way as she rolls down the window to hand over fifties and hundreds?

She drives in such a way that her dad says it is the car driving her rather than the other way around.

Lahore's hubs and centres change as the city grows; the Old City's walls are taken down. Individual houses have walls built around them. Gated communities spring forth within the affluent areas.

But if the walls can't contain the contemporary city, can they contain the future city?

Conceive of an utterly space-age urban Lahore, and know that it already exists, waiting to be brought forth from the earth. A Lahore with America-town, UK-town, China-town, Korea-town, Little Italy. With a distant enough vision, you can see the city's assimilation into the global, even as it imports the world's cultures.

LUSS is derided already as the Manhattan of Pakistan, for its existence outside any sphere of reality or connection to the rest of the country. All that remains is the extrapolation of the idea—the unfurling of the future.

This is the university's summer trip to the base of the Himalayas after their junior year. In the line of buses going across Lahore just before dawn, Omar and Sara are in the third bus, and after an hour the line is still snaking its way slowly within the suburbs of the sleeping city.

The excitement of finally leaving the campus behind has dissipated. Those on board are now hunkered down in any spot that offers comfort from the biting metal and frayed cushion of their seats. They have settled in for the long haul.

Next to Omar in a double-seat behind the driver sits a young and misfit business school professor who is not wearing any deodorant, and is witless about the students wanting the bus to themselves. Here, in this seat, is where Sara wants to sit.

But she sits in the back on a single seat, across the aisle from Nadia and Mehreen. It isn't just a coincidence. She deliberately waits for Nadia to fall asleep before she pulls her move.

It is four in the morning. The sky outside is beginning to get paler but the bus is still within the city limits.

Outside, on the empty roads, crates of the season's first ripened mangoes are lined up on the donkey carts waiting to be tugged in the opposite direction back into the city. The shuttered fronts of the various shops they cross have slogans and posters that advertise help for male sexual dysfunctions, the area's National Assembly candidates from the election two years ago and phone numbers for a variety of services like D.G. Cement, Pepsi distributors, ceiling fan repair services, land for sale and many other services and products. All these things trundling along, kept alive by the seepage of business outward from the various hubs within the city. A galaxy of other people's lives at the crumbling edge of Lahore. All this is becoming illuminated in the early morning aerosol spray of blue light.

Omar tries to breathe through his mouth and rests his nose on the cool window for respite. His pungent companion shifts and lets more odour fly. There is no respite. There are more than eighteen hours left until they arrive in Karimabad, at the foot of the Himalayan mountains. With the AC running, over the next eighteen hours the business school professor's stink will become exponentially worse with the accumulation of sweat. Omar struggles to breathe only through his mouth, so his olfactory nerves can remain untriggered.

In the back of the bus, Sara sneaks out of her seat and pulls her backpack out from under it. She looks across the aisle; Nadia is sleeping on Mehreen's shoulder. She doesn't look like the Nadia Sara knows, not in this sleeping form. Not so pretty or intimidating with her mouth hanging open. Mehreen and Sara's eyes meet. There is some recognition there. She doesn't say anything to Sara, but there is a Mona Lisa-esque smile in her eyes. Sara breaks off eye contact first as she turns towards the front of the bus.

Ahead of her, two chairs are folded out into the aisle, and each has a boy sleeping on it.

Sara thinks for a moment that she will falter and sits back down in her own seat. It is a delicious moment that throbs out in an instant a lifetime replete with the fear of failure and a branch into the unknown life, one that she will never lead, now that she chooses to move forward. She taps the first boy's shoulder. He is a sophomore. He gets up, folds his seat, and moves out of her way to let her go past. She mouths a *Thank you* at him, so as not to wake anyone else. She moves forward two steps and looks at the back of Omar's head again.

Something takes over her stomach, something anti-gravitational, something that suddenly makes her giddy. She feels as if she's swallowed a bit of outer space, and those laws now apply to her. She taps the shoulder of the next boy in the foldout chair. This one is fast asleep. He shifts and brushes her hand away without opening his eyes. She taps again, but he just shrugs and grunts.

Sara doesn't try to wake him again. Instead, she uses a force she's received and launches herself onto the edge of his backrest with her left foot, and forward, over his head with her right leg.

Shocked by her own actions, she looks back to see what she has just done—what has felt like a leap for the stars. Her head never touched the bus's ceiling, though she felt she leapt much higher. But it is only three feet up, three feet forward and three feet down that she has moved.

She feels like telling Omar about this, and she believes she will tell him as soon as she gets to him. But in the next instant, she forgets. She walks up the aisle, and taps the smelly professor's shoulder. He turns and looks at her, and she says in a whisper, 'Sir, this is my seat.'

Sitting next to the window, Omar turns to see the young

professor stand up, release more foul air, and then walk on to the back of the bus. For Omar, this is a mystical experience. He feels magnetized. There is something that clicks into place when Sara sits down next to him; there is a spark in her eyes even though she arrives with a deadpan expression on her face.

She pretends it is nothing, her being in the seat next to him. She acts as though it isn't seas parting, or the dead being raised to life again, or a mountain glowing with more than its allotted portion of divinity. But that's what it means to Omar.

She does not look at him too long. She knows there will be time for that. With over eighteen hours of the ride still left, there will be enough time for Nadia to wake up and notice where Sara has gone, and for the stinking professor to come back and try and take his seat again. There will be time for doubts about whether to sleep or touch his hands or read a book or talk to him; time for doubts about him to come and go; enough time to build shared memories of this trip together. She wills time to pass and not pass. She sees all this reflected in his eyes.

They choose not to speak.

The window offers a place to rest her gaze. The light outside is dark blue still, but the colour will soon lift. Roadside shops and houses rush by, but in the now frequent gaps between the buildings, she can see a fair distance. Rice paddies and fields of corn open up as they begin to leave Lahore behind. Tube wells gush out water. A few farmers gather in a field, stripping its green. Cows and dogs come into view and from this distance seem fixed in time and space, but slowly disappear behind them. Cycles of life have been spinning here on the outer edge of Lahore too, and they will keep doing so.

Sara sits next to him, their shoulders barely an inch apart. They have hours and hours, and then days once they get to the mountains as well. A year ago, when leaving Lahore on a similar bus for the same trip to Karimabad, he had ached for this. He aches again, and this time feels fulfilled for his wish has been granted. But only a part of him feels at rest. He tries to emulate what he believes is her way of looking at things. He knows there is an epic difference between Sara's view of the world and his own. She doesn't colour what she sees outside of the window with feelings of inadequacy like he does. When she sees the donkeys, the cows and the dogs, the farmers and their mud houses, the trees and shrubs—she sees life in them. She sees they are full of actual daily life and drama. Whereas he sees them only as they are framed in the window: objects that come and go, and leave in their wake the absence of themselves. He wants to look at the world like she does, and when she is this close to him it seems almost easy to do so.

The buses merge onto the Grand Trunk Road where the city ends. More cities and towns will come and go by. Eventually, they will get on to the Karakoram Highway, and the hours will pass as hours do, and the road will end as roads do, and they will reach the lush green heaven on earth at the base of the mountains.

With less than eighteen hours to go, the buses wheel past the city limits, each full of its own set of dreamers, all dreamers leaving a different Lahore behind.

Sophomores
At the Still Point

Sara's room was off-limits for the boys, so they sat in the formal drawing room, the three of them. Hayyan and Omar and a cousin of Sara's whose name Omar forgot instantly after being introduced. There were uncles spread out on the other side of the room. Omar was dressed in white and blue, and the room had a décor of the same colours: lapis lazuli plates, blue pot pourri in a bowl, a blue tinge in the coffee table's glass top, the white walls, and the white lights.

He sat quietly and became a part of the furniture. He thought about when his own mother would die; would things be like this?

Hayyan talked to Sara's cousin about what he was studying and why. It was a practical discussion between two adults but it seemed out of place. Wasn't silence called for? The uncles sitting at the other end of the living room, all of them with paunches, discussed politics and death. They were all saying banal things against corruption; they were all resigned to the futility of life and the inevitability of death.

Omar had not gone for a run that morning. He should have because without it he felt agitated, restless. Sara needed him to be free of agitation though; that is, if she needed him at all. He wondered if he would get to see her.

Upstairs, the real story was being played out. God knew what Sara's mom thought, or if she had any inkling of what the fuss was about. Her still breathing but drugged body had been returned from the hospital to live out its last few hours or days at the place she called home. It was her husband's choice, not her daughter's. She lay half covered by a rose-patterned quilt; her arm white as a sheet, tubed to a drip that eased a few drops of diluted morphine into her bloodstream every five seconds. Perhaps the drug had let her loose among memories of better times, for her gaunt face was lit faintly by a smile.

Across the hallway sat Sara, on a couch in her own room, while Nadia hovered at the dresser fixing her hair. Mehreen was lying on the bed with her eyes closed. Her lips moved constantly, which meant she was probably praying. None of them had spoken for a while.

What was there to say? Weren't they all waiting for someone in the house to stop breathing? Didn't they have to be extremely quiet to hear the silence that would come?

Sara tried to remember her mother's good days, but none of them seemed un-diseased. The cancer had always been growing inside her, hiding and rising. So the picnics and the daily kisses and snuggles with her in the morning when she was younger, the recipe she had modified for French toasts and berries, and the magic of her eyes that her father had fallen for, all of it had been a death-trap.

Sara felt wrong thinking like this about her mother, but she felt she had been wronged more than wrong. That was the issue here. She couldn't help feeling that if she had to die sooner rather than later, her mom should have died years earlier. These were crucial years for Sara. The person she was going to become had already been decided, and even if the exact parameters of her future self were not privy to Sara now, they were already set in motion.

Why take away the one person who had set the stage for Sara's act in life? Why remove her before the play began? It just didn't make sense. Wouldn't Sara be stranded with a fright she wouldn't ever overcome? Or a rage she couldn't control? Which was worse: the fear, the anger, or the despair that would follow both?

Nadia, her hair brushed into straight lines, came and sat next to Sara. 'Zafar's coming to pick me up,' Nadia said. 'Will you be okay?'

Sara wanted to tell Nadia to *shush* so she could hear the last gasp for breath her mom took, which could be anytime now. The exact time might mean something significant in the future. Sara nodded and just mouthed a yes.

'Look, Sara,' Nadia said, putting her hand on Sara's knee, 'if there's anything you need.' Sara shook her head, relishing from Nadia the ugliness of the incomplete cliché. Nadia was a terrible actress because even though she cared, she tried not to show it. It was weak to care and Nadia didn't want to let weakness show. 'You know. Anything,' Nadia said. Sara nodded and held back a chuckle that nearly escaped.

'Where are you going?' Mehreen asked from the bed. She was sitting up now.

'I have to go,' Nadia said.

'You just got here,' Mehreen said, innocently, as if she believed there was a specific amount of time to be spent at Sara's house on this specific day.

'I know,' Nadia said. 'I know,' she repeated. Her phone tingled out a tune as soft as a whistle, all bells and chimes.

But in Sara's head, that melody travelled the length of the room and from the gap under the closed door across the hall and into the keyhole of the door to the bedroom in which Sara's mom lay, slowly making her way towards death.

It felt like the secret tune that could fix everything. It felt like the world's first music. It was Nadia's ringtone for Zafar's calls and texts. It was the sound of devotion.

'That's your signal,' Sara said. Nadia nodded and gave Sara a big hug while Sara kept sitting and returned the hug half-heartedly. Nadia waved to Mehreen.

'Okay, call me,' Mehreen said.

As she softly pulled the door behind her, Nadia called out from the diminishing gap: 'I will.'

Downstairs, Omar saw a girl looking like Nadia cross the doorframe of the drawing room and he tensed up, thinking Sara would follow. The girl was in red and black from head to foot, and she rushed past. The front door opened and closed but nobody else followed.

'Son, what do you do?' one of Sara's uncles asked Omar, looking directly at him, as if noticing him for the first time since the half hour they had sat across the room from each other. The conversation had become duller among the other participants. And Omar's tensing up had made it seem as though he had emerged from the background of the room, conjured into existence.

A direct question was aimed at him and Omar was obligated to speak even though he didn't want to. It was against everything he held sacred. Especially here, conversation should not be about the prosaic and everyday nonsense that people got up to. Someone was dying. Didn't these people understand that? Omar stared at the uncle's salt-and-pepper moustache that needed a trim and chose not to say anything.

'He studies business, uncle,' Hayyan answered for him instead. Omar nodded, grateful to Hayyan for not mentioning history instead. That would have started another round of questions Omar would not have answered—yes, he was convinced he would not talk. He would look away from the questioner, outside the window into the distance and look at the grass and the late afternoon sky of this sad day, to show he was in mourning, and questions about mundane things did not hold his interest at the moment.

He believed his grief to be so strong and his conviction so pure. There was faith's blind leap in there somewhere.

But what if he were cornered by Sara's dad with a question? Would he answer? He had no story ready for that.

For now though, mercifully, the word 'business' from Hayyan elicited only a nod of boredom and a grunt of approval from the avuncular man who had asked the question. And Omar could lean back again because Sara wasn't coming after all. She was still in a room beyond his reach. Only the servant girl with glasses full of Pepsi and Fanta and a tray full of pastries kept coming with replenishments from some room in the interior of the house, and she brought not a whiff of Sara with her.

Mehreen got off the bed in Sara's room and came and sat on a chair across from Sara. Nadia would never do what Mehreen did next. She took one look at Sara's blank face, got off the chair she was sitting on and knelt in front of Sara. Nadia would never relinquish a position of comfort to console anyone. Here was Mehreen, putting herself lower than Sara, or that was what it seemed at first.

Taking Sara's hands, Mehreen pulled Sara forward on the couch and sat on the floor in front of her. 'I have to tell you something,' Mehreen said. 'I've been wanting to tell you this for a whole year.'

Mehreen's hands sweated around Sara's dry ones. 'Oh, okay,' Sara said. This didn't sound like Mehreen. She usually *asked* what was important. She never said anything of significance. Maybe she was going to begin contributing more to the group dynamic.

'I haven't even told Nadia this,' Mehreen said. Her eyes were wide, solemn. Her palms greasy with sweat against the back of Sara's hands.

'Okay,' Sara said.

'You can't tell Nadia,' Mehreen said, blinking her eyes and opening them wider. 'Okay?'

'Okay.' Sara nodded. She was ready to bite her tongue should she feel like laughing dismissively once Mehreen was done saying what she had to.

'Okay,' Mehreen said, 'I'm going to tell you.'

'Maybe you shouldn't,' Sara said, giving Mehreen a chance. She wanted some peace and quiet, even though she didn't want Mehreen to leave. Mehreen's departure would mean Sara would have to go and sit in her mom's room, waiting for the worst thing to happen. With Mehreen around, waiting was still easier.

'I need to do this right now,' Mehreen said. 'Nadia isn't here. I've been waiting for that.'

Sara nodded. 'Okay,' she said again.

'You know my mom's restaurant on campus?' Mehreen asked, her hands loosening. Sara resisted the urge to pull her hands away to wipe them on the couch.

'Yeah,' she said. 'Of course.'

'You know my mom's partner at the restaurant?' Mehreen asked. She put her palms on Sara's knees, and Sara felt the warmth of them through her jeans. This felt good.

'Yeah,' Sara said. She had seen the partner. A thirty-something man with a goatee. Some of the girls at LUSS found him quite attractive.

'My mom is having an affair with him,' Mehreen said. She said it calmly. Only her eyes were locked open, not blinking. And her hands gripped Sara's knees tightly.

Sara did not register Mehreen's words, only her wide open eyes and her tighter grip. Then the words hit. The goatee, the hands of the man with the goatee, thin hands, touching Mehreen's mom's flesh. Mehreen's mom's big thigh came into Sara's head, and the goatee rubbing against it aggressively. She could picture a motel room. Dim lights. Roughness. The roughness of an affair. The scratches and biting of ears. Saliva, wild sex. Affair. Out of marriage. This was something that happened to bad people. It was the crack of unhappy marriage. Years of repressed impulses along with blame games. The excuses. The dirt.

'What?' Sara asked. 'Why?' She wanted to ask why Mehreen was telling her this.

Mehreen's face twisted. 'I don't know,' she said. 'He's so ugly. I don't know what my mom sees in him.'

Mehreen was answering a different question. She thought Sara was asking why the affair was happening, and not why Mehreen was telling Sara about it. Sara understood that and did not ask her own question. It would be rude and might make Mehreen think this confession was irrelevant to Sara's life. But wasn't it?

'How do you know?' Sara asked.

'I just do,' Mehreen said. Her eyes were normal again and she had let go of Sara's legs. 'I have known for a long time.'

'And your dad?'

Mehreen nodded. 'Yeah, he knows too,' she said. Mehreen's dad was a floppy, effeminate man. Sara had stopped herself from thinking he was gay whenever she had met him. In her mind, Mehreen, her two younger sisters and their parents had always constituted a semi-functional family of not-too-bright but very happy people. Blooming idiots, but giddy ones.

Who would have thought that even within that family, the wife had been on the prowl? And the husband knew. It all grew dirtier with Mehreen's dad knowing about it. It grew sordid.

Sara's mom was in the other room, dying, and Sara's heart was racing, thinking of Mehreen's mom having sex with someone.

It seemed unreal. The world was off-balance, or the centre of its gravity had never been where Sara had thought it was. Mehreen's mom's big hips had shifted it further off its axis. The thought crossed Sara's head that if Mehreen's mom could get herself a lover, anyone could. She shook that thought off her mind. It wasn't productive or kind to go down that route.

'Okay,' Sara said.

'Yes,' Mehreen said. 'I wanted you to know.'

'Okay,' Sara said again. She did not want Mehreen sitting right in front of her. But there she was.

'And please don't tell Nadia,' Mehreen said. 'I mean that.' A conspiracy. They recognized a shared fear of Nadia's capabilities.

Sara nodded. 'I won't.' So be it.

'You know why I'm telling you, right?' Mehreen asked.

'No,' Sara replied.

Mehreen leaned back and sighed. Sara also leaned back, as if given permission by Mehreen's movement.

'Because the grass is always greener,' Mehreen said. She looked away from Sara, her eyes glazed. She said, 'I don't mean that I would rather have my mom dying than her having an affair.'

'Of course not,' Sara said, and wondered if she should have said anything.

'But, I mean,' Mehreen said, 'is it not worse in a way, having your mom alive and sleeping with someone other than your dad?'

'Oh,' Sara said. She took an instant to surrender to disgust, and in that instant she was repulsed by the comparison that Mehreen was making. Death versus passion. Death versus betrayal. Death versus a lapse of reason. Death versus abandonment. Which was it? What set or combination of dichotomies did Mehreen mean to compare? How dare she equate death with anything less than death?

Then an imaginary clip of Sara's own beautiful, gaunt mom—with an incipient cancer rather than the metastasized one blooming inside her—in the arms of Mehreen's dad, sneaked into her head. His girly hands, with their long and tapered fingers, caressing Sara's mom's arms. What a mishmash this was. How bizarre the world would be.

'Yeah, you're right,' Sara said. Could she imagine her own rage if her mom was having an affair instead of dying?

Were those the only options: alive and fucking around, or dead and dignified? What about all the good years? Had they been leading to this split in her mom's life? Had her mom, on some metaphysical level, chosen death over an affair? 'You're right,' Sara said, entombing her mom in another layer of nobility. 'You're so right.'

'I am?' Mehreen asked. 'I thought you might get angry with me for saying something like that. But I had to say it. Death may not be the worst thing to happen.' Mehreen got up from the floor and sat in the chair across from Sara again.

Sara had the feeling for a second that Mehreen was playing both her and Nadia, that it was all a game for her just the way Nadia and Zafar were a game for Sara. Maybe Sara, Omar, Nadia, Zafar, mothers, affairs, death, bombs, balloons, all of it was just a game for Mehreen. Mehreen with her chubby arms and chubby mom, always pretending to be kind and goofy, while deep down she was conniving and cruel. Sara felt trapped, suffocated by all the trickery and potential double-crossing in human beings other than herself.

She was being paranoid, she knew that. And if she looked far enough down the line of people and beings who were tricking her, at the chain's origin would be God. And He wouldn't be so cruel, would he? Taking away her mom to upend her life was one thing. But leaving her not even with the sense that she could have something that wasn't booby-trapped? How cruel could God be? Surely not this much.

A door opened in the hallway. Sara's dad had come out of the room where the imminent corpse of her mom lay, still breathing. For now. For how long? At least for now. A nurse was still in there with her, standing next to the bed, measuring drops of morphine passing down a drip's plastic tube. There was no pain. That's what counted now. There was nothing left to be gained from keeping the body alive, keeping the spirit trapped.

Sara's dad coughed like someone who had been crying and walked past Sara's door to the drawing room where the uncles, Sara's cousin, and Omar and Hayyan were sitting. Sara could picture him meeting Omar for the first time, and Omar not liking him. She was conscious that she was more embarrassed by her dad than by Omar.

❦

In the drawing room below, when Sara's dad walked into the room, all the men stood up first, and then the boys. Hayyan and Sara's cousin went up and shook hands with him, and came back and sat down. Omar hesitated only for a second, but in that second Sara's dad said, 'Let's go to the other room,' and led the uncles out of the drawing room into the lounge.

The boys were left behind in the drawing room. They arranged themselves on separate two- and three-seaters, and faced a table on which lay a bowl of nuts, their drinks and fried patties and samosas. Hayyan leaned forward and grabbed a big handful of nuts, held it to his chest, and picked at it with his free hand. Sara's cousin picked up a samosa.

Omar watched them munching at the snacks like it was something okay to do and listened as they began talking about the latest cricket match in which Pakistan had won against New Zealand, thanks to Afridi. They paid no attention to Omar. It was as if his sense of intense gravity rendered him invisible.

Zinc tinges of white light were hurting Omar's eyes, making him blink more often. The walls had paintings of abstract landscapes, mostly in blues and reds. On the mantelpiece, among the plates of lapis lazuli and a heavy blue-tinged crystal that seemed like a paperweight but could have been just an odd decoration at an odd place, was a framed picture of a young couple, in old-fashioned wedding clothes.

Omar got up from the sofa to look at it. Maybe it was Sara's mom. He would get to see what she looked like. The picture was set in an oval wooden frame with a strip of silver running through it. It showed a much younger version of Sara's dad standing next to a woman in a red and gold wedding sari. They looked young, happy, nervous and wide-eyed with wonder. As if they were not actually getting married, but only playing at it. Well, it played at them right back, didn't it? The woman, who did not look like Sara, was beautiful in many ways, but not the way Sara was.

Behind Omar, Sara's cousin and Hayyan kept chattering and chewing. The air was thick with death and their conversation was just as lifeless. Still talking cricket. What did cricket have to do with anything? Nothing, of course. It was an absurd sport and to discuss it in this setting was ridiculous. If only Sara could hear them. What would she say? She would scream that her mom was dying. Like she had screamed it at Omar over eight months ago.

Was it that long ago? August or September on the tracks, that was. The day they had walked around in the storm and she'd left after throwing a fit. He had run for hours after that—ruined his shoes, destroyed QT's iPod. He smiled wistfully, thinking about that night. And here they were, in May of the next year already. Sara's mom was finally going to die. All that sound and fury of the year, of a life, going cold.

A surge of anger threatened Omar's overflow of grief. He had never got to meet Sara's mom. He never got to call her 'Aunty'. He didn't get to tease Sara in front of her mom. He never insinuated himself into Sara's family life. He would have teased Sara so much. Made her miserable with the imitations and mockery of her prim and proper behaviour.

Since learning about her mom's illness, Omar had prepared scenarios where he would visit Sara's mom on her sickbed and entertain her with stories about Sara—some made up, some real. He had created visions in which Sara's mom got better incrementally, miracle after miracle. There were sequences in his mind's reel in which she pampered him, baked him cookies and made him delicious food, needled him about Sara, ganged up with him against her own daughter, and laughed and laughed like a little girl in her middle age.

But the picture of the healthy, though overly thin, woman he held in his hand was a picture from long ago. Too much had happened to her, to that body, to the being that was Sara's mom. And Omar was angry that he would never get to feel all the things he wanted to feel about Sara's mom. What a waste of possibilities. He slowly put the picture back.

As he stepped away from the mantelpiece and sat back on the sofa, he began to think about it all from Sara's perspective rather than his own. In place of his fury, pity took root. How had Sara grown up? Had her mother loved her more than anything in the world, like moms were supposed to? She had not talked about her relationship with her mom at all, just given him updates on her mom's deteriorating condition over the past few months. It had been something they had glossed over, as someone would discuss a bad film or an average meal. It had been like paperwork; necessary and depressing.

He wondered if Sara knew how much she was going to lose with her mom's death—had already lost, in fact, since her mom had been in the process of leaving the world for over a year now. Did it register before the person left?

He tried to imagine his own mother dying. But he couldn't.

It wasn't that. He could actually do it. He easily could, and had imagined his mom and dad dying in many different ways and at many different points in his life. Even wished them dead, sometimes.

Hayyan and Sara's cousin, though speaking softly, were still discussing sports. They had moved on to tennis and were discussing some match between Djokovic and Nadal. How bizarre. How very bizarre.

If my mother dies, Omar thought, I'm not going to invite these people. How bizarre a thought that was as well: inviting people to a death.

But couldn't they just be here and be quiet? Couldn't they just sit and be quiet and just think, even if not about Sara's mom's death, but death in general? Were Djokovic or Nadal or Afridi or Tendulkar not going to die too? Of course they were. So?

Omar's hand by reflex was going to reach for an almond. He stopped the impulse and leaned back. How bizarre it was to desire the taste and crunch of an almond when Sara's mom was dying.

Sara and Mehreen walked into the drawing room. Omar was sitting hunched, looking at his hands. Here he was, dressed in white and blue, like the lapis lazuli plates on the mantelpiece.

Sara walked over and sat down next to him on the three-seater sofa. The gap of the middle seat separating them was just enough for her to be comfortable sitting next to him in her own house.

Omar looked up at Sara and pursed his lips.

She smiled at him. He gave her a weak smile and puppy-dog eyes.

Mehreen sat next to Sara's cousin. Hayyan and Sara's cousin both waved their hands at her. They were talking about the

Australian Open from last year. Had Djokovic won, or Nadal? They couldn't remember.

'Google it,' Sara said. She meant that as a helpful tip because they both had their phones out on the table in front of them, and Sara's home had a fast wireless connection.

'No,' Hayyan said, 'that's not necessary. But I think Djokovic won.'

'It was definitely Nadal,' Sara's cousin said.

Sara's cousin's face resembled Nadal's. Maybe that was why he was so adamant. Omar relished judging Hayyan and Sara's cousin. He believed Sara had suggested a Google search to shut them up. This was a house of pre-mourning. It didn't need petty squabbles. They should have had the decency to stop their blabbing once Sara had walked into the room. Omar turned his body away from them and faced Sara. 'How are you holding up?' he asked her. He clenched his jaw to show that he was here to support her and ready to console her the moment she needed it.

'I'm okay,' she answered, wondering what he was so fretful about. Was Omar sad about having to leave in two days? His eyes were red and he was staring at her.

Sara and Mehreen exchanged a look. It was a look only girls can send and interpret, a signal about the boy in their vicinity, a signal that a rescue is needed from some boy getting desperately attached.

Immediately after sending that signal, Sara was consumed by a flush of guilt and confusion. She had just signalled to Mehreen that Omar was acting desperate, jumping over the edge, and that she—Sara—wanted a rescue. But it was true, wasn't it? She did not wanted any of his intensity right now.

'How is she?' Omar asked. He didn't say the words 'your mother' or 'your mom'. He couldn't. Abysmal sadness overtook him when he realized, conceptually, just as he was framing the question, that Sara was about to become half an orphan within hours.

'She's without pain,' Sara said. She watched Omar nod deliberately, as if she had revealed something profound. A part of her wanted to shake or slap him for acting so grave.

'Neither of them,' Mehreen suddenly said. 'It wasn't even Federer. It was the British player who won. I remember because they said he would never win a Grand Slam but he did.'

'Who? Murray?' Hayyan asked.

'No way,' Sara's cousin said.

'That's good,' Omar kept his conversation with Sara going. 'She shouldn't be in pain.' He pictured himself in an echo chamber with Sara, where none of this talk of tennis tournaments interfered with what they had to say to each other. He filled his words with what he felt was meaning deeper than they would carry if they were used in other people's ordinary conversations. The word 'pain' took on dimensions other than physical, mental, spiritual and spatial. Pain became the song of history, entwined in ribbons around itself like a helical substructure that perpetuated the cycle of life and death. Sara's mom should have no pain because she should not need to suffer resuscitation or rebirth. She should rest in the cosmic space that was the floating existence beyond isolated, cyclical truths and part of the absolute one that need not spin or revolve. Just be.

'Yes,' Mehreen said. 'It was Murray, and he beat Djokovic.' She said this with finality.

Sara thought back to last year, but she couldn't picture Andy Murray winning any tennis Grand Slam. How was Mehreen so sure about this? It made her uneasy. The unnerving feeling came back that Sara did not know everything there was to know about Mehreen. That Mehreen was not so simple after all. It upset Sara. It threatened her. This meant Sara was just like Nadia deep down, just another power-hungry girl out to protect the status quo hierarchy.

Omar's cosmic limbo had physical laws that allowed Sara to look away before looking back at him. She was allowed that gift. But only when she faced him once more did the moment become truly significant once again. He felt like he had smoked a joint and was on a trip. But this was real. This was no substance-driven state of mind. This was abject clarity and focus that were delivered to him as a byproduct of the tragic circumstances. He thought back to the explosion on the day they had first met. That was contained in this fissure. So was the attempted balloon blast in their freshman year and also Sara's outburst on the track during which she had told him about her mom's illness.

These cracks and fissures were the openings that let the light come in and fall on reality, illuminating all the dark corners of it. What a waste an ordinary life would be, thought Omar, in which the surface never broke and the light from the outside never got a chance to brighten up the areas forever lost in shade. For he knew now, and he knew however temporary it was, that he could feel his soul tethered by strings of unhappiness and disaster to the soul of Sara. This dark string keeping them together was neither good nor bad. Only this, that it became visible when destruction and death were close, and when danger or remorse threatened either of them.

In this given light, Omar saw that he would never ever be able to fulfil the role of a hero in her life. Sara's grace was all her own and not of the same kind that would be given to him. He would never recognize the centre of her being, even as he gravitated willingly in its direction.

The sofa with its three seats felt immense and vast, the short distance between them seemed to span a light-year.

'Did you meet my dad?' Sara asked.

'Yeah,' Hayyan answered.

'He came in here,' Omar said, making sure to ignore Hayyan,

override his words. Hayyan thought he had a chance with Sara. He was always trying to be around her, trying to insert himself into her daily life. How could he have a chance with Sara? How could Sara give him a chance? Why would she? She had no reason to.

But a chance at *what* did Hayyan think he had? Her hand? Her heart? Her core being? Omar was losing the plot. Why, from the sadness of the occasion, had he gone off track to try and find a way to sever Hayyan's tenuous connection with Sara? It was stupid of him. She needed friends at this time, all the friends she could handle.

'Did he say anything?' Sara asked.

'Your dad?' Omar asked.

'No,' Hayyan said.

'No, he didn't say anything,' Omar said, still trying to cut off Hayyan. He did not *want* to cut him off. He did not feel the need to because he believed his own connection with Sara was unaffected by Hayyan's attempts. But he felt guided to do it, as if some external force were taking charge, letting him know that the effort he applied to cordon Sara off from Hayyan would pay dividends in the future. Either way, Hayyan did not seem to notice or he did not seem to mind even if he did.

It didn't matter if he did or didn't mind. Hayyan didn't matter. He would disappear into the background noise, the monotony of daily life with its commonplace conversations.

There was a silent pause after that, as each person ran out of things to say next. Tennis was covered and cricket before it. Politics didn't seem appropriate, given that an entry into the topic would make an exit difficult.

But this was Omar's favourite part of the evening so far.

For in that silence he heard the echo of a distant wheeze from the inner architecture of the house. That could just as well have been Sara's dad or her mom, or even some machinery in the kitchen making tea for the guests. But Omar imagined it to be a gasp of despair from the house itself, as it settled down for the death within it.

'You guys leave tomorrow?' Sara asked Omar.

'Yes,' Omar answered, 'tomorrow late night, so early day after tomorrow.' He didn't want to talk about the LUSS Adventure Society trip to Karimabad that he now wanted to back out of just in case Sara needed him once her mom did die. Because she was going to die within the ten days while the group would still be in the mountains.

'What will you do there?' Sara asked.

'I went last year,' Hayyan said, before Omar could say what he wanted to. 'It was awesome up there.' Omar waited for him to finish. 'There's hiking and fishing too,' Hayyan added, 'and lots of other things to do. The best food I've ever had is up there at Hotel Karimabad.'

'Really?' Sara asked. 'The best food you've ever had?'

Omar waited.

'Yup,' Hayyan said. 'The best lamb korma and chicken karahi I ever had. Oh man, I wish I was going again this year.'

Omar waited to say what he had to say.

'I couldn't get tickets this time,' Mehreen said. 'They run out so fast.'

'Yeah,' Hayyan said, 'you have to get in line two days before they start selling the tickets. I couldn't get them either.'

Omar's stretched patience, the conversation's dullness and his bottled-up words were thinning the air out. It was like holding your breath underwater. But the surface wasn't close yet. The people around him weren't done with their prattle, their noise.

'How did you get the tickets, Omar?' Mehreen asked him.

'I, I think I was tenth in line,' Omar said.

'Really?' Mehreen asked.

Omar nodded.

'What else can you do up there besides fishing and hiking and eating?' Sara asked. She asked because she wanted to know what Omar would be doing the next few days. She wanted to picture him in the mountains while she sat at home. Knowing his whereabouts would be some solace.

Why was Sara dragging this on, like it mattered? Omar could draw hardly any breath. The room was becoming a cave too full of people, and too loud with the echoes of their incessant chatter.

'There's a kind of local alcohol up there,' Hayyan said. 'It's called Hunza Water. It tastes like apricots because that's what they use to make it.'

'Apricots?' Sara's cousin, whose name Omar still could not remember, asked. 'That sounds flavourful.'

'Yeah,' Mehreen said, 'I like apricots. They're the yellow ones, right? I always get them mixed up with peaches.'

'What else?' Sara asked Hayyan.

'Oh, I forgot the best thing of all,' said Hayyan. 'There's the Attabad Lake. You have to go there, Omar. It's this long lake that was formed by a landslide. And you can cross it by boat.'

'Boating?' Sara asked. 'That sounds like fun.'

'You have to go there, Omar,' Hayyan said. 'But don't drink the water. Make sure you don't.'

Omar nodded, no longer waiting to say what he wanted to say. He exhaled and sank deeper into the sofa. What else was there to do in defeat? He couldn't ask Sara a simple question: did she want him to stay back? He could not ask that in front of Hayyan and Mehreen and Sara's cousin.

'Why shouldn't he drink the water?' Sara asked. She made a mental note to text Omar every day not to drink it.

'Because it's poisonous,' Hayyan said. 'The lake was formed by an avalanche over a village, and there are dead bodies in the lake. In fact, there are whole houses and farms you can see from the surface.'

'No way,' Mehreen said, her eyes wide open, a hand theatrically up at her mouth.

'Yup,' Hayyan said. 'A whole village. You can see it all from the surface. And someone in our group drank the water from the side of the boat because he was getting thirsty.'

'What happened to him?' Sara asked.

'He got food poisoning,' Hayyan said. 'He threw up all over the place, and for hours. It was very bad. He was nearly hospitalized.'

Omar felt hollow. He felt thirsty. He hadn't eaten all day, since Sara had told him in the morning that she would like him to come over to her house as her mom was back home from the hospital. He had refused to eat, as if to commemorate the gravity of the situation. He had drunk water all day. And then his hunger had vanished. But he could not stop feeling thirsty. His throat felt parched. The conversation added to it. It was dry and dull and without meaning or consequence. He felt the anchor of his life lifting and he saw himself drifting off, for years to come, without purpose or direction, neglected by the fortune that was in everybody else's allotted fates.

If Lake Attabad had been in front of him at this ebb, he would not only have quenched his thirst but he would have dived straight in, all the way down to the bottom, where he would enter the first waterlogged house he came to and live out the rest of his life there. In the silence and the depth, maybe, the slithering conversation's incessant flow would be checked. Down there, where nothing shallow could be discussed.

A kind of peace came over him with this resignation. He was glad he hadn't asked Sara if she wanted him to stay back for her mom's funeral. What if she had said yes?

'You look really tired, Omar,' Mehreen said, and Omar registered this.

'Yeah,' Sara added. 'You look like you could use some rest.'

'I'm fine,' Omar said.

'We should get going,' Hayyan said. He stood and picked his cell phone and keys from the coffee table. Sara's cousin also got up. Omar did too.

'Nice to meet you again,' Sara's cousin said, and shook hands with Hayyan. Omar would have leaned forward to offer his hand too, but the cousin only nodded at him and left the room to join the uncles in the lounge.

'I should get going too,' Mehreen said.

Sara wanted Omar to stay, to be himself, but maybe that was too much to ask. It was his first time in her house. Now that he had seen what her dad and her house were like, and that those would be the only people left after her mom died, would he still feel the same things about her that he did before?

She had asked him to come over only because she couldn't leave the house, because her mom was imminently on her way out. This was the only way she could see Omar before he left for Karimabad. Should she have asked him to stay back? Maybe go next year? The Adventure Society went every year, after all. But it looked to her as though she had made the right decision. He looked needier than she felt. He should go.

First he would leave and then her mom.

Everything would change after that. The loss of her mom would finally hit her and she would feel guilty at last. She was waiting eagerly for the guilt to set in and the processes that stood between now and that desired state seemed tedious. She got up too. Everybody should leave.

'You should go too,' she said to Omar. 'Get some rest.'

He looked at her with half-pleading eyes.

She refused to see anything of consequence in them.

Omar nodded, reluctantly. 'Okay,' he gave in. 'I'll get you something from Karimabad.'

'Get her some dried apricots,' Hayyan said. 'Those are the best. Get some for me too, if you can.'

'Me too,' Mehreen said.

'Yeah, sure,' Omar said, just to have something to say.

They walked in line out of the drawing room, and Sara held open the front door for them.

'Goodnight, guys,' Sara said. 'Thanks for coming. It means a lot.' She tried to give Omar a look that would say more than thanks, but he wasn't looking at her. So she just looked down at her feet. At this moment, Hayyan seemed a much better person to her than Omar. At least Hayyan could make small talk with a stranger. At least he could fill up a room with something other than weight. She looked up and saw Hayyan and Mehreen walking to the gate, already deep in conversation.

Omar looked down and walked a few steps behind Mehreen and Hayyan. He waved his hand as he went past Sara and thought about giving her a hug. To his regret, he didn't. 'Take care,' he said. He imagined it to mean more than it did.

Her mom stopped breathing late the next night, while Sara was with her, and her dad was sleeping in the room next door. He had stayed up for thirty hours straight, keeping vigil, eating very little, pacing up and down the corridor, praying under his breath. By the time he had slept, he had begun to look half a century older than he really was.

After her mom passed, Sara waited ten minutes before she woke up the nurse who was curled up and asleep on a chair. She did this just to be sure that the nurse wouldn't be able to resuscitate her mom. She'd suffered enough. The nurse was paid well, so she got up without fuss and checked for a pulse as well as signs of breath, and then detached the morphine drip.

Sara and the nurse stood at each side of the bed and covered the body with a white sheet. After that, they sat there for a while.

Sara prayed in her own words.

She told the nurse not to wake her dad up for at least two more hours. Then she left the room and walked upstairs to the terrace; from there she climbed the ladder to the roof.

The lights were turned on all over the neighbourhood, and she could hardly see any star in the sky. She sat on a raised ledge and breathed in and out, blanking out for a while, trying to accept her motherless state of being.

Sometime near dawn, Sara texted Omar: 'She's gone.'

Omar was on the bus, only four hours out of the city, when his phone vibrated in his pocket. Everybody except the driver was asleep. Omar was drowsy too, but he woke up, and registered Sara's name on the text message list.

But he didn't open it. He couldn't.

He would wait eighteen more hours, until they got to Hotel Karimabad, where he would put his gear in the room and then walk up to the nearest hill; he would climb it no matter how much time it took, no matter if it was the middle of the night and pitch dark, and even if he couldn't find a torch he would climb that hill and would reach one or two false crests. He would keep going until he surmounted the real one, until the sky was open above him, and he could see the peaks of the Himalayas in all directions. That's where he would open the text message.

He tried to wait. He tried to fall asleep. He tried to distract himself with music.

He turned his phone off.

Mere minutes went by.

The rattle of the bus, his exhaustion, his cold and thin travel pillow, and the sweat frozen all over his body created a cocoon of vibration that made him check again if his phone was off or not. It was. He pressed the power button to turn it on. He went to the text messages list, and the message from Sara was still there, still unopened. He didn't turn off the phone this time. He stared at Sara's name. 'Sara,' he whispered.

Omar looked around. The AC was on and the cooling mechanism was just effective enough to make the interior temperature just below lukewarm. It was perfect to sleep in. The twenty-six other non-driving passengers lolled weightlessly in their seats.

The bus drove on and on through the darkness and cars overtook it at random intervals. Three lanes went each way. There was no vehicle going in the opposite direction. Omar couldn't look outside for too long before he had to look back at the phone and make sure the message was still there.

It was.

He couldn't wait for Hotel Karimabad or the hours of uphill climbing before doing what he did next. He opened and read the text.

'She's gone.' That was Sara's message. She's gone?

Gone across the chasm. Sara's mom was dead. Her body would soon be in the ground and her spirit … in the infinite abyss.

He had been afraid to open the text but he was relieved that the fear was gone.

He didn't type out a reply. Sara's mom left his thoughts. He felt his shoulders relax. It was over. Good for Sara. He felt no sadness anymore; there was nothing left to be sad about. Sara was free.

That didn't sound right in his head, but those were the words that came of their own volition. She was free.

He looked at the text again. 'She's gone.' He felt no need to send her a reply. He put the phone back in his pocket, closed his eyes, and drifted into a deep and dreamless sleep.

Sara's dad made all the arrangements. Flowers, tents, food, phone calls and guests—he took care of it all. On the morning of the funeral, the sun was out in full glory and there was a light breeze. Around a hundred people showed up to pay their respects. Sara's grandparents hugged and kissed Sara again and again, and with their infectious sadness made her cry several times.

She longed to go up to the roof and stay there while the circus of her mom's death played out. She wanted to be alone and remember some of the good times. Because now they *were* good again, not ailing from her dead mom's cancer.

Sara felt like a whole person now that her mother was dead, but she couldn't tell anybody that. Maybe Omar would understand, but definitely not her own family.

They came in, raised their hands and prayed for her mom's soul. Sara prayed too, deep down. *Love her, God. Show her your love. Be kind to her. Love her more than I love her. Love her even more than she loved me. Forgive her. Give her one of the best houses in heaven.*

The body still lay in Sara's parents' room. It was wrapped in several white cotton sheets with rose petals scattered on top, and more flowers on and around the bed. The air conditioner was turned to its highest setting and incense had been lit up in the corners of the room and all over the house.

The men in the gathering formed a line on white sheets in the garden outside to pray. The women formed rows inside the lounge.

After the formal prayers, her dad came over to where Sara sat, took her aside, hugged her and cried into her hair. He was trying to say something, but he keep sobbing. Sara hugged him tightly.

'It's okay, it's okay. It'll be okay. She's in a better place. You don't have to worry anymore.'

Several cars followed the ambulance in which they drove the body to the graveyard. Lifting it onto a stretcher from the ambulance, some men shouldered the sheeted corpse and the rest took turns, three on each side, relieved often, to carry it all the way to the designated empty grave at the back of the graveyard.

Sara's dad stood beside her as her cousins and an uncle lowered the body into the grave. Everyone threw in a handful of dirt. Sara threw two handfuls gently at the feet of her mom's body.

The undertakers took over and filled up the hole efficiently, professionally. They made a mound on top of which her relatives scattered red rose petals with prayers and sobs.

Some of the guests left while others stayed back and prayed. Sara and her dad stood together, thanking people for coming. Her grandparents had to leave early as well. But they promised to come by the house later and to bring food. Sara's maternal grandmother, her Nano, kissed Sara several times on her forehead. Sara gave everything she could muster in hugging her back. It was the least she could do.

On the LUSS Adventure Society trip that year there were two hundred and thirty-nine students, including nineteen LUSS Adventure Society members who controlled the money, the food and the daily activities of the group once it was split up into smaller numbers; thirteen drivers spread across, and sharing duties of, ten buses; three professors, including Professor Zaidi, Omar's Academic Adviser and history professor; Professor Zaidi's eldest daughter on vacation from Stanford University, where she was in the middle of a long PhD in political science; seven and a half tons of cooked and canned rice, chicken and lentils; nine large cauldrons in which to heat up the food; more than thirty-five tents and canvas for the mini-trips to be taken out from the hotel into the surrounding hills and up to various mountain base-camps; maps and compasses for hike leaders; emergency radios with long-range antennas; and the things that the people carried with them in their knapsacks, including cameras, clothes, snacks, hiking boots, cell phones and cell phone chargers, laptops, board games and incessant texts from Lahore: from friends who could not be on the trip, and from parents who would not leave their kids alone.

After two stop-overs along the way for food and rest, at mid-morning on the second day, they reached Hotel Karimabad. The buses needed airing out and light maintenance. Their drivers went about these tasks.

The students picked up their bags and trudged up to the rooms: six in each double-bed room. Except the professors and their families, who had their own reservations, with more space per person. Then there were the LUSS Adventure Society kids, who slept all together on mattresses in the hotel's large lobby.

Omar put his bag on a corner bed by the window of a room full of boys. He changed into his hiking shoes, grabbed his jacket and left the hotel after letting one of the Adventure Society people know he was heading out. The girl waved him away, as she and the others were busy unloading all the group's food and gear.

He walked up the road past a cafe that looked too upscale for its mountain village location. It looked like a tourist trap. Further up, there were stalls for t-shirts and sweaters, dried apricots and mulberries, and trinkets and baubles. The shopkeepers and other people in Hunza caps with green and grey eyes smiled and waved, and he smiled and waved back at them, saying 'Salaam' now and then. He could tell how much some of them just wanted him to stop and shoot the breeze. They could probably talk for hours, these mountain people. Their conversations would be meandering and slow. There was no city rush here.

The road forked two ways, up and down. Omar took the path leading up to the crest of the hill. The market and its smell of roasting masalas gave way to terraced gardens and more lush greenery than he had thought possible.

He huffed uphill, pacing himself, slow enough to not lose breath. The locals went past him and came down from the hill at more than twice his speed. There were more salaams. A few minutes later, without his noticing, cooking smells were replaced with natural ones. Freshly cut grass, clean mountain air, a hint of manure, animal hide smells and even some mineral odours he had not experienced before to know what they were.

He looked back down and it seemed he had come up a long way. He looked up the hill, and the top was still just as far as it had been ten minutes ago. It was going to be at least an hour's walk, zigzagging up a dirt path. He could do it if he tried. He could.

First, he needed some rest. The air was cold, but the effort had made him sweat. Omar took off his windbreaker jacket, put it on the grass and sat on it. He took out his phone. It was nearly discharged. 4 per cent battery left. He opened Sara's text again.

'She's gone.' He read that. He read it again. 'She's gone.'

He checked the signal. It was full. Karimabad, of all places, received full cell phone signals. This was impressive.

There were no more messages from Sara or anyone since that one. Why hadn't he replied?

He had thought about not replying at all, and getting off the bus in Islamabad, only five hours out of Lahore, and buying a ticket for a bus ride back, and attending the funeral. Even after they had passed Islamabad, he could have told the Adventure Society people it was an emergency. They would have dropped him off at a rest stop.

But why hadn't he got off? And since he hadn't got off, why hadn't he replied to Sara?

Should he now? What could he say? *Sorry*? Was 'I'm sorry. I hope you are okay', enough? Shouldn't he write a much longer text explaining what he really thought, or a longer text saying what she needed to receive from him?

That would take all night to type. He would write it at night. The battery was now at 3 per cent. So there was no point trying to write a long text right away.

Also, there was no point climbing any further. He did not want to get lost without a phone. Of course, this was an excuse. He had hours of daylight left, and the path led visibly up to the top. Abandoning the hike was cowardice; he knew that. He excused it as being careful. You can't be too careful. His clothes were quick to dry up, and he started the walk back to the hotel, not once turning back to look at the climb he was abandoning.

At the hotel, he plugged his phone into a wall socket next to all the other plugged-in phones and typed out a text to his parents: 'We've reached Hotel Karimabad. Getting some rest. Will call later.' He pressed send. Then he lay down on the window side of the double bed and fell asleep.

Being the one who leaves is so much easier.

Sara sat in her room after the funeral and thought about last year, the flights to New York and San Francisco. There would be no long journey this year for Sara; only short trips to the graveyard and back.

She looked at her phone again. He still hadn't replied to her text.

Should she have stopped him from going? But under what pretext? He wasn't her boyfriend after all. Or was he? He felt like one sometimes. But did he also think that she felt like a girlfriend occasionally?

I can't think about this right now, Sara thought. Not now. I'm confusing the issues. Mom is dead. My mom is really dead. No longer dying of a long battle with cancer. She's dead now. The battle is over and she's gone.

She tried to remember her mom saying something to her long ago, over the telephone. 'And take care of your dad.' That's what she had said whenever she was away.

The words were hers, but Sara couldn't remember her voice. What did she sound like when she was well? Her mom's giggle was something Sara hadn't thought she would ever forget. But where was it now? Why couldn't she access the memories she wanted to?

It was Omar's fault. He had to go away and distract her. He just had to be away and even at her mom's funeral make Sara think about him. She checked her phone again. No messages. She checked the inbox. No, he still hadn't replied. She went to the sent messages and saw that her text had gone out to him. Maybe they don't have signal in the mountains, and he never received it. Or maybe he did reply and it never came through. No. He would have called. They had phones in Karimabad. She was sure of it.

Something else was gnawing at her, a fainter memory, back when she had just turned twelve. She was a shy and awkward girl who had just hit puberty and thought of herself as one of the ugliest girls in school. Too long a face, too thin a body, no size yet where it mattered, while her friends were getting the appropriate bumps and curves she envied.

Her dad had taken her to his ancestral village near Chichawatni, to acquaint her with a flavour of where and how he had grown up. At first, the stink had been intolerable. She could still remember how repulsed she had been after smelling so much manure. Her dad had not even flared a nostril. He hadn't turned the car around and fled. Sara had desperately wanted to.

They had stayed six days in her dad's cousin's villa in Chichawatni which had a huge brick and cement courtyard, charpoys for sleeping, and hukkahs and dhotis.

Memories of that and the smell of manure were more intact than the remains of Sara's mom's good years. That would change over time, Sara knew. Things would eventually come back to her from nowhere.

But for now, it was the village she thought about, over a third of her life ago. A boy from that village had seen her in the courtyard. He had climbed over a wall to retrieve a cricket ball that had come inside. The boy and his friends with their cricket bats and wickets and his bald head and their naked feet, and them running in the mud, all of it came back. She'd loved him at first sight because he had kept staring at her and she hadn't thought to look away from him. It had felt so comfortable, being admired like that. It was like a sense of belonging.

Over the next five days, the boy had come again and again to retrieve cricket balls, to give her fresh earth-baked bread, to give her yellow flowers from the meadows, to bring her a glass of lassi, to watch her while she sat and chatted with her cousins, who had also been crushing on her, she now reasoned. And then her dad and she had left the village, just like that.

She had been heartbroken, but resigned. Life was like this. It would always be like this. She would like people and then not get anymore time with them.

Part of what she gathered as a lesson from this memory applied to her mom's departure too. Her mom had been taken away, just like that boy had been taken away from her.

But Sara didn't linger there, in that nostalgic distillation of her memory, of the sadness of her loss.

More vivid to her was the abject, unquestioned infatuation she had felt for that boy. Her first and perhaps last crush. She had dissected the feeling over the years, to discover what it was, how it worked and if it could be repeated. There were certain patterns she had observed in this and in her friends' stories about similar experiences: when you leave your comfort zone, your senses are heightened; in that heightened state, things and people may seem more important than they are at other times; a crush, even love, is ridiculously easy when you're in that state of displacement.

Omar was away now, in the hills. There were many other girls on the trip as well. Omar was in a state of displacement and so were these girls. The headiness induced by thin mountain air would add to all this. The cold would wake them up further. All their senses would be alert. There they were, vulnerable and raw, charged and hot like sparks that could kindle a fire if they came into contact.

If Omar fell for someone up there in the mountains, he would never be Sara's again. Should she have made him her boyfriend? She suddenly missed him intensely.

She sat on a chair in her mom's room, resting in the middle of sorting a pile of clothes on the bed where her mom had died, and her heart ached.

Why had she let him go? She could have asked him to stay. She could at least have asked him if he wanted to stay; that wasn't asking for too much, was it? Why wasn't she his girlfriend already? What were they waiting for?

Omar slept through lunch, and one of the Adventure Society members woke him up for dinner once group alliances had already formed. There were the obvious couples trying to remain inconspicuous in front of the others by hovering at the fringes of larger groups, the buddies who had come up only for Hunza water and 'good times', and some larger clumps of students whom Omar could join as anonymously as he wanted.

But it would be awkward to try and get along with students he did not hang out with back at LUSS. Why bother at all, especially if he got stuck with an annoying group of people.

Instead, he looked for Professor Zaidi. He told himself he wasn't looking for Professor Zaidi's daughter, but only for her father, that he wanted advice on his future as a history major. He assured himself that it wasn't the daughter's face he scanned for in the crowd of students; it was a coincidence that she was pretty, and that the attractive set of eyes and her dark red lipstick that he'd noticed earlier didn't figure in his standing at the door of the large dining area, sifting for Professor Zaidi's long grey hair. Omar found him at one of the back tables near the window. His daughter was with him too. Merely a bonus, Omar made himself believe, since now he could ask her about graduate programmes in political science, which was one of the natural extensions of a history major at the undergraduate level.

'May I join you guys?' Omar asked. The professor waved him to a seat while his daughter smiled. She was a happy person, Omar could tell. She had a constant smile and her face was incredibly pleasant to look at. He smiled back.

She introduced herself as Sonia. He kept saying her name in his head while talking to her. *Sonia*. They ate rice, chicken, lentils and salad, followed by kheer and green tea, and after dinner Professor Zaidi smoked a clove cigarette without a filter as they took a digestive walk down the dark road in the mountain air.

A hundred thousand stars lit up the night. There were more lights twinkling up there than Omar had ever seen before on a single sighting of the sky. He kept looking up as he walked next to Sonia and his professor. Sonia's father told them about the multiple times he had been up here in the mountains over the years, how it was the last spot of paradise left in Pakistan, and how he hoped his grandchildren and their grandchildren would be able to come here and see what he had seen. They walked up the road to where it forked and then made their way back.

As was inevitable, Professor Zaidi grew tired before Omar or Sonia and excused himself, telling Sonia to get rest soon. She had her own room next to her father's, she told Omar.

After her father left, they walked in the other direction, descending, though knowing they would have to climb back up each step they took down.

Sonia was twenty-seven and she was at least two inches shorter than Sara. Sonia also smiled more often than Sara. With Sonia he felt no pressure at all.

The night was theirs. There were dark trees, a bright moon, the blanket of stars and easy conversation full of light moments, smiles and comfortable pauses. They descended all the way down to the bank of a large lake.

Only one vehicle passed by them on the way down. Otherwise it was idyllic and the whole world seemed to have quietened down to its lowest volume, except for the gentle rippling of the water in the lake.

They sat on the grass by the bank and talked about the different countries she had been to, the pace of life in academia versus real life, the beauty of vacations and why she didn't think she could ever live in Pakistan even though her degree was focused on the politics of South Asia in general, particularly Pakistan.

He mentioned he liked to go running while she described her yoga and meditation. He brought up his love for literature, and she mentioned all the independent bookstores where she spent hours. She said he was different from all the other students on the trip; he shrugged and said maybe he was and then immediately turned red. He was glad it was too dark for her to see him squirm. He was smiling uncontrollably at what she had said. He *was* different. He stood out. She had noticed that. The night was turning out to be perfect.

They made the uphill climb in more silence than conversation. Soft sounds of the water surrounded them and Omar pretended to be less winded than he was as he kept pace with her. Yoga must be better than running for a walk in the mountains, he thought.

Sonia was thin and lithe; he felt he could put his arms around her and lift her over his head in one breath. With her he felt strong, able to do more than he had ever done before.

But it was just a walk and Hotel Karimabad was closer than he'd anticipated; return journeys always seem shorter, probably because the distance has already been covered, already been fathomed.

He walked her to her room and she asked if he had any plans the next day. He replied that no he didn't, except for a long hike with a group. Then she said good night and closed her door.

Omar walked to the roof of the hotel where some chairs were laid out and a few couples and groups were sitting in their own spaces. He found a metal chair in a corner and wanted to sit there in the cold for a couple of hours, looking up at the stars to empty his mind of anything negative.

Five minutes passed and the cold bit through to him. He felt the chill of the metal through his jeans, past his boxers and his skin and muscles, to the very marrow of his bones.

He went and lay down on his bed and checked his phone. There was a missed call from his father and a text from his mother saying 'Stay safe, darling. Bring back some of the famous Karimabad apricotts.' He smiled at her misspelling, but did not reply. Instead, he went back to his inbox and pressed on the message from Sara again. 'She's gone.' He read it again. 'She's gone.'

Only a very small part of him wanted to spend the time

composing a long text telling her all sorts of lies. Because that is what they would be: lies. He did not want to think about grief. It took too much energy out of him to empathize with Sara's sadness at the moment. He felt a sense of lightness and freedom from any cares. He didn't want to change that. If Sara were here, he would have hugged her and rocked her to sleep and watched over her. But if he wrote that to her, she wouldn't understand what he meant.

Instead, he lay awake for most of the night, unable to sleep, envisioning a future far away from Pakistan, a future in which he would be a PhD student in a fantastic political science programme, concentrating on South Asia. Maybe he could focus further on political parties—why they didn't bloody work—and he would be married within the PhD's third or fourth year to a fellow student in the programme. Someone just like Sonia. But, of course, he would be friends with Sara for life. That was given and didn't need deliberation.

⚜

Some of the distant relatives at her mom's funeral had asked Sara's dad if she was still single.

Hayyan had texted Sara and asked if he could come over and spend time with her.

To get away from the discomfort that the queries generated as well as to escape the general thickness of the air at home, Sara said she had to retrieve something from her locker at LUSS. She drove there, parked under the shade of a large oak in the empty parking lot and walked through the heat from one building to the next, savouring alternatingly both the AC-cooled rooms and the wafts of scorching summer heat.

Eventually, she made it to the library, which was thankfully open. The air conditioning was coolest there and she sat pretending to read a newspaper, but instead watched the library's front desk. A man and a woman were sitting there. Both were unattractive and middle-aged, both seemed married—not to each other—and there was clearly no chemistry between them whatsoever. It seemed as if their life played out in the most boring permutations possible. Sara watched them and gloried in the pity she felt for them. They just sat there, in the nutmeg smell of the building, surrounded by books every day.

The news in the papers was duller than it was depressing. And Sara's store of pity was quickly drained.

She got up and moved around the stacks. She started with the boring ones first: commerce and electrical engineering. These were the driest and most difficult subjects for her. Physics, on the other hand, she could still manage, and astronomy more so. Some of the titles were intriguing enough for her to pull out the books and shuffle through the pages. *A History of Arabic Astronomy*, *A Brief History of Time*, *String Theory*. She pulled the books out, carried them halfway across the library and set them out on a desk. She decided she would check these out with her card.

She browsed through the economics section next and then finance. *Barbarians at the Gate* stood out and she thought about taking it down, but chose not to. She walked away from the religion and Pakistan studies shelves, and went to look at the literature aisle instead.

There was no semblance of order that she could find. Some Jane Austen books stood next to Umberto Eco's, and Kafka's *Metamorphosis* was shelved next to Arundhati Roy's *The God of Small Things*. It was not alphabetized, not arranged by size or colour, and even the codes ran anywhere from PA to S3 along the spines, in completely random order.

Every book intrigued her because of these odd juxtapositions.

She was looking for books she had seen in Omar's hands. She

remembered *Love in the Time of Cholera*, *Cloud Atlas* and *The Unbearable* Something *of* Something.

The books were covered in dust from disuse and the lack of cleaning. Oddly enough their smell reminded her of her mom, and she imagined her mom lying in her grave reading a funny book and laughing. As morbid as that sounded, it wasn't an altogether unpleasant thought. Wouldn't she rather imagine her mom reading than getting infested with worms?

But that didn't scare Sara, the decomposition bit. It was natural, of course. Her mom's body needed to disappear through the natural process. Only after the body disappeared would she truly become a part of the abyss.

Sara's phone rang out loud and trembled in her hand.

She gripped it tightly and stared at it. She'd forgotten to put it on silent mode when she had entered the library.

The screen said Nadia calling ... Good thing the library was empty, but Sara still felt ridiculous. She answered just because she didn't want it to ring anymore.

'Hello,' Nadia said.

'Hey,' Sara whispered, and covered her mouth. 'Nadia, I'm in the library.'

'Hello?' Nadia asked again. 'Sara? Hello?'

'I'm in the library,' Sara said a bit louder.

'Oh,' Nadia said. 'Are you on campus?'

'Yes,' Sara replied. 'I'll call you in a few minutes. Let me go outside.'

'No, no,' said Nadia. 'I'll come there. Wait for me.'

'Are you on campus?' Sara asked. But Nadia had hung up.

Sara turned her phone to silent and walked down the line of books. She kept her eyes on the spines, but didn't know what she was looking for anymore.

Kipling's *Jungle Book* lay next to Bapsi Sidhwa's *The Crow*

Eaters. Toni Morrison's *Beloved* sat next to an anthology of African and Australian aboriginal writers. Clearly, the system was purposefully insane. Who could come up with these combinations otherwise?

And then there it was: *Cloud Atlas* by David Mitchell. It was a medium-sized novel. Sara didn't like novels, but Omar had said this was more of a physics book than a novel. He had said something peculiar about it that had stuck with her: the chain of causation is more of a loop or a cycle, rather than a straight line; how *Cloud Atlas* was a study in the future influencing the past. That had stayed with her for a year and only now that Omar was not around did she think to pick up the book herself. Because why would she bother reading it when he could tell her about it if he were around.

But he wasn't here now, was he?

And like a cough building up inside her, a cough that would make her spew her insides out, she knew what was making her sick. She could easily discard the thought of her mom's rotting body, but Omar was inside her like an infection.

And what if he returned from the trip and said he had fallen in love with some girl in the mountains? What then? Because wasn't that inevitable? She would lose her best friend. She would lose whatever Omar was to her. What *was* he? Why was she afraid of losing him? What made him so important? Nobody else had seemed that important to her so far.

Her phone buzzed again. It was Nadia. The text message read: 'I'll be there in five minutes. Meet me outside library.'

And what if Sara didn't want to meet Nadia right now? She could tell her to lay off for today, maybe even for a few more days. She could use her mom as an excuse ... no, she couldn't use that now. Not after all the wrong things she'd used it for already.

She opened *Cloud Atlas* and went past the title page to the first section, 'The Pacific Journal of Adam Ewing'. Sara put a finger there, closed the book around the finger and with her free hand typed out a reply to Nadia. 'Come inside. Reading.' She pressed send hard and took *Cloud Atlas* to the sofas with the newspapers and opened the book.

'Thursday, 7th November...

'Beyond the Indian hamlet, upon a forlorn strand, I happened on a trail of recent footprints. Through rotting kelp, sea cocoa-nuts & bamboo, the tracks led me to their maker, a White man, his trowzers & Pea-jacket rolled up, sporting a kempt beard & an outsized Beaver, shoveling & sifting the cindery sand with a teaspoon so intently that he noticed me only after I had hailed him from ten yards away. Thus it was, I made the acquaintance of Dr. Henry Goose, surgeon to the London nobility. His nationality was no surprise. If there be any eyrie so desolate, or isle so remote, that one may there resort unchallenged by an Englishman, 'tis not down on any map I saw...'

What a wonderful way to spell 'trowzers' and such an easily readable book this was. Sara read the passage again. She noticed the mini-alliteration and sing-song rhythm of 'cindery sand'. David Mitchell could definitely write well. The opening sentences were fun. They made her think of something like *Robinson Crusoe*, which had been the first unabridged book she had read in high school.

She was going to read this book right away. And to think she didn't even like novels.

Nadia's shadow loomed across Sara's book. Here she was already, wearing a black dress with pumps, not heels. This was unusual for Nadia. Maybe she had known the campus was empty, so she didn't feel the need to be her ostentatious self.

'Hey, Saroo,' Nadia said, putting a hand on Sara's shoulder. Sara closed the book. Here come the consolations, she thought.

'Hi,' Sara said, 'How are you?'

'Not good, babe,' Nadia said. 'Not good at all.'

Sara didn't say anything. She waited for Nadia to admit feeling guilty that she had abandoned her; to say she felt horrible and wanted to make up and would now be at Sara's beck and call.

Nadia sat down across the table from Sara and leaned back. 'I feel horrible,' she said, with a grotesque smile. It was evil.

Sara looked at Nadia and tried to hide her fear, but her eyes only grew wider. What was Nadia playing at?

'What?' Sara asked and instantly regretted it. Nadia was toying with her again. Sara couldn't even use a period of mourning to get out from under Nadia's foot. Nadia kept up her smile, making Sara squirm. 'What?' Sara asked again. She felt weak and spent.

'We,' Nadia whispered, pausing to bite her lower lip. 'Zafar and I,' she paused again. It seemed theatrical. She hammed it up by winking at Sara.

'What? Zafar and you what?' Sara whispered back. 'What?' she said louder this time, as if demanding an apology. That was exactly what she was demanding. But it was off-topic. The topic, without Sara's wanting it, had shifted back to Zafar. Fucking Zafar.

'Zafar and I,' Nadia started again, leaning forward, 'we did it.'

'Did what?' Sara asked. Of course. As soon as the question left her lips, Sara knew the answer. She'd predicted it a year ago. Nadia had proved Sara right. I could have bet my savings on this, Sara thought. 'You did it, as in, you had sex?' she asked. She had to confirm.

Nadia nodded, smiling wider.

'Did you use protection?' Sara asked.

'What?' Nadia said. 'That's your first question? Did I use protection? Of course I did. You think I'm an idiot? Don't you want to know how it was?'

'Yes,' Sara said, giving in, playing Nadia's game. 'But first I want to hear you swear that you used protection. And I want to know what kind.'

'I swear I used all the right things,' Nadia said. 'But I want to tell you what it was like.'

Sara looked over at the librarians sitting at the front desk and imagined the middle-aged duo getting horny listening to these two sophomore girls talking about sex in the library. She imagined the woman winking at the man and both of them going at it behind the counter. What an image that was. Good thing they were just far enough for Sara and Nadia to talk about this softly and not be heard.

'Are you sure you want to talk about this?' Sara asked Nadia. 'I mean, isn't it very, very personal?'

'Sara,' Nadia said, 'I've been dying to talk to you about this.'

'Okay,' Sara sighed. 'So how was it?' She wondered how it would be for her and Omar. It would probably be good the first time and they could eventually get really good. Why was she thinking this? Did she plan on having sex with Omar? Was that going to happen? Was it a *given*? What about the ambiguity? Would that end before or after the sex? What about saving herself for marriage and all that old-fashioned stuff? Didn't that mean anything? Didn't it mean more than the ridiculously nebulous thing she had with Omar? Why was she questioning herself? Of course she wasn't going to have sex with Omar. But then again, why 'of course'? Didn't she find him attractive?

'It was horrible,' Nadia said.

'Huh,' Sara said. 'Really?' Okay, that meant Sara would not have sex with Omar. She was flooded with relief at having the choice made for her.

'Not the sex,' Nadia said. 'The sex was good. It was really good, in fact.'

'Okay,' Sara said, confused again. 'Okay,' she repeated.

'Yeah, the sex wasn't horrible,' Nadia said. 'It was everything else that was horrible.' Nadia waved her arm in a circle around her head, a loop which could indicate the racks of books, the shelves of periodicals and the cluster of computers in the library. 'Everything else,' Nadia said, 'it just didn't make sense anymore.'

There was a moment of silence between them. Sara and Nadia looked directly into each other's eyes and sat in silence for a while. They could hear the AC vents spewing cold air, which played at turning the page of a newspaper lying on the table between them.

'What do you mean?' Sara asked cautiously.

'I don't know how to say it,' Nadia said and looked away. 'It's weird.'

'Say it,' Sara said. She leaned forward. 'Say what you mean.' Did Nadia have more depth than Sara gave her credit for?

Nadia looked at Sara again. She leaned forward too. Up close, Sara could see how Nadia had smeared some of her eyeliner. Her red lipstick also ran off from one corner of her mouth. It was possible, Sara thought, that Nadia had come to LUSS right after having sex with Zafar.

'Okay,' Nadia said, 'It's this feeling I had, you know. Like nothing I'm doing is because I want to do it. I feel like that with, you know, Zafar. I feel like I'm in some game that I'm playing or is being played with me.' Nadia paused and looked away.

Sara kept staring at Nadia's eyes, not daring to shift. She could feel Nadia reaching a breakthrough. She didn't want to spoil the moment by saying anything just yet. Staying still, Sara coaxed Nadia on with her thoughts: *Say what I'm thinking; go on, say what I'm thinking. You can do it.*

'I mean,' Nadia said, 'this whole thing with Zafar and me, and with you and Omar, with everyone here in college, even with your mom dying and how you feel about that, and how Mehreen and I are supposed to help you out, you're supposed to grow out of it, and we're supposed to graduate. Then God knows what. Isn't all of this just us acting out some sort of script, no matter what we do?'

Bingo, Sara thought. Nadia had hit the nail on the head. *Finally*. After two whole years of college, after losing her virginity to a sleazy bastard, Nadia had come of age. She had crossed the threshold and could see what Sara saw, what Sara had *always* been able to see.

'Hmm,' Sara said, looking down, as Nadia's eyes met hers again. 'Hmm,' she said again. Nadia had taken Omar's name, she thought. She had equated Nadia–Zafar to Sara–Omar. This meant that Nadia thought it was a given that Sara and Omar would be banging within a year or so. That wasn't an unpleasant thought though, not completely.

But it wasn't a thought Nadia should have expressed, or even thought up in the first place. This was not her decision. It was Sara's and Omar's. For now, she decided, she didn't want to meet Nadia halfway.

'I don't know what you're talking about,' Sara said. She looked deep into Nadia's eyes, pretending not to understand. 'I really don't understand.'

'You don't?' Nadia asked. 'Yeah, right. Of course you understand.'

'Look,' Sara said. 'I'm sure what you're feeling has something to do with having sex with Zafar.' She made her voice sweeter and nearly sang the rest. 'I've never had sex, so I don't think I'd understand. Maybe you should go talk to your mother. You know. I mean, since you still *have* a mother.'

Nadia looked as if Sara had swiped at her with a sharp blade. She got up slowly. 'I'm sorry about your mom,' Nadia said. 'I really—'

'Thank you, it's okay,' Sara said, loud enough for it to sound dismissive. It was Nadia's fault. And instead of apologizing up front for leaving Sara alone after her mom's death, Nadia was audacious enough to try and wrest control of Sara and Omar's life story. How dare she? Oh, *oh*, she dare not.

Nadia withered and disappeared. She left some stale perfume in her wake.

Sara sat where she was for twenty more minutes, reading the praise on the cover of *Cloud Atlas*, opening it at random pages, and reading the chapter headings. 'Letters from Zedelghem', 'The Ghastly Ordeal of Timothy Cavendish', 'Sloosha's Crossin' and Ev'rythin' After'. Another world waited for her inside this novel. A world within a world within a world within…

All the universes could open up again now.

The morning after their late-night walk, Omar and Sonia hiked up a hill to catch a view of the Himalayas. They were with a large group and her father, Professor Zaidi, was leading the pack. Omar and Sonia walked near the rear so she, an experienced hiker, could keep an eye on the stragglers. She and Omar talked politics, but with subtext, he thought.

She admired his stamina aloud while he commented on the depth of her thoughts and kept silent about her physical attributes, which he also admired. She asked him if he had a girlfriend or a boyfriend. Hearing this he laughed and said no, he didn't have either.

Near a precarious ledge, where he held out his hand for her to clamber up after him, with trickles of water making the stones slippery for their heavy boots, Sonia refused to take his chivalrously extended hand and joked that she was too old for him. Omar laughed uneasily but let it pass. Though it lingered at the back of his mind. Did Sonia think he was hitting on her? Wasn't he just being kind to the daughter of his favourite professor by keeping her company? Sure, he enjoyed what time he was spending with her and she was pretty after all. But wasn't she the one asking all the flirtatious questions? Was this her way of being coy and coquettish?

Later, at a lunch stop during their hike, he sat next to her eating a sandwich. She blurted out an awkward question: Did he like any of the girls on this trip? Without waiting for him to answer, Sonia exclaimed that her Chilean boyfriend was back in San Francisco and she missed him.

Omar considered telling Sonia about Sara, but then dismissed the thought. He didn't look at girls like that, he said stupidly, and then felt ashamed that he had basically confirmed he didn't have a girlfriend and might never end up having one. What was Sara to him then? A hobby?

He also wondered why Sonia needed to let him know she had a boyfriend. Did she seriously think Omar was hitting on her? Or maybe she was reminding herself, while letting him know at the same time, that there stood somewhere between them a line that shouldn't be crossed.

While walking again, still at the back of the group and nearing their destination, Sonia said something she had also said the night before: he was different from the rest of the boys on the trip. This time, he told her he was the same as them and it just looked like he was different because he didn't have any friends. The vehemence of his response felt good. She had insulted his attempt at friendship with her and he didn't need that while his best friend was in Lahore, grieving for the loss of a loved one.

Before he could release any more indignation against Sonia and perhaps ruin his professional relationship with her father, Omar decided he would keep away from her for the rest of the trip. He decided he would not go on any more hikes with the group either. Instead, he would go hiking and running on his own.

That was just what he needed. That was just what he had been missing. He needed to purify himself again, to wash off the confusion. Running through the hills in the thin cool air, battling his lungs against the steep mountains, it would be the perfect thing.

Of course, he couldn't run uphill for long on the first day he tried. A few minutes of thunder in his heart and lungs, breathless gasps led to collapsing onto his knees, and then he was forced to walk and scramble up the rest of the way.

His cell phone in his pocket was a constant reminder that nearly half the vacation was over and he still hadn't replied to Sara's text. All the days that had slipped by, all the time sagging under its own weight. Impatience was shooting through his body.

It was too late to send simple condolences in a text message. He was too far away to drive over to her place and apologize. Five days to go, or thirty-six hours if he started back now, on his own. And Sara hadn't texted him after that. She had waited. Maybe she was still waiting. He was making her do just that.

Did he want more from her? She hadn't given him much, just a two-word text. 'She's gone.'

The sun was shining bright and the air was warmer the next morning. A group of twenty-five students were trudging out for a day-long hike. Professor Zaidi and Sonia were not up for breakfast yet. Omar thanked his luck that he kept avoiding them. He skipped breakfast and went for a run and then a hike, taking a small sling with water and snacks along.

He jogged all the way down to the valley to the lake, picked a track with a gentler slope and put on his iPod which he had bought right after exams, especially for the trip.

All the music he had on the player were two thirty-minute qawwalis: '*Ghorak Dhanda*' and '*Behad Ramzaan*'. The good thing about qawwalis was their metronomic beat kept up by claps and dhols, which after fifteen minutes put him into the rhythm he needed in order to forget he was running at all. The lyrics, the music, everything tuned out, and he entered the beat to become one with the road. He zoned in and out, breathing harder if he went too hard and softer if he eased up. Things were holding together now, beginning to make sense.

Sara woke up on the sixth day after her mom's death and looked at her cell phone. No messages; nothing from Omar still. She smiled. It didn't hurt her that he had not replied to her six-day-old text. She felt okay because by now she expected it. Anything else would have been worse. Sara had been distanced from Omar for long enough for her withdrawal symptoms to weaken.

She wanted to discuss with him the ending of *Cloud Atlas*, especially with reference to what he had said about the past being dependent on the future. It made sense to her, but she didn't know how to put it into words yet.

Half the trip was over. Omar would be back in five days. She was at the end of her rope with her other friends, and a large part of her was growing numb.

Omar would make things better. He knew just how to.

She went into the washroom, splashed some water on her face, tested a smile in the mirror and could not tell if it was fake.

For two more days, Omar ran up and down some steeper hills, drank water from the melting glaciers, snatched some apples and blackberries from the trees, and snacked on the nuts and dried apricots he carried in his pockets and his sling. He ignored the many students from LUSS that he came across on the roads and trails and kept out of the way of the villagers and the other mountain people.

Next year, he promised himself, he would come again and talk to the locals to know them better. Maybe Sara would be with him then.

To cleanse himself while he was running to qawwalis with lyrics about purification and self-denial, Omar thought about what kind of life he was living.

He believed himself to be a perfectly well-rounded individual on the surface: he could run for hours, he could excel at school if he wanted to and he was taking both business and history classes, thus becoming a potentially valuable member of society. The skin-deep Omar seemed to him an entity worth keeping on the planet for the sixty to eighty years of life he might yet lead. That was his rough estimate, of course. Accidents and diseases could happen to anybody.

He suddenly imagined a cancer growing somewhere in his body, something like bone cancer. But his bones were strong and they firmly held up his body as he ran among the hills. No, there was no cancer in him. Not a physical one at least.

But his mother was overweight. She had frequent flu-like symptoms when the weather changed too suddenly. Was there a cancer in her somewhere? Ovary? Breast? Bone? Blood?

He put all the special moments with his mother at the core of one of his runs. She would die one day. That was inevitable. She would die and he would be bereft of a mother.

His mother never had a central role in Omar's life. She was loving but aloof and always misunderstood him. The communication gap between them had grown over the years. He had always considered her somewhat peripheral to his future.

But why then, when he tried putting her at the core of his life, did she develop more meaning for him rather than when she was at the periphery that he had always imagined her at? It was the concept of motherhood itself that he held important, rather than his own mother. He had always kept looking for another woman, one who should have been his mother but wasn't.

This was why the death of Sara's mom hit him so hard. He had wanted his own mother replaced in some way. He had almost wished his mother had taken the place of Sara's at the deathbed, and that Sara's mother had lived on.

But even if his mother was ever diagnosed with cancer, he could not imagine her dying. He could imagine her funeral, but not her body passing from a living thing to a non-living thing. He skipped the process of his mother's death, and thought ahead, directly to the stage of her funeral.

A film played in his runner's second-winded mind in which he stood around as a mute observer, feeling himself acting catatonic, but misleading the viewers with his stillness. Even then, he would not be in the moment, but in the act of performing his grief on a stage. As if it could be rehearsed.

But he knew it would not be like this. He would not have a flower and blades of grass in his hand while standing next to her grave. He would not be left alone and in silence. He would not get to sulk. There would be preparations, chores, constant movement and transactions for flowers and food, seating arrangements for guests and other practical things to occupy his time.

Sara's mom was already gone and Omar had never even got to meet her.

He looked in through the window of his imagined grief and sighed at not being called, not being needed. He snapped back to reality and wondered why Sara hadn't just called him after not receiving a reply to her text. She had given him two words worth of rope: 'She's gone.' And that's where the rope ended. She could have given him more. His head ached with the complaint. He wondered if he would have done the same had it been his mother.

Maybe Sara needed him now more than ever and just didn't know how to say it. But she *did* know. Didn't she?

The various things that needed doing were occupying her, of course. Flowers, food, and ceremonies of prayer and blessings for the dead; keeping vigil with recitations of the Quran beside the grave; quieter moments of grief alone in her room looking out of the window and finding nothing that could give solace; and loud sessions of dredging up of memories with distant relatives and friends who had long ago drifted away from her mom. Sara was going through all that.

He saw these days for her in his head and made himself believe they were the real thing. In his innocence and self-beguiling naiveté, he never imagined how much he condescended while creating for her a world, an ecosystem in which, for however little time, he felt comfortable letting her exist as if the call were his to make.

Running was simple like that. It allowed things to be reduced. But he was projecting the simplicity of it onto something he would never understand.

The music was getting in the way so he began to run and hike and clamber without it. He was made more vulnerable to sounds from the outside world, but he was also better able to connect the processes of running with those of real life around him and in his past.

Sometimes a single moment played out in his head, sometimes a series of moments. They lasted between seconds and hours in his head as he ran for miles. Thoughts about him and his school and his education, his parents teaching moral lessons to him, his blessing and curse of being lonely, loneliness leading him to meeting QT and becoming his friend, losing his friends from the past over a series of hormonal acts and, of course, moments with Sara.

At LUSS, the run was circular. He had to run around the same dirt patches in the track that he had completed hundreds of times before. But in the mountains, he had different, thinner air, and the trails went all over the place, climbing or dipping as they went. Here the world opened up.

That didn't mean, however, that all runs were not begun with a starting point that also served as the finishing marker. Even the non-circular runs were loops. They just stretched out, and there was always a going and a coming to them, a circularity, however distorted.

At LUSS, the chase and the escape on the track had been simultaneous He had always been running away from his thoughts while pursuing them at the same time. But in the mountains, the illusion of the circuit being more open enabled him to put at the centre of his runs any one thing he wanted to run from or towards without it being both.

The meditative *zone* of running didn't come of his own volition, for if he tried, he could never really get into it. And he tried hard for hour after hour. But either he couldn't do it or it couldn't be done. The thing always stayed on the track, behind or ahead of him, or held by invisible threads to the centre around which he ran.

Frustrated by the effort, he would give up the chase and the pursuit, and in that act of giving up, he denied himself the ability to defeat himself. Something washed over him and he was transported to meditations on matters he had been chasing all along. A clarity of vision accompanied these moments and no matter how long they lasted, the effect and memory of them lived for hours afterward. In these moments, the thing could be a still point in the chaos, thereby becoming his beacon.

Omar was human, of course. He gloated to himself about the second wind, zone or hallelujah state he was able to achieve. That made it harder the next time around. A cycle of hubris and humility, layered and hidden in the miles he covered on the road. What a gift he was given. How could he explain this to someone? How would someone believe him?

During one of his runs, having reached the zone while winding his way around a mountain on a level incline, he was able to detach himself from meditating on the differences between Sara and Sonia, and realize that he had nearly ended things with Sara for a silly mountain crush.

Just past that realization, he was given a glimpse of what and who he really was. The truth of his self, resplendent and visible. A vision he knew he would have a hard time forgetting or remembering clearly.

He had always been chasing this person just out of reach, wanting to believe he could be, truly *be*, this person. To begin the transformation, he believed he needed to run harder than he had ever run before. But this no longer meant a physical run.

The physical run was not the end in itself. It was only a means of achieving the spiritual purification that running allows, the lustre of which is a reflection of the single glinting point where Truth, Beauty, Justice and Goodness converge to deliver the simplest, yet most profound epiphanies. It is the spark of a single metamorphic instance in the growth of a human being that contains the mysteries of infinity, and they are understood and assimilated within the runner, the meditator, the samurai, the calligrapher and their kin, only for that one instance before being forgotten.

When Omar was able to experience that feeling and to glimpse Truth with its capital T, he recognized at once how flawed his actions had been. He understood how much more of himself he needed to offer to Sara as a friend. Without expressing any need for her affection, he was to surrender his ego at once.

Omar decided he would not equivocate on rhetorical questions anymore. If he knew the answer, he would not only say the answer but he would also live it out.

He no longer wanted to grieve over the long silence that followed the text sent by Sara.

After his run, he sat on the roof of Hotel Karimabad in the early evening and finally sent her this reply: 'Mountain air is pure and purifying. I'm thinking of you and your mom, and her next journey. Praying for her, and for you. Wish you were here, finding the peace you need. Miss you.'

He felt clear of all doubt and he reasoned that he had achieved this clarity by purifying himself. He thought back to what had initiated his feeling unclean and sullied in the first place, and recognized that he would not have felt the need to clear his conscience unless Sonia had goaded him. So he thanked his professor's daughter without vocalizing his gratitude, since she probably didn't even know how she'd helped him.

Sitting at dusk on the rooftop in his sweat-laden clothes, watching the clouds roll across the mountains, Omar felt propped up by luck. He felt there was some entity blessing his life, leading him to a higher purpose. He felt his life would be a series of successes that would feel like fortune handing him a victory at the moment of their occurrence, when in fact they were the acts of a map laid out for him long ago in the stars. This was a story he would never be able to read himself, even though it was written already and witnessed by the entire universe.

Feeling so connected to the cosmos, he went out for a stroll that night and ate at a restaurant with some of the other students, even managing a conversation about the hills and running through them. One of them asked him why he liked to run so much. He shrugged and said, 'I don't know. It feels good.'

They latched on to other topics and their inside jokes, and he ate his delicious dinner of meat and gravy. He then returned to his room and fell asleep.

In the middle of the night, his phone buzzed. It was QT with a cryptic note: 'I have seen the moment of my greatness flicker … in a minute there is time for decisions and revisions that a minute will reverse…'

Omar wrote back saying, 'Good one, bro.'

His phone buzzed again. QT wrote: 'Not me, T.S. Eliot. He is the man. Check him out.'

On his phone, Omar googled 'T.S. Eliot greatness flicker' and skimmed the poem 'The Love Song of J. Alfred Prufrock'. Some of it made sense. The women coming and going, talking about Michelangelo, the moment of greatness flickering. And the lines 'No! I am not Prince Hamlet, nor was meant to be/ Am an attendant lord, one that will do...'

I'm not even the hero of my own life, Omar thought, not yet, at least. There was defeat in knowing this, but there was something restful about it too. He didn't have high standards to maintain. There was no dramatic push required. Running in the mountains was good enough by itself. The distance run was itself the purpose. Itself the destination.

Maybe now that QT had graduated, Omar thought, it was time to break free of intellectual and self-involved cyclical thinking. It was time, perhaps, to not try so hard to think about the flaws in everything and just let go. Just *be*.

Omar clicked on the links to other some other poems on the website. Click by click he switched over from one page to the next until a line stood out: 'Things fall apart; the centre cannot hold.' Much of the rest of the poem, 'The Second Coming' by William Butler Yeats, was about something else. But this line was about running around a single track. It was about going around yourself again and again, not knowing how many false coverings you were moulting, or how many strands you were adding to thicken the noose to hang your own self.

Yes, it was time to let go. A knot came undone just behind Omar's forehead at the thought of letting go. It was a knot that he didn't know existed and its undoing let him fall into a deeper sleep than he could have wished for that night.

When he woke up, there were three more days left in

Karimabad. He went for his usual solo hike and spent five hours out among the valleys and slopes. He wanted to rest his legs for longer, harder runs on the last two days so he walked most of the time. Which is why it took him so long to get back.

When he did return to the hotel, the buses were loaded with all the stuff the LUSS Adventure Society had arrived with in Karimabad. Omar was confused, so he asked what was going on. He was then pointed out to everyone in loud voices and was surrounded by the Adventure Society representatives.

They demanded to know where he had been.

They scolded him for negligence because he hadn't taken his cell phone with him, and he hadn't told anyone where he had gone.

He was baffled, they realized, and so they filled him in: 'There's been a bomb blast in Karachi, a huge one.'

'Also, there was a gun fight between the army and the Taliban in Chitral. Three tourists were killed; two Japanese and one American.'

Chitral was ten hours away by bus, but it was also in the mountains and tourists throughout the Himalayan ranges had been told to protect themselves.

'We're going back to Lahore right now,' one of the girls from the Adventure Society said.

'Go get your things,' she added. Everyone standing around in the lobby was called to board the bus since the missing person had been found.

Omar shoved all his things in his bag and didn't bother to double-check whether he had taken everything from the hotel room.

Tourists had been killed. There were bullets and explosions—this was never going to end. These fucked-up things would keep on happening and keep getting closer and closer.

Someone I know will die, Omar thought, because of nothing. And that's when it will hit home.

At the start of the return journey, seventy hours earlier than planned, the bus was quiet and everyone was awake and keeping to themselves.

Those first two hours of the drive down from the mountains, Omar sat in his window seat and charted in his mind the zigzagging, groping and clambering routes he would take to the crest of each hill that passed. He could see footholds in the rock face, and even the straight boulders held some crevices if he looked carefully enough. His muscles ached because of all the running and hiking the past few days, and for all the running and hiking left behind.

QT's Speech

Hello everyone.

My name is Qasim Waqar Tiwana, and everyone at LUSS knew me as QT.

I graduated from LUSS two years ago. That was the last time I was on this stage. I am up here again now and not for reasons I want.

There were times I thought I would never leave this place. Yes, academically it was tough, but that's not what I mean. I would say that part of me never left this place. Though it is difficult to explain, I will try my best.

Omar was my best friend at LUSS. We met over three years ago, right after that blast on campus during his freshman year, which was my junior year.

We never had the same classes. He was a history major with a minor in business while I majored in anthropology. We were two years apart, both loners, which is probably the main reason we got along so well.

I don't want it to come across as a bro-mance. It wasn't a comfortable friendship. At least not for me.

I was used to being alone before Omar came to campus. I knew almost everybody here and almost everybody knew me because, well, just look at me. I stand out like an electricity pole.

I had plenty of acquaintances. We'd say hi and make small talk about tennis, football, the model UN, the classes and professors, the tough workload, the weather and all that. But that's where my interaction with the other students on campus ended. I didn't like having meals with anyone and I didn't like having conversations about grades, GPAs or the desirability quotient of any given professor, teaching assistant, or student. That kind of talk was not what I wanted to be part of. I emphatically pulled away from all that in my first year here.

But the first two years of my college life were miserable because of it. I didn't feel like I had anyone to talk to.

I didn't like what was being taught in the classrooms. Most of the professors—and I'm sorry to say this—set a low bar for succeeding in their classes. Blurting out anything, relevant or not, counted for the class participation grade, and everything on the tests and essays required either repeating memorized nonsense or going along with already established theories to produce predictable essays. And then, the conversations I was being pulled into by students, and even the professors, were always about grades and GPAs and things like that.

Don't get me wrong. I graduated with a 3.87 GPA, near the top of my class. I knew my priorities right from the start. But I never imagined it was something that needed to be talked about.

And today, being given this platform and opportunity by my best friend, and what happened to him, I want to say this: it doesn't matter what your GPA is. To hell with it if it's above the minimum required to maintain your scholarship or your admission in college. Damn your GPA.

I see some of you nodding. Good. That's a start. I don't know if you completely understand my frustration. I didn't understand it for the longest time myself. At least not until Omar came to LUSS and I finally had someone to talk to.

I can't give you a complete picture of our friendship. It started with an explosion and now it has ended with one too. It seems life is like that. Only the good go young.

Omar was good. Sometimes he was very good and other times, not so much. At times he was other things: arrogant, self-centred, self-righteous but honest, incredibly smart, curious, energized, devoted, and a helpless and hopeless romantic. He had these ideals in his head about the kinds of things education would do for him.

Most of you must have seen him running on the track or around campus early in the morning. And if you were driving through the city late at night, you may have seen him running on the Lahore roads in the middle of the night, especially during the summer. He was such a strong, fast, constant runner. He ran a lot and he became really good at it. The more he ran, the leaner and more machine-like he looked.

But I knew him from when he couldn't run a single lap around the track. When he started, all he could manage were one or two rounds; only eight hundred metres. He would walk two laps, then run two, and then walk two again; then he would be done, sweating and panting. He was chubby back then, but he was determined. Every single day, he would run more than the previous day, overcoming the need to walk in between. And then nothing could stop him once he didn't need breaks between long stretches of running.

And man, could he run. I saw him at his swiftest and leanest, and felt the most jealous I had ever felt of any person, dead or alive.

When we became roommates in my senior year and his sophomore year, he was already doing twenty to thirty laps, and sometimes forty. That's ten miles on a four-hundred-metre track. Can you imagine the kind of resolve needed to get over the boredom of running that kind of distance in repetitive circles on a 400-metre track?

He used to wake up at four in the morning, sometimes at two or three at night during the summer to avoid the heat, and I would curse and fling things at him if he woke me up, but then he would be gone and I would go back to sleep. Sometimes—very few times—I got up and went with him. I would do my walk and jog, and he would go past me again and again. He would switch directions and pass by me even quicker, until I made him stop so we could go have breakfast, or until I got bored with how focused he was and how I couldn't compete.

Omar's dedication to running was incredible. He went to the track every day, and every day he ran intensely. Often, he showed no sign of getting tired as he glided across the track with athletic grace. All his muscles rippling, his body moving like poetry. Perfect. Humanly perfect.

And that's what we talked about. That is all we talked about: perfection. Our entire friendship was about just that.

And I'll tell you about that. But first I will tell you what little I can about Sara.

She and I were never friends, but we knew each other. I saw her on campus, hanging out with her friends Mehreen, Hayyan and Nadia; sometimes Omar was with them.

You can tell when two people like each other. It's in their voices, their eyes, their body language and their comfort with each other. Once I gave it some thought, it was easy to figure out that Omar liked being around Sara. He was happier. It was also plain to see that she was at least interested in him.

It's not my intention to belittle her emotional involvement by saying she was only curious about Omar while he was more invested. Here, I want to make a distinction between Sara and most girls here at LUSS. Because if Sara was able to attract Omar, it wasn't just because of her physical appearance or something on the surface. In fact, if you will allow me to hypothesize, I don't think Sara's friends knew her at all.

Let's face it. We've all had a crush on Nadia at some point in college. I bet there's not a single girl who isn't jealous of her. But

Nadia and Sara were friends without Nadia knowing who Sara really was. I always guessed that much and Nadia confirmed it for us today.

That's not a slight on Nadia. It's just who Sara was.

I believe that Sara was the one person made for Omar. I know, I know, they were still growing up, they were just college kids. But given all that, and given that I didn't know Sara very well, I still believe she was perfect for Omar. However, I don't think he was right for her.

My friend brooded a lot. He played around with ideas and ideals of perfection. He was absolutely smitten with Sara but he never talked about her. He talked of romance in the abstract, as if trying to intellectually understand the feelings that he had, rather than to just feel them. He wanted to know himself and to be his best self. He didn't let himself just exist.

The most passionate and charged up I ever saw him was on many occasions right after he had finished a long run and come off the track. But the happiest I ever saw him, the most relaxed, was when I saw him walking with Sara or sitting with her on the campus lawns.

Omar became happier with every passing year here. He became less of a brooding loner, and I think that's because I graduated before he could spend too much time with me. After all of our discussions on abstract ideas, Omar and I needed to split up and go in different directions. I'm glad I graduated when I did, especially for his sake.

I also give credit to Sara. She helped him out of his abstractions. She must have done so.

But Omar and I never talked about Sara. He never told me if he was in a relationship with her or if the thing between them was as ambiguous as it seemed.

Instead, we had conversations on the meaning of the Higgs-Boson discovery for the humanities, or the possibility of our random sophomoric visions about world peace and Pakistan's prosperity coming about. The nutritional value of the cafeteria food was of constant interest as well. There was zero nutritional value, of course, negative even. We decided that quite easily.

Most of all, we discussed education. The education at LUSS too of course, but mostly education in general.

We never discussed grades or GPAs. That wasn't education and we both knew it. Omar and I hypothesized that education at LUSS happened while everyone was paying attention to the GPAs and grades and relative versus absolute grading systems. We believed it was the wrong kind of education taking place. So, since we were so intent upon debating ideals, LUSS was hardly ever a topic of discussion.

We started from scratch. Given no constraints, what would the ideal education be for any individual in the twenty-first century? We believed it would be heavily influenced by Plato's *Republic*, Thoreau's *Walden* and Iqbal's poetry about the *khudi*—the self, or the ego.

Here was our vision:

Children would concentrate on physical play and games, gaining proficiency in many languages and becoming adept at mental maths exercises until their early teenage years. This would be followed by lessons in philosophy, literature and history that would never abate even as each student began to pursue a specialization in one or two areas. In their late teens and early twenties, the students would practically begin running the school itself to guarantee a hand at applying principles taught in class.

That's the kind of student life we envisioned at first. It would be a system that started from kindergarten and went up to a university Omar and I would build together, should anyone ever let us make a place like that. That was the first grand idea, our joint dream for an institution of true education in Pakistan.

But that turned out to be an exercise only to get us going, to get us excited. That was the ideal, given no limitations. We then imagined a system that was hindered by realistic constraints.

We started on a large scale: a country like Pakistan. We thought about the income and expenditure on and of various sectors such as agriculture, textile, dam-building, security, defence, and so on. We wanted to determine the best kind of life livable by a person in the ideal Pakistan.

But once we got into the details of the country's operations, such as budget for forestry, the amount of corruption by highway police versus city police, the amount of annual copper imports required and other intricate matters, we couldn't hold the system together. It brought us to a conclusion that if we couldn't do it, nobody could.

And that meant the country was off the charts.

So we decided to scale back. Not the province of Punjab, not even a city like Lahore. Cities have similar, seemingly minor factors that just add up. We scaled further back, down to a campus the size of LUSS. We scaled back to our own lives.

We began to apply our abstract ideals to our own surroundings and to our own lives. We started to question what the best kind of institution possible could be, given the resources and constraints that LUSS has. What would be the ideal life lived here?

It took us a long time to develop this idea. More than six months of research, I believe. We scoured the library for articles. Data was available on the Internet as well. But all of that needed processing. Sometimes it took us weeks to break down esoteric numbers and statistics. But we were adamant. And the data from other institutions was only a launch pad for our own vision.

Omar would suggest ideas after a run. I would jot down all the students' complaints I overheard and wonder how to address them appropriately. In some classes, I would pretend to take notes while writing down alternatives for the best possible mass-scale nutrition we could offer at the cafeteria.

Food is important after all. Food is where it all starts.

The unused land at the back of the campus fields could be used for growing vegetables and fruits that the students would cultivate themselves. They would learn things about the soil. They would use their hands. They would learn the value of water.

We had other ideas as well. Building design, ideal dorm locations, sports schedules according to seasons and available space. An institute for languages and the budget for yearly stationery supplies for the staff. Ideal administration to faculty to student ratios, gardening funds, course design, consultancy fees and summer and winter training camps for executives. There would be student clubs, classroom decorations, light and shade designs in every corner of the campus, landscaping. We would take care of maintenance costs, salaries, income streams, endowments and medals, scholarships, student loans, student jobs.

We didn't leave anything out. We wrote it all down, rearranged and organized it into something that made as much sense as possible. And once we had a full picture of an ideal university, we began comparing it to the real LUSS.

Given our enthusiasm for our own imagined, ideal university, LUSS lost out in every category. Apologies to the vice chancellor, Mr Khurrana. But it did.

That shouldn't surprise anyone here. LUSS is far from perfect, as we know, and the institution's resources can be used much more efficiently.

I can look back and remember that even when we discussed our ideals, Omar and I always saw room for improvement even beyond our vision. We saw that things could be endlessly tweaked. After a while, though, perfection becomes a matter of preference.

So who were we, two loners, to decide what was perfect? How objective could we possibly be? Not very, of course.

Obviously, Omar and I favoured the humanities and social sciences. It was the same way anybody from an MBA class would think studying entrepreneurship was central to education. What could subjects like rhetoric and philosophy be for such a student? They were extrinsic for sure.

So we changed direction yet again. Given everything as it was, no changes in the system or direction of LUSS, there was only one question to ask: who was living the best possible life at LUSS as it was?

We were looking for students immersed in the system, making the best of it and yet not investing themselves in it. Students who had a grasp of how to sift through the layers of deception and manage a true education despite everything. Individuals who could rise above the hype of being at LUSS and still manage to connect with reality.

If you were to look at us back in those days, you would know that Omar and I were definitely not students making the most of the system.

Omar believed Sara was living life in the best possible way at LUSS; she was making the most of being here. She had friends, she had connections within the system, but she was always aloof, tuned into something within herself. He thought nobody else could see that about Sara.

I prodded him about this, to understand why Sara meant so much to him, but he wouldn't respond. That was the only time Omar mentioned her. I tried to bring her up sometimes, just to tease him or to find out what exactly he felt about her but he would always change the subject.

I had my own crushes, my own emotional baggage, which I needed to unleash on a friend. But like with Nadia and Sara, I could open up to Omar without him saying anything to me about Sara at all. I admired that, even if it pissed me off occasionally.

But now that I think about it, I can say that the two of them had something special.

That's not praise at all. I say 'special' as in fragile, vulnerable, most easily breakable.

It was problematic because it wasn't the usual girlfriend–boyfriend thing, nor was it a morbid fake sister–brother relationship. It was hard to place them. It was definitely not just friendship. There was something in the air when they were together; some electric circuit being completed and creating magnetic pulses. It was quite unique.

I don't envy what they had. In fact, I pity it because it was never meant to last.

But another part of me hates that it ended, that it just remained a promise of things to come.

And speaking of promises of things yet to come and of things that never happened, I would like to share something more personal.

Bear with me a few more minutes, please.

I have been, since this past January, the regional specialist of human resources at a multinational corporation that many LUSS graduates apply to every year. I am one of four such regional specialists.

I want you to consider this question: what can an anthropology major know about human resources?

Yes, the anthropology majors among you are thinking, 'Everything, of course'. And that's right. You can know everything there is to know about human resources. Anthropology is, after all, the study of humans, past and present.

But I didn't know that when I was graduating. Trust me, when I was in your shoes, one day before the graduation ceremony, I was willing to do anything it took not to enter the real world. I was going to request my professors to give me F's in two courses, even though I had A-minuses in them, so I could continue being a student here. I thought about taking four more courses and completing a minor in economics or sociology, just to be able to stay on. I even thought about telling the registrar I had plagiarized one course so I should be made to repeat it. I thought about all of this on the last night, walking around on campus, envying everybody else's happiness at graduating. I was terrified, and lonelier than ever before.

Now I know what it was I was feeling that night. The bubble had become too comfortable. The campus was easy. I knew the system, even if I didn't like it. Plus, I had Omar if I needed to discuss ideas.

But at the time I didn't know all that. All I knew then was panic. I was going to leave the gates with a paper in my hand, forced to figure out what I needed to do with my life.

I knew I would need to get a job and that scared me to death. Going to some office early in the morning, pulling levers or pushing paper, making money for someone in an executive seat, someone I would never see, the thought of it terrified me. My life would waste away because it wouldn't be consumed by the pursuit of knowledge and truth. It would fritter away behind a desk. I would come home every night, turn on the television and numb myself from the pain of living without meaning anything to anyone.

The maze I pictured in my mind was so linear, so narrowly focused on the job and the meaninglessness of it that I forgot to consider that I would still have volition.

It was the lashing criticism of consumer society in films such as *Fight Club*, documentaries such as *The Corporation and Capitalism: A Love Story*, and the complete despair in Arthur Miller's play *Death of a Salesman* going round and round in my head.

Being afraid of rejections, I had not applied to graduate schools. And being anti-corporation, I had refused to apply to any jobs either, because everything seemed influenced by the overly money-driven corporate ecosystem. I had nothing lined up and I needed to do something after graduation, of course, because my family could not support a bum forever.

At LUSS, I was on scholarship and loans. One or two more semesters here would have been taken care of easily. In that time, I could probably have even completed an economics minor. So given all these backup reassurances, I had blocked out my graduation until it happened.

But then the time came and I was about to take the walk in my cap and gown.

There I was, the night before graduation, wandering around campus, tired and scared.

After a long walk, during which I found no answer, I went and sat outside the mosque around midnight. I thought the mosque's door was closed, so I didn't try opening it. But after a while someone came out through the door. The door was open; the mosque was open. It was just the sign I needed. I got up and went inside. The air conditioner was on and it was much cooler inside. A few students lay sleeping in corners, taking advantage of the best AC on campus.

I don't think I prayed though. I just sat there for a long time, in the large prayer hall, looking around but not really seeing anything. I was trying to slow my racing heart and to get God to help without my saying anything.

Because I didn't have the words. I couldn't say 'God, I don't want a job because I am afraid I will lose my soul if I get one', even though that is exactly what I wanted to say. It would come out like a tantrum but it wasn't meant to be. I was in serious conflict about my soul and the corporate slavery I would be offering it up to if I became a 9-to-5 man. And not to mention the third-world sweatshop exploitation chain that I would become a part of as just another link.

Omar couldn't have helped. That's why I didn't go talk to him about this. He couldn't have helped me at that point even if he tried because it wasn't reassurance I needed. Something much bigger was taking hold of me.

It was the system. It had me marked and I was about to become part of the matrix. Indentured, a slave to the machine, chained, inserted into the production automaton. My personality removed and a cyborg transplantation made.

I even pictured myself standing in an assembly line to get a chip installed at the back of my neck. That and a barcode. My new identification number, my new identity. A slurping sound would accompany my soul being sucked out of my body.

I remember thinking: I need to sort through this chaos in my mind. I need to calm down. I need to register what is real and separate it from the panic I'm feeling. I needed to talk to Omar. He would understand.

I was dependent on him to help me process my thoughts. A codependency, if you want to call it that. It could easily be called that. But deep down, I knew that talking to Omar couldn't really help. Nothing could.

And finally something like a miracle took shape.

The buzz of the air conditioner, the muffled riffs from a guitar, a chorus of voices singing somewhere far away at the other end of the campus, the dim lights and the subtle suffusion of incense in the mosque, all of it played tricks on my nerves. There was some Divine help at work too.

A wave of sleep washed over me and pushed aside my worries until they did not seem like concerns at all, but more like ants that had crawled up under my shirt, tickling my spine, and which needed to be brushed aside.

Something had just brushed them aside. A moment of clarity followed, one that I still remember and will probably never forget.

Omar wasn't there, but he did not need to be. His ideas and my own, the classes I had taken the four years, the plans we had made to find the right people to fill the right slots in the ideal university we would one day build—everything arranged itself as a piece of the larger puzzle.

At the time, I could not understand what was happening to me because I was just an observer. But since that night, over the past two years, I have been able to dissect what happened and reconstruct the processes of it.

Imagine your thoughts as blocks, compartmentalized into separate, physical objects.

Now imagine that the shapes fit together in many different ways but that they fit in one way that is best of all, most compact, like pieces of a puzzle snug and tight. Liberating the space that remains unused.

You computing students call it a defragmentation.

That's what happened to me sitting in the mosque that night. I didn't ask for it. It just happened. And as the chaos evaporated, so did the fear. I had a moment of complete clarity. Everything made sense, even my fear.

That is why it disappeared: because we can't fear anything that makes sense.

What I understood, as if for the first time, was that corporations, their decisions, their stores and services, branches and chains, products and brands, were created by people. Human beings, imperfect beings. So they couldn't be perfectly manipulative, even if they wanted.

Of course, given our capitalist paradigm, humans at the top of the production chain would want the bottom line of profit to be better at the expense of all other factors. But maybe I could add the things to consider important at the bottom line. I could make the final calculation have more factors in it, which caused more gears to turn before getting the answers.

Things clicked. I could become an agent of my own agenda. I was an activist planning a stealth takeover of a polluting factory to clean up its operations from the inside, so to speak. I could build a meaningful life made of wilful actions. These actions could be carried out with the interest of growing myself rather than spending myself. And they could be made to benefit other people as well.

I still had volition and I was not going to get a chip implanted in my body. Neither would my soul get transplanted.

Nothing is permanent. So the illusion of traps was just that: a temporary hindrance.

A job could never trap me for long if I didn't like it. Any job, even a bad one—especially a bad one—would most importantly provide experience. I would eventually, over the years, get incrementally closer to the goal of conceiving and building a pragmatic, progressive educational institution. All I had to do was keep the dream alive, keep stoking my desire for it and bring it to life with increments of tangible action.

And what about the books, films and documentaries that warn us about capitalism and corporations? The answer to that, too, was made clear to me: the art is all exaggeration for effect, to warn of dangers. The truth is somewhere in the middle, but made clearer by warning through extremes.

I was sufficiently warned and I could act with those warnings heeded. And nothing—nothing—is as bad as the dystopias we see in fiction and films. Some specific aspects can be that bad, but they are mitigated by aspects that are not.

Plus, only by being within the system could I influence it. So I was ready to be plugged into the matrix, metaphorically, through a connection at the back of my head.

But then there's the danger of losing yourself. And here came the direct message from Omar, even if he didn't mean it for the occasion at which I needed it most: Sara. Be Sara. Understand and access the system but don't buy into its lies. This is the world. Be in it, but don't give *in* to it.

I would not burn out at a 9-to-5 job. I would remain unburnt.

I would not come home, plop myself on a sofa and turn on my TV and lull myself into a slumber.

I would read. I would take classes. I would learn for life, not trivia, but useful things.

I would learn how to manage a small enterprise, how to differentiate between schools of thought, how to find the right kind of people for certain jobs.

I would learn, on and off the job, how to manage people and get the best out of them. How to motivate without pushing too hard. How to build team culture.

I would figure out systems. Banking systems, especially. The best loans for small and medium-scale enterprises.

That was it. I would learn systems. I would learn to work within them, but not be worked *by* them. Flirt with traps, be as wise as serpents, but as innocent as doves. I believe Jesus says that in the Bible. And I also believe it applies at college and it certainly applies in the corporate world.

I saw that I could cope with having a job. In fact, I needed a job.

But sitting there in the mosque, fixing the shape of thoughts in my head to take a new form, it occurred to me that before anything else, I needed to drown out the ego that I had developed in college.

Let me explain.

My 3.87 GPA plays a role in this.

You know how they say college is supposed to make you ready for life? Well, it doesn't.

You come to LUSS and LUSS tells you to apply your best. So

you do. But either it's not enough or it's not aligned right. Your best effort doesn't get you the grade you want because your effort has to be aligned with how the system wants it shaped. Before college, the high-school system rules you and that's what you are used to. You learn the college system and the way to get the grade you want, and you start applying the system. You think you have done your best because you achieved the highest grade possible. And you think you deserve a medal for all the time you spent studying because you have become the best you possibly can at achieving the highest grades in college. But all you have done is learn a system.

And the same system doesn't necessarily exist everywhere in the real world. Real-world systems are different and at best can only be mirrored by analogy to the university's way of working.

In the real world, every time you do something new, you have to start over, from scratch, with a beginner's mindset. You have to be in a state of Zen while starting every phase in life, without ego, without feeling like you deserve a free lunch.

You have to be in love with starting from scratch.

College can make you forget that. I had forgotten that over the four years.

So I emptied out my ego there, in the prayer hall, and walked out. I came out of the mosque that night a new person. I was now someone who understood and had integrated the education he had received in those four years.

Omar played a huge role in my understanding at the time, but I don't think even he could understand what he had given to me and what I had gained from him without him knowing it. I don't think I could have prayed for the kind of understanding I received that night. I would not have known what to pray for.

And I'm telling you all this because I believe Omar had similar doubts about graduating and entering the real world. He wasn't feeling great about leaving LUSS and I think it was partly because he and Sara still didn't understand what they were to each other.

You would think four years in college would have helped them sort out what they wanted from each other. But it didn't seem that way. It was, as far as I know, still ambiguous, still up in the air. One of the reasons I know that is because he still wouldn't talk about Sara.

So what did he talk about instead? I'll tell you.

Fifteen days ago, right after the end of exam week, Omar called me. I was at work, so I didn't pick up. But he called again. I texted him telling him I was heading into a meeting. But Omar wrote back to me, saying, 'You need to hear this. Step out of your meeting.'

It was not very typical of Omar to send such a message.

So I went outside and called him. When he answered, he said, 'I get it now. I understand.'

I asked him what he understood.

He said, 'I am going to graduate in twenty days. And I know what you went through.'

I began to walk up and down the office driveway, watching the gardener go about his routine of watering the plants with a pipe and trying to look relatively busy. I felt the knot of my tie hit my Adam's apple as I swallowed nothing. My throat was dry.

'You mean, you understand why I didn't want to graduate?' I asked Omar. The uncomfortable memory of my doubts washed over me.

'Yes,' he said. 'I understand completely. I went through the same thing just last night.'

I asked him what had happened.

'Life, man,' he said. 'It's going to begin and I'm not ready.'

Just then, someone came out from my office. It was time for the meeting. I knew I had less than thirty seconds left on the phone.

'You're ready, Omar,' I said, starting to give him a pep talk which I thought I would continue later. 'You, of all people, are ready.'

'I'm going to run,' he said.

Those were his last words to me.

My boss was looming behind someone standing in the doorway and at that moment the necktie felt like a leash with its end in his hands.

As I ended the call, my last words to Omar were, 'Gotta go; boss.'

I like to believe that when I said those words, I was calling Omar my boss. Or at least that he felt I was.

I like to believe that everything I felt, all my doubts about graduation, moving on to work, and all the other doubts about growing up, also coursed through him and made him fear his lack of preparation. And then, I hope, that just like me he was gifted a kind of peace that would never leave him.

This was my hope because at the time he called, I could not tell him how the two years since that night had helped me understand what I had been through just before graduating. I just hope he knew, somehow.

But, when all is said and done, things have happened.

Omar is gone now. Nothing is going to change that. I think what we can do is remember him for what and who he was, and for the people and the things he admired. He cared about Sara; that was certain. But he also loved meaningful education. That's another thing.

A form develops out of the person who I miss and try to construct again and again through memories of him.

I think that missing a loved one who has moved on is best expressed by someone who was a favourite author of Omar's, Robert Pirsig, wrote in *Zen and the Art of Motorcycle Maintenance* that his own deceased son Chris was 'not an object but a pattern' and that 'the pattern was larger' than the person in ways that cannot be understood. It is not just a matter for the intellect but also one for spirit and faith to understand and assimilate.

So, I want you to do Omar an honour. I want you to remove the conception of yourself as flesh and matter struggling with the set of thoughts called your mind. Release the mental and emotional picture of yourself as a human being with limits and constraints.

Instead, think of yourselves in the abstract. As sets of patterns interacting with other patterns in your world. As certain sets of energies gathering and flowing, moving and consolidating. And now ask yourself: what does this pattern mean?

Maybe this exercise will help you discover the direction you need to take in your life, especially now that so many of you are graduating.

I hope you will also keep in mind that the ideas and patterns of Omar and Sara will remain open in all directions. Even as we leave them behind, we do know the immense possibility they once held.

And to end this long tribute, I want to thank you all for coming tonight and for honouring my friend Omar and his friend Sara. They were unique individuals; maybe two of the best among us.

Omar's last words to me were, 'I'm going to run.'

And I like to believe that after we talked he put on his running shoes and his favourite yellow Nike running shirt, and went for that run like he said he would.

And I like to think he is still running somewhere, facing the wind and breathing without a sound, as if all that motion requires no effort at all.

I picture him running on a long, empty stretch of road, with a smile on his face, thinking of Sara, letting his feelings for her just exist for once.

Running with Sara on his mind; that's how I will remember him.

Thank you.

Juniors
Space for the Act

5.15 a.m. The first rays of the sun were just beginning to break through the darkness of night. Old Lahore's mosques and havelis were coated in a film of dark blue light. There was a late October chill in the air. From pitch darkness, light and dark shadows were beginning to emerge. But there was already a break in the peace of the night. In the distance, the drone of rickshaws could be heard. Beat-down labourers clanged along on their beat-up bicycles on the main roads and back alleys.

Sara, Omar, Nadia, Zafar, Mehreen and Hayyan hunkered in their shawls and jackets on wobbly plastic chairs outside Haji Sahib. They had just finished gorging themselves on nihari, maghaz, nalli, mirch, adrak, naan and lassi for breakfast after staying up all night on campus, and then driving down to the old walled city.

Zafar smoked a cigarette while Nadia playfully frowned at him, trying to catch his eye. He didn't seem to be aware of her though. Hayyan and Mehreen sat peacefully at their end of the table, too full and too cold to start a conversation. The night was over, the laughs were over; they sat all joked out, buzzing from the heavy beef and lack of sleep.

Omar was wide awake. He had adapted to the all-nighter weekend routine by now. Just before they headed out for breakfast, he had gone for a five-mile run and his body was craving food. The cold air and the hot food had woken him up.

Sara sat next to him, wanting to lean her head on his shoulder, but the unstable plastic chair would tip over if she shifted her weight. So she bunched up within her shawl and sucked on a piece of mint.

'Should we walk around today?' Sara asked. She was dreadfully tired, but they had not toured the Old City on foot on any of their previous visits.

'Sure,' Omar said, 'I'm up for it.' His fear of accompanying the girls on a tour of the Old City was mitigated by Zafar's bulk and Hayyan's presence. There were enough boys for the three girls to feel protected from the leering crowd he imagined would gather if only he and Sara were walking among the ancient mosques and villas.

'I was hoping you would say no,' Sara said. 'Aren't you tired?' She punched him playfully on his shoulder without pulling her hand out from under the dark brown shawl.

'Omar is never tired,' Hayyan said. Omar forced a smile. Hayyan just had to speak if Sara did. He had the disease even now. He was still trying to be Sara's backup option in case things with Omar didn't work out. But Hayyan was needed now if all of them were to walk around the Old City at dawn, and his own neediness could be ignored.

'What about you, Nadia?' Sara asked. She wanted Nadia to say no just so she wouldn't stick around and complain.

'Zafar and I were thinking of heading back,' Nadia said, and Zafar looked at her for the first time since driving down across the city from the campus.

Sara knew what Nadia was thinking. She wanted to go and spend some alone time with Zafar. There was no indication of it in Nadia's voice, but Sara knew it.

'No,' Zafar said. 'I'm going to stay here. I want to walk around a little. You can take my car if you want.'

'Oh, no,' Nadia said, 'I'll walk with you if you want.' Zafar smiled and shrugged, and looked away from her to his hand with the cigarette in it. He took a long puff.

Mehreen and Sara exchanged a look. Their friend was such a doormat. Sara could tell that Mehreen also felt it. Nadia was suffering; Zafar was not. There was nothing mutual about what was going on between them.

'Hayyan? Mehreen?' Omar asked. 'Are you guys in?'

Mehreen nodded, opened her mouth and yawned into her shawl.

'What's there to see?' Hayyan asked.

'So much,' Zafar replied. He stood up and stretched, the half-smoked cigarette dangled from his mouth. Nadia's eyes never left his body.

Sara looked at her friend with pity and sadness. Nadia was such a beautiful and perfect girl, on the outside. But what an absolute mess she was deep down. Sara didn't bother looking at Mehreen to confirm her thoughts. She just knew she was right.

Omar gathered the money and paid at the counter, then grabbed a toothpick to keep in his mouth.

Sara didn't say anything, even though she didn't like this toothpick dangling act. The thing that irked her about it was that it seemed he was copying it from a film. It was like some attempt to come across as a strong, silent type of hero.

Mehreen grabbed a jacket from Zafar's car, while Hayyan checked to see if his own Land Cruiser Prado was locked and secure; then they walked out into the narrow lanes which led to the Data Darbar Complex.

Mehreen and Sara walked with Omar. Hayyan and Zafar

walked with Nadia. In threes at first, and then in a single file past an open drain along one side of the alley.

They reached a dead end where there was a pile of garbage heaped up against a wall. Omar turned around and told Zafar to take over the navigation from the front. He knew his way better. They went past carts full of leather shoes, and carts and stalls full of oily, fried papads and milky chaats.

Through a hole in the wall of a building, Sara saw a fat man in only his underwear lying down on a charpoy, watching TV. She smiled to herself and looked away.

Omar watched an odd-shaped shopping bag stuck in the gutter. When they came closer to it, he realized it was a dead bird. He stared into the eyes of that grey and black pigeon until he couldn't see it even out of the corner of his eyes as they walked past.

Out of one alley and into another, this one had young scruffy, bare-chested men hanging out at the counter of a small general store and a line of shops with alchemical bottles full of 'homeopathic medicines'.

Once they turned the corner into this lane, Zafar put his arm around Nadia and the girls covered their heads with their shawls. Their procession went past a large group of men and most of them paid it little attention. It was too early to start staring at women. One of them stared anyway. He was too conditioned not to.

'I'm zonked,' Mehreen said. 'It's my bedtime.'

'It's 5.30 in the morning!' Sara said.

'Yeah,' Mehreen said. 'Bedtime.'

Hayyan was walking ahead of Sara and Mehreen. He half-turned and asked, 'Are we walking around the whole area?'

'Yes,' Omar said. He wanted Sara to be with him as the sun slowly rose over the Old City.

'At least to Data Sahib's,' Sara said.

'And Wazir Shah's mosque,' Omar said.

'That's in the other direction,' Hayyan said, 'and it's pretty far away.'

'You know the way?' Omar asked.

'No,' Hayyan said, 'but I've been there once before.'

'When?' Mehreen asked him.

'A few years ago,' Hayyan said.

'How long ago did you come here last?' Omar asked Sara.

'I don't remember,' she said. 'Maybe two years.'

'When we went together?' Mehreen asked her.

'Yeah,' Sara said.

'That was five years ago,' Mehreen said. 'I remember now. It was just before my mom's forty-first birthday.'

'I haven't been to Data Sahib's in eight months,' Omar said. He was sad about the number of months and days that he had spent away from the shrine. Not because he cared for any of the activities at the shrine: the abject worship of the graves with prostrations and other borderline blasphemies, the langar where an unending mass of poor people gathered in haphazard lines with open shopping bags to get a share of charity in doles of biryani, sweet rice or aloo channay.

No. He was sad because this was his city. The old and new parts of it flowed seamlessly together to make one glorious city. But he hadn't crossed over in months from what he considered his half, the more developed half, the one progressive and future-oriented rather than locked in the past. And to think, these people he was with, they hadn't come here for years. It left him feeling cold, separated from the city, its people at large and the people with whom he had come as well.

Now that he thought about it, it was the dead pigeon that had triggered the change in his mood, making him feel so grim.

Despite the piles of discarded newspapers and stains of

chewed-up betel leaves on the sides of the road, the crisp early morning air made the Old City feel cleaner than it was. There was an earthy and cool smell in the air. The sky now glowed blue and orange over the top of the buildings in front of them.

Zafar and Nadia were a few steps ahead of the rest; maybe they were talking or maybe they weren't. Zafar still had his arm across her shoulders. Sara watched the arm and then looked away to read the words painted carefully on the shutters and the walls. They were political slogans and posters mostly, and advertisements and phone numbers. It was a different world. She didn't belong here.

'Whenever I come here,' Sara said, 'I feel like I'm either doing an experiment or I'm part of an experiment.'

'Yeah,' Mehreen said.

'What do you mean?' Hayyan asked.

'I don't know,' Sara said. She wanted to explain that in LUSS, every day was like a well-rehearsed performance. You came to college, you hung out and you went to class just like everybody else. But in the Old City, it was like she was being watched by the very thing of which she was an observer. 'There's too much voyeurism,' she said.

'Hmm, yeah,' Hayyan said, yawning. 'But isn't LUSS also like that?'

'Yeah,' Sara said. She disagreed, but vocalizing her disagreement would require too much effort.

They came onto a main road and saw cauldrons lined up along one side of the street. Zafar led them to the right and they neared the main cross-section.

'What the hell!' Mehreen exclaimed.

'What's wrong?' Omar turned to see if someone had grabbed Mehreen or touched her or thrown something at her.

But Mehreen didn't stop. She kept walking, looking up and pointing at the bridge in front of them.

'Mehreen, are you okay?' Sara asked.

'No,' Mehreen said. 'What's that?'

Omar looked at the bridge. It was not falling or cracked, it didn't have anything extraordinary about it. The underside was covered in soot and filth and cars were whizzing along on it.

'The bridge?' Sara asked. She looked at Omar for help and behind him saw two people sitting on a bench. They looked at Mehreen and then turned to stare at the bridge. They scanned it and looked back at Mehreen. Sara looked up at the bridge again.

'Yes,' Mehreen said. 'There's a bridge there.'

Zafar and Nadia had gone ahead while the rest had slowed down to stay with Mehreen. They turned to see what was happening. Mehreen was moving, but very slowly.

'What's wrong with the bridge?' Omar asked. He scanned it again.

'Why is there a bridge there?' Mehreen asked.

'What do you mean?' Hayyan asked.

'You mean,' Sara said, getting what Mehreen meant, 'you didn't know they built the Ring Road Bridge here?'

'When did this happen?' Mehreen asked.

Sara felt tired from being up all night and also at a loss because Mehreen never knew anything about current affairs in the world, or in the country, or even in the city. She was oblivious to danger or news.

'The bridge has been there for a long time now,' Hayyan said, shaking his head at Mehreen.

'Not so long,' Omar said, 'only a few months.' He now remembered why he hadn't come to this side of town for so long. They had been building this bridge and much of the area had been closed off.

'It sucks,' Mehreen said.

'What?' Hayyan asked. 'The bridge? Why? What's wrong with it?'

'It's so awful,' Sara said, joining Mehreen's team. Even though the bridge and the Ring Road enabled a less congested route into the Old City, the bridge was completely out of place in the Old City. It stuck out; the whole Ring Road stuck out. A super-highway next to 200-year-old havelis. Next, they would probably be putting up a McDonald's or a Burger King next to Haji Sahib's. Or worse, right beside Data Sahib's shrine.

'I feel sick,' Mehreen said. She stopped moving.

'It's not *that* bad,' Hayyan said. Omar gave the back of his head a glare. Hayyan had driven them till there a little too fast and a little too smoothly over the bridge in his car. So he would say that. He probably cared more for the convenience of the drive than for the disharmony in the elements that Mehreen had noticed. Now that he looked at the bridge, Omar could see it as something that definitely did not belong here.

'Are you okay?' Sara asked Mehreen. She saw that the locals all along the street were beginning to look at their group and sense how foreign they were. Maybe it was better for them to go now.

'I don't feel good,' Mehreen said. 'Maybe I'll go sit in the car.'

Zafar and Nadia had walked back by now to join the others, and heard some of their conversation.

'You mean you never noticed the bridge?' Nadia asked. 'We drove on it every time we came here.'

'She's not feeling well, Nadia,' Sara said. 'Don't...' and trailed off. She was afraid of saying too much.

'Let's just go back,' Omar said. A part of him still wanted to stay there and walk with Sara, but Mehreen was Sara's friend. Plus, Mehreen's reaction was just right: the bridge felt *wrong*. The horror of the bridge juxtaposed against the rest of the Old City was made too obvious and it could not be unseen now. What a jarring sight it was.

'No,' Nadia said, 'Let's stay. Mehreen, we can stay, right?' Zafar's arm was still around her. She was clearly high on that.

'I feel nauseous,' Mehreen said. 'It's the food. I ate too much. I need to sit down.' She waved a hand in front of her face.

'Let's go,' Sara said, put her arm around Mehreen's shoulder and turned her around. She looked at Omar.

Was she asking for support? She didn't need to ask. He moved and Hayyan followed him. Zafar led Nadia slowly after them. He had his own car. Let him come as slowly as he wants, Omar thought.

They walked through the meandering alleys back to the cars. Hayyan clicked open the locks to his vehicle; the fresh leather smell of the seats was artificial and antiseptic.

She couldn't take the food, Sara thought. They had been eating too much of it. At least once every weekend—sometimes both Saturday and Sunday mornings—since the beginning of their junior year, they had been coming to Haji Sahib's to eat. It was too much for Mehreen's system, clearly. It was a wonder the rest of them weren't sick already. If not the questionable hygiene of the food, the amount of fat and cholesterol in the nihari was terrible enough for their bodies. But then, the beef melting in their mouths had felt so worth the gobs of weight and hazard it also threatened.

Omar went to sit in the front passenger seat.

'I want to sit there,' Mehreen said, pointing to the same seat. 'Please. I'll feel sick otherwise.'

'Sure,' Omar said, and opened the door for her. 'Here you go.'

Sara and Omar sat at the back. Hayyan started the engine, breaking the early morning silence.

They idled, with the heat on low, until Zafar and Nadia walked around the bend in the road and got in Zafar's Honda Civic.

Hayyan pulled out of their parking spot and started driving through the narrow lanes, turning onto the main road that led to the bridge.

'I'm sorry,' Mehreen said from the front seat, 'I didn't want to spoil the walk.'

'It's okay,' Sara said, 'we can always go next time.'

'Yeah,' Omar said, and he let himself feel as tired as he was. 'It's okay,' he yawned.

'You know,' Mehreen said after a few seconds, 'it wasn't the food. I couldn't stand seeing that ugly bridge there, right in front of Data Sahib's shrine. It made me want to puke.'

'This is the same bridge now,' Hayyan said. 'What's so ugly about it?' He turned his car onto the bridge as Mehreen and the others stopped talking.

Sara looked down at the large marble courtyard of Data Sahib's shrine, with the tombs of lesser saints and other graves surrounding it. It felt wrong to watch the monument from above. The bridge felt like a symbol of false progress from which she was looking down at a relic of ancient and simpler virtues.

Hayyan's car glided smoothly along the bridge. Its passengers didn't feel the joints pass under the tyres.

Mehreen was awake and quiet in the front passenger seat and Omar felt himself drawn to feeling the same way about the construction as she did. No matter how comfortable it was, no matter how much easier it made travelling between the Old City and the rest of Lahore, the bridge did not belong where they had built it; those visionless idiots.

'Are you okay?' Sara asked Omar.

'Yes, I'm fine,' he said, smiling widely, faking it a bit too much.

She could see through it though.

He could tell she could. Still, he kept the act up like an elaborate act of defence against her penetrating gaze.

'Mehreen,' Hayyan said, 'we always come down from this bridge. Every single time we come here. Didn't you ever see this before?'

'No,' Mehreen said. 'I mean, I know we crossed a bridge on the way, but I didn't know it was so close to Data Sahib's. I thought it was at the edge of the Old City.'

Sara had looked down while crossing the bridge before, on a few of their earlier trips. And she was looking down now. Next to Data Sahib's were the langar stalls set up for food distribution among the poor people who seemed to live at or around Data Sahib's shrine. She pitied them, but she didn't understand them, didn't know how to think about them. The problem of poverty in Pakistan stretched too far back for her to see the root cause that could be addressed. Maybe it stretched to the one-billionth of a second after the Big Bang, when all atoms and molecules were aligned in one specific arrangement and no other.

Omar was looking out of the window again. He was not happy and he didn't want to be around Hayyan, Nadia or Zafar. He liked Mehreen as a friend though. He thought she was a cheerful and goofy girl who sometimes said profound things, just like today. Did Sara see that, he wondered.

He turned and looked at Sara and saw the soft glow of blue and red light on the curve of her cheek and the shadows that sketched out the contours of her neck. He was sad about the distance that seemed to still exist between them.

Sara's body ached with exhaustion and she was glad they had skipped the walk. The Old City's sense of being something separate and the complex issue of who belonged where and who was watching whom from the outside or inside—it took too much energy to process. Soon enough they would be back on campus, and she would go with Nadia and Mehreen to sleep in a hostel friend's room.

Nadia wouldn't come though; Sara knew that. She would go

with Zafar and do whatever they needed to do. Sara tried to avoid thinking about what would happen after she woke up later. She would have to go back home and be with her grandmother, her Nano, who had taken over her mom's room. Sara loved her Nano, but her Nano had become too sad since her mother's funeral. She couldn't bear to leave Sara alone and stifled her with care and concern. It was like having another disease in the house, one which hurt Sara more, because for how many years was Nano going to live anyway?

Hayyan put his car on cruise control on the highway and put on some sad orchestral music.

Hayyan and his pretentious music, Omar thought. This one sounded like a variation on either the theme of *Braveheart* or *Gladiator*.

Omar was bored of Sara's friends. He did not understand what she saw in any one of them except Mehreen, who was a sweetheart. He couldn't understand Nadia's significance to Sara. So what if they were friends since childhood—now they had nothing in common. It was time for Sara to actively shed Nadia from her life because they were unable to naturally drift apart.

Of course, Omar was biased. He saw that himself. He saw that he had lost all his high-school friends quite suddenly, over the course of a year and a summer vacation. He recognized his bias against keeping friends who were ripe with the potential for betrayal. That bias didn't make him wrong, though. He knew Nadia's kind well enough.

Nadia was the beautiful girl with all the world's luck by her side at birth, but no vision with which to make the best of her fortune. She would always get trapped by the next instant gratification; the next distraction was always round the corner. Without long-term goals, that's what happened to most people at LUSS who made no plans.

But Omar had a plan. The first part of it was to leave this group. He admitted to himself that he had joined the wrong people for the wrong reasons. Sara was not reason enough to suffer through the boredom, claustrophobia and ill health when he stayed up all night talking, rather listening, because he never felt comfortable enough to initiate conversations around them. Then there was the disease-laden and system-crashing breakfast to top it all. It was time to remove these people from his life.

It was time he let go of people rather than them letting go of him. He felt the force of this decision gather in his full and queasy gut and wondered how much of Sara he would have to let go.

The sun was dim yellow and there was a haze of smog behind them. In that direction lay the Old City, which they had just left behind, having escaped it just in time, before the crowds and the pollution set in. Soon enough, they were turning off an exit into Defence via the Ring Road, and then headed in through the LUSS gates.

Omar and Sara kept staring out of their own windows until they came to a stop. Mehreen had dozed off and had to be woken up. Nadia and Zafar didn't come within the next three minutes, which is how long they stood waiting.

They all felt the inertia of being unable to escape each other's company. They believed that their weekends would always be just so, eternally recurring loops, until their exhaustion would reach newer heights and the sense of fun and spontaneity would get whittled down to nothing. Finally, in complete silence, they separated, waving to each other.

Hayyan drove to his house. Omar walked back to his hostel while Mehreen and Sara went to wake Zainab up in her room, so they could roll out her floor mattress and collapse on it.

Before falling into bed, Omar brushed his teeth, washed his face and looked into his eyes in the mirror. I could lose her, he thought. He knew the boy in the mirror didn't need to hear the words inside Omar's head out loud.

If I let go, he thought, I let go completely.

I stayed back at LUSS for her, I didn't transfer. And now I have to let her go. She wasn't worth it, he thought. It was a question he tried to frame as a statement, to deepen his resolve.

If he could have, he would have run. But he was tired and still full of food and had already been for a long, hard run a few hours ago.

No amount of running would lead to the right answer. It wasn't an oracle. It was just a process that enabled a clarity of vision on other processes. Time spent with Sara was not a process but a place out of time, a comfortable dimension that felt close to Omar's concept of home.

But it was becoming sour because too many other people wanted to inhabit the space as well. Those were the people with whom Omar couldn't coexist. Barring Mehreen, of course. She was the only one Omar could stand to be around.

After spending so much time with Sara's friends, Omar had started to compare them to his own.

He still missed them, his Aitchison boys. Sometimes he had to try and miss them, and then at other times he had to try not to. He lay on his bed thinking about that. And in the spin-drift of these thoughts, it occurred to him that even though he would never be part of that group again, somewhere along the way he had forgiven them for excluding him.

He could think of only one reason for this forgiveness: they had done something good by excluding him from their collective decision to ease their hormonal surges with transacted sex.

They had never pressured him because they had not wanted to

relive, even vicariously, the crossing of the threshold from *being* right to *doing* wrong.

Across campus, Mehreen threw her shoes into a corner of Zainab's room, pulled out the floor mattress with Sara's help, lay down and instantly fell asleep.

Sara sat at Zainab's computer and checked her email and Facebook, clicking softly so as to not disturb the sleeping forms of Zainab, Zainab's roommate and Mehreen.

There was enough space on the mattress next to Mehreen but Sara did not want to sleep despite being utterly exhausted. It was the kind of tiredness that brought absolute clarity on what to do in life from that point onwards in order to fix it and live it right. But the clairvoyance would not survive the passage of sleep that was imminent.

Sara knew what was wrong. It was Nadia, yes, but it also wasn't Nadia. It was mostly Sara herself. She was doing the things she had done before her mom died. She was letting people take her for granted. She was going along with whatever everybody else wanted to do, and apparently everybody wanted to kill themselves from sleeping less and overeating globs of fatty beef. The self-destructive impulses started with unhealthy living, but they also extended to unhealthy thinking.

Sara clicked on Nadia's profile on Facebook. The bitch was pouting in her profile picture. Yeah, you look so cute, Sara thought. Such an adorable slut. But the problem wasn't Nadia, Sara reminded herself. Even then, she clicked through five more of Nadia's profile pictures, noticing the hundreds of 'likes' on all of them.

Her choices of clicks were toxic. This clicking Sara was participating in was the opposite of therapy. It reduced clarity. She had to get up. She had to stop.

She took a deep, long breath, logged out of Facebook, put the computer to sleep, put on her shoes again, wrapped her dark brown shawl around her shoulders, and stepped out of Zainab's room.

Omar lay on his bed, dreaming lucidly about lying in such a bed, in such a room, on such a morning. He savoured it all, waiting to drift off from a conscious dream to an unconscious one.

Rays of the sun dodged the swaying eucalyptus leaves outside, seeped in through the translucent white curtain, and cast a play of shadows on the wall he was looking at.

It was still early on a Saturday morning. He loved the peace that he imagined ran through the entire campus and extended, to some degree, into the city as well. His body ached from running and overeating. Both the aches would vanish once he woke up. So he lay savouring them while they lasted, and while it was still cool enough without the ceiling fan turned on at full speed. The day would only get hotter and brighter from here on and he would wake up sweating. But for now he was in a pleasant drift of floating thoughts.

Sara waited for ten long minutes outside Zainab's room, wondering if she was ready, if it was the right moment. It was cool and breezy in the corridor.

She thought about what she was going to do, but then it didn't make sense to only think about it. She couldn't keep acting the way she was anymore. It was over. She had to do it. There was no other option.

She walked down the stairs, two steps at each lunge, then slowed down to take one step at a time. She walked the length of the empty corridors of the social sciences building. A janitor she recognized waved to her and said 'Salaam'. She nodded and kept walking, quickly now, past the dining hall, the Admin building and behind the power generation unit.

Omar's hostel was looming straight ahead. There it is, Sara thought. This is it. This is where they stop me, she thought. I'll never get to do it. The security guard will be sitting at the window just inside the hostel, and he'll see me, and then it's game over. They've already got me.

When she reached the glass door, she hesitated. Why bother if it's going to fail anyway, she thought.

But failing was less scary than not trying and then being left with the question: what if it hadn't failed? She pulled the handle.

The door wasn't locked like the ones to the female hostels always were. She took one step inside. Two boys sat on the stairs straight ahead and a third was reading a noticeboard. The building had a different layout than the girls' hostels. It seemed older and there was a musky smell in the hall. The smell of sweat and stale socks parsed through a citrusy cologne. The light in the security booth was switched off. Sara stepped further in. There was someone in uniform flopped on a sofa in the booth.

Sara walked quietly up to the boys sitting on the stairs.

'Hi,' one of the boys said to her. He obviously recognized her, but she didn't know him. But that didn't matter.

'Omar Kayani's room?' Sara asked. She liked the authority in her voice. She liked that she hadn't said anything unnecessary.

'What?' the other boy asked.

'Omar Kayani's room,' Sara said again. The force was too deliberate this time. It felt off-kilter.

'312,' said the boy who knew her. She nodded thanks at him. 'Third floor,' he added. She gave him a quick, half-smile and nodded again. There was an elevator, but Sara didn't use it. She made to get up the stairs past the boys. They parted, and let her go through.

She realized why she had done that. Her heart was galloping at a hundred thousand beats a minute. She could not have waited for the elevator to slowly open and clang close while the boys looked at her.

She was scared out of her mind.

312. 312. She kept reminding herself of the number while she climbed the stairs. *312. Third floor.* She reached the second landing and looked up and down the corridor at the numbers to check where she was. The numbers began at 201. She went back to the stairs and up another floor. 301, 303. So it would be on the opposite side. 306. 308. 310. *312.* She knocked and then turned the door knob. It was open. She entered, looking down at the floor, and closed the door behind her. Then she locked the door behind her.

'Omar, if you're not wearing any clothes, please put some on,' she said. 'I'm not looking.'

The bedding came off, and then bare legs and a t-shirt.

Omar blinked and moved his head from one side to the other and blinked. He wasn't dreaming anymore. Sara was in his room. 'How?' he asked, and noticed he had only boxers on below his t-shirt. 'Is everything okay?' he asked. Maybe something had happened to Mehreen. But then Sara would have called. There it sat, his phone, on his bedside, not blinking.

'Yes,' Sara said, still looking down at her feet. 'Just please put your jeans on.'

Omar grabbed a pair from the foot of his bed and pulled them on, all the while looking at Sara.

'What's wrong?' he asked. She didn't answer. He was alone in his room with a girl. They could get kicked out of LUSS for this.

He had to hide her. Under the bed? Down the hallway? In the common bathroom? In his closet? In his head, he saw an inspection committee finding them guilty of breaching the laws of LUSS. Handcuffs figured prominently in the vision. But he cut off that film before it got going.

Why was she here?

Calm down, calm down, he told himself, let her tell the reason herself. He pulled out his desk chair. 'Here, sit down,' he said.

Sara looked up cautiously. Omar was dressed now. He had on a red t-shirt and dark blue jeans. Okay, she told herself, this is it. She stepped into the centre of the room and sat on the chair facing Omar, who sat on the bed with his feet on the floor. He forced his eyes open, blinking repeatedly.

He was waiting for her to begin.

She took her time adjusting the hem of her shawl and thought about chickening out, but that was a stupid thought now. She pushed it aside. 'I need to tell you some things,' she said, looking straight at him. She watched him raise a protective shield in the pupils of his eyes. He was ready to become absolutely quiet, like a wall, if she attacked him. But those day were done. She wasn't here for that. With a smile, she disarmed him. 'I need to share some things with you,' she said.

Omar's ears were picking up bird sounds from outside the window and he could also hear his own heart drumming. He was so alert that the slightest sound other than her words distracted him. She was doing this right now, according to a plan. She was going to tell him he was not welcome among her friends and she didn't want him around anymore. He wouldn't put up a fight. So be it. He would let go lightly, no matter what. He steeled himself for her words.

'Okay,' he said, trying to keep his voice neutral.

Sara looked away, then at her hands, which she had taken out from under the hem of her shawl. She caressed the handcrafted edge of the lace at the hem. 'Girls lie, Omar,' she said suddenly, as a crow cawed outside the window. 'Girls lie mostly to other girls. But they also lie to boys.' She looked up at him.

He didn't say anything.

She looked down at her hands again. 'Girls cheat each other, but they also cheat boys,' she said. 'Girls don't ever tell the full truth if they're scared.' She didn't look up at him again, even though she wanted to see how much she was scaring him. Probably a lot, even if he was trying not to let it show. 'Okay?' she asked, wanting to hear his voice.

'Okay,' Omar said.

'Boys lie too,' she said. 'All girls know that. But boys don't know how to hide their lies. They work too logically with their lies. It's like they're programmed by computers. We can almost always tell when a boy is lying.'

Omar didn't say anything. He tried to keep a straight face, but wondered what he had lied to Sara about recently. Had he lied to her at all? Was she talking about another kind of lying? She knew how he felt about her. That's what this was. She was going to draw his feelings out into the open. What better place to do that than in his own room, where he was most vulnerable? A place he would begin to associate with whatever he told her. She had him completely cornered.

He had to keep his wits about him. This was not going to end with him being nailed to the wall. He was going to remain stoic about whatever she said. He would simply let it wash over him and she would not checkmate him. If anything, he would back up far enough to force a stalemate. He pulled his legs up from where they were dangling and folded them on the bed.

'I know what you're thinking,' Sara said. 'You're thinking: she's gone crazy, running into your room and admitting how she feels. Well, you're right if you think that. I needed some madness to do this, and to come here and tell you all this.' She stopped, gulped deeply, theatrically. 'But here I am, mad or not.' She gave him a weak smile.

'What are you saying, Sara?' Omar asked. It was best to get her to blurt out her accusations, if possible. Then he could defend himself.

'I'm saying I like you,' she said. She looked up, directly at him, deep into him. She saw the cowardly shake she had given him with those words. His head was cocked back and his eyes were full of fear. This wasn't worth it. It was never going to be worth it. She should have known. 'I mean,' she said, 'I like you the most out of all the people I have ever liked.' I need to backtrack immediately, she thought.

Omar did shake inside. With her words, simply her words, she had woken up a pride he thought would never come back. He had given up on it. Pride was the wrong word for it. It was a dot of fire in his stomach, and was growing into a small ball of flames. He felt a jolt in his head as he grew more awake than he had been for months. 'What?' he said. 'You like me?' A wave of selfish pleasure spread across his face, lit up his eyes and rested smugly as a grin across his lips.

Sara looked at him, and nodded. 'I do like you, but—'

'Wait,' Omar interrupted her. The grin disappeared, not only because of the 'but' she had introduced into her sentence, but also because he realized that here she was, in his room, and she didn't want to crucify him for something he had done. She had come to admit that she liked him. It was enough. It made sense. Everything over the past two years fit together.

'I like you too,' he said, glad that he hadn't used the word 'love' just yet, though he was glowing inside with it. She had given him so much. So, so much. 'I,' he started and then shook his head and looked down at his hands, which had somehow joined together, as if they were praying on their own, 'I've liked you for a long time,' he finished.

He wondered if he should add that he had liked her from the moment he had seen the bun on her head the first day of classes. He wondered if he should make a quip about the explosion that took place on campus long ago.

No, no, let her talk, he told himself. She's the one who deserves to talk. I've just held this all inside and she's the one who had the courage to come here and say this.

So this is how friendship turns into something else, he thought. The fire was spreading its glow and heat throughout his body.

'I know,' she said. 'Boys can't hide things.' She smiled at him, teasing him. He looked down and then back up at her again because he couldn't keep his eyes off her. He was falling. She turned and faced him, and leaned forward on the chair. He put his hands out and she put hers on the bed. They were inches apart. They closed in.

This is how it all evolves, he thought.

This is where I have to stop it, she thought.

'I,' Omar said, looking at her hands like he was seeing them for the first time but he didn't know what he was going to say, so he stopped, just in case he would say something stupid like *I want to touch your hands.*

I should stop this here, Sara thought again.

Could she have if she had tried?

The length of her fingers ran up his palm and her hands folded themselves inside his. Only then did he look up, meet her eyes and breathe.

'Wow,' he said. He was going to say how beautiful she looked, which she did. But he never got the chance.

'I need to say something else,' Sara said.

'Okay,' he said, his thumbs carefully gliding over the soft skin on the back of her hands.

'I can't be your girlfriend,' she said. There, I said it, she thought. I finally said it.

Omar's throat felt dry and his eyes narrowed. He stopped caressing her hands, and his hands where they touched hers felt too hot. He didn't know whether to grasp her wrists or let go quickly. 'Why?' he asked. 'Why not?'

With her eyes looking into his, Sara said, 'Because even though I like you the most out of all the people I have ever liked, I am not ready to commit to anything. I can't do it. I know how this sounds. Here I am, telling you that I like you, and also telling you that you can't have me.'

'What do you mean?' Omar asked.

'You know, as a girlfriend,' Sara said. 'I—'

'Wait,' Omar said, pulling his right hand away from her left, balling it into a loose fist, and placing it on his chest. 'You're telling me it doesn't matter if we like each other?'

'Yes,' Sara said, 'There's something—'

'No, wait,' Omar said, pulling his other hand away as well, so she had both her hands untouched by him. 'I need to understand something. You're telling me that out of all possible outcomes, the one situation in which we *don't* become more than just friends is if, and when, we both like each other. Is that what you're telling me?' His voice had lowered to a whisper, with the hint of a croak.

He felt the heat and venom in his words as he said them. She had drawn him out. She had done it. It had all been a game. It was too late for him to say *ha ha, tricked you* because she had already done it. The joke couldn't be told twice.

'No,' Sara said. 'You need to hear me out.' She could see his defences going up. He was beginning to shut her out. She had to change tracks. 'You need to listen,' she said.

'Okay,' Omar said, 'I'm listening.'

'Not like this,' she said. 'Not with anger, not with this attitude. You have to listen to me and try to see where I'm coming from.'

Sara's hands were still on the bed. She opened them up, reaching for his hands, asking for them.

'Sara,' Omar said and shook his head. He took in a deep breath, slowly letting it out. 'Can I tell you something?'

'Sure,' she said. 'But can I finish first?'

'No,' he said. 'I need to say this now or I won't say it.'

'Okay,' she said.

He took both her hands into his. 'I decided to let you go this morning,' he said. He gave a dramatic pause because he felt what he had stated required one. The silence was not so silent. She still breathed and so did he. 'I was lying here in bed trying to find peace after my decision was made.' Her hands were no longer just beautiful hands to him. They were also like crutches he was holding limply. 'Then you came in here and I thought, "How can I give her up? She's a miracle."' He smiled and looked away from her, out of the window, as if he expected Divine Grace to part the curtains and shine heaven's rays on their hands. 'And now, you're telling me that you like me—'

'Yes, I'm telling you that,' Sara said. 'But I'm also telling you some other things that you need to hear.'

'Oh, Sara,' he said and took a deep breath as he exhaled. 'Okay, tell me what you have to tell me.'

'I will,' she said. She felt the strength of her conviction that she was doing the right thing. 'But first I'll tell you why you decided to let go of me this morning. You did it because of my friends. You think I don't know that but I do. You don't like them. You like Mehreen, but you can't stand Nadia, Zainab, Hayyan or Zafar. I know this.'

She was right, but he wasn't about to give in.

She kept looking at him. 'But you also know that they are not my real friends. They are people I spend time with, but I don't love them.'

'Yeah,' he said. This healed some of the hurt. But she had also played him.

'Omar,' she said, 'I can't commit to anything right now. My mom's death is only just beginning to sink in. I'm beginning to understand how much she suffered and how much my dad suffered. You know what I mean? It was so much pain and I wasn't any help at all. And I have all this guilt inside from wanting my mom to go quickly rather than suffer through a long illness. It's all started to make sense. You see? I have things I need to do at home. I have to be with my dad. My grandmother needs me too. I can't start something new without fixing the old things.'

Omar nodded, but then thought of a counter-attack. 'Why tell me now, though?' he asked. 'Why not wait until you were ready to start something?'

'I don't know,' Sara said, and she put her thumbs on top of his, pinning them to her palms. He let her play with his hands. 'Maybe I sensed you were going to distance yourself from me.'

'Hmm,' he said. 'Okay.' She released his thumbs and then pinned them again.

'I also wanted to be completely honest with you,' she said.

'Okay,' he said again, and nodded. He wanted to ask her when she would be sure, how much time she would take; not now didn't mean not *ever*, did it? But he didn't. He didn't want to *ask* anything; he wanted to be the one to *tell* her. Asking seemed too weak. Why was he offering himself up to her anyway? Why did he always have to be the one giving so much?

'I'm not taking anything away from you,' Sara said. 'Nor am I asking for anything. I'm just letting you know I like you the most.'

'The most out of anyone you've ever liked,' Omar said. 'Right?'

'Right,' she said. 'Exactly.'

'Me too,' he said.

'Okay,' Sara said, 'I'm glad it's mutual and I hope the future has something good in store for us.' She smiled and punched his hand playfully. She pulled her hands away and leaned back in her chair. 'Now I have something more serious to ask you.'

'More serious?' Omar asked, as he too leaned back against the wall on the other side of his bed. 'What could be more serious?'

'Sex is serious,' Sara said and watched him squirm. She felt queasy herself, if she were to admit it. She even smiled playfully and showed that she too felt uneasy about what she was going to say.

'Okay,' he said, frowning despite feeling aroused. 'Where did that come from?'

'It would hurt me a lot if you were getting it on with someone else,' she said.

'What do you mean?' Omar asked. Did Sara know about the young and pretty chemistry research assistant who kept showing up at the jogging track every morning, sitting there and watching him through his stretches before and after his circuits? Did Sara know every time he even supposedly flirted with other women? Were they after him as much as he wanted them to be? The possibilities in her question spiralled out of control.

'I mean just what I said,' Sara said. 'It would hurt me.'

'I've been to the den,' Omar said. He blurted it out like it was an admission of guilt.

'The den?' Sara asked.

'That Persian professor's flat,' Omar said. 'He rents it out to horny couples.'

'What's it like?' Sara asked.

'Filthy,' Omar replied, remembering the smell of dirty pots and pans in the kitchen, and the stink of multiple layers of sweat and bad incense in the room. It was a dark and crass place, full of people from outside LUSS, and the party he had briefly attended there had been a sausage-fest. There wasn't a single girl. It was well known that this professor ran a prostitution racket. No self-respecting LUSS girl or boy would go into that room.

'Why were you there?' Sara asked.

'I went with QT once or twice,' he said. 'He had to collect some booze and dope from there for someone.'

'Right,' Sara said.

'Anyway,' Omar said, 'don't worry. I won't be having any sex with anyone. I'm not desperate for it.' He believed it when he said it. He was stoic, monkish. 'Running keeps my libido in check,' he said, repeating something he had read on the Internet. It was something that ought to work, but didn't. He knew he could run all he wanted to, play one hour after another on the pavement and track with rhythm and wind sprints. But the one thing that running could not do was process desire. Omar could not outrun it. He could not quench it.

'I envy you,' Sara said. 'You become a different person after running.' His mood usually did change for the better, but Sara was not too sure about his basic human impulse as a growing man. He had to be lying. 'If you feel like you will lose control, let me know.'

Omar smiled. 'Why should I tell you?' he asked.

'Because I know a girl who likes you,' she said and winked.

'Ha, ha,' Omar said, feeling uneasy about discussing something dirty with her and pretending he was not thinking such thoughts, that he was the cleanest person she knew just because he was the person she liked most.

'Okay,' Sara said. 'I should go.'

Omar reached for her hand and she gave it to him. He held her wrist lightly. It was so boney beneath her skin. He had imagined it to be softer.

He opened his eyes wide and said, 'Don't talk about sex with your boy and just leave.'

'Are you my boy?' she asked.

'Are you my girl?' he asked.

'I am your something,' she said.

'Good,' he said. 'See you later then, my something.'

'Omar,' she said, getting up and wrapping her shawl around herself, 'don't be awkward around me because of what I just told you.'

'Why would I be awkward?' Omar asked. She was on her feet now, stepping towards the door.

'Maybe I will be the one who is awkward,' she said, looking around at him.

'Well, don't be,' he said.

'Okay,' she said, opening the door. 'I'll try.' She listened at the door for a second, waved and smiled at him, and then quickly slipped out.

The walk back was just as uneventful. Nothing happened. But inside her head she was tripping over her own thoughts.

Did he understand? Of course he didn't.

Did he get what she meant? Of course, he only got half of it. And that was worse than not getting any of it.

She didn't go back to Zainab's room to sleep on the mattress next to Mehreen, and she didn't call Nadia to ask her where she was. She called her dad and asked if he could pick her up. Meanwhile, she found a spot on the front steps of the social sciences building that was getting some of the feeble sunlight, and tried to keep herself warm.

⚜

Omar sat on his bed looking at his hands, smiling to himself. He couldn't get over what had just happened. Sara liked him. She really liked him back. That he liked her had never been doubtable. How she got him. Oh, how she got him.

Her hands were so soft and smooth, and her fingers so full of life.

But they couldn't be a couple.

But that didn't matter. That was okay. Even though they couldn't legitimately do the things a couple did.

Of course his mind centred on sex first, and backtracked from there. Why need sex at all, he thought. Wasn't sex superfluous at this point in life?

Of course it mattered. Everything mattered; sex more than most things.

Her hands, eyes, face and body loomed in his thoughts, and a buzz ran through his body and mind: why does the span of skin allure? What sheet of magnet is it? Her perfect form. Thoughts such as these ran circles in his mind.

With his energy spent, Omar lay down again and covered himself, half hoping Sara would come barging into his room again. He blinked and slowly fell a sleep.

His eyes opened hours later when his phone rang. QT was calling. Omar picked up.

'Hey,' QT said. 'You free for lunch?'

'Yes,' Omar said. 'Come, pick me up.'

'Okay,' QT said. 'You alright? You sound dead.'

'Yeah, I'm just tired,' Omar said. 'Hey,' he thought about how to ask QT the question that was riding his head. 'I need to ask you something without specifics.'

'Okay,' QT said. 'Right now or when I come?'

'Right now,' Omar said. 'I don't want to talk about it later.'

'Okay, shoot,' QT said.

'If a girl likes a boy, and the boy likes her back, but they don't do anything about it … what does that mean?' Omar asked.

'A waste of time,' QT said.

'Right,' Omar said. His head felt lighter with an answer. Maybe any answer would have done but this one felt correct. 'That's what I thought. Should one of them force the issue?'

'Force doesn't work when you like someone,' QT said. 'It gets ugly.' It was uncanny how he knew exactly what Omar was thinking.

'Okay,' Omar said. 'But is there something that can be done to smoothen the initiation of a relationship other than friendship?'

'Of course,' QT said. 'There's always something.'

'Okay,' Omar said. 'How long does the window of opportunity remain open?'

'You want to talk specifics?' QT asked. 'Is this about someone I know?'

'No,' Omar said. 'You're right. Thanks. There's always something that can be done.'

In trying to be accommodating, perhaps he'd blown the one chance he would ever have had with Sara.

He hung up the phone and climbed out of bed, feeling somewhere between holy and an idiot for doing what was right for Sara. Because by doing that, had he not also denied himself? By pretending to be holy, he had forced himself to become chaste and proved himself to be an idiot. A holy, chaste idiot.

Holy.

Chaste.

Idiot.

Pakistan
The Country

Pakistan feels incomplete. For over sixty years, it argues over Kashmir with India. The original reasons are now no longer brought up or even disputed.

Some things do happen though.

East Pakistan breaks away and becomes Bangladesh.

Most maps of the world award Kashmir to India, and only Pakistani maps, optimistically, mark it as a disputed territory. Onward thrums the constitutional bandwagon in both states.

Meanwhile, Balochistan, the largest province in Pakistan, wants nothing to do with the rest of the country. It would rather be its own state. Pakistan, the state, tells Balochistan, its province, to shut the fuck up in several ways. It:

- Extracts and takes away all natural resources, and lets the locals deal with each other's tribal brutishness for the dust left behind.
- Picks up any suspected dissidents and shoves them into empty rooms in holding cells throughout the country. Lets them rot.
- Makes excuses and feigns ignorance. People go missing all

the time. Can the federation be expected to keep real-time information on every citizen's whereabouts?

- Shows that there is always a nuclear option. #JustSaying

Karachi, Lahore and Islamabad. The three main cities of the country.

Karachi is where people actually work.

Islamabad, the capital, is where foreigners actually live, even in these turbulent times.

Lahore is where people eat a lot, complain about the regular power outages, pretend to work, then work their social calendars around a fixed matrix of people, compare their pouts and attires with Hollywood and Bollywood stars and subscribe to magazines full of pictures of people in Lahore who are preoccupied with these activities.

All three cities fare well in terms of planning. Even though Islamabad and Karachi have water access issues and Lahore has power outage issues.

Karachi, once called the Dubai of Pakistan, is the point of import and export of solid commodities like rice and computers; it is the hub of financial activity and upheavals and it breeds and exports pedigreed acts of violence.

Partly Mumbai-like, quasi-Sicilian, almost Beirutish, Karachi violence is a brand of its own. The structure works like a thriving corporation. All main orders come from the self-made CEO self-exiled in London. Hands-on staff maintain and secure neighbourhoods, receiving protection money and unquestioned allegiance.

Recently, the model has been copied and pasted by rival parties, including the Pakistani Taliban. And why not? The model works, even if there is no Excel sheet being tweaked somewhere. In fact, the model of Karachi's import and distribution of violence should be studied in business schools for efficient organization and management of labour.

Islamabad can be boring, though. The city shuts down at 8 p.m. It isn't restaurants or the streets where the action in Islamabad is. You have to know the right people. You need access to the right people's connections, to their basements, and to their swimming pools. Several circles and orbits can be tapped into and easily tapped out of too.

Pakistan has cheap labour. There are millions of people not thought of as people by the ones who employ them. Other than day-labourers, there are the multitudes of drivers, cooks, handymen, gardeners, cleaners, maids, laundry crews and their children. Those who can afford a combination of these, part-time or full-time, keep a small force on hand, set them up in quarters on the roof or in a corner of the garden, or just tell them to go away once their work is done for the day.

Throngs of villagers live in the slum areas of the big cities and have done so for ages. Their new generation, though, is savvier because of the Internet, the hundreds of TV channels and the nouveau riche who can't help but flaunt what they have.

The children of servants don't want to be cleaning rugs and dusting bookshelves for the rest of their lives. Some of them have a clear vision beyond the pitiful 'education' trickling down to them in the worse than mediocre schools. The theory in their textbooks does not match reality.

The streets where they grow up, the shops where they can't afford much, the households where they apprentice, the despair at the disparity—that is their source of practical education.

The rich get richer, the poor get louder. One day the dam will burst from their complaints, even if none of the destitute lifts a finger. The problem isn't that they lack motivation. Every day, there is more reason than yesterday to rebel, to buck the trend of remaining an indentured or disenfranchised slave of the state. To take up arms and ammunition, open the gates to the village haveli, the city mansion, the upscale shop's glass door, and let the bullets fly.

Bang! Bang! Bang! The soundtrack of muzak and kitsch drowned out by the reality of the gunshots. Not to kill anyone but just to wake them up.

Sometimes Pakistan thinks it is the centre of the world. When the national team wins a cricket match against the Indian team, or an unsupported and self-driven girl wins a medal at the Asian Games, the Commonwealth Games or the Olympics—it doesn't even have to be gold, just *any* old medal will do—Pakistan's streets fill up with Bhangra dancers. A week of celebrations ensues.

Pakistanis collectively have won two Academy Awards and two Nobel Prizes. The Oscars are not even in an acting or feature film category. They are for short documentaries, which will never be released in the cinemas. The Nobel Prizes are in physics and peace, and those are quite nifty.

But one just has to marvel at Pakistan's puffed chest. As if its universities are making cutting-edge research with Quranic physics, and as though showing its tortured and scarred underbelly on camera is something still avant-garde. And does the Peace Prize matter if there is no peace?

From this high a vantage point, with an ultra-high-definition view of the whole country, it looks as though the boy, the little speck running on a track, is turning around himself. And that centre is the still point that serves as an axis to the whirling dervish of LUSS.

Deserts, access to a sea, rivers, forests and mountains. The country has everything, from gold and coal deposits, to fertile soil and climate conducive to optimal cycles of labour and sloth.

Pakistan exists for a blip in the cosmic scale of things, between the big bang and the collapse of the universe. With its thrust-out chest, it takes itself so seriously. As if perspective is something other nations need to develop. As if Pakistan already knows how things stand.

Over the course of a single year, Pakistanis live through constant news alerts of internal and cross-border acts of terrorism, bankruptcy in the central bank's vaults, similar tales of woe at the exchequer, two government changes without any elections, five ousters of chairmen of the Pakistan Cricket Board, the constant threat of a military coup, massive gastroenteritis, cholera, malaria and TB outbreaks, localized but rampant dengue fever contagions, a hockey world cup semi-final loss to Australia, deranging floods that uproot the same twelve million that were uprooted the previous year plus another seven million (don't worry, they will be back to resettle and start the whole process again as soon as the water clears), a Test cricket win against world number one South Africa, a nationwide ban on firecrackers and pillion-riding and dropping holy rosaries and copies of the Quran on the ground even if by accident, the launch of fifty-five new brands of indigenously designed and produced saris all to be exported to Paris and London and sold at thirty-three thousand times the labour and material cost, the opening of Burger King outlets in five major and one minor city, the inauguration of the East-West-North-South Mega Highway project to build sixteen-lane expressways from Karachi to Kashmir and from Quetta to Delhi (India's sign-off is pending on the latter half of the project), bomb blasts and grenade hurls and violent protests and political assassinations and drone strikes and gun battles galore, the targeted killings of scores of Ahmedis and Shias and Hindus and Christians across the country, a 350 per cent increase in beggars and hawkers on the roads, a 550 per cent increase in vehicles on the road, seven billion dollars coming in through foreign aid, a nearly seven-billion-dollar scandal involving the two major political parties and one obese religious figurehead, the invention and dismal failure of a local YouTube equivalent to make up for the real one being banned, major Facebook privacy changes that remain a mystery, a rupee-to-dollar devaluation by 15 per cent, an increase in infant mortality for the first time since the birth of Pakistan in 1947, national chagrin at U2 touring five cities in India, no progress on laws against honour-killings and rapes and child marriages, continued ignorance of women's rights over their own bodies, an increase in Islamophobia and Islamophilia, an exponential growth in the number and variety of economic and social hardships leading to a huge decrease in public participation, the birth of a supposed messiah, the death of thousands who waited for salvation, and the collectively exhaled breath of hundreds of thousands who will, one day, try their hand at the same game.

Under a muted TV at Gate 24 in the economy lounge of the Islamabad Airport, sits a sleep-deprived, bent-back, white-haired gentleman. Three hours to his flight. His five children are spread out all across the world: Hong Kong, Berlin, Cincinnati, Austin, and San Mateo.

The old man is returning from his visit to his sister and her family in Islamabad after years of living in the United States where he has been flitting from one of his children to another every six months.

He now sits and recognizes that he is losing the battle to keep calling Pakistan home. It isn't just the distance and his being close to seventy-five years old. It is also the place. The people are louder, the cheating more brazen, and his own children have flown off to grow new branches to the family tree.

The ticker for him shows more death than life looming. All his old friends are dead and gone.

He grew apart from his sister years ago—it was all the property she didn't let him inherit. He has let all her deceptions drift into the past, but she guards them like secrets still unrevealed to him. She has turned bitter, refusing him a good room in her house. At this age she made him sleep on the sofa. But at least the sofa cushions were softer than the mattress. So he needn't complain.

He knows he partially *wants* to feel hurt. He knows he can also dwell on his sister sitting at the foot of the bed on the last night, rolling her fingertips around her swollen knuckles while she spoke about the old days and about how little time is left for either of them.

It is like wanting to fall out of love because it hurt so much. He sits measuring the decades of difference in progress between his childhood street in Pindi and the one where his son lives in the suburb of San Mateo.

But why complain? And why fret so much over giving up his claim to be Pakistani first and foremost?

Because he was *told* to worry. He was *told* to love Pakistan. Really *love* it.

He was told by his mother when she was young, and he was just a child, and Pakistan was not even ten years old.

Then by his comrades in the Party when he signed up to do his part in saving the country from the evils of capitalism.

It never came to that though. He was quickly disillusioned. He went abroad on scholarships and fellowships because he was good at maths and then mechanical engineering. His father also sent money to him in London.

But the seeds of patriotism were planted too early, and the roots they dug into him could not easily be uprooted. Reason and logic are poor tools to unburden himself of such emotional baggage.

He loves Pakistan. He cannot help it.

He sits watching the news ticker run from right to left in Urdu, his eyes no longer quick enough with the script to catch all of what is going on.

They will call his flight in two hours and fifty minutes.

He imagines a life on the roads in Islamabad as a renegade seventy-year-old. He tries to recall if he ever saw a beggar in the old days who looked like he does now. Because he always believed the beggars were versions of himself from another timeline, another life, so he always treated them well. He always gave them something, even if it was just a smile.

Sleep-deprived, nostalgic, lost in time, he gives up the ghost of reason. He roams in his memories the street where he grew up. There, on the tree-lined government house where his father used to smoke in secret behind a jamun tree, he imagines himself as a child running up to his father and hugs his leg.

'Baba,' he says in the crowded and noise-filled airport. Nobody turns to him. He is clutching his handbag to support his frame. Its fabric feels for a moment like the raw cotton of his father's long, untucked shirt. He could swear he was just breathing the air from that street only a moment ago.

There is a sweet fragrance of freshly cut grass and ripe mangoes. His personal Pakistan, a universe revolving around itself, a centre long ago blown apart, a centre still holding fast.

They fit like perfectly carved pieces of a puzzle. And yet, the lines and weights of what has become India and what has tried to become Pakistan is also, in many ways, arbitrary.

Staged at repose, the rectangle of Pakistan has its centre of gravity teetering over the brink of its base and into the land of its origins. India, with its bear-belly thrust out in support of the fall, also extends a hand on which to let Pakistan perch.

But it will still tip over.

On its southern end, Pakistan fans out and lays anchor on the banks of the Arabian Sea. As if water were meant to be stood on. What a country it is.

A caravan of buses rolls onward to the north of the country.

Sitting next to the window, he shifts so he can face her while all the others on the bus are asleep. He wakes her up. These few hours will be the best part of their journey. Everything else is the need and not the clasp.

Hands folded into hands on each other's lap, playing whisper-loud claps. Squeezes, pokes and giggles. Shoulders and arms meet across fabric. Watching each other with abandon, sharing headphones and songs.

And then as the passengers begin to yawn and stretch and wake up, Sara leans and falls asleep on his shoulder. Omar turns to look out of the window and glows with the recognition of how beautiful and perfect his country is.

Juniors
Bangs and Whimpers in the Dark

It was 3.15 a.m. and pitch dark. A drizzle had started but soon stopped, leaving the road wet and shiny. The roads were dead and empty and a few cars and rickshaws were parked outside shuttered shops. Any soundtrack could set the mood, the night was that malleable.

Omar had soft, sad music playing in his ears as he jogged slowly up the Defence Main Boulevard. He was already fifteen minutes, just over a mile, out of the LUSS gates. Every second wind was filling up his lungs. Through the low volume of a Sarah McLachlan song, he could hear the droplets of rain falling on the ground. For the second time in the song, McLachlan sang these lyrics: 'It doesn't mean much/It doesn't mean anything at all/The life I've left behind me/Is a cold room.' The song faded out and ended soon after, and he kept jogging through the silence between songs.

It was not a serious kind of night. He didn't take the lyrics to heart and try to make them mean something to him. They provided him with a good beat, just like the music did, for a long and slow run. The open city was good for that—for taking off into at night, for breaking the campus-bound conception of himself as a tiny human being trapped in a small circle.

The vastness of the city did not bother him. Its juxtapositions of squalor and mansions did not create anger at discrepancies or

Marxist outrage and cognitive overflow in his head. Not on this night.

Here, now, tonight in the empty city, bent a few degrees forward towards the pavement, using gravity and muscle to propel himself at a speed that the night itself dictated, feeling the intricate mechanisms and processes of his body and will, Omar felt sufficient unto himself.

This was the thirty-eighth night in a row that he had left the LUSS gates to run into the city. He should have started this a long time ago. The LUSS track didn't offer anything over the open road except safety. But safety was just another word for confinement.

Lights loomed up ahead. Even though the early summer load shedding had begun, the petrol stations still managed to get state electricity. There it was, the Shell station he would run past. It was the quarter mark of his shorter runs, but today he was doing a longer loop and he would go past the eight miles. He would know when to stop; his mind and body would tell him after conferring. For now he felt quite sure he could go on for a while longer.

Thunder rumbled faintly overhead. But there was no flash of lightning, no brightening up of the sky, no torrents of water gushing down. It was just the sound, like a bomb going off in the faraway sky. Omar's heart skipped a beat and then raced faster. He slowed down to calm himself, barely jogging. There was even more thunder, and it seemed closer.

Was that thunder?

It couldn't be. It was much too close to be that and it wasn't overhead either. He pulled out his right earphone and cocked his head, still jogging.

Gunfire. It had to be gunfire.

Someone was firing a strain of bullets from a machine gun. But there were no screams, no human sounds at all.

Omar ducked low and pulled out his other earphone. He

crouched on the road, listening to the rattle of bullets. Another bang followed. This was no thunder. It was a shotgun.

He could sense the general direction of the sound. It was not on the main road, but just off it, coming from a clump of houses behind a few very tall trees.

At least two different machine guns rattled and crackled back and forth. The sound of such rapidly discharged bullets was very unnerving.

Omar was exposed on the empty road and he was wearing a bright yellow shirt. He was far too easy to spot even in the darkness.

Any stray bullet could strike him.

There was no place to hide unless he climbed into someone's house.

'What the f—?' he said out loud. There was a shower of bullets. More bullets. A bang followed. It was that shotgun again. It was either really loud, or really close, or both.

Omar looked at the petrol station again. It was over two hundred metres away. Should he make a run for it? 'Fuck,' he said. 'Shit.' Adrenalin was pumping hard through him.

Stay or run. He had to pick one.

He made up his mind, got up and ran as fast as he could. The yellow and red petrol station, the dark wet road with its grains of tar and white lines that had faded from the rubber of millions of tyres rolling over them—this combination of things was the last thing he would see before he was lowered into the grave and then raised up to be judged good or bad enough for heaven or hell. And the last thing to enter his hearing would be his own panting breath along with his heartbeat on the insides of his inner ears.

He was no closer to the station. Maybe it would always stay suspended this far away.

The bullets had stopped. But Omar didn't slow down to catch

his breath. Maybe it was over. Maybe he didn't need to run so fast. Maybe the danger was over.

Or maybe the people with the guns were coming onto the main road.

He pushed harder on his legs, on his lungs, on the road. He broke his own speed barrier.

The petrol station was fifty metres away.

Forty. Then thirty and then twenty.

Omar still didn't slow down. He ran until he thought his heart would swell with blood and burst out of his chest.

The station's all-night convenience store was open. Most of the lights inside were on, which was why it glowed in the darkness like a phosphorescent mushroom in a forest.

Omar dodged past the pumps and went straight for the store's door. A bell tinkled when he pulled it open.

There were aisles and aisles of snacks and sodas and newspapers and pirated DVDs but there was nobody inside.

'Hello?' Omar called out loudly. He ran around a stack of magazines and looked out of the windows and the glass door. The emptiness of the shop felt eerie and Omar was about to shout out again.

'Hello, sir,' a man said. He was standing behind the counter, rubbing one of his eyes. He must have been sleeping on the floor down there. He was a wisp of a thing, dark and lean, like all he had were bones.

'There is firing outside,' Omar said. 'Guns. Lots of bullets.' He wondered if he was making enough sense for the man to follow his line of thought. He caught his breath, but his heart was still racing hard inside his chest.

'Oh?' the man said.

'Yes. Lots of guns. Lots of bullets. Should we call the police?' Omar asked.

The man yawned. 'Yes, sir,' he said. 'You okay, sir?' He pointed at Omar's knee. Omar looked at his scuffed right knee, where a cut was running thin streams of blood down the inside of his calf.

'What the—' Omar said. He must have scraped it when he was crouching on the road outside.

The man, whose badge said 'Yasir', picked up his phone and dialled a number.

There was music was playing in the background, on low volume. Omar could just hear a hint of the song. He recognized it.

There was no more gunfire, or at least it could not be heard inside the store. So the music was the only sound other than the faint dial tone from Yasir's phone.

Omar looked down at his knee and the dangling earphones next to his foot. That's where the sound was coming from. Omar's iPod was still on. The song it played was from the soundtrack of the film *Drive*.

'A real human being. And a real hero,' the song ran. Omar turned his iPod off.

'Police coming, sir, someone else call them,' Yasir said, as he held out an unwrapped bandage. 'Sir, you are LUSS student?'

'Yes,' Omar said. 'Thank you.' He took the bandage and bent to put it over the cut on his knee. The sound of a siren blared in the distance.

Omar stood up and walked around to calm himself down and to take more cover.

'Sir,' Yasir said, following him behind the aisle of cereal boxes, 'you scared?'

Omar looked at Yasir, the tiny man with his anorexic frame. He was short and thin, most likely because he had been hungry most of his life. He had probably never been able to afford a nutritional meal—no meat, and very little rice and bread. Poor thing. And here he was, asking Omar if he was scared.

With one punch, this man, who could be anywhere between seventeen and forty-five years old, would have cracked ribs and a broken backbone.

Omar felt like hugging him, feeding him, telling him not to worry; telling him that he had never felt hungry before going to sleep; telling him that maybe he had been eating Yasir's share of food all his life. It was a pity that Omar couldn't do anything with the pity he felt for Yasir. And yet, Yasir was genuinely concerned, asking if Omar was scared.

'I'm okay,' Omar said. He hunkered behind the aisle as the sirens grew louder. Finally, the police were getting in on the action.

'Sir, guns fire here almost once a month,' Yasir said. He wasn't scared, not that Omar could tell. He stood up to his full five feet behind the shelf, like he was surrounded by a bulletproof shield. He wasn't afraid at all.

But Omar felt justified in his precaution. Shell's store was the only lit-up place this side of Defence. Wouldn't it be the most obvious target for armed people to attack next? Wasn't the light also a danger?

'Here they come,' Omar said, as two cars with flashing lights on their roofs crossed the span of the glass wall. The police had arrived.

'Police here, but police no good,' Yasir said, as he followed Omar's gaze out of the window.

'What do you mean the police aren't any good?' Omar asked, getting up slowly.

'Oh sir, you know,' Yasir said, 'police part of problem.' Yasir walked up to the shop's front door and wall of windows and Omar followed him, feeling strangely protected by the tiny man leading him. Like he knew things Omar could never know; a shaman at the Shell store.

Why hadn't Omar stopped at the shop during his previous

runs? He had always thought the yellow and red Shell sign was some kind of warning, with its branching rays of alarm.

The sirens had stopped somewhere among the houses and some of the treetops were speckled with strobing blue and red lights.

'You are safe here, sir,' Yasir said. Omar looked at him and nodded. 'You are safe, but I am not safe,' Yasir said.

'Why not?' Omar asked.

'This danger happen every day, sir,' Yasir said, and shrugged. His gesture was one of dismissal. As if he were saying that he had so many dangerous things to contend with that he couldn't begin to worry about them.

Omar felt the weight of his own problems diminish, problems which included girls—a girl—and a future with too many options.

He needed to get back to campus. This wasn't his world.

He didn't belong at a petrol station in the middle of the night. He had an education at LUSS to finish and then a postgraduate degree to pursue. He couldn't face the streets, not even from inside the petrol station's shop.

A part of him was praying to get out of this alive. A tiny hidden part. He didn't want to pray for real unless he had a gun pointed to his head. The guns which probably weren't all that far off. And to think that he had been running every day past some trouble or the other.

'Police not solution, sir,' Yasir said again, breaking into Omar's thoughts. 'My two cousins killed by police fire while police trying to kill robbers.'

'Wow,' Omar said, 'I'm sorry to hear that.'

'Police not sorry, sir,' Yasir said. 'Police say these things happen.'

'I guess they would say that,' Omar said. He wondered if he should leave soon, or settle down in the shop for the rest of the night. How dangerous could it be with the police already here? The sirens seemed louder than before. Omar had heard no bullets fired since he had entered the shop but if he had been outside, running, maybe the police would have shot him down as a suspect.

He felt safe here with Yasir. From inside the shop, the situation felt like an adventure.

Yes, that's why he wasn't praying. He was living the adventure he would get to talk about later. He would tell Sara, of course. She would be the first person he would tell. 'Guess what happened last night during my run outside campus at 3 a.m.' Even the setup was exciting.

He hadn't told anybody about the late-night runs off-campus. Of course the guards knew because they opened and closed the campus gates for him. But it wasn't like they actually cared what he was doing. It wasn't their lives on the line. And he hadn't told his parents because they would have said the sensible thing: 'Stop running in the middle of the night outside the college campus.'

'One of my cousins, he killed by ten bullets. Police say it is accident.' Yasir was going on with his story. Omar was beginning to feel irritated with Yasir's sob stories, and also he was ruining Omar's adventure by listing them out loud and concatenating them into a litany.

'Right,' Omar said, not looking at Yasir now, not encouraging him in the least.

'It was tragedy, police said,' Yasir went on.

'Right,' Omar said again, reminding himself not to say anything when Yasir stopped talking, even if the pauses became awkwardly long. Yasir was standing behind the counter again, and Omar walked away from it, increasing the distance between them so that the conversation would peter off. The bandage on Omar's knee felt awfully tight.

'My sister also, police trouble her,' Yasir said. 'She said to police to help her husband find his motorcycle that was stolen. Police said they don't register case unless she pay 5000 rupees. See? Police part of problem.'

Omar was near the back of the shop now, near the line of beverages in the fridge. He faced the window again and thought about how he would open the story up for Sara. He could lead into it as a character study by describing Yasir's size, shape and colour. Tell her all the gruesome things his family had suffered at the hands of the police.

Or he could start with the empty road, the sounds and the sirens, and then end the story with his entry into the store. Yasir would not exist in that version of the story. Nothing at all would be said about Yasir.

But Yasir had become such a key element.

Then, without warning, a car pulled into the petrol station.

Omar's throat got caught mid-swallow.

But it was a police car, with its siren and overhead lights turned off. A policeman in uniform got out of the passenger side and came up to the store's entrance. Omar walked slowly with a bottle of apple juice in his hand towards the counter.

The policeman was big and tall, with a bush for a mustache. In any other clothes, he would look like a deranged criminal. But in the cop's getup, he was a delight to behold.

'Sir,' Omar said, 'is everything okay?'

The policeman turned and looked at Omar. His badge said 'Sub-Inspector Shabbir Ahmed'.

'Yes, son,' the policeman said. 'Just some idiots with guns trying to get into a house that had security cameras. We caught most of them.'

'Thank God,' Omar said. He looked at Yasir, who stood behind the counter with a constipated smile. Yasir, the boney, tiny man with hundreds of personal tragedies. That's how Omar would describe him to Sara.

'We got a call from here,' the police officer said, turning back to Yasir. 'Did you call?'

'I asked him to call,' Omar said. 'I heard the bullets and told him he should call.' Omar saw himself for the credit-taking bastard he was, even as he was speaking that thought out loud. He felt no shame. He told himself he was saving Yasir from interacting with the police because Yasir hated them. It was a good deed he was doing.

But Omar's mind felt split at the seam that joined its two halves. He was now unsure of his intentions. They were so suspect.

'You don't want to be involved, son,' the policeman said over his shoulder. 'I hear you but you don't want to get mixed up with this.'

Omar opened his mouth to say something. He looked at Yasir, but Yasir with his small beady eyes was looking down at his hands and grinning widely, eager to please.

'Sir, I called police,' Yasir said. He raised his dark and thin face to meet the policeman's eyes. The smile never left his face. 'I am glad to be helpful, sir.'

'Right,' the policeman said. 'What time was it that you called the police?'

The questions were simple: what time, why, who else was around. For the last question, Yasir said, 'Nobody else, sir.'

'Wait outside in the car, son,' sub-inspector Shabbir told Omar.

Having been turned into a robot with commands to follow, Omar left the shop without looking at Yasir again. He went and opened the back door of the car. It smelled of stale smoke and spilled liquor. The driver, also in police uniform, was smoking a cigarette.

He was parked at a petrol station and he was smoking a cigarette.

Omar didn't say anything, just breathed in and out, and let the smoke enter his lungs and stay there with the rest of the polluted self that he had. He felt the driver look at him in the rear-view mirror, giving him a once-over. Omar looked down at his hands holding the unopened bottle of apple juice.

The shop door suddenly opened and out walked the policeman, Shabbir, with Yasir. They looked akin to a rhino being tailed by a mouse. But the cop waved him off and Yasir stopped at the door.

Omar wanted to get out and pay Yasir for the apple juice with the 1000 rupees he had zipped up in the pocket of his running shorts, but he knew he wouldn't get out. That payment would have to wait.

Shabbir got in and the policeman driving started the car, and reversed out of the station.

'Sir,' Omar said, 'where are you taking me?'

'You are a student at LUSS, right?' Shabbir said, without turning around.

'Yes,' Omar said.

'That's where we're dropping you off,' the cop said.

'What's going to happen?' Omar asked.

'Nothing,' said the cop. 'Nothing ever happens in these cases. We either kill the robbers or they escape.'

'And what happened this time?' Omar asked.

'Some were killed but some ran away,' the cop said.

Omar looked out of his window, hoping to see some robbers fleeing, so they could run the car over them. But he saw only darkness and dirt, and it felt like the darkness extended into him.

'You jog in Defence a lot at night,' the cop said. 'We see you on our regular shift.'

'It's not so hot at night,' Omar said.

'It's also not safe at night,' Shabbir said. He lit up a cigarette too.

'I guess not,' Omar said. He knew he would not step outside the campus to run again in the middle of the night. All his miles on foot, for months to come, would be confined to that one circular track on campus. He sat back in the seat, looked out past the two policemen and the windshield, and waited for the LUSS campus to appear.

He had hoped, one day, to go walking through the city in the middle of the night with Sara. He wanted to show her everything one missed when driving by in a car. He had always thought he would feel vulnerable with her walking next to him in the city at night, but that the vulnerability would also bring a sense of power, a heightened awareness and an agility and looseness that would help him attack, like a whipped-up Bruce Lee, any predators that would try to harm his girl. But then again, guns were several notches above leering men and slime.

Omar had seen the city for what it could do, and it wasn't something he could deflect from anyone, not even from himself. The indignation at being confronted with unwanted danger did not override the fact that the threat was real and it was not something he could mess with.

The nightmarish images of more bombs and gunfire encompassed him. It was as if the violence was circling around him, waiting to find him inattentive before closing in at last.

The ride was silent for a while, except the police radio crackling. The LUSS gate finally arrived and Omar opened the door and got out, ready to say thank you and go. He walked around to the front passenger seat window and was about to speak. But he didn't get a chance.

'Son,' the big cop said, 'if you're worried about that attendant at the petrol station, don't be. He will be fine. I know him well.'

'Okay,' Omar said, 'thank you, sir.'

'Also,' the cop said, 'there's no reason for you to be outside these gates. Get your degree, get out of this country. There's nothing left here for people like you.'

Omar didn't say anything and the cops didn't look at him. They left him outside the gate and drove off.

A part of Omar wanted to go running at this moment, into the darkness of the open road, again the one mile to the petrol station no matter how much gunfire interrupted him. It was a small part that suddenly became quiet though, as if choked by the rest of him.

I'm useless, Omar thought. I have nothing to offer but this story to give to Sara, he thought.

And then a thought occurred to him: why should he tell her about it at all? It didn't have anything to do with her. There were other worlds in him than those that had to do with Sara.

He sat just outside the LUSS gate, on a raised pavement, in full view of the guards inside. He decided he was not going to unload it all onto Sara. He needed to keep it inside himself. It pleased him to think of himself as that strong. As if in this way he were still protecting her.

Omar smiled. Always, always, playing the hero.

For more than an hour after the power went out, Sara lay in her bed, hoping it would come back so she could fall asleep. It grew hotter and stickier and soon she was sweating.

In one month, it would be a year since her mom had passed on. She lay thinking about her mom's bed, where her grandmother, Sara's Nano, was sleeping. Her dad had moved into the study since Nano had moved into the house, a month after the funeral.

All of that seemed so long ago now. The ancient history of last year.

Sweating, dry-mouthed and leaking unwanted tears, Sara got up to go to the kitchen. An envelope of darkness followed her slow walk to the kitchen's swinging door, next to which sat the water dispenser. She picked up a glass from the table next to it, and poured some fresh water for herself. The glug-glug of the water machine was followed by a shuffle behind Sara. She turned around.

Her grandmother was sitting with her feet up on the long sofa in the living room.

'Nano,' Sara said. 'You're awake too?'

'Just about,' Nano said. 'Come, sit.'

Sara grabbed another glass and filled it, and put it on the coffee table in front of Nano sitting across from her.

'I couldn't sleep in this heat,' Sara said.

'Yes,' Nano said. 'I can understand. But the heat is good for my bones.'

'Oh, right,' Sara said. She could hardly make out the woman lying down on the sofa. A few years younger, a few inches thinner and taller, the voice a little less hoarse, and it could have been her mom. An ancient silence came between them. Maybe Nano saw Sara's mom in Sara as well. In the darkness it was hard to tell where her face was. But there was a ghost of a feeling in the air.

'I was thinking about the old days,' Nano said, 'when your mom was not born. This feels like that.'

'Hmm,' Sara said. 'I forget what she was like sometimes.'

'Yes,' Nano said, 'sometimes, I don't think she even existed. It's strange. It feels like she came here only so you could be born and she could help you grow up, and then she had to go back into becoming nothing.'

'But I feel her all the time,' Sara said. It surprised her to say that because it was true. It was as if her mom was being reborn, cell by cell, inside her.

'What worries me is that I love you more than I ever loved her,' Nano said. 'Even now that she's been gone a year, I don't miss her as much as I miss you when you're away from me.' Her words felt like an embrace that was much too tight.

Sara had two options: she could surrender and be warmed by it, or struggle against it more. She felt limp.

'Sara,' Nano said, 'tell me what you're thinking these days.

What do you think about and what do you worry about? What makes you happiest these days?'

Darkness enveloped the old woman's questions. They were benign questions designed to draw out who her granddaughter was. Since Sara had begun to spend more time at home, a new kind of life had filled the house; even with her mom's absence, it seemed enough that the three generations of very different people were able to coexist. Things and events filled space and time, until time meant more than just what happened on a clock, soon becoming a series of fresh memories.

Her dad's movements were different from the old days, but day by day his walk had grown less tentative. Her Nano's hand-cut bowls of fruits on the dining table and the warming aroma of her cardamom kahwahs every few hours had blunted a dark and violent sadness from taking over the house.

Pictures of Sara's mother had remained in their frames and her dad had often sighed while walking past one of them, sometimes stealing a quick glance at them. But his injured looks had also begun to ask for permission to be happy.

'I like a boy,' Sara said.

'You like a boy?' Nano asked. 'Well, it's about time.'

'Yes,' Sara said. 'But he's immature.' She felt unkind saying that about Omar. Unkindly honest.

'In college?' Nano asked.

'Yes,' Sara said. 'He's in my year.'

'Does he like you too?' Nano asked.

'Even more than I like him,' Sara said. 'I keep him worried.'

'Good,' Nano cackled in the darkness like a jolly witch.

'He's a good boy, Nano,' Sara said. 'He's really a good person. But he's not grown up yet.'

'It's good you realize that distinction,' Nano said.

It had been close to three hours since the power had gone

out across the neighbourhood. Many people had woken up because their air conditioners had stopped working. Some kept on sleeping because they could afford to run air conditioners on fancy power supply units or diesel generators. Many kept on sleeping because they could not afford air conditioners in the first place. The absence of power for them meant only the absence of fans whirring overhead. Others had woken up for reasons other than the heat: insomnia, guilt and fear were some of these reasons. Sara's dad drew a breath and entered the room.

'Tell me about this immature boy,' he said. 'What do you mean by immaturity?' He had walked quietly, in his self-effacing shuffle, to the door of the living room, and he had been standing there for a whole minute before he had spoken.

It was the darkness that helped him speak his mind. It was the darkness that helped Sara overcome her fear of talking to her dad about a boy. Had her mom been alive and well, Sara would have talked about boys generally and specifically only with her. But that had been taken away from Sara and she had since then thought she would one day get married after maybe falling in love, and that would be the first time she would talk to her dad about boys. Or maybe not even then.

'He's still a boy, Dad,' Sara said. 'He doesn't know what he wants.'

'And Sara knows what she doesn't want,' her grandmother said. It was true. Sara did know that she didn't want some things. For instance, she didn't want to spend her life with Omar as he was.

'That's silly,' her father chuckled. 'What's wrong with not knowing what he wants?'

'He's always looking for approval,' Sara said. 'It's like he wants me to keep congratulating him for everything he does.' She felt like she was taking an extreme position, playing devil's advocate. She wondered if she was trying to make Omar in some ways more palatable for her dad and her Nano by talking against him, just so they would be on his side.

'Sara,' her Dad said, 'what do you think boys want?'

'Are you sure this is what she needs to hear right now?' Nano asked.

'I'm serious,' her dad said. 'And no, I'm not saying what you think I'm saying. That crass thing that people say boys want is exactly what I'm arguing that boys don't want. Tell me, Sara.' She could feel his eyes on her silhouette.

'Okay, good,' Nano said.

'I think,' Sara said, 'boys want to be loved a lot. They want to be unconditionally loved the way their mothers love them.' She realized that this was something her mom had told her about her dad. She had told Sara this once her illness had taken over. She had prepared Sara for when she wouldn't be there anymore by telling her that she would have to be like a mother to her widowed father.

That memory nearly spilled a teardrop from her eye, but Sara didn't blink it into a stream, and refused to flick it out of her eye. It was dark and they couldn't see. It wouldn't matter. But it did.

'You're nearly right,' her father said. She could imagine him holding his hands folded under his chin. 'You're very nearly right.'

'She's absolutely right,' her grandmother said. Sara smiled; her Nano couldn't help it even now. Up in arms against her son-in-law's opinions.

'Just hear what I have to say,' Sara's dad said. '*I* am the man here, not you two.'

Nano giggled while Sara smiled. Her father had a swagger even in the dark.

And, for an hour, Sara's dad waxed poetic—at intervals interrupted by Sara's Nano, of course—about what boys want. 'Girls think boys want to be loved,' he began. And then he went on to say that this was only a natural deception. Pretending to want love was part of the trick. Some boys deceived even themselves with that layer and forever remained stuck as boys. And a boy is nothing if not an attempt at being a man. After all, a man is everything a boy wants to be.

Look at the stereotyped images of masculinity: power, a gruff voice, big muscles, the ability to provide for his family. That surface holds within itself a tender root, the essence of a boy's desire: to give love.

That's what a boy wants. He wants to know someone or something that is worth giving all of his love to. It is a simple desire that gets cloaked up, right from childhood, in the garb of a desire to acquire and possess people and things.

Many boys fall by the wayside, collecting always, thinking things and beings will give them love because they *have* these things and these people. But they forget that the cycle starts with *giving*, not taking or receiving.

Naming your toys is an act of favour. It is an act of giving. Building collections of soldiers or airplanes or trucks is a pivotal point. If a boy understands that these things are his only to guard so he can share them, he is already well on his way to becoming a man.

But if he hoards and denies access to his toys to other children, if he refuses to think about sharing when it is part of being a man, he is losing the battle. He is regressing. He is a man becoming boy.

Such boys will want to possess beauty, truth and love. They will never know that these are things created within the act of giving them to someone else.

Nano did not buy this, however. She fought over definitions and details. The darkness kept all three of them in a confessional mood and the conversation they had was more with the darkness than with each other.

At length, a pale light began to creep in through the curtains.

It was close to dawn; what photographers call the magic hour was at hand. But to Sara it felt as though the magic were seeping out rather than pouring in. The house felt like a leaking vessel.

Her dad's eyes were closed against the light. He was lying down on the chaise as if he were a psychiatrist's patient. Her Nano was also lying flat on her back on the three-seater. Sara sat with her legs folded under her on a wing chair.

'If he likes you,' Sara's dad said after some silence, 'and especially if he likes you in the right way, he's a good boy. I was a good boy. I cared deeply for your mom. She was just like you are now.'

Sara believed that. She saw her mom in herself. But she had not known that other people saw that in her as well. She had thought it was just a way of keeping her mom alive. But it was more and she was glad that it was.

'So what do you think I should do, Dad?' Sara asked.

'You said he's immature,' her dad said.

'Yes,' Sara said. 'He will become mature, I'm sure of that. But it will take him some time.'

'Good,' Sara's dad said. 'I was like that with your mom. She was always teasing me about being a child inside. It was her way of telling me to be a man.'

The power suddenly came back on and the room was lit up by lamps and an overhead light. Sara and her dad blinked. They saw Nano's body rise and fall slowly with her mouth slightly open. She was fast asleep. She was well covered with her shawl and looked comfortable on the sofa, so Sara and her dad switched off the lights and left her there, and walked to Sara's room where she got into her bed and her dad kissed her forehead and patted her on the cheek. He turned off the lamp, closed the curtains and stood in the doorway to leave.

'Don't worry too much, Saroo,' he said. 'Boys grow up. And the good boys are always trying to be the best versions of themselves.

I know you. You're not the kind of girl to like someone for surface things like looks. And I'm sure you won't pick an idiot, or a hero type with an inflated sense of self. You're like your mom that way. You like the quiet and strong type. Like me.' He grinned.

Sara wanted to hug him, but she was tired and the bed was cool. But what if this is the last time I ever see him like this, she thought. There has to be something I can do to show him how much I love him. She smiled wide and closed her eyes tight. Had it still been dark, had he not been able to see her, she would have said she loved him without feeling embarrassed.

'Thanks, Dad,' she said. 'Thanks for telling me about you and mom.'

'Your mom and I,' Sara's dad said, 'we love you.' He didn't say 'loved'. She loves me, Sara thought. Wherever she is, she loves me. 'We trust you,' he said. 'She is watching you become a woman.'

'Dad,' Sara said, 'what do girls want?'

'God knows,' he said, and laughed, cracking up. Sara giggled at how boyish he looked when he laughed. His youngest possible self showed on his face. 'If he's the one, he'll figure it out,' her dad said. 'That's his job. And your job. Good morning, sweetheart. Get some rest.'

'Good morning, Dad,' Sara said.

He left, closing the door quietly. Soon, she was falling asleep and the picture on her bedside table, of her as a one-year-old laughing baby in her mom's arms, was the last thing she saw before closing her eyes.

In the picture, holding Sara, her mom was frowning playfully at the camera. Sara had hundreds of stories for that frown.

She was already sitting near the front when Omar entered Auditorium 3. The lights were dim and the overhead projector was on standby. The professor stood at the head of the room with his eyes on a small computer screen. He was going through the slides that he would soon transfer onto the big white screen by turning on the projector.

Omar swerved around some seated students and settled in next to Sara.

'Hey,' she said, looking up at him, smiling.

'Hey,' he said, 'how are you?'

Sara nodded and yawned, slowly blinking. She waited until he sat down and then stared at him. He was trying to look like he wasn't hiding anything from her. The story inside him was brimming on the surface, but he was corking it tight.

He looked at her and stared back, but didn't make a funny face. She waited for it.

He didn't ask her why she was staring at him, or crack into a smile or an awkward laugh. And he didn't tell his story from last night. He kept looking back at her. He was no longer squirming under Sara's gaze.

Maybe he would grow up. Maybe he would find out how much he needed to give her.

Even if he didn't, at least they had a whole year together still to go.

The lights dimmed further and the projector sprang to life. The screen showed the first slide, which had the words *Sociology of Evil: Last Class* written in a red Gothic font against a black background.

In the ninety minutes of darkness and flashes of light on the screen, interrupted often by the professor's excited antics, Sara and Omar sat next to each other like an old married couple at a movie theatre, neither fidgeting with desire nor falling into a sense of false hope for the future.

It was enough for her to be next to him. And sure, let him daydream while he could.

Professor Aurangzeb Muneeb's Closing Thoughts

Assalamu alaikum, friends.

As some of you may know, my name is Aurangzeb Muneeb and I am an associate professor of sociology at the university.

I have been asked by the vice chancellor, Professor Najam-ud-Din, to say a few words about Sara Shahjehan and Omar Kayani. Of all the faculty members, my name came up because I am the only professor who taught both Sara and Omar. Together, they took my course, sociology of evil, in the spring of their junior year and they were both my teaching assistants last semester. I was close to both of them and that closeness went beyond that of any ordinary teacher–student relationship.

Let me tell you how.

I am thirty-seven years old and I am a widower. My wife died five years ago in a car accident in Karachi. She could possibly have been pregnant at the time. I don't know. We had been trying to have a child after two years of being married. She was twenty-eight at the time. I was in the middle of my second post-doctorate and offers from universities all over the world were beginning to pour in.

There I was, with a fantastic start to both career and family. Life was great.

And then my wife died, and life was anything but great.

I have heard the rumours about me. Thirty-seven and single. Some dirty stuff goes around the campus. I know. I've heard strange things about myself and about my colleagues. I could tell you stories.

But no.

The simple matter is that my wife died and here I am, very alone.

Now you must be wondering: why is he telling us all this? Because you need to know this to understand my relationship with Sara and Omar and what they represented to me.

Sara and Omar were in love. I don't think that is up for dispute. I will tell you what I saw of that. But before that, I will tell you what I didn't see.

I didn't see them hold hands and I didn't see them sitting on a bench with their eyes locked on each other. I didn't see them giving heart-shaped chocolate boxes to each other on Valentine's Day. Theirs was not the run-of-the-mill, ordinary, uncomplicated romance.

Now you look at me and wonder: what does he know? Maybe they did exchange gifts and celebrated each other's birthday and held hands while they walked on the jogging track.

But I know.

I know because they showed me that the feelings they had for each other were much more complicated. They didn't have it easy. They were insecure about the complications and they needed constant guidance and assurance that it was okay to have the complex feelings that they were experiencing.

I know Sara and Omar's relationship because it was very similar to what I had in college with a girl. A very pretty girl. The most beautiful girl I ever knew.

People think I listen very well because I don't say much. Especially my students. They often come and sit in my office and talk to me about issues that they face: stress, family problems, you name it. I guess I do listen. Even if I am working on a paper, or in a hurry for a meeting, I will set up a time to talk to them later.

And you all know us college professors. We have a reputation for sitting around twiddling our thumbs.

Well, sometimes this is the case. Sometimes I do work as a means of passing the time until a student comes in and distracts me from my work and my thoughts. Because sometimes, even when I'm fully committed to my research or preparing for a class with five different texts in various stages of being dissected on my table, even hours after classes are over and the hallways are quiet, and there isn't a soul stirring on campus, I am sitting in my office, thinking about her.

Let's call her M.

M was never my girlfriend. With a girlfriend I would have had a spoken commitment, people would have known about our mutual ownership of each other.

But between M and myself there was none of that.

We were in college, a small liberal arts one, in the US. We were both humanities students. Everything had to be theorized and categorized into 'isms' and 'ologys'. Everything had to be parsed through the lens of feminism and Marxism and neo-liberalism. There was so much to read in the sociology and history courses we took. So much to understand and then respond to. It was overwhelming; just like academics in college ought to be. There was always more to learn and so little time to learn it all.

Somehow, along with the massive workload, the development of my understanding of the vastness of the cosmos of knowledge didn't bother me when I was with M, discussing banal things.

And speaking of banal things, I still remember her favourite green cardigan. She seemed to wear it every day in the winter of our last year in college. I can picture her with her long hair and her long strides across campus even today. How she always managed to be four minutes late to every class. The way she laughed sometimes like a little girl if I did something stupid like slip on ice, or fall down and say 'Yowza'.

She wasn't afraid of laughing.

With her, the everyday things were enough. When I was with her, I felt at home. I felt at peace.

I've always believed that unless you're in love, you're a cynic. It's fruitless to discuss love with such a person. So, unless you have been in love, I can't convince you of my feelings, especially now, after the passage of time and the changes that my life has gone through. But I can tell you that I was in love with M. She was truly the love of my life.

We took some English courses together, and we spent time discussing Dostoevsky, Nabokov, Steinbeck and other great writers because literature was where our academic and personal interests converged. I remember lectures from our course on Russian novels like they took place last week. M and I both loved the professor of that course. He was a hero to us and the one who made me want to become a professor.

We used to go to his office and sit and talk to him about the gossip circulating the campus. He used to be scandalously open about other professors and share their embarrassing stories. We would often play Scrabble with him. M or I would usually win. He was great about losing. Sometimes I think he used to lose on purpose.

You're probably wondering again: why am I telling you this?

I'm telling you all this because that is what my relationship with Sara and Omar was. They would come to my office just to say hello and they would leave hours later, after playing cards or Scrabble, after finishing the almonds and chocolates from the snack tray in my office, having discussed bits of Hemingway and Ondaatje, taking down books from my shelves and reading passages aloud, then playing another round of Scrabble or chess before leaving. I would go easy on them, remembering M and my own professor, and our long afternoons of playing word games and sharing our musings on literature.

I think about M a lot more since my wife died. I look back and think about that time in college as the beginning of some fork in the road, where M and I went our separate ways. She, with her green cardigan, packed up her suitcases and went to live somewhere else in the United States, where she could focus on producing and analysing literature.

I sold my things, said goodbye to the US, and moved to England for a doctorate.

We kept in touch as much as we could. We wrote emails to each other, called when we could; she even came to England, but at the time I was visiting my parents in Pakistan. We were eager to reconnect, and we even met once more, the year before I got married when I stopped by her apartment while at a conference in Boston.

But it was not the same. It never is after all the years that have passed. I was not the same and neither was she. All of it was different.

M and I didn't stay together after college for various reasons. Financial considerations, of course, played a part. I didn't feel ready to marry someone right after college, and the kind of work I was pursuing led me away from the cities she wanted to live in.

God only knows what she must have felt at the time. We never talked about any deliberate steps to take, to keep us in the same city. It just never got to that.

You see, M and I breathed each other's presence. We became so used to each other that at any given moment, I would know which part of campus she was at.

Not in a way that, 'Oh, it's 4 o'clock, she must be in her 3.30 class.' It was more. I could feel her presence and absence. I knew when she would turn the corner around the library and come sit on the grass where I would be reading some book.

She knew my appetite for sushi and chicken karahi, and learnt to make both for me on my birthdays. I knew which horror films she did and didn't like. I knew what music would cheer her up, no matter what, even if she had never listened to it before.

It was like we had tuned into each other's frequencies.

The professor who taught us the Russian novels used to call us 'the entwined'.

We used to feel sorry for him that he didn't have anyone else to talk to. There was a rumour on campus that he was a homosexual. Not that it would have affected us in any way. It didn't matter if he was or wasn't. But maybe he was, like I am now, someone with rumours rather than truth shaping his life.

There were some distasteful things said about him, some of which may have been true. But then there have been some scathing rumours about me too, none of which are true.

If I knew back then that I was going to turn into my old English professor, I would have asked him many more direct questions. I would have asked him if I should risk my friendship with M and ask her to marry me. He knew I liked her.

He knew why we came to his office again and again even though we had other friends on campus we could have spent that time with. There was no shortage of that. But those friends couldn't have given us what M and I were truly searching for. We were looking for approval.

We trusted him to know whether it would work out for us.

He guided us without even knowing it. Or maybe he did know. He was a shrewd old fox. Maybe he knew what M and I had was a great thing. Maybe he knew it was something profound that couldn't be stenciled into just any sort of conventional relationship.

What we had was bound by time and space. It was in the bubble of that campus that our romance thrived. The location provided us with that intense connection.

Those two hundred acres and those four years. It was all we had.

We weren't college sweethearts though we were the centre of each other's revolutions.

But our orbits couldn't stay that small forever. A campus is a few hundred acres of space, a city is a million more. Eventually, the four years passed, the two hundred acres became small. M spun off, and I left as well.

I got married halfway through my doctorate. You could say it was a kind of love: very practical and based on our compatible lifestyles and my financial readiness. She was studying medicine to become a pediatrician.

Our hours away from each other gave us enough energy and warmth for each other to compensate for all the loneliness that life brings. And life brings such deep loneliness, such a thirst for the company of someone good to hold, and for them to hold you tight at the end of the day. Just to make you feel that it's all worthwhile.

My wife was a good human being. She made me want to give her all my love. Which I did, sometimes. For the last few months we were married, she was my only love, the only one who occupied my sense of home.

But then, things happen; whether they happen for a reason or not, I don't profess to know.

My wife died in a car accident that was another person's fault, and my life completely changed.

After the funeral, I was in a completely different world from the one I had inhabited with my wife. It was as though marriage had been a dream and the memory of my wife began to seem more and more unreal over the weeks and months that followed.

All I could focus on were questions about my memories of M and college: whether I should have said something all those years ago. Whether not doing anything had been a conscious or subconscious choice. What had separated us?

I was haunted by the kind of questions that never get answered well enough for you to stop asking them.

I looked her up on the Internet again five years ago, a few weeks after my wife died.

M was married; she was a high-school teacher of literature, like she had always wanted to be. She had a daughter and her husband was working at Siemens in Ohio.

That settled it. A future together was impossible now without disrupting her life.

But I continued to think about her even as I did all the right things in my own profession. I completed my second post-doc, received job offers from universities in Lahore, Karachi, London, South Bend, Lancaster, Saskatoon, Brussels, Toronto and even Leeds.

I chose Lahore because this is where I am from, this is the city I thought I would always return to. No other place felt right, even with the higher salary offers I received from almost everywhere else.

I came here thinking I would be able to put my memories of M to rest somehow. The work would help—hundreds of students to teach, so many conference papers and books to write and such little time to do anything else. I might even get married again, I thought.

Yes, extended family members have got me in touch with women whose requirements I match as a thirty-something-year-old professor whose wife has died.

But how do I explain that it's not my wife I am mourning? How can I explain that what I am grieving for is the ambiguous relationship I had in college, the one that led me to become such a patient and caring husband? How do I explain that I listen so well because I am still tuned in to my memories, and the look of attention I give out is partly a gaze back in time and across the world?

I cannot explain it to the women who want to marry someone like me. So I choose not to. I just never go further than small talk.

And that is where I was for the longest time: in that rut, if you would see it like that. I was piecing together the memories of moments I had spent with M, trying to dissect the magic given to us on that campus during our four years together.

That is what occupied me, trying to pick apart the best years of my life at the seams, to see what was inside them.

I would like to share a quote with you that will probably help you understand how I felt. It's by one of my favourite poets, Fernando Pessoa. 'To feel today what one felt yesterday isn't to feel—it's to remember today what was felt yesterday, to be today's living corpse of what was yesterday lived and lost.'

That was me, willing myself to become a corpse of memories. Decomposing my future by investing it in the past.

I was near breaking point when I met Sara and Omar. The feeling of being alone had overwhelmed me. It was no longer a joy to sit in my dark office with a small lamplight, looking out on the grass where the students lay sprawled, and looking past them and thinking back to my strolls with M across that faraway campus. It was no longer a joy to imagine the green cardigan she wore with such ownership. It was an obligation now. Something I had to labour with, but a struggle in which I made no progress despite my untiring effort.

My colleagues in the anthropology and sociology department

know that my work suffered. I was encouraged and ready to take an early sabbatical simply to go and recuperate.

On the day I was to apply for a sabbatical, to take a year off from work, I was checking the last few term papers from an intro to sociology course. And this one paper ended with the line, 'Therefore, evil does not exist—it is a construct of the fear and anger that become misplaced, which leads to evil building up.'

It seemed an odd line to write in that paper because the rest of the paper was not about evil, but about anger. Even fear had not been mentioned in it before. It was completely out of place. But it made me wonder if the thought behind the sentence was something arguable.

So I began to look up the causes of evil and went to online journals and used the library's resources to see what experiments and research had been done on this.

I found examples like the notorious Stanford Prison Experiment, which posed everyday students as guards and prisoners to see what would happen. Evil things did happen. The 'guards' became belligerent if their orders weren't followed and the 'prisoners' became more subdued over time.

Similar experiments were carried out to determine whether all the Nazis in Hitler's army were evil. Maybe they were just following orders. There were many indications that they were, indeed, just following orders. Anyone in their place would possibly have done the same evil things they did.

The first thing that struck me about that was my own way of thinking, my own existence.

And there it was, finally. A moment of grace in my being able to see myself with a somewhat objective perspective.

You see, this is what I began to ask myself: every time I would lock myself in my office in the dim light to look out of the window and think of M, wasn't I just following orders as well?

The habit had become a set of orders, a set pattern of processes. Automatically, I used to switch off the lights, turn one lamp on, put away every other article of work except a bottle of water and a glass, a bowl of almonds, and a journal in which I jotted down any breakthroughs.

There weren't that many entries even after all those months. Maybe twenty pages of scribbles at the most. Even the notes I did make went round and round in circles around that significant switch from when I had her in my life, to when I didn't.

I recognized that I was facing something that had started out as love, but was fast becoming fear and anger, and which would devolve into something worse. Something, perhaps, evil.

One of my students had helped get me to this point by writing that incongruent last line in her essay. God bless her. She knows who she is, and she is here tonight. I thank you for the grace of that line.

It was because of that one line I began designing a course on the sociology of evil. I wanted to include readings which explored the existence and occurrence of evil in misdirected vision or a lack of vision, and linked that negative force to the mindless following of orders.

You are perhaps asking yourselves, again: why is he telling us all this? This night is about Sara and Omar. Why is he boring us with these irrelevant details?

Well. You give a professor a microphone...

I will come to the point shortly, I promise.

When I had created the outline and syllabus for the course on the sociology of evil, I could not stop thinking about it. And I just couldn't apply for a sabbatical.

The head of my department had already told me that the sabbatical would be approved. All I had to do was fill one form out and write a cover letter.

But now the despair in me shifted positions. I simply *had* to teach this course. And I had to teach it immediately. It was fresh and it challenged the notion of evil as an external entity.

And yes, it was also something which, finally, held more significance than my memories of M. It pulled me away from the past and gave my future some purpose.

So I didn't apply for the sabbatical. Instead, I pitched this course to the academic committee and they approved it within a week. It was put up on the next semester's list of offered courses.

I went for a three-week winter break to Karachi to enjoy the breeze on the beach, refresh myself and get away from my office. I came back ready to face my demons, ready to turn away from the dread of nostalgia and to teach my students what despair and rage can turn into.

And that is where Sara and Omar came in. They were there from the start, right from the very first class.

But I saw that only in retrospect.

At first, I was completely in thrall of the subject matter itself. Many of the students seemed surprised to learn about evil as an internal rather than external process. The Islamic concept of evil entities existing independently from humans has been taught to us for so long that as a society we attribute all actions other than good ones to demonic influence or actions of other entities conducted through us. Yes, we believe that some other people are evil, but never ourselves.

I won't lecture you now, I promise. I'll just tell you that the class was all business and the business was engaging. The subject matter was different from other sociology courses and even personal for many of the students.

The course started on just the note I would have wanted. I used to find myself walking across the campus lawns after class, smiling and thinking about something a student may have said.

It was not a smile from something M had said long ago, but from something new. 'But isn't Hitler completely evil?' someone would ask in class while another would respond, 'No he isn't. He killed Zionists. How can that be evil?' I was glad most of us were too much in shock to respond to that thought. Incredible prejudices came to light as did incredible insights.

Sara came to my office first. The first thing she said was, 'Professor Muneeb, you look very different this semester.' I asked her why she thought that and she said, 'You look happier.'

I had not noticed it until then. I was truly happier. I was waking up earlier just to read more about evil, and good, trying to come up with more readings we could complete in class, to give us even more perspectives to discuss. Then I would go for a long walk around campus just after dawn.

I often saw the silhouette of someone running on the track during the early mornings; once I knew it was Omar, we would wave to each other from far off.

Everything was beginning to click now.

My work life improved. I brightened up my office with more lamps.

The next time she came, Sara brought Omar to my office and introduced him as a friend from class. Obviously, they were more than friends. It isn't possible to hide that kind of thing. The room's energy would change when they were both there. The physical and the alchemical. All energies, in fact.

They came many times to visit me. We talked about education, literature, the cosmic battles between the forces of light and darkness.

When they would leave my office, I would feel blessed again. It was as though the best part of M and myself had somehow lived on and become something else for two new people.

Omar was especially interested in how the university could be improved. His friend Qasim Tiwana pointed out that Omar was always arguing about how LUSS was messing up opportunities to create true visionaries and leaders.

Many would argue that Omar was way ahead of his time. But I don't agree with that. He was of this time and of this place. He belonged here.

Another way to look at him could be that he was impatient and idealistic. There is nothing wrong with that. If you aren't going to be idealistic in college, when are you going to dream big?

... Sara was the daughter I never had with M.

She read a lot. She was smart, beautiful, kind. She used to suggest faculty members I could date. And the way she giggled at all my excuses.

She gave me good, pleasant and graceful company.

I often thought of speaking to them both about myself and M because I knew why they came to my office so often. It was the same reason M and I used to go to our English professor in college. We thought he was great to talk to and that with him we could be ourselves.

But, in all honesty, we were really there to ask him what we should do.

I often wondered whether I should have gone to him alone and asked him about M.

I could tell that Sara, when she came to see me alone sometimes, wanted to say or ask something that she didn't know how to articulate. I was the same when I was in college.

You see, I had always wondered if the campus, the college life, those four years were all M and I would have; even if we pushed and tried, would that have been the best we could have made of the time we had together? I especially wondered this after it was over and after my wife's accident. I thought about it for years.

Somehow, Omar and Sara answered that for me.

The answer was not a yes or a no. It was that M and I were in a state of grace. We were given a gift. What lay on us was not to ask, but to receive; not to question, but to accept with our own act of grace. Somehow, by circumstance, we had managed to do that.

Only, I had transgressed by looking back with something less than gratitude. I had begun to want more grace than was in my allotted portion.

I look at you all tonight ... parents, students, people from the administration and staff, and members of the faculty, and I picture myself among close friends on one of the saddest nights at this university. And yet, I still wonder if I should have said all the things that I have said.

Maybe I have disclosed too much. Maybe I should not have said anything about myself. It could be that I am just an old has-been trying to find connections where there are none.

But I don't think so. I believe Sara and Omar were, and are, in some way a reincarnation of M and myself. A reincarnation in meaning, if nothing else. Like that trite phrase 'history repeating itself', they were something like history brought back to life.

I cannot bear the grief of discussing with you what has happened to Sara and Omar. In a way I am glad Vice Chancellor Professor Najam-ud-Din has restricted us from speaking about the tragedy and asked us to focus instead on the lives that Sara and Omar led, so we may remember them for who they were.

I will restrain myself from the questions I have. I will do it even though I am eager to find out what became of them and whether the worst is even true. Or whether, like I want to believe, they instead eloped and took the one final leap of faith that M and I never did. I want to know but I will rest that desire for now.

Tonight, after all that I have already said, I will share just one moment with you because the rest are for myself.

I was given grace and help when I needed it, and Sara and Omar were the agents of that grace. I owe them so much for bringing me out of my despair, for making me believe that I did not live my life wrong. But I also owe them for what I believe to be the truth.

In my eyes, the truth goes beyond time and space. It is a thing of beauty that only an unflinching belief in idealism brings out. And unless you are in love yourself, or have been, and remember it, I don't think this moment will mean much to you. But I will try and make you see what I saw.

This happened in April of last year, the second semester of Omar and Sara's junior year.

I had not stood at my office window for the longest time. There had been no reason to. I didn't miss M and I understood and realized that the intense nostalgia was not good for me.

But that April afternoon, it was raining after months. It wasn't heavy rain, but it still felt like a shower of blessings. The romantic mood set by that unexpected rainfall made me want to repeat the old ritual.

I turned off the lights, put on that one lamp on the table, cleared everything from my desk except for a bottle of water and a glass, and stood at the window looking out. I tried thinking of M. I tried reviving her.

Minutes passed and so did students. Some of them carried umbrellas while others rushed past without any protection, getting wet. It was an amusing sight. Some of them seemed to mind getting even slightly wet. Others, not so much.

What pleased me the most was that I couldn't conjure up an image of M from the past. That ghost had finally left. I tried to revive it a little, not too much. I prodded my memories of that campus and I stirred up what I could remember while standing in my office, stoking the embers to see what was left of that warmth.

It was all cold. I remembered a cardigan, but couldn't get the shade of green right in my mind. And this time I saw no face.

The fire was out, I realized with relief, and I kept looking out at the rain.

Seconds or minutes may have passed.

And then it flared up in an instant.

There she was, walking across the LUSS campus.

It was a sharp jolt I felt and I remember its effect on my body, the ache I felt in my shoulders and my back from an immediate build-up of tension.

But, of course, it wasn't M. It was Sara. She didn't even walk like M. I had just associated her with M in my mind, and that is what had hit me. That, and the fact that Sara was without an umbrella.

I remember that, standing there, feeling the distinct sensation of déjà vu.

This had happened before. Even as I raised my hand to wave to her, whether she saw me or not didn't matter as much as completing something from long ago.

There was rain; she was wet and she walked slowly across the span of my window, twenty metres or so from where I stood behind the glass. She walked as if the rain was of no consequence. She wasn't dressed for the cold, but she didn't seem to care. There was something on her mind.

I was going to put my hand down, but then she looked up, and at my window, and smiled and waved. I waved again, and then she was gone.

I was grateful she had seen me and that she had returned my greeting. It is one of those moments that live with you as a professor, as a spontaneous gesture exchanged with a favourite student outside of class.

But there is something even more amazing in that moment and my having been part of it.

I remember, over fifteen years ago, in my own junior or senior year in college, walking across the campus in the rain. I was missing Lahore, missing M who was away for the holidays at the time, and I was walking in the rain thinking about her, trying not to think about her. I had decided what I was going to do. I walked past the library, where I could have taken shelter from the rain—and it was a heavy downpour.

But I kept going past even the government and philosophy buildings, where some of my friends worked and where I could have stopped to wait out the rain.

My thoughts kept swivelling around that one point: was it worth losing her friendship just to have something that officially meant we were supposed to be in love? The pendulum would go one way and then the other, and in those minutes of decisions and revisions, I was lost and in love with the rain and the cracking clouds that gave me such music and cold, stinging bites in which to walk across the campus.

Near the English building I looked up and saw that a few windows were lit up. But only one window had someone standing at it. Our English professor who taught us the Russian novels. He was holding up a hand and he was smiling at me. I remember how good it made me feel to forget my worries and to just wave back. That one gesture.

I didn't know what it meant at the time, but I remember the relief it gave me from my worries, from my wanting to make a decision. It was as though the right person at the right time gave me the signal that it would all be okay no matter what I decided or did not decide. I was in a moment of grace and the best thing I could do was be grateful.

I hope that when I waved from my window to Sara that day just a little over a year ago, I was able to give her that same relief from her worries. She smiled like a little girl, I remember.

I will always be grateful to her and to Omar.

I have since last year been released from the grasp that the memories of M had on me. Since then, I have been able to grieve for my wife. My friends and family labelled it a long period of denial, followed by acceptance. But they did not know what I went through. I did not tell them. I did not tell anyone.

But I have told you everything tonight. I have done so only to help you understand what Sara and Omar meant to me. They were not just my students. They were part of my return to life.

... Our professor never answered the question M and I did not ask. And I did not answer the question Sara and Omar did not ask me. I think I followed the tradition as I was supposed to. And I hope and pray that somewhere out there, despite what we all believe, Omar and Sara will live on and take this tradition one generation forward; perhaps this time it will be a different ending.

Perhaps they will be together in an office, even as they advise another young, frightened and daring couple about Tolstoy's love of tradition in *Anna Karenina*, or the extraordinary ability for ordinary individuals to overcome and defeat the capacity for evil within themselves.

I wish them well, wherever they are.

As for all of you ...

Thank you, friends. For your patience, for your memories, and for coming together to celebrate two good people who will live on within us even as they go on without us.

Thank you. God bless you all for being here tonight.

Seniors
Moments Leading Up

The relative peace of the last few years was threatened in the summer before Sara and Omar's senior year by increased sniper fire across the Pak–India border.

The governments and armies were playing politics on both sides of the border and big slogans like democracy and peace-building were preceded and followed by shenanigans and hooliganisms.

Attacks on Waziristan in northwest Pakistan by US drones launched from Saudi bases continued as well, even escalated. So did the Pakistan Army's supposed operation against suspected militants throughout the country.

Bombs went off in Karachi, Khyber-Pakhtunkhwa, and all along the western belt between Afghanistan and Pakistan, killing scores of civilians. The responsibility for the explosions were claimed by splinter groups of the Taliban and the Al Qaeda subsidiaries.

The mayhem and the grief continued apace. It was unrelenting, unending.

The summer ended with four Pakistani soldiers killed near the Lahore border.

Schools and colleges opened up again because the summer was over and life had to go on.

The senior class was beginning to splinter by October. Some fretted over how they would talk to their parents about talking to another set of parents about proposals and engagements after graduation.

Girls were discarding more boys than the other way around. Most were doing this because the boys didn't amount to much after years of investment. And some because they had invested too much in the girls.

The delicate balance of being someone worthy of interest and being aloof enough to not come across as needy was carried forward from LUSS by only two couples in that year.

Sara and Omar were seen as still trying to get together after the fact.

It was strange though that to the 'liberal' kids, Sara and Omar came across as conservative hypocrites and to the more fanatical parties, the uncoupled couple were a symbol of degeneracy.

⚜

Even Mehreen and Hayyan hooked up by the end of the junior year and they went through a summer fling while the holidays lasted. They only tried each other out because Sara didn't zone out of Omar enough to give Hayyan a chance.

He lingered in Sara's orbit until the inevitable happened. Mehreen thought he was good enough to pursue, at least as a meanwhile proposition.

Hayyan vocally compared Mehreen to Sara constantly and didn't hide that he was unhappy he had a lesser person than he wanted. Often when they fought, Mehreen and Hayyan would both seek out Sara but not speak about how her existence was wedging them apart.

Once college opened up again, they tried to extend the fling into a longer version of itself. That did not work out so well. The fizz with which it dissipated left streaks of acid on both sides.

Omar's tiny, fully automatic Suzuki Mehran was a loan from his parents for his senior year on campus at LUSS. It turned out to be a group joyride and Sara's friends took the most advantage of it.

Often, they would pick and drop Nadia and Mehreen from their homes, or Sara and Omar would go for long drives across Lahore, listening to her collection of music. Being together, talking about who and what and where and how and when of things. Making plans.

They created scenarios about their futures. In one, they would meet years later in some foreign country—him: a rock star in leather pants and a guitar slung across his back; and her: a nuclear archaeologist excavating hidden artifacts using precision explosions.

The outlandish schemes of their futures lay far away from their preposterously ordinary lives. It was all for the giggles. It was all to keep the despair of the end of college at bay.

Days when they couldn't tap into their shared worlds were spent with other people around them occupying their energies and distorting everything. Mehreen was all right. She could be all right. But Nadia was the cat who wanted too much and gave nothing in return. She purred in the back seat about her and Zafar and what their future plans were. The diamonds were specifically large in Nadia's yet-to-be-taken engagement photos. The bouquets all would be white, because, as predicted, she pretended to be a virgin damsel. Of course, Zafar had yet to propose. But why wouldn't he? Any time that Nadia spent with Omar, Sara and Mehreen, she made sure to emphasize how magnanimous and generous she was being by giving them her company.

Zafar called her over to his place one night on a weekend and refused to pick her up, citing his tiredness. 'Get your friends to drop you,' he said.

Sara, Mehreen and Omar were already in his car, heading to catch a George Clooney film about outer space. When the request was relayed to him, Omar told Sara that they could drop Nadia off a couple of hours early.

When they arrived at Zafar's place, the muscled lank of him was standing outside his own gate, arms draped atop the hood of a car in which sat a dashingly pretty young girl. He was seeing her off.

Nadia didn't get out of Omar's car and told him to drive on, which he did. They parked seven gates further down and Nadia looked out of the blurry back window at Zafar canoodling with the girl through her open car window.

They waited quietly in the car, Sara refusing to say 'I told you so,' because why the hell should she even bother.

Mehreen broke the silence by saying, 'Is that his cousin?'

The girl left in her car and Zafar went into his house. After that, ten minutes passed. Everyone knew the score: Zafar–1: Nadia–1. Courtesy demanded that nobody say anything out loud.

Omar kept stealing glances at Nadia in the rear-view mirror. He wavered between pity and disgust. Of all the things he wanted in those ten minutes, what he wanted most was to get Nadia out of his car. She wasn't crying or raising a fit. So there was nothing to console her about. She wasn't breaking at all. The mask had become the person because it had stayed on too long.

Sara and Omar began talking about the film, which would start in five minutes. They didn't want to miss the previews since those would also be in 3D and Sara asked Nadia if she wanted to come along with them to the cinema. It was a get-out call.

Nadia didn't take the bait. She sat a further five minutes in absolute silence, all her negative energy focused on something inside herself.

Poor Zafar. What an idiot. He had Nadia as his robot and his slave. What else did he want? What else could he, or anyone, want?

Anything but her, Sara thought.

Without a word, after all those minutes, Nadia opened the car's door, walked the fifty metres back to Zafar's gate, unlatched it and went inside.

Sara, Omar and Mehreen went to the theatre and were told they couldn't enter the hall because it would disrupt the film. It was the last night that *Gravity* would play in the cinema and they had already bought the tickets.

They went to have dinner instead and wondered how ugly the fight between Zafar and Nadia was going to be.

Nadia never spoke of that night again. It was a defeat she refused to acknowledge. Zafar and she were back together the next day and the size of the diamond in the imminent engagement did not change. Nadia never asked Sara to request Omar to kindly drop her off at Zafar's home again. She also made it a point from then on not to arrive earlier or later than the time Zafar said they should meet.

Omar's circles spiralled out again and he started running along the outer walls of the campus. Garbage and broken bottles strewn across his path were easy to dodge during daylight.

But on a gloomy day full of clouds, he lost his footing on a bottle cap sitting on a brick and twisted his ankle. After hollering from pain, limping and hopping, he still tried running on it for ten nerve-jangling minutes. That did not work out so well.

In the five-week rest he was prescribed for his sprained ankle, he would feel his feet kick out into a strut at any given moment—

walking, sitting or sleeping—as if his legs couldn't believe they were even temporarily out of commission.

He was forced to be home during those weeks of rest because the hostel elevator wasn't reliable.

Since he was available all the time, Omar's parents began to talk about his future whenever they were in the same room. They hit him with a bag full of keywords: senior year, GREs, grad school applications, prospects, programs, and the like. He wished he had no future to talk about. He wished for stasis. He was miserable outside the campus and away from Sara.

Sometimes, with his foot immersed in ice-cold water, waiting impatiently to heal, he wished he could remain forever on that cusp between not knowing Sara and knowing her, that fine edge of a point on either side of which lay a remarkably different state of existence.

⚜

To cheer him up during his convalescence, Sara gave Omar a CD of songs she had re-sung herself. Some of them were covers of his favourites: Third Eye Blind's '*Semi-Charmed Life*', Pink Floyd's '*Wish You Were Here*', Smashing Pumpkins' '*Crestfallen*', Pearl Jam's '*Wishlist*', Junoon's '*Mitti*', Del Amitri's '*Driving with the Breaks On*'. She deliberately sang them out of tune and out of rhythm, to tease him about his morbid taste.

As a bonus track, she included a cover of the Dire Straits song '*Romeo and Juliet*', in a husky voice he didn't take for hers at first. Despite his repeated requests, she refused to sing it to him live. Not until his next birthday at least, she promised.

Once Omar had healed, he ran with that track on repeat on his iPod and couldn't stop. He didn't know whether to laugh or ache from what she had given him.

⚜

As an impending graduate of LUSS, smart and beautiful—someone worth handing over the house's keys to once she was clubbed and bagged—Sara was 'a catch'. Her dad was rich, to boot.

A 'decent interval' after her mom's funeral, Sara's extended family and their acquaintances began to send semi-formal proposals.

Her dad had amusing ways of dealing with the most persistent, and most unlikely, prospects. Over a 'polite' third cup of tea in the drawing room, he would blurt out things like: 'Sara is only going to marry a 6-foot-5-inch Kashmiri with blue-green eyes because that's who her mom saw as Sara's groom in her last dream before she passed on to the next life.' He would say this with such a straight and sombre face that the desperate prospects sometimes suggested compromises—surgeries, contact lenses and the like.

Sara's Nano disapproved of her son-in-law's tactics at first, but eventually came to realize that it was for the best. She came up with hyperbolic excuses of her own. Once, she told the mother of a candidate that Sara was an avid conspiracy theorist, a vegan, and she was looking to marry someone bald who had to have a mole on each earlobe.

On the two occasions that her dad and her Nano's defences broke down, and they thought the boys were worth meeting, Sara refused on the grounds that she needed to graduate first and then think about anything other than college.

Even then, the external parties countered it with: 'It's her last year. Graduation will arrive sooner than you think. Let's start the meeting process. The whole thing takes a long time.'

Sara did not bring up the topic of those proposals in conversations with Omar, even in moments of weakness when she felt absolutely sure she would. There was some force that kept her going.

She did not want him to feel threatened or pressured into

sending his own parents to her house. It had to spring from within him and it had to remain within the space they allowed each other. The decision had to be theirs before extending it outward.

During their last semester, everywhere around them, freshmen, sophomores, juniors, conservatives and liberals—bearded, scarved and otherwise, were coupling up, grouping together. Either as friends or as lovers. They clumped together at concerts, hangouts, all-night vigils outside the cafeteria, and even in political rallies and class discussions that got too heated.

Everyone seemed to have someone special to share their best years with. New hierarchies began to take shape that mirrored, in distorted ways, the older ones.

And the seniors also reshaped themselves. They aligned themselves in an imitation of the world 'out there' that sat in judgement on all impending graduates.

Most of the seniors regretted something about their college years, but not enough to wish the past to change.

Some however, did. They would wallow in regret over getting caught plagiarizing or over falling for the wrong girl or over not being able to convince the right boy or not taking advantage of someone who had wanted them abjectly.

Some of the graduates looked ready to throw in the towel and jump off a building. Their hashish majors and alcohol minors showed in their spider-webbed eyes and in the stammers with which they articulated their scattered thoughts. Very few of them were able to latch onto the pity of the bleeding hearts and artists who were out to make a better world through acts of selfless charity.

The cult of musicians who had brought their guitars to campus every day to jam together—they chilled out at last, having broken through individual barriers of music development or having realized that they were playing just to get some attention.

Three of the seniors were already national celebrities: a model, a singer and a television actor.

The model wanted to go to graduate school. Or so she said. The singer wanted to go to India to launch her second album. She even had the right contacts by now. The television actor was not getting enough work other than cell phone company advertisements. But he was determined, and his college friends were sure they would see him on the big screen soon. At LUSS, these three were part of couples and groups, needled and poked enough by their peers to keep grounded. But once they were out of the gates, their egos began inflating.

There were some solo acts.

A nerd or two, here and there, who had remained nested in the library, emerging only to perform bodily functions. They butterflied out from their monkish cocoons to claim 4.0 certificates from the registrar. Gold medals would follow at the ceremony. Having not squandered a moment of their four years at LUSS, they were wasted individuals indeed.

On Valentine's Day, Omar sent Sara a text asking what time she would be on campus and if she would like to go out for fresh juice at the H-Block market after classes.

Lahore was so full of red heart-shaped helium balloons that it seemed the city itself would lift off from their collective skyward effort.

Sara and Omar made fun of the couples they drove past and also while they sat on the second floor of a shack where they ate samosas and jalebis and people-watched for a while.

There were countless boys staring at Sara. Desperados, almost all of them. Sara watched Omar glaring at the boys staring at her. Her desperado hero; he was all hers.

In March, a day *after* Sara's birthday, Nadia started planning a surprise party for Sara. She said the two-day delay would be the automatic surprise.

She told Omar what his only job was: bring Sara to the upscale Chinese restaurant, Yum, in Y-Block. All he had to do was nonchalantly drive over with Sara around dinner time.

Omar would have done exactly that, except he knew Sara would want to know if it was Nadia's plan. So he told Sara about the element of surprise in his offer to take her out to dinner.

For three hours, Sara fretted over whether to go or not. She wanted to skip the entire thing and go elsewhere for dinner. But the spite would then show on Sara's side and the fault would lie with her as well. What was she to do? She wished Omar hadn't told her.

She wished it out loud, so he almost apologized, but thought better of it because eventually she was more likely to not hold it against him. He again felt the need to apologize while she sat in his parked car and calculated the results of each alternative.

They picked up Mehreen, who said she knew of no surprise dinner at Yum, and they showed up at the appointed time outside the restaurant.

Sara deliberately walked in front, keeping a nonchalant look on her face. When she opened the door at 9.03 p.m., there were no shouts or whoops of joy. No balloons shot up to the roof and no confetti popped and rained down on Sara.

Nadia wasn't even near the front of the restaurant and it wasn't a mistake. She was at the back, standing next to Zafar in one of the many spotlights that lit up the restaurant's floor.

Zafar's friends and their friends by extension, around twenty of them, filled up more than half of one end of the long table laid out for the reserved party in the middle of the room. They were already well into their soup. Other than them, there were no customers at the restaurant.

Nadia waved the new arrivals over to one end of the long table, away from Zafar's friends. Sara, Mehreen and Omar took those seats and Sara immediately began planning their escape.

On the surface, she remained unfazed. That was the key here. Don't act like you know this was supposed to be a surprise but it isn't, she kept telling herself. Inside, she was boiling with indignation. It came in waves, the anger, and it smelled like burnt chicken corn soup.

The floor was full of Zafar's crew. The restaurant's doors opened and three boys and two girls entered. They were sophomores and juniors. Nadia went up to them, gave them pretentious pecks on the cheek, and led them past Sara to their seats.

No one wished Sara a happy birthday. Sara felt like she was still in high school, still being bullied with passive aggression.

Omar asked Sara if she wanted to order a soup.

Sara didn't answer and didn't look at him. She put a hand on his lap and nodded. Hold on, that meant; let me think, let me sort this out. Mehreen was on her phone, which Sara understood was Mehreen's way of keeping herself from asking embarrassing questions like, 'Hey, wasn't this supposed to be your surprise birthday dinner—so where's the surprise?'

Nadia walked over to them once Zafar went to his friends and ignored her for a few minutes. She hugged Sara from behind and let out a fake laugh and said, 'Happy birthday again, Saroo. Hey Omar, thanks for bringing Sara. Hey Mehreen, good to see you too.'

Mehreen waved without looking up from her phone.

'Thanks,' Sara said, 'we just stopped by. But we have to head over to my aunt's. She's not feeling well.'

'Oh no,' Nadia said, stretching out the '*no*' to Pinocchio proportions. Soon, she was back with Zafar and Zafar's extended universe.

Omar and Mehreen, led by Sara, made a quiet exit. In the car, Sara apologized to Mehreen for the embarrassment and Mehreen waved it off.

They drove the short distance to the H-Block McDonald's where they had burgers, fries, onion rings and sundaes.

The bad feeling from Yum lifted by and by, replaced with relief and laughter. They made fun of Nadia's 'oh no,' with the long o's at its end, until it became a refrain for everything. 'Should we have more food?' 'Oh noooo.' 'Should we go back to Yum?' 'Oh noooooo.' 'Should we throw eggs at Zafar's car?' 'Oh nooooooooo.' 'Should we throw a surprise birthday party for Nadia and make it fail miserably by inviting nobody she knew or wanted to be with?' 'Oh noooooooooooooooooo.'

They overdid it and it slowly grew less funny. They had to force themselves to laugh at it. But they had the night and they had no care or misery dragging them down.

The city's bright lights, the loud, cheap music in the car, the all-night tussle of city traffic—the safety of Defence—it was theirs.

After making stops to have juice, paan, kulfi and chai, Omar asked if they wanted to get something else to eat and Mehreen croaked out the 'oh noooo,' and it was funny again.

Poor Nadia. Poor, lost and foolish Nadia.

They were giddy, the three of them, from the excessive sugar and silliness. Everything was covered with a surface layer of seeming all right. With the laughter came a renewal of the pact to not take themselves too seriously.

They felt inspirited with the idea that they were still just college kids, still living in the possibilities of the people they would eventually become.

On their third set of drinks, once back at LUSS and sipping lemonades, Sara said she didn't think Nadia had meant to come across as selfish.

'Yeah right,' said Omar.

'Oh nooooo,' said Mehreen.

'No, no,' Sara said, after suppressing her giggles. 'I mean it. Maybe she just doesn't know any better.'

'You mean,' Omar said, 'Nadia is actually a very nice person deep down and she's just stupid and doesn't know how to act around people?'

'Yes,' Sara said. 'That's sort of what I mean.'

'You're right,' Mehreen said, then turning to Omar. 'She's right.'

'Oh noooooo,' Omar said, and pretended to run away from them. 'It's contagious.'

Rather than continue arguing her point and defending Nadia, Sara let it go. The back of her mind churned on the thought that Nadia was only trying too hard to keep high-school hierarchies intact, but destroying her old friendships in the process.

But, anyway, it wasn't like Sara wanted to hang out with Nadia after college was over. There were only a few more months of the madness to go. In that sense, with regard to Nadia, it was a blessing.

The three of them walked around the track and not once did Mehreen act like a third wheel. It was more comfortable with her around because with the three of them, one person's silence was okay for some time, while the other two talked.

When time came for them to sleep, early the next morning, Omar was the first to head up to his room. Mehreen and Sara kept going around the track for another thirty minutes, for the first time feeling like the close friends they had become without knowing how or when.

Was there anything better than the cold rainy night drive through the lit-up city of Lahore with the darling and beautiful girl, drowsy and draped in a shawl on the passenger seat?

How about when the drive was interrupted by a police checkpoint off the main road and a set of uniformed paunchy traffic cops waddled over to the window? One of them tapped longingly on the glass, to have it lowered, to ask who the girl was and what two young and good-looking people were doing out in the middle of the night?

He hesitated only for a flicker. 'She is my wife and we are going home,' he said in a deeper voice than his own. The cop sensed he could pursue this, but the boy stared like the man he could one day become. The cop adjusted his belt and waved his partners off.

The rest of the rain-soundtracked ride was pleasantly awkward for her.

He felt this could be a fork in the road. But he was comfortable with that. He had stated his needs.

At Sara's house, late one spring afternoon, Mehreen and Sara walked barefoot on the grass in her front lawn. Only Sara's Nano was at home and she was resting inside.

Mehreen's mother was still having her affair with the co-owner of her cafe at LUSS, but it had cooled into domestic levels of boredom. Talking about it was like going in closed circles because Mehreen's parents had come to some sort of arrangement; they were amicable with each other. It was as though Mehreen's mother did not have hidden chapters in her life at all.

Mehreen's younger sisters didn't know the truth, though. They'd been spared the confusion. Mehreen, in her own way, had shirked off the responsibility that had fallen on her shoulders once the adults hadn't held it up at their end. She pretended at home that everything was okay with her. She also pretended at LUSS that everything was all right back home. How many cracks could one person hide, though?

Here she was, confessing to Sara on their looped barefoot walk that she was glad to graduate and head on out to the shitty Ohio university to which she had just got accepted. Her parents were going to pay the full tuition for her MBA. Mehreen was using their guilt to her full advantage.

Sara asked her, 'Do you remember comparing your mother's affair to my mom's death?'

'No,' Mehreen said. She looked shocked and almost stopped mid-step in their amble across the lawn. 'Why would I do something like that?'

'You did compare them,' Sara said. 'I remember it clearly. You said you wished you could exchange places with me. And I have to tell you this: I think you were right.'

'So,' Mehreen said, 'you think a dead mother is better than a mother who is having an affair?'

'No,' Sara said, 'not better. Just less complex.'

'Hmm,' Mehreen said, 'maybe.' They were quiet and it was just as quiet inside Sara's head. This was something Sara had never experienced with Nadia. With Nadia, words were weapons, always poised for attack or deflection.

Mehreen's company brought something very different with it: peaceful coexistence. An ability to let go of thinking about the permutations of the conversation.

'You know,' Sara said, after another figure-eight loop around her garden chairs and table, 'the most complex thing in my life is my friendship with Omar.'

'Yeah,' Mehreen said, 'that does seem very complex.' Sara felt good hearing the word *very*. It meant this wasn't just inside her own head.

Had Nadia said the same thing the same way—oh, God knows what Sara would have felt.

Mehreen went a little bit further. She asked Sara why she did not do something about it, since it was obviously mutual. What was keeping Sara? What was keeping Omar? Wasn't it confirmed to be something more than infatuation after more than three years?

'It's the explosions,' Sara said. 'Every time Omar and I are together, feeling what we have is special, it's because a bomb explodes or is about to explode. It's either bombs getting us together or us getting together that makes things explode.'

They both let the matter rest on that note. But thinking about what she had jokingly said made Sara wonder if it were true. Did she feel close to him because of the heightened sense of surviving bomb blasts and epic tragedies while he was around? Even her own mom's death, for that matter.

And then, what if the tragedies ended and the equation between them became completely different? She would no longer be the damsel in distress and he would no longer be the hero he so wanted to be. Would she still like Omar? Would he still like her? Would liking each other be enough?

Because that was the feeling of domestic dullness and eventless-ness in the bomb-less, bullet-less and danger-less future she envisioned for herself.

College was all fun and games, and sleepless nights and tricks for grades, and skip-roping over tightropes into the future by fluke and random preparation. Life beyond college wouldn't be that way, or at least it shouldn't be.

And so, why risk everything on one roll of the dice?

That is exactly what they were doing, Sara thought. They were holding on to the fortune and virtue that each of them had and they were helping each other keep back from the brink of a colossal mistake.

Sara and Mehreen walked in the garden past dusk, swatting mosquitoes and sipping lemonade, wading with comfort through topics that once, with Nadia, would have dredged up nothing but barbs and thorns of grief and resignation.

❦

On the last day of college, their exams over and done with and their dues and courses cleared, with nothing left but the annual concert and the graduation ceremony in a few days, Sara and Omar sat on the entrance steps for an hour after she finished printing and handing in her honours essay. It was something she had once held dear. But oh, how it fatigued her now.

Not many students lingered on campus that hot day in early May. The graduating class would return to campus in a few days to go through the motions of saying goodbye to LUSS. Until then, Sara and Omar had the campus almost entirely to themselves.

They talked about the old days, the days when college had just begun. He told her he remembered what she looked like on the first day they had met: she was wearing a blue dress and her hair was up in a bun on her head.

She told him she had never worn her hair in a bun and never would. She said he must be confusing her with someone else.

But he insisted on the bun.

She didn't remember it like that and said she had probably worn a blue dress that day, but definitely not her hair in a bun. It's not a thing that would suit her at all. It would look and feel tight, and out of place.

He dropped the subject and, in his memory of that first day, readjusted the tight bun of hair into a straight cut, the one in which he liked her best—even though he knew better.

Four years filled up the cocoon of memories that swelled between Sara and Omar. The more they remembered, the larger the cocoon grew. The elastic surface of it was made of the pain and the regret of things not done, the words not said.

In the centre of it all were the countless moments they could no longer recall because the past, which distorted images of joy and loss, and erased the memories that no longer resonated emotionally, held them at bay.

Their history and the future, both equally obscure, hovered in the air like solid but invisible things.

They got up from the steps and, though they started on the other end of campus, their path would always lead to the track.

After they had rounded the circle several times, conjured up enough of the bygone days to invoke and dispel the bitter taste of nostalgia, and were about to head back to the buildings, Omar asked Sara if she could smell garlic in the air.

She couldn't, but she did hear a mechanism roll into place with a *ping*.

Seniors
Where the Dance Is

In the thick of the winter, once the late-December fog had begun to roll over early morning Lahore and its outskirts, after Nadia had asked Zafar to propose to her already for it had been months since the incident, beyond the police and the army and the agencies' investigations and cover-ups of the event during which they had bungled up the evidence by mixing clay with bone and blood and what smelled like garlic without using such elementary equipment as a centrifuge, their centred approach and long-standing war still focused in the northwest of the country, even after all the passive-aggressive gestures of reconciliation with the US, India, China, Afghanistan, Russia and Iran—border skirmishes and daily crossfire-induced bloodshed with neighbouring countries notwithstanding—besides the generous doles of militating funds from the Saudi princes continuing to steadily trickle in, a hundred million dollars at a time, and trickling out on the political conveyor-belt to numbers-only Swiss bank accounts, once the case of gross negligence Omar's parents filed against LUSS went into limbo, but before it exited that legal whirlpool to land a decision firmly in one party's favour, before the campus gear ever shifted to security concerns being communicated to the students, despite two explosions in the heart of its fields, but beyond the reach of policy that thwarted drones or lobbed grenades or student stink-bomb pranks escalated to a whole other level, before the fog that rolled in had a chance to be cleared away by the winter sun, to reveal a girl become a woman seated beside two mounds of earth in a cemetery full of marbled encasements for the long-forgotten dead with dry flowers weighing them down, and beginning to fret about the possible end to his future in Pakistan, an old man at the Islamabad Airport sat watching TV and responded with an outburst to someone in his past while those around him took for madness what was its opposite. After revelation, long after revelation, long after the apocalypse of a certain set of lives, but long before the world's end from its own evolved processes and accoutrements of destruction, crouched on prayer mats and with broken hearts all across the bomb-and-bullet-strewn Land of the Pure, sifting through the remains of what remained, long after and before and, in the endless cycle of the violence, spinning out into the widening gyre and feeling light and woolen like dust that wouldn't settle, departing from this life to that, and cleaving from that to this, a land on which there walked, on the Land of the Pure that teetered ever closer to the brink of falling off a cliff, there walked, on the thrust-out screens of TVs turgid with breaking news of the latest attack and the biggest, most record-breaking calamity yet, there *walked*, long after the vultures had become extinct from the city's skies and there was nothing to clean the meat off the bones of all that was discarded, once *there walked*, once the clean water receded deep into the earth, and the rivers flooded annually with dark swirls of roiling mud, and the biannual earthquakes in the mountains to the north avalanched people to the lowlands to look for relief, which was just counting the disasters without human agency, and after the gap between the poor and the rich was spread so bleak and stretched so thin that mirages cropped up to illusion even the disillusioned, the teetering on the brink and ever closer to the abyss, this Land of the Pure suspended in its faith, held aloft at the start of a pirouette over the chasm, a land on which once *there walked* a boy turning into man, a girl more than woman already.

Their eyes surfed the dust and pebbles and gravel on the track without seeing what they scanned. Outer peace, inner rust and the graze of the noonday sun on their bronzing arms and hands.

A pebble had got into her shoe, but it wasn't at a sore spot. With each step she took she rolled her foot a little to feel its curved surface under her big toe.

What struck her most was that it was a day just like any other day. To be expected, of course. Though from the moment she had begun thinking of this day, two years ago in her bed, while she had slowly fallen into deep sleep in the room next to the one in which her mom had been dying, she had listed and arranged several hundred words to say during this moment. Not a farewell speech like the ones at the last day of the graduation week. Something more lasting.

'Can I say something?' Omar asked.

He was interrupting the flow of thoughts that would have led her to break the silence first.

'Hmm, yeah,' Sara said, without looking up from the track, and without slowing down or speeding up.

They kept turning left, with her on the inside of the circle, the pebble disappearing at times from under her toe to the empty spaces within her shoe.

'I want you to know something,' Omar said. A flicker of doubt made him stop there and reconsider. He wanted to blurt it out, fling it into the air between them.

He could take her hand in his again, their fingers entwined, as they had been a few minutes ago when he had held her hand and released it.

He could also lean over and kiss her forehead. He could brush away the lock of hair from her temple, and lightly flick her earlobe as he tucked strands of it behind her ear.

Omar could even see himself kneeling before her, taking her hand and asking a question. He could say the three words that neither of them had said so far.

But there was something else.

He knew the pause was getting longer, but the afternoon was bright and dull and appeared endless by itself. The deep and dry heat, his parched lips and the crunch underfoot, all were good enough to last, and they did. He waited out the gap in conversation, patient and knowing that the right moment was just around the corner of his thoughts.

Sara looked at his shadow and turned her head a little so she could see his face. He wasn't looking at her, but that didn't mean anything.

'What?' she asked, because the silence was becoming solid now. She saw him lick his lips, open his mouth to say something and then close it. Like a fish making air-bubbles. Like a mime, with his eyes over-expressing something.

No, he couldn't say it. He just couldn't. She wouldn't understand. He took two more steps with her and then stopped. She stopped mid-step too and she was still looking at him. He looked up at her, smiled, and said, 'Let's go the other way.'

They turned to start walking on the empty track in the opposite direction. Turning right now, instead of left, with her still on the inside of the track. The sun still as hot, the day still as dull and the end just as looming.

Like a spindle on its own revolutions. The thread invisible to them, unwinding and then winding back.

The pebble in her shoe had disappeared after they had turned. Still, she could picture it, the shape of it certain to her. It wasn't lost; it would always exist.

In the waves of heat that late afternoon, a guard cycled from one end of LUSS to the other, changing his post on the hour. He thought he saw a couple walking while holding hands on the track. His cycle drifted forward, he stopped peddling for a second, during which a forbidding part of him battled with the memories of his own first love, and the park—so long ago—where they used to meet, where he would walk about and lay in the grass with her next to him, holding hands and making promises.

The guard pedalled on, not knowing that the hands he saw were not clasped together, but separate and swaying in sync, though they would brush each other now and then.

Only sometimes would Sara tangle Omar's knuckles with her own.

Otherwise, all that seemed to exist around them were the sounds coming from under their feet and the glare of the sun overhead.

With so many revolutions around the track, their long walk was in equal measure a release as well as the ache from which they sought the release.

For a long time, they did not speak and each was lost in separate thoughts. Though somewhere, their musing must have overlapped because when the silence broke, it was when one of them, replacing three other words that had been fenced for so long, said their equivalent, 'I don't know if you'll understand this, Sara. But I have to say it. Spending time with you is like being at home in the universe.'

And the other replied, the spring in her step coiled and ready, 'Yeah. I know what you mean.'

Acknowledgements

This novel was conceived in solitude, but it was nurtured from idea to published volume by Divine support and the great work of many people other than its author. My wife Sheema was the first, most critical reader. Claire Alexander and Faiza Sultan Khan were other early, encouraging readers. Bilal Tanweer, my author friend, was constantly available as a sounding board. The Winquist family, especially Martin, helped crystalize the final form of the book. Agents Sridhar Gowda and Geraldine Rose championed the novel across continents, and found just the right team at HarperCollins India. Rea Mukherjee, my fantastic editor, sieved much rough material to help refine the story. I am grateful and humbled by the hard work put in by all the professionals who contributed to the creation of this novel.